DARKEST HOUR

Also by James Holland

FICTION
The Odin Mission
The Burning Blue
A Pair of Silver Wings

NON-FICTION
Fortress Malta: An Island Under Siege, 1940–1943
Together We Stand: North Africa 1942–1943 – Turning the Tide
in the West
Heroes: The Greatest Generation and the Second World War
Italy's Sorrow: A Year of War, 1944–1945

DARKEST HOUR

JAMES HOLLAND

BANTAM PRESS

LONDON · TORONTO · SYDNEY · AUCKLAND · JOHANNESBURG

TRANSWORLD PUBLISHERS
61–63 Uxbridge Road, London W5 5SA
A Random House Group Company
www.rbooks.co.uk

First published in Great Britain
in 2009 by Bantam Press
an imprint of Transworld Publishers

A CIP catalogue record for this book
is available from the British Library.

ISBN 9780593058367 (cased)
9780593058374 (tpb)

Addresses for Random House Group Ltd companies outside the UK
can be found at: www.randomhouse.co.uk
The Random House Group Ltd Reg. No. 954009

The Random House Group Limited supports The Forest Stewardship
Council (FSC), the leading international forest-certification organization. All our
titles that are printed on Greenpeace-approved FSC-certified paper carry the FSC logo.
Our paper procurement policy can be found at
www.rbooks.co.uk/environment

Typeset in 11/14pt Caslon 540 by
Falcon Oast Graphic Art Ltd.
Printed and bound in Great Britain by
Clays Ltd, Bungay, Suffolk

2 4 6 8 10 9 7 5 3 1

Mixed Sources
Product group from well-managed
forests and other controlled sources
www.fsc.org Cert no. TT-COC-2139
© 1996 Forest Stewardship Council
FSC

For Sue, Bill and Giles Bourne

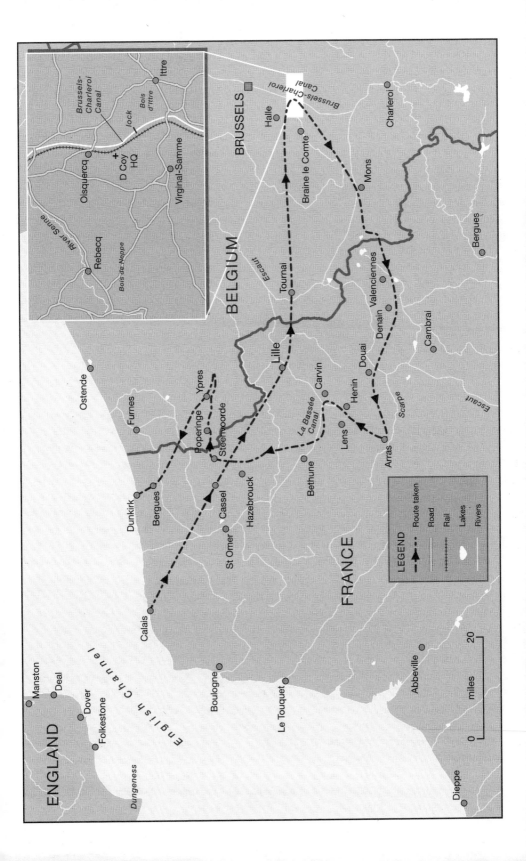

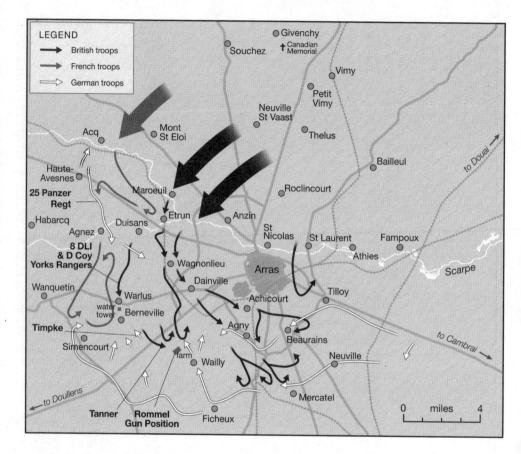

LEGEND

→ British troops
→ French troops
⇨ German troops

Givenchy
✝ Canadian Memorial
Souchez
Vimy
Petit Vimy
Neuville St Vaast
Thelus
Acq
Mont St Eloi
Bailleul
to Douai
Haute-Avesnes
Maroeuil
Roclincourt
25 Panzer Regt
Etrun
Anzin
Habarcq
Duisans
St Nicolas
St Laurent
Fampoux
Agnez
Athies
Scarpe
8 DLI & D Coy Yorks Rangers
Wagnonlieu
Arras
Wanquetin
Dainville
Tilloy
Warlus
water tower
Achicourt
Berneville
Timpke
Agny
Beaurains
Simencourt
farm
Wailly
Neuville
to Cambrai
to Doullens
Mercatel
Tanner **Rommel Gun Position**
Ficheux

0   miles   4

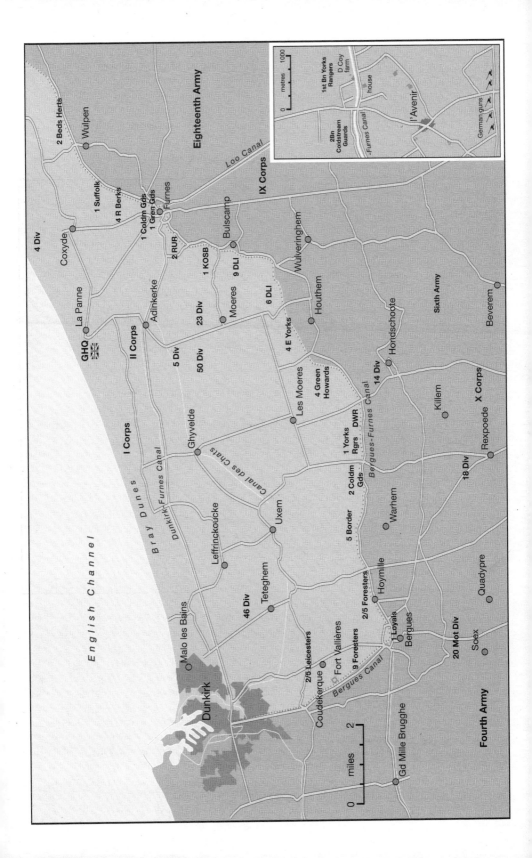

English Channel

Bray Dunes

Malo les Bains

Dunkirk

Gd Mille Brugghe

Coudekerque

Fort Vallières

9 Foresters

2/5 Leicesters

46 Div

Teteghem

Leffrinckoucke

Uxem

Ghyvelde

I Corps

II Corps

GHQ

La Panne

Coxyde

4 Div

Wulpen

2 Beds Herts

1 Suffolk

4 R Berks

1 Coldm Gds

1 Gren Gds

Furnes

Adinkerke

2 RUR

5 Div

50 Div

23 Div

Moeres

Les Moeres

4 Green Howards

4 E Yorks

1 KOSB

9 DLI

6 DLI

Bulscamp

Houthem

Wulveringhem

Eighteenth Army

IX Corps

Loo Canal

Dunkirk Furnes Canal

Canal des Chats

Bergues-Furnes Canal

1 Yorks Rgrs   DWR

2 Coldm Gds

5 Border

Warhem

14 Div

Hondschoote

Sixth Army

Beverem

Killem

Rexpoede

X Corps

18 Div

Quadypre

Soex

20 Mot Div

Bergues

1 Loyals

Hoymille

2/5 Foresters

Bergues Canal

Fourth Army

miles
0   1   2

1st Bn Yorks Rangers

2Bn Coldstream Guards

D Coy farm

house

l'Avenir

Furnes Canal

German guns

metres
0   1000

1

A little after half past ten in the morning, Thursday, 9 May 1940. Already it was warm, with blue skies and large white cumulus clouds; a perfect early summer's day, in fact. It was also quite warm inside the tight confines of the Hurricane's cockpit, even fifteen thousand feet above the English Channel, and Squadron Leader Charlie Lyell was wishing he hadn't worn his thick sheepskin Irvin over his RAF tunic but the air had seemed fresh and crisp when he'd walked across the dew-sodden grass to his plane just over half an hour before. Now, as he led his flight of three in a wide arc to begin the return leg of their patrol line, the sun gleamed through the Perspex of his canopy, hot on his head. A line of sweat ran from his left temple and under the elastic at the edge of his flying goggles.

Nevertheless, it was the perfect day for flying, he thought. It was so clear that he could see for a hundred miles and more. As they completed the turn to head southwards again, there, stretching away from them, was the mouth of the Medway, shipping heading towards and out of London. Southern England – Kent and Sussex – lay unfolded like a rug from his starboard side, a soft, green, undulating patchwork, while away to his port was the Pas de Calais and the immensity of France. Somewhere down there were the massed French armies and the lads of the British Expeditionary Force. He smiled to himself. *Rather you than me.*

Lyell glanced at his altimeter, fuel gauge and oil pressure. All fine, and still well over half a tank of fuel left. The air-speed indicator showed they were maintaining a steady 240 miles per hour cruising speed. He turned his head to check the skies were clear behind him, then back to see that Robson and Walker were still tight in either side of him, tucked in behind his wings. *Good.*

Suddenly something away to his right caught his eye – a flash of sunlight on metal – and at the same moment he heard Robson, on his starboard wing, exclaim through the VHF headset, 'Down there – look! Sorry, sir, I mean, this is Red Two, Bandit at two o'clock.'

'Yes, all right, Red Two,' said Lyell. He hoped he sounded calm, a hint of a reprimand in his voice, even though he was conscious that his heart had begun to race and his body had tensed. He peered down and – yes! – there it was, some five thousand feet below, he guessed, and perhaps a mile or so ahead. It was typical of Robson to assume it was an enemy plane – they all wanted the squadron's first kill – but the plain truth was that most aircraft buzzing around the English coast were British, not German. *Even so.*

'This is Red One,' he called, over the R/T. 'We'll close in.' At least the sun, already high, was behind them, shielding them as they investigated. Lyell pushed open the throttle and watched the altimeter fall. His body was pressed back against the seat, and he tightened his hand involuntarily around the grip of the control column. A few seconds later and he could already see the aircraft ahead more clearly. It appeared to have twin tail fins but, then, so did a Whitley or a Hampden. The brightness was too great to distinguish the details of the paint scheme or symbols on the wings and fuselage.

Ahead loomed a huge tower of white cloud and together they shaved the edge of it, so that Lyell fleetingly lost sight of the plane before it appeared again and then, in a moment when it hung in the shadow of the cloud, he saw the unmistakable black crosses. His heart lurched. *Christ*, he thought, *this is bloody well it.*

Pushing open the throttle even wider, he closed in on what he could now see was a Dornier. It appeared not to have spotted them yet, but as he was only around seven hundred yards behind and a thousand feet above, Lyell checked that Robson and Walker were still close to him before he said, 'Line astern – go!' Still the enemy plane continued on its way, oblivious to the danger behind it. Lyell turned his head to see Robson and Walker now directly behind him.

Taking a deep breath, he flicked the firing button to 'on' for the first time ever in a real combat situation, then said into his mouthpiece, 'Number One Attack – go!' Opening the throttle wide he dived down on the Dornier. As it grew bigger by the second, he pressed his thumb down hard on the gun button and felt the Hurricane judder as his eight machine-guns opened fire. Lines of tracer and wavy threads of smoke hurtled through the sky but, to his frustration, fell short of the enemy plane. Cursing, he pulled back on the stick, but already he knew he had misjudged his attack. Seconds, that was all it had taken, but now the Dornier seemed to be filling his screen and he knew that if he did not take avoiding action immediately, they would collide. He pushed the stick to his left and the Hurricane flipped onto its side to scythe past the port wing of the Dornier, just as a rip of fire cut across him. He could hear machine-guns clattering, Robson and Walker shouting through the airwaves – all radio discipline gone – and saw tracer fizzing through the air, and then he was away, circling, climbing and scanning the skies, trying to pinpoint the enemy again.

Lyell swore, then heard a rasp of static and Robson's voice. 'Bastard's hit me!' he said.

'Are you all right, Red Two?' Lyell asked, peering about desperately for the Dornier and conscious that several enemy bullets had torn into his own fuselage.

'Yes, but my Hurri's not. I'm losing altitude.'

'I've got you, Robbo.' Walker this time.

Damn, damn, damn, thought Lyell, then spotted the Dornier again, a mile or so ahead, flying south-west once more. 'The bloody nerve,' he muttered. 'Red Two, turn straight back for Manston. Red Three, you guide him in.'

'What about you, sir?' asked Walker.

'I'm going after Jerry. Over.' *Damn him. Damn them all*, thought Lyell. He glanced at his instruments. Everything looked all right; the plane was still flying well enough – it was as though he had not been hit at all – but the fuel gauge showed he was less than half full now. It was a shock to see how much he had used in that brief burst of action. *Well, bollocks to him*, thought Lyell. He was damned if some Boche bomber was going to make a fool of him or his squadron. Applying an extra six pounds of boost he climbed five hundred feet and turned towards the Dornier.

He was soon catching up and, making sure the sun was behind him again, waited until the German plane began to fill his gunsight. Then, at a little over four hundred yards, distance, he pressed down on the gun button. Again, the Hurricane juddered with the recoil and Lyell was jolted in his seat despite the tightness of his harness. Lines of tracer and smoke snaked ahead, but the bullets were dropping away beneath the Dornier. Lyell pulled back slightly on the stick and continued pressing hard on the gun button. His machine-guns blazed, and his tracer lines looked to be hitting the German plane perfectly, but still it flew on. It was as though his bullets were having no effect.

'Bloody die, will you?' muttered Lyell. Then tracer was curling towards him from the Dornier's rear-gunner, seeming slow at first, then accelerating past, whizzing across his port wing.

'For God's sake,' said Lyell, ducking his head.

Suddenly the Dornier wobbled, belched smoke, turned and dived out of Lyell's line of fire. 'Got you!' said Lyell, then pushed the stick to his left and followed the enemy down. Not far below and away from them there was a larger bank of cloud. So that was the enemy's plan – to hide. In moments, the Dornier was flitting between puffs of outlying cloud, all signs of black smoke gone, but

Lyell was gaining rapidly, the Merlin engine screaming, the air-frame shaking, as he hurtled towards the enemy and opened fire again.

Just as the lines of tracer began to converge on the German machine, Lyell's machine-guns stopped. For a moment, he couldn't understand it – could all eight really have jammed? But then it dawned on him. He had used up his ammunition. Fifteen seconds' worth. Gone. More than two and a half thousand bullets pumped out and still that bloody Dornier was flying. Lyell cursed and watched the German disappear into the cloud. Following him in, he banked and turned reluctantly towards home, a strangely bright and creamy whiteness surrounding him, the airframe buffeted by the turbulence. Suddenly, it thinned, wisping either side of him and over his wings, and moments later he was out in bright sunshine, the Kent coast ahead. Trickles of sweat ran down his neck and from beneath his leather helmet, tickling his face.

He throttled back, lifted his goggles onto his forehead and rubbed his eyes. He felt sick, not from being thrown about the sky but from bitter disappointment. The squadron's first kill! It should have been his – a sitting duck if ever there was one. And yet, some-how, it had got away.

From the corner of his eye he noticed feathery lines of grey between the cockpit and the starboard wing. He glanced up at his mirror. It was filled by the enemy plane bearing down on him, pumping bullets, its ugly great Perspex nose horribly close.

Christ almighty, thought Lyell, momentarily stunned. Then something clicked in his brain. He remembered that a Hurricane could supposedly out-turn almost any aircraft and certainly a lumbering twin-engine Dornier. Jamming the Hurricane to its full throttle, he turned the stick, added a large amount of rudder and opened the emergency override to increase boost. The Hurricane seemed to jump forward with the dramatic increase in power. With the horizon split between sky, land and sea, Lyell grimaced, his body pressed back into his seat.

In no more than half a circle, he could see he was not only getting away from the enemy but creeping up on the Dornier's rear. Again, the German rear-gunner opened fire. *Jesus*, thought Lyell. *How much ammunition do these people have?* The two aircraft were circling together now in a vertical bank. Lyell wondered how he would get away without the German rear-gunner hitting him, but a moment later the firing ceased. He pushed the stick to starboard, flipped over the Hurricane and reversed the turn, breaking free of the circle and heading out of the Dornier's range as he did so.

Although he was certain the enemy aircraft had neither the speed nor the agility to follow, Lyell glanced back to make sure the German pilot was not coming after him. The Dornier was banking away from the circle too, levelling out to return home. And as he straightened, he waggled his wings.

'Bloody nerve!' exclaimed Lyell. Was the enemy pilot saluting or sticking two fingers up at him? Either way, he had foxed three RAF fighter aircraft – out-thought, out-flown and out-gunned them.

About thirty miles away, a fifteen-hundredweight Bedford truck turned off the Ramsgate road that ran through Manston village, almost doubling back on itself as it entered the main camp at the airfield. The driver swore as he ground down through the gears, the truck spluttering, jerking and rumbling forward, past two hangars on the right, then towards several rows of one-storey wooden huts. He turned off the road, brought the truck to a halt and, letting the engine idle, said to the sergeant beside him, 'Hold on a minute. Let me find out where they want you.' He jumped down from the cab, and strode to what appeared to be an office building.

Sergeant Jack Tanner stepped out and went round to the back of the truck. 'All right, boys?' he said, to the five men sitting in the canvas-covered back, then pulled out a packet of cigarettes from the breast pocket of his serge battle-blouse.

'It's certainly a nice day for it, Sarge,' said Corporal Sykes. 'Not bad up here, is it? I've always had a soft spot for Kent. Used to come as a boy.'

'Really?' said Tanner, flicking away his match.

' 'Op-pickin' in the summer. Quite enjoyed it.'

Tanner made no reply, instead turning to the open grassland of the airfield. A number of aircraft were standing in front of the hangars to their right, bulky twin-engined machines, their noses pointing towards the sky. Further away to his left, he saw several smaller, single-engine aircraft that he recognized as Hurricanes. A light breeze drifted across the field. Above, skylarks twittered busily.

'It's all right round here,' said one of the men, a young-looking lad called McAllister, 'but give me Yorkshire any day.'

'Nah,' said Sykes. 'It's always bloody raining up there. Every time I go to HQ it bloody pours. Half my kit's still damp. And the air's a lot cleaner here than it is in Leeds.' He breathed in deeply and sighed.

'I meant the Dales, Stan,' said McAllister. 'The Dales are grand, ain't that right, Tinker?' He nudged another of the men, a short, fair-haired boy.

'Don't know, really,' said Bell. 'I suppose. I like our farm well enough.'

Tanner smiled and took a drag of his cigarette. A faint hum caught his attention and he looked back towards the coast. The sound grew louder and he stepped away from the truck, a hand to his forehead to shield his eyes as he looked up into the deep blue sky.

'Sarge?' said Sykes.

'Aircraft,' he said. 'Sounds like one in trouble.'

Immediately Sykes leaped down from the truck and onto the road beside Tanner. Together they scanned the skies.

'There,' said Tanner. Hepworth and McAllister were out of the truck now too. Two Hurricanes were approaching the north end of the airfield, one above and gliding effortlessly towards the grass strip, the other belching dark smoke, a grey trail following. The engine of the stricken aircraft groaned and thrummed irregularly, the airframe slewing and dipping, the port wing sagging.

The men watched in silence as the crippled plane cleared some buildings on the far side of the 'drome, dropped what seemed like fifty feet, recovered briefly, gave a last belch of smoke and crashed into the ground. The port wing hit the soft earth first, the under-carriage collapsing and the plane ploughing in an arc through the grass. Its propeller snapped and the fuselage buckled.

'Come on – get out, you stupid sod,' muttered Sykes. For a moment there was silence. Then the pilot heaved himself out of the cockpit, jumped onto the wing and sprinted away from the scene for all he was worth. He had not gone thirty yards when there was an explosion and the broken Hurricane was enveloped by a ball of angry orange flame and billowing black smoke. Tanner and the others flinched at the sound, saw the pilot fling himself flat on the ground then watched the fire-wagon, bells ringing, speed out from the watch-tower and hurry to the scene.

'Look, 'e's getting up again,' said Sykes, who had taken it upon himself to be the commentator.

'Good lad,' said Tanner, as the other Hurricane touched down safely behind them.

The truck driver returned. 'One's still not back. The CO an' all. Station commander's not at all happy.' He clicked his teeth and indicated to them to get back aboard. 'You're just down here,' he added, as Tanner clambered into the cab beside him, 'the other side of the parade-ground.'

He took them to the last of a row of long wooden huts. 'Here,' he said, pulling up. 'Make yourselves at home. The CSM'll be along shortly.'

Tanner undid the tailgate, waited for his men to jump down, then grabbed his kitbag and rifle. Like all British rifles, it was a Short Magazine Lee-Enfield, a No. 1 Mark III model, and although the newer No. 4 version was now coming into use, Tanner had no intention of surrendering this personal weapon. The son of a gamekeeper from south Wiltshire, he had learned to shoot almost as soon as he could walk and with it had come the well-drummed-in lesson of looking after a gun, whether it was an air rifle, twelve bore, or Lee-Enfield rifle. But, more than that, Tanner had made an important modification to his.

He had done it almost as soon as he had returned to Regimental Headquarters in Leeds back in February after nearly eight years' overseas service. Having been issued with new kit, he had gone straight to the Royal Armoury where he had had a gunsmith mill and fit two mounts and pads for an Aldis telescopic sight. They were discreet enough and few people had noticed – no one in authority, at any rate, not that he imagined they would say much about it even if they did. The scope had been his father's during the last war and Tanner had carried it with him throughout his army career. Although he had never attempted to become an army sniper, he had certainly sniped, and on several occasions the Aldis had proved a godsend. Slinging the rifle and his kitbag onto his shoulder, he followed the others into the hut.

Jack Tanner was twenty-four, although his weather-worn and slightly battered face made him appear a bit older. He was tall – more than six foot – with dark hair, pale, almost grey eyes and a nose that was slightly askew. He had spent almost his entire army career in India and the Middle East with the 2nd Battalion, the King's Own Yorkshire Rangers, even though he was a born and bred Wiltshireman. This last Christmas he had finally returned to England. Home leave, it had been called, not that he had had a home to return to any more. He had not seen the village where he had been brought up for over eight years. *A lifetime ago.* He wished he could return but that was not possible and so he had spent the time in Yorkshire instead, helping a gamekeeper on an estate in the Dales; it had reminded him how much he missed that life. Four weeks later he had presented himself at Regimental Headquarters in Leeds and been told, to his dismay, that he would not be going back to Palestine. Instead he had been posted to bolster the fledgling Territorial 5th Battalion as they prepared for war. In Norway, the Territorials had been decimated; Tanner and his five men, along with a few others, were all that remained of the 5th Battalion. A fair number were dead, but most were now either in German hospitals or on their way to a prison camp.

Tanner had hoped he might be allowed back to the 2nd Battalion now, but the regimental adjutant had had other ideas. The 1st Battalion was with the BEF in France; new recruits were being hurried through training and sent south to guard the coast. Men of his experience had an important part to play – all the veterans of Norway did. The 2nd Battalion would have to do without him for a while longer. Forty-eight hours' leave. That was all he and his men had had. The others had gone home, to their families in Leeds and Bradford, or in Bell's case to his family farm near Pateley Bridge, while Tanner and Sykes had got drunk for one day and recovered the next.

The hut was more than half empty. Just ten narrow Macdonald iron beds and palliasses were laid out along one wall, but otherwise it was bare. Tape had been criss-crossed over each window. Tanner slung his kitbag beside the bed nearest the door, then lay down and took out another cigarette.

'What are we supposed to do now, Sarge?' asked Hepworth.

'Put our feet up until someone tells us where we're to go,' Tanner replied. He lit his cigarette, then closed his eyes. He was conscious of another Hurricane landing – the engine sound was so distinctive. *Bloody airfield and coastal guard duty*, he thought. *Jesus*. He told himself to be thankful for it. They had escaped from Norway by the skin of their teeth so a soft job would do him and the others good. In any case, the war wasn't going to end any time soon, that much was clear. Their chance would come. Yet part of him yearned to rejoin his old mates in Palestine. For him, England was an alien place; he had spent too long overseas, in the heat, dust and monsoon rains of India, and the arid desert of the Middle East. Before that he had only ever known one small part of England, and that was the village of Alvesdon and the valley of his childhood. He still missed it, even after all these years. Often, when he closed his eyes, he would remember the chalk ridges, the woods on the farm, the clear trout stream, the houses of thatch, cob and flint. But both his parents were gone, and dark events from his past ensured there could be no going back.

He sighed. Long ago, he had resigned himself to exile, but it still saddened him. That long train journey south from Leeds: too much time to think, to remember. Tanner chided himself silently. *No point in getting bloody maudlin.* What he needed was a distraction. Activity. It was, he realized, barely a week since they had returned from Norway yet already he felt as though he had been kicking his heels for too long.

Soon after, he dozed off, the others' chatter a soporific background noise that lulled him to sleep. He was awake again, however, the moment his subconscious brain heard a new voice in the hut – a distinctive one: a deep, yet soft Yorkshire accent that was strangely familiar.

'Morning, gents,' Tanner heard, followed by a squeak of springs and the clatter of boots on the wooden floor as the men stood quickly to attention. Tanner swung his legs off the bed.

'All right, lads,' said the newcomer. 'As you were.'

Tanner's eyes widened in shock. A big, stocky man of nearly his own height stood in the doorway. The bright sun behind cast his face in shadow, but Tanner would have known him anywhere. *Blackstone. Jesus.* He groaned inwardly. That was all he needed.

Blackstone stared at him, then winked and turned back to the others. 'Welcome to Manston, lads,' he said, 'and to T Company of the First Battalion.' He had a lean face, with deep lines running across his brow and between his nose and mouth. He was in his mid-thirties, with thick sandy hair that showed beneath his field cap.

'I'm Company Sergeant-Major Blackstone,' he said. 'Captain Barclay is the officer commanding of this training company, but as far as you lot are concerned, I'm the one who runs the show. So if I were you I'd try to keep in my good books. It's better that way, isn't it, Sergeant? Then everything can be nice and harmonious.' He grinned at Tanner. 'Now,' he continued, 'I'm going to take Sergeant Tanner here away with me for a bit. Later on you'll meet your platoon commander and be shown about the place. For the moment, though, stay here and get your kit together. All right?' He smiled at them again, pointed the way to Tanner and said, 'See you later, boys.'

Outside, he said, 'Well, well, my old friend Jack Tanner. Fancy us ending up here like this.'

'Fancy,' muttered Tanner. 'You recovered, then.'

'Oh yes, Jack. You can't keep a good man like me down for long.' He chuckled. 'I'm taking you to see the OC.' He took out a packet of Woodbines and offered one to Tanner. 'Smoke?'

'No thanks, sir.'

'Don't tell me you've given up the beadies, Jack.'

'I just don't want one at the moment.'

'You mean you don't want one of mine.' Blackstone sighed. 'Jack, can't you tell I'm trying to be friendly? Come on – let's have no hard feelings. It was a long time ago now. Let bygones be bygones, eh?'

Tanner still said nothing. Blackstone stopped and offered him his packet of cigarettes again. 'Come on, Jack. Have a smoke. Water under the bridge, eh?'

They were now at the parade-ground. A platoon of men was being drilled on the far side, the sergeant barking orders. Tanner looked at Blackstone, then at the packet of cigarettes being held out towards him. Briefly he considered taking one.

'Look here, Jack,' said Blackstone, 'we're at war now. We can't be at each other's throats.'

'Agreed,' said Tanner, 'but that doesn't mean I have to like you.'

The smile fell from Blackstone's face.

'A few pleasantries and the offer of a smoke,' Tanner continued, 'and you think I'll roll over. But I was never that easily bought, Sergeant-Major. Trust and respect have to be earned. You prove to me that you're different from the bastard I knew in India, then I'll gladly take your bloody cigarette and shake your hand.'

Blackstone stared at him, his jaw set. 'Listen to you!' he said. 'Who the hell do you think you are? I offer you an olive branch and you have the nerve to spit in my face.'

'Don't give me that crap. What the hell did you expect? You

listen to me. Whether we like it not, we're both here, and for the sake of the company I'll work with you, but don't expect me to like you and don't expect me to trust you. Not until you've proved to me that you've changed. Now, I thought you were taking me to see the OC so let's bloody get on with it.'

Blackstone laughed mirthlessly. 'Oh dear,' he said. 'You always were an obstinate beggar. I can promise you this much, though, Jack. It's really not worth getting on the wrong side of me. It wasn't back then, and it certainly isn't now.'

'Just as I thought,' snarled Tanner. 'You haven't changed.'

'You're making a big mistake, Jack,' said Blackstone, slowly. 'Believe me – a very big mistake.'

2

By the time he reached Manston Squadron Leader Lyell was already in a bad mood, but his spirits fell further when he saw the wagons dousing the flames of Robson's Hurricane – or, rather, what was left of it: the fuselage was nothing more than a crumpled black skeleton. Then, clambering out of the cockpit, he saw Cartwright, his rigger, examining what was evidently damage along his own fuselage.

'Don't worry, sir,' said Cartwright. 'Only a couple of bullet holes.'

'I didn't notice any difference,' Lyell muttered.

'No – looks like they went clean through. Soon patch that up.'

'What about Robson?'

'Believe he's all right, sir. His kite didn't blow until he was well clear.'

'That's something, then.' He began to head back, but Smith, his fitter, called after him.

'Did you get it, sir? The Dornier?'

Lyell stopped. 'Put it this way, Smith, I doubt very much that it will have made France.' As he walked on across the grass, he decided to continue with the lie, but it did little to improve his mood or assuage the humiliation and anger he felt at having been foxed by a lone German reconnaissance plane. Christ, how many times had they practised their aerial attacks? Almost every day since the war began! Each attack procedure had been assiduously drilled into every pilot, yet the first time they had tried the Number One Attack – which was also the most straightforward – it had failed hopelessly. He had been thrown by the Dornier's return fire, but what had really shocked him was the ineffectiveness of the .303 Browning bullets. Was it the range, or their velocity? He wasn't sure. And his ammunition had run dry so quickly. Fifteen seconds had always seemed a reasonable amount during gunnery practice, but in the heat of combat, it had gone by in a trice. Had their training been wrong or were the German aircrew simply better?

As he neared the dispersal hut he saw Dennison, the intelligence officer, hovering by the doorway, itching to ask him about the sortie. Lyell felt a further flash of irritation.

'So what happened, Skip?' Dennison asked as Lyell dropped his flying helmet into a deck-chair in front of the wooden hut.

'Did you get the bastard?' asked Granby, the commander of B Flight.

'I caught up with him, all right,' Lyell told them. The other pilots were also listening now. 'He was a wily sod, though, making the most of the cloud. Still, I managed to get in a couple of bursts and I'm pretty sure I knocked out his port engine. Must have got the rear-gunner too because he shut up shop pretty quickly. Anyway, she was losing height and trailing a fair amount of smoke when she disappeared into a large bank of cloud.'

'Probably in the Channel by now, then,' said Granby.

'I'd have thought so.' Lyell glanced up at the almost perfectly clear sky above them. 'Bloody weather. Why couldn't it have been like this all the way to France?' He looked at Dennison. 'Don't worry,' he said to the IO, 'I know we can't claim it.' He paused to light a cigarette, exhaled and said, 'I hear Robbo's all right.'

'Bloody lucky,' said Granby. 'Another few seconds and, well, I hate to think.'

Reynolds, the adjutant, now approached Dispersal. 'Station commander wants to see you, sir,' he told Lyell.

Lyell sighed. 'I'm sure he does.' He ran his hands through his hair. 'I think we should have a few drinks tonight.' He addressed this comment to Granby, but it was meant for all of the pilots. 'We should celebrate Robbo's narrow escape, commiserate over the loss of a Hurricane and raise a glass to our first almost-kill.'

'Hear, hear,' said Granby.

'And I don't mean in the mess. Let's go out.' He turned to the adjutant. 'Come on, then,' he said. 'Better face the music.'

Tanner had followed Blackstone to a brick office building at the far side of the parade-ground. In silence they walked up a couple of steps and through the main door, then along a short corridor. Blackstone stopped at a thin wooden door, knocked lightly and walked in.

'Ah, there you are, CSM,' said the dark-haired captain from behind his desk. 'And this must be Sergeant Tanner.'

'Yes, sir,' said Blackstone.

Tanner stood to attention and saluted, while Blackstone ambled over to a battered armchair in the corner of the room and sat down, taking out another cigarette as he did so. Tanner watched with barely concealed incredulity. *Jesus*. He was surprised that the captain should tolerate such behaviour.

'At ease,' said the captain. He was, Tanner guessed, about thirty, with fresh, ruddy cheeks, immaculately groomed hair and a trim moustache. Beside Tanner, sitting stiffly on a wooden chair in front of the desk, was a young subaltern. The room smelled of wood and stale tobacco. It was simply furnished and only lightly decorated: a coat of whitewash, a map of southern England hanging behind the desk, a metal filing cabinet and a hat-stand, on which hung a respirator bag, tin hat and service cap.

'I understand you know the CSM,' said Barclay, taking his pipe from his mouth.

'Yes, sir.'

'In India together?'

'Yes, sir. With the Second Battalion.'

'Good, good.' He nodded. 'Well, let me introduce you to Lieutenant Peploe. You and your men will be joining his platoon.'

The subaltern next to him now stood up and shook Tanner's hand. 'How do you do, Sergeant?'

'Well, sir, thank you.'

Peploe smiled. 'Glad to have you on board.' It was said sincerely. The lieutenant had a rounded yet good-looking face, blue eyes and a wide, easy smile. His hair was thick strawberry blond, slightly too long and somewhat unruly, as though it refused to be tamed by any amount of brushing. His handshake was firm and he looked Tanner squarely in the eye; it was something the sergeant liked to see in an officer. He hoped they would get on well enough.

Barclay tapped his fingers together and shifted in his seat. 'I see you've been decorated, Sergeant.' He noticed the blue, white and red ribbon of the Military Medal sewn above Tanner's left breast pocket.

'A few years ago now, sir.'

'Do you mind me asking what it was for?'

'Nothing much, really, sir. A bit of a scrap with some Wazirs, that's all.'

Blackstone laughed from his armchair. 'Such modesty, Jack. Honestly, sir, Tanner's single-handed defence of Pimple Hill is the stuff of legend – at least,' he grinned, 'the way he tells it. Isn't that right, Jack? I've heard the story a few times now and it gets better with every telling – especially with a bit of the old sauce inside.'

You bastard, thought Tanner.

Blackstone laughed, and shot Tanner another wink, as though it was nothing more than friendly ribaldry between two old comrades.

Barclay raised an eyebrow. 'Well, I'm sure you deserved it, Sergeant.'

Tanner shifted his feet, aware that he was betraying his discomfort. What could he say? He knew Blackstone was baiting him, daring him to rise. He had never spoken of that September day, four and a half years before, in the hills around Muzi Kor – not once – but Barclay wouldn't believe that now. He cleared his throat. 'I was proud enough to be awarded it, sir, but there are many brave deeds carried out in battle and most go unobserved. And there were certainly other men braver than me that day.'

'Yes, well, I'm sure you're right. In any case . . .' Barclay let the words hang and fumbled for his tobacco pouch. 'So,' he said at last, 'were you briefed in Leeds, Sergeant?'

'The regimental adjutant told me that this is still really a training company, sir. That most of the men have been hurried through formal training and have been sent here to do coastal and airfield guard duty.'

'That's about the sum of it. Since Norway, everyone's expecting Jerry to make a move against us in the Low Countries. With the Second Battalion in Palestine and the poor old Fifth in the bag, the First Battalion's a bit stretched. The idea is that our recruits can do a bit of soldiering of sorts and carry out more training while they're about it. But, of course, we need experienced men like the CSM here and yourself.'

'And the men Sergeant Tanner has brought with him, sir,' added Peploe.

'Absolutely.' Barclay lit his pipe, a cloud of blue-grey smoke swirling into the still air of the office. 'I hear you had quite a time of it out in Norway, Sergeant.'

'Yes, sir.' Tanner knew the captain wanted to hear more, but he was not going to indulge him. Not in front of Blackstone.

'Sounds like you were lucky to get out.'

'Yes, sir.'

'I don't know how you do it, Jack,' interrupted the CSM. 'Most of the Fifth Battalion get themselves put in the bag, but you manage to get yourself safely back to Blighty.' He sniggered. 'I tell you, sir, Tanner's one of those lucky soldiers. Always gets himself out of a tight fix.'

Tanner glared at Blackstone. Then, too late, he saw that Peploe had seen.

'We need men like that,' said the lieutenant. 'If what the CSM says is true, Sergeant, I'm very glad to have you in my platoon.'

'Thank you, sir,' said Tanner.

Barclay put another match to his pipe. 'Yes, I'm sure we can all learn something from you, Sergeant. Anyway,' he leaned back in his chair, 'what else do you need to know? We're a small company. Three platoons, most not quite at full strength although Mr Peploe's will be, now that you're here. We rotate duties between training, guarding the airfield and a stretch of the coast at Kingsgate – do you know it? Between Broadstairs and Margate. Big castle there. It's a hotel and, incidentally, out of bounds to service-men. Not very taxing stuff, I'm afraid, but important work all the same.'

'So, do you think we'll be going to France, sir?'

'Yes – I meant to say. That's the point of us being down here. In effect we're the reserve for the First Battalion. A hop across the Channel and we'll be right alongside them. Now,' he said, placing his hands flat on the desk. 'Is there anything else?' He turned to Blackstone, who was absent-mindedly picking at his fingernails. 'CSM?'

Blackstone looked up. 'Shall I brief the sergeant on duty rotas, or will you do that, Mr Peploe?'

'I can do that, thank you, Sergeant-Major,' said Peploe. 'I want to meet Tanner's men in any case.'

'Very good, sir.'

Barclay clapped his hands to signal the end of the interview, then suddenly said, 'Oh, yes – I almost forgot, but there is something else you should know. I'm afraid we've had some thieves here at the airfield.'

'Sir?'

'Two nights ago a dozen barrels of fuel were stolen. Understandably, the station commander's livid about it. He rather wants us to get to the bottom of it.'

'It's those Poles, sir,' said Blackstone.

'I really don't know how you can be so certain,' said Peploe.

'You'll see, sir,' said Blackstone. 'I'd put good money on it.'

'Poles, sir?' Tanner asked Peploe.

'Yes. Former soldiers and pilots, mostly. They've come over since the fall of their country, poor devils. They're being housed here for the moment.'

Barclay raised an eyebrow at Peploe, then said, 'We've got several dumps here, you see, Sergeant. Lorries deliver the fuel in barrels – presumably from a refinery somewhere – a couple of times a week. They're taken to the fuel stores and then the bowsers siphon the petrol from there. One of these dumps was broken into and the barrels swiped. Of course, the fuel's got dye in it but that hardly stops people using it. After all, once you've put it in your car or what-have-you, who's to know? It's all high-octane stuff but apparently that's of little concern on the black market.'

'Why do you think the Poles are responsible, sir?' Tanner asked Blackstone.

'I saw several of them skulking around the store in question the other day. And a number of them are employed around the airfield and camp, some as drivers. You couldn't nick all those barrels without a number of men being involved, and I can't see any of the military personnel doing it. We've a war to fight and win, not help lose by pinching fuel needed for the aircraft here. No, it's those Poles, all right. Certain of it.'

'Anyway, the point is, Tanner,' added Barclay, 'we need to be vigilant. You see anything suspicious, you tell one of us right away.'

'Yes, sir.'

Barclay dismissed Tanner and Peploe, but not Blackstone. To Tanner's surprise, the CSM took out another cigarette and settled back in the armchair next to the OC's desk. *Blackstone.* Tanner sighed. Christ, but that man had made his life difficult during the

Nowshera Brigade days, yet when the CSM had been wounded he'd thought it would be the last he'd ever see of him. Of all the luck! And he was just the same – five minutes in front of Captain Barclay had proved that. Tanner clenched his fists. He had an urge to hit something very hard.

Neither Tanner nor Peploe spoke until they were outside the building and standing in the parade-ground. The sun still shone brightly and Tanner squinted. A sudden roar of aero-engines from behind the office block made both men turn. Through a gap between the buildings, Tanner saw a Blenheim take to the air, followed by two more, then another three a few moments later. The two men moved to where they could see the bombers better and watched as they climbed into the sky and away towards the coast.

'Beasts of aircraft, aren't they?' said Peploe. 'Six-oh-oh Squadron. I've learned there're three squadrons here – the Blenheims, the Defiants of 264 Squadron and the Hurricanes of 632. I've often wondered what the world must look like from up there. Pretty bloody amazing, I should think.' He smiled. 'Have you ever fancied flying, Sergeant?'

'Like you, sir, I wouldn't mind being able to look down on the world, but I think the Army suits me better. I prefer to have my feet firmly on the ground rather than relying on a machine up in the sky.'

'I suppose there's something in that – although I wouldn't have minded flying fighters. At least then it's just you and your plane. No men to worry about. Actually, the OC of 632 Squadron is Captain Barclay's brother-in-law, Squadron Leader Charlie Lyell. Apparently it's a total coincidence that they should both end up here, but it seems very cosy to me.'

'It's a pretty small world in the military, sir, even during wartime.'

'Yes, I suppose so. Like you and the CSM being thrown together again.'

'Exactly, sir.'

Tanner turned to head back across the parade-ground but Peploe scratched his head and said, 'Look, would you like a quick tour of the place first? A sort of orientation? No one ever bothered to give me one when I first got here, but I wished they had.'

Tanner readily agreed. He was curious about the fuel theft and had intended to look at the Polish quarters and the fuel stores anyway. Peploe had seemed to doubt Blackstone's conviction about the Poles' culpability and certainly it struck Tanner as somewhat odd. After all, how would these men, presumably only recently arrived in England, know where to sell petrol on the black market? Or were they hiding it for later?

First, Peploe wanted to show him the airfield itself. There were, he explained, effectively two airfields, the Northern Grass and the main field, which were bisected by the road leading to Manston village. As he led Tanner to the far side, where the watch office stood, he said, 'I hope you don't mind me saying this, but I couldn't help noticing that you looked rather taken aback by the way the sergeant-major lounged in that armchair.'

'I suppose I was a bit, sir.'

'He's certainly very chummy with the OC. I don't have a yardstick by which to judge these things – as you've probably guessed, I'm new to the Army – but I can see it's perhaps not the normal way of things.'

'I suppose that's between him and the OC, sir.'

Peploe looked thoughtful. 'I also got the impression you don't much like CSM Blackstone.'

Tanner grinned ruefully. 'I'm afraid he wasn't my favourite person out in India.'

'He's very popular here. The lads seem to think the world of him. So does the OC. To be honest, Blackstone is absolutely his right-hand man. I suppose it's because he's such an old hand – but he's a strong character too. Rather clever, in his way.'

'Oh, he's that, all right,' said Tanner.

Peploe laughed. 'So speaks a man who knows. Well, in any case, I'm certain experience must be the best kind of training. It's why I'm delighted you've joined the platoon.'

'You're right about experience, sir,' replied Tanner. 'You can be the best soldier in training but until you've been under fire you haven't been tested.'

'I'm sure you have much to teach me, Sergeant Tanner. I was at university before the war, and come from a farming family with no military background whatsoever, so being a soldier is still very much a novelty to me.'

'Your father wasn't in the last war, then, sir?'

'No – he stayed on the farm. So did my uncle.'

'Well, there's not much to it, really. I'll bet you know how to use a rifle, sir.'

'I know how to *use* one, Sergeant. To a farmer's son, shooting is part of the growing-up process. I wouldn't say I'm an especially good shot, although it's certainly not for want of practice. And what about you?' he asked, pointing to the embroidered badge on the forearm of Tanner's battle-blouse – two crossed rifles crested by a crown and ringed with leaves. 'Forgive my ignorance, but I'm guessing that's a marksman's badge of some kind.'

Tanner smiled. 'The Army likes badges, sir.'

'But it is a marksman's badge?'

'Skill in Shooting, sir. But it doesn't mean much.'

'Where did you learn to shoot? With the Army?'

'Like you, sir, I grew up with it.'

'A farmer too?'

'Not as such. My father was a gamekeeper.'

Peploe nodded – *that explains it* – then said, 'But not in Yorkshire, I take it. Somewhere down south, guessing from your accent.'

'South Wiltshire, sir, A while ago now. I joined up as a boy.'

Peploe adjusted his cap. 'Forgive me, Sergeant, all these questions. I'm a nosy sod, aren't I?'

They had almost reached the far side of the airfield. A number of Defiants were lined up in front of the watch office, their ground-crew tinkering with them. In one, a man was testing the hydraulics of the gun turret, swivelling through three hundred and sixty degrees, the electronics whirring.

'I'm sorry to bring up CSM Blackstone again,' said Peploe, as they paused by the watch office, 'but I hope whatever argument you have with him won't be a problem for the platoon – or the company, for that matter.'

A warning, albeit gently made, but still Tanner felt his heart sink. *Damn, damn.* Blackstone had already caused him to get off on the wrong foot with this new posting. 'It won't be, sir. It's true I don't like the man, but I won't let that get in the way of anything.'

Peploe nodded. 'Good.' He smiled at Tanner again. 'You know, Sergeant, I think you and I are going to get along just fine.'

Good. Tanner relaxed a little. He felt rather the same. *Just so long as Blackstone doesn't get in the way.* But, by God, he was going to have to watch his step.

Inside the hut it was warm and still, the sun pouring through the windows and capturing a million tiny dust particles disturbed by the arrival of the men. Aware that to step outside was to court unwanted attention, the five had taken off their battle-blouses, rolled up their shirtsleeves and settled down to a game of poker around one of the unused beds.

More than an hour after they had begun, two – Bell and Kershaw – had fallen by the wayside, although they were still there as spectators.

Sykes glanced at his watch. Tanner was taking his time, he thought. He put his cards face down on his knee and rolled himself a cigarette, while keeping half an eye on the other two players. Hepworth was fingering his cards, knowing he was beaten but evidently hoping that by shuffling them repeatedly, the winning combination would miraculously reveal itself. McAllister, on the other hand, clearly believed he had the hand of his life.

Sykes smiled to himself. 'You know, Mac,' he said, 'you could be quite a good player, but you're so bleedin' easy to read. The point of poker is not to give anything away.'

McAllister jigged his knee up and down. 'I don't care. No one can beat my hand.' He chortled. 'Come on, Hep. Get a move on. You're dead and buried, mate, so why prolong the agony?'

'It's your bloody crowing,' said Hepworth. 'It's driving me mad.'

There was now seven shillings and fourpence on the empty bed that was doubling as a card table – a tidy sum and more than any of them, even Corporal Sykes, was paid for a day's soldiering. Sykes wondered what hand McAllister had – a straight flush, perhaps? Had to be something like that. He licked the cigarette paper, ran a finger down the seam, then put it to his mouth.

Eventually Hepworth sighed and laid his cards face up on the bed. Three of a kind. 'Go on, then, Mac, let's see what you've got.'

McAllister grinned, then slapped down his cards. Seven, eight, nine, ten and jack of clubs. As Sykes had suspected, a straight flush.

'Very good, Mac, very good,' said Sykes. He held his cigarette between his thumb and index finger and stroked his chin.

'Swallow your pride, Stan,' said McAllister. 'Just accept that this time a miracle's happened and you've lost.' He looked round at the others. 'He knows he's beat. Ha – look at all that lovely lolly! That'll keep me in fags and booze for weeks.'

Sykes remained impassive. He was not a tall man, with a wiry frame, a narrow face and always immaculately brilliantined hair. But he had long, slender fingers and a sleight of hand that could fool most people, and certainly the young Yorkshire lads in his section.

'All right, Mac,' Sykes began, and McAllister leaned forward to scoop up the coins in front of him. 'Here's my hand.' He fanned his cards on the bed, a smirk stretching across his face as he did so.

Hepworth laughed. 'It's a royal flush! Ha! Unlucky, Mac!'

'What?' exclaimed Mac. 'How the hell did you manage that?'

Sykes grinned. 'Like I said, Mac, you're too bleedin' obvious.' He picked up a coin and flicked it to McAllister. 'Here,' he said, 'have half a crown. Runner-up's prize.'

A moment later, Tanner returned with Lieutenant Peploe.

'Don't get up,' said Peploe, from the doorway. 'As you are.' He eyed them all and, seeing McAllister putting away the cards, smiled. 'Who won?'

'Corporal Sykes, sir,' said Hepworth. 'McAllister here thought he'd nailed us all, but it weren't to be.'

Sykes shrugged.

'You want to watch the corporal, sir,' said Tanner, standing beside the lieutenant. 'He can do very clever things with those hands of his.'

'What are you suggesting, Sarge?' said Sykes, feigning indignation.

Peploe cleared his throat. 'An introduction,' he said. 'I'm Second Lieutenant John Peploe and I'm your new platoon commander. I know you had quite a time of it in Norway and I'm sorry you've not had more leave. However, your experience is much needed here – we're primarily still a training company – and I'm extremely glad to have you in my platoon. There's every chance we'll soon be joining the First Battalion in France, but in the meantime we need to help the recruits so that if and when we do get to join the BEF we might be of some use.' He glanced around the men. 'You'll meet the rest of the platoon on the parade-ground at four o'clock – or, rather, I should say, sixteen hundred hours – and then we'll be heading off to Kingsgate for some coastal guard duty. Right – now I need to know who you are.' He stepped from the doorway into the hut and approached each man in turn, shaking hands and reiterating how glad he was to have them serving under him. Then he spoke briefly with Tanner, straightened his cap, and left them to it once more.

Sykes came over to Tanner, who had made a beeline for his pack. 'He seems all right. So did the CSM for that matter.'

'Mr Peploe's fine,' agreed Tanner. 'It's early days but I'd say he was a good bloke.'

Sykes thought a moment, conscious that the sergeant had made no mention of CSM Blackstone. He hadn't known Tanner long – a few weeks only – but he believed a friendship had been forged in Norway, founded on mutual trust and respect, and developed during a difficult trek through the snow and the mountains. The enemy had dogged their every move yet they had made it to safety, rejoining the rest of the British forces as the final evacuation was taking place. In many ways they were very different, both physically and in character, but although neither had ever spoken of it, Sykes had recognized early that they shared one thing in common. Both were outsiders among these Yorkshiremen, and there was a tacit understanding of this between them: while most of the Yorkshire Rangers were drawn from the northern cities of Leeds and Bradford, Tanner was a countryman from the south-west and Sykes a working-class boy from Deptford in south London. And these differences revealed themselves every time they spoke – Tanner with his soft south-western burr, Sykes with a Cockney lilt.

'And the CSM?' he asked.

Tanner said nothing.

'Sarge?' Sykes persisted.

Tanner stopped fiddling with his pack and turned to him. 'Let's just say there's some history between us.'

'Before the war?'

'Yes – in India. He may seem a right charmer, but take a piece of advice. Watch how you tread with him around, Stan.'

'All right, Sarge. I'll bear that in mind.' For a moment, he thought about asking what that history was exactly, then dismissed the idea. He already knew Tanner well enough to sense he would get no more out of him now. Eventually, though, he would get to the bottom of it. He promised himself that.

It was around one a.m. on the morning of Friday, 10 May, when Stanislaw Torwinski woke to find a hand pressed hard across his mouth, a hand that smelled of old tobacco and oil. No sooner had he opened his eyes to the almost pitch dark of the hut than two more hands grabbed his shoulders and dragged him out of his bed. He tried to speak, but the hand across his mouth merely pressed harder.

There were only three of them in the hut, the overflow from more than a hundred of their compatriots who were housed in identical huts alongside. More Poles were on their way to join them, they had been told, but in the two weeks since they had first arrived at Manston, it had remained just the three of them.

Torwinski was conscious of Ormicki and Kasprowicz struggling too. As his eyes adjusted, he was aware of a faint hint of light from the open door, then a voice said, 'Get dressed,' and a torch was briefly turned on, shining at the clothes laid out on the empty bed next to his own. The hand released his mouth.

'Tell the other two, but otherwise don't say a word, understand?' The unmistakable muzzle of a pistol was thrust into his side.

Torwinski nodded again, then spoke in Polish. 'What do you want with us?' he said, conscious of the tremor in his voice. A fist pounded into his face and he gasped.

'I told you not to speak,' said the same voice again. 'Now get dressed.'

Torwinski did as he was ordered. Quivering fingers fumbled at buttons. His head felt light, his brain disoriented. There were several men, but how many exactly, he could not be certain.

'Hurry!' hissed the voice, then the torch was flashed on again.

Torwinski squinted in the sudden light then glanced briefly at the other two – Kasprowicz grimacing angrily, Ormicki with terror on his face. As Torwinski bent to tie his laces, he was shoved forward. Stumbling, he was grabbed by the collar and pushed roughly towards the door and out into the night. 'Where are you taking us?' he said. 'What do you want with us?'

Hearing his comrade speak, Ormicki began to ask Torwinski questions and also received a blow to the head.

'I told you,' said the man, in a low, steady voice, 'to bloody well keep quiet. Now shut up – I don't want to hear another sound.'

'Why don't we gag them?' said another.

'You can keep your bloody trap shut an' all,' said the first man. 'Now come on, let's get going.'

Slowly, Torwinski's eyes adjusted to the night light. There was no moon, but the sky was clear and millions of stars cast an ethereal glow so that he could see the dark shapes of the huts, the trees near by and the track that led towards the Northern Grass. His heart was hammering as they stumbled on in silence. There were four men, one ahead, the other three behind. All wore their helmets low over their eyes so that it was impossible to tell who they were or what they looked like other than that they appeared to be and sounded like British soldiers.

Torwinski prayed they might see someone else – a late-working mechanic or a guard, perhaps. He was certain that whatever these men wanted with them it was not authorized. How could it be? What had they possibly done wrong? He could think of nothing. But not a soul stirred. As they neared the Northern Grass, a row of Hurricanes loomed in front of them, but then they were pushed to the left, along the airfield road until they reached a series of stores and a parked lorry, which, from the cylindrical shape of its load, Torwinski recognized as a fuel bowser.

'Get in,' growled the first man, opening the cab door. Torwinski climbed up, the other two following. The same question kept repeating in his mind. *What can they want with us?* His stomach churned and sweat ran down his back, chilling him. Inside the cab it was darker again, and one of the soldiers opened the other door. Torwinski turned to look, and as he did so the butt of a rifle was driven into the side of his head. His vision and other senses left him. By the time he had slumped forward against the dashboard, Ormicki and Kasprowicz had been knocked cold too.

Standing on the cliffs at White Ness just a few hundred yards north of Kingsgate Castle, Sergeant Tanner had been staring out to sea when he heard a lorry, followed by muffled yells from the men guarding the roadblock.

'What the hell?' he murmured and, calling Hepworth and Bennett, one of the new men, he ran towards the main road that led to Kingsgate. He could hear the lorry thundering onwards, then saw the slit of beam from the blackout headlights as it approached the bend in the road before the castle.

'What the bloody 'ell's going on, Sarge?' said Hepworth, breathlessly.

'Some damn fool's driven right through our sodding checkpoint,' Tanner replied. Standing in the long grass at the side of the road, he unslung his rifle and levelled it towards the bend.

'What are you going to do, Sarge?' asked Bennett.

'Shoot the bastard's tyre.'

'Do you think it's a Jerry?' Bennett was young, only eighteen.

Before Tanner could reply, the lorry ploughed straight on at the bend, smashing through a fence and a hedge and crashing to a standstill as it hit a tree.

Immediately Tanner was sprinting down the road, Hepworth and Bennett following. As he leaped through the hole in the fence and hedge, he heard groaning from the cab, then saw a figure stumble out, stagger across the young green shoots of corn and collapse.

Hurrying to the prostrate figure, Tanner knelt beside him and put his ear to the man's mouth.

'Ormicki and Kasprowicz,' the man mumbled.

'What?'

'In the lorry,' slurred the man. 'They are in the lorry.'

Christ, thought Tanner. Hepworth and Bennett were beside him now and shouts were coming from the road. He stood up and was about to hurry over to the ticking lorry when there was an explosion and the vehicle was engulfed in flames.

'No!' groaned the man. 'No!' Tanner dived back to the ground. The flames now lit the sky, and as the sergeant raised his head he saw the shape of two men engulfed in the inferno.

'Let's get out of here,' he said and, with Hepworth's help, hoisted the man to his feet. 'Here, Hep, grab my rifle, will you?' he said. He lifted the man onto his shoulder and carried him across the field to the road. There, they met Lieutenant Peploe and Corporal Sykes.

'A petrol bowser, sir,' said Tanner, as he laid the man carefully on the verge. 'Two dead by the look of it.'

'Bloody hell!' said Peploe. 'What a stupid waste. Our fuel thieves?'

Tanner shrugged. 'Maybe. Here, Hep, shine your torch on him, will you?' He looked down at the man, and saw a livid gash across his forehead. Blood was running freely down the side of his face. Quickly, Tanner delved into his pocket for a field dressing, tore it open and took out the first bandage. He pressed it against the wound, then wrapped the second around the man's head. 'Where are you hurt?' he asked.

'I'm all right,' murmured the man, making an effort to sit up.

'Steady there,' said Tanner. 'Just stay where you are for the moment.' He peered up at Peploe, standing beside him. 'At the very least this cut needs attention, sir. We should get him to the MO.'

'I'll run down to the hotel,' said Peploe, 'and use their phone to get an ambulance and a fire-wagon. Hepworth, go back to the checkpoint and get the truck. I'll meet you back here.'

'That fire will burn itself out before a fire-wagon can get here, sir.'

'You're probably right, but I still need to report this straight away.'

Tanner nodded. 'Shall I organize another roadblock here, sir? We don't want anyone going near the site, do we?'

'Good idea, Sergeant.'

When the lieutenant had gone, Tanner turned to Sykes and said, 'So why the hell wasn't he stopped at the checkpoint?'

'He just went straight through, Sarge. Nearly knocked Mr Peploe over.'

Tanner sighed, then turned back to the man lying on the ground. 'Can you hear me?'

The man groaned.

'What's your name?'

'Torwinski,' murmured the man. 'I am from Poland.'

'And the other two?'

'Yes – also Poles.'

'That fuel lark you was tellin' me about,' Sykes said, turning to Tanner. 'Perhaps the CSM was right.'

'No,' gasped the man. 'We were taken.' He groaned again and grimaced in pain.

'Easy, mate,' said Sykes. 'Easy.'

'What do you mean?' asked Tanner.

'We were all asleep. Some men came in, woke us up and ordered us to get dressed. They led us out to the truck. Then they hit us. The next thing I know the truck has been driven into the tree and I wake up. I knew I had to get out. Then the explosion.' He put his hand to his eyes. 'I don't know why this happened. I don't know what they wanted with us.'

'Did you see these men?'

'It was dark. Whenever they shone their torches they did so in our faces so we could not see them. But they were soldiers. British soldiers.'

Tanner stood up, walked a few steps away from the prostrate Torwinski, then pushed back his helmet and wiped his brow. 'Bloody hell, Stan. This is not good. Not good at all.'

'What I'd like to know, Sarge, is what the hell a fuel bowser was doing on this road anyway. If you want to hide nicked fuel, why drive towards the coast where there's bound to be roadblocks?'

'God knows. Looks like someone's trying to stitch these lads up, though.'

Sykes stepped away onto the road. 'You believe his yarn, then?'

'Don't you?'

'I dunno, Sarge.'

'He's a bloody good liar if he isn't telling the truth.'

'Christ, Sarge, you know what that means?'

'Yes, Stan. Those Poles were murdered.'

3

Tanner stood over Torwinski as he waited for Lieutenant Peploe to return. Even from seventy yards away the flames of the bowser cast a low orange glow. He pulled out a cigarette and offered one to the Pole but he had his hands over his eyes. Tanner passed the packet to Sykes and struck a match. Blood was already seeping through the bandages on Torwinski's head, Tanner noticed, but the fellow seemed more tormented by grief than by his physical injuries. There appeared to be no broken bones, though; he'd been lucky.

For a short while, Tanner and Sykes stood in silence. It occurred to Tanner that it had been a mistake to suggest that Torwinski should see the medical officer. The man needed to be taken somewhere out of harm's way – a place where his would-be murderers couldn't make a further attempt on his life. Lieutenant Peploe would be back soon, but he had only known the officer half a day and was uncertain how much he should say about his suspicions.

A thought struck him. He told Sykes to wait with Torwinski, then clambered back through the fence and hurried towards the still burning bowser. He could see the charred corpses in the cab and stepped past the tree so that he could see more clearly their precise position. The flames were dying down but as Tanner walked around the bowser he felt the heat on his cheeks and ears. He studied the blackened bodies; it was as he had suspected. He headed back to the road.

'Listen, Stan,' said Tanner, as he rejoined Sykes, 'we don't both need to wait with him, and that second roadblock needs setting up. Sort it out, will you?'

'Right away,' Sykes replied. 'But, Sarge, we need to get him somewhere safe.' He hurried off to fetch some men.

A few moments later, Tanner heard running footsteps and Peploe appeared. Rather breathlessly he said, 'The MO and fire-wagons are on their way, and so are the RAFP. Jesus, I'm exhausted. What about that second roadblock?'

'Corporal Sykes is organizing the men now, sir.'

Peploe looked down at Torwinski. 'How is he?'

'He should be in hospital, sir.'

'Really? I thought he'd just cut his head.' He squatted beside Torwinski. 'Are you hurt anywhere else?'

'No,' mumbled Torwinski. 'I don't think so. I just want to get the bastards who did this.' He pushed himself up.

'Steady, mate,' said Tanner.

'What are you talking about?' Peploe asked Torwinski. 'Get who?'

'Sir,' Tanner interrupted, 'can I have a word?'

Peploe stood up. 'What the bloody hell's going on, Tanner?'

'Sir, this man says he and the other two in the truck were forcibly taken from their hut, marched to the bowser and knocked un-conscious. He says he doesn't know how they got here.'

'Sounds a bit far-fetched, doesn't it?'

'Maybe, sir. But if these men did steal the bowser, what are they doing here by the coast? According to my map, this road leads to Kingsgate only. It's hardly the place to shift stolen fuel, is it? And how would they know where to sell it anyway? They've only been here a couple of weeks.' He took a pace away, then added, 'What bothers me, sir, is that if he's telling the truth, the Poles've been framed to look like the thieves.'

Peploe rubbed his hands over his face. 'And if so, Sergeant, this man's life is presumably still in danger. Christ, what a mess.'

'Yes, sir.'

'But in hospital he might be safer?'

Tanner nodded.

Peploe sighed. 'And what do you think?'

'Something makes me believe him, sir.'

'Who else could have done this?'

'Any of the troops here.'

'How, for God's sake?'

'Must have jumped out of the cab. I had a look at the wreckage, sir. Neither of the two dead men was driving.'

Peploe scratched the back of his head, then pulled a slim hip-flask from his battle-blouse, unscrewed the top and offered it to Tanner. 'Slug of Scotch, Sergeant?'

'Not for me, thank you, sir.'

'Well, don't mind me, Sergeant. I find it helps me to think straight.' He took a couple of sips, then put the flask back. 'All right, Tanner. I'm going to stay with this man. You get one of the others to bring the truck down and I'll make sure he gets to hospital in Ramsgate. But for the time being don't breathe another word about this to anyone. The last thing we want is rumour and wild speculation flying around – and we should be careful not to endanger this man's life further. Understood? I'll speak to Captain Barclay about it later.'

'Yes, sir. What about the Snowdrops, sir?'

'Snowdrops?' Lieutenant Peploe looked confused.

'The RAF Police, sir. What should we say to them? There might be other police as well.'

'Damn – I hadn't thought of that. You must, of course, tell the police, but no one else. And in the meantime let's make sure both these roadblocks are properly manned. We don't want any more tearaway lorries ploughing through them.'

*

As Tanner had predicted, by the time the fire-wagon had arrived, the flames around the bowser had all but died out. The RAFP arrived, took a few statements, including one from Tanner, placed a cordon around the scene and left one of their men on guard. Torwinski had already been taken to hospital by Lieutenant Peploe so no one else was any the wiser – for now, at any rate.

With a second roadblock set up under the command of Sykes, Tanner walked back to the first where McAllister, Bell and a number of the new men were positioned across the road.

There were, of course, rumours and wild speculation aplenty among the men about what had happened. Peploe could do nothing about that, although no one doubted that the Polish men in the bowser had been the fuel thieves. Instead, debate raged over what they had been doing there and how they had come to crash. Tanner said nothing, listening to their theories without comment and shrugging in response to their questions. He would have found it amusing had it not been for his growing unease.

It was tempting to think that Blackstone was behind it somehow. Tanner had known him to have been involved in various scams in India – not that he had ever been able to prove it or that Blackstone had ever been caught. Yet the more rational part of his brain reminded him now that this could have been the work of any number of people and, in any case, no matter how much he disliked the man, that did not make Blackstone a murderer.

Not for the first time since it happened, Private Ellis was recounting the moment the truck had sped towards him and thundered through the roadblock. 'I still can't believe it,' he said. 'I shouted out for them to halt but the sodding thing was still coming at me, wasn't it? So I jumped out of the way and I swear he missed me by inches. I didn't join up to be run over by one of our own.'

'But they're not our own, are they, Billy?' said Private Coles. 'They're Poles. It's cos of them we're in this bloody war in the first place.'

Tanner wandered a short way from the roadblock, in the

direction of Manston village. 'When did you first notice the bowser?' he called to Ellis.

'What do you mean, Sarge?' Ellis was taller than most of the others, a lanky youngster with a thin, heavily freckled face.

'Did you see or hear it first?'

'I dunno, Sarge. It came round that sharp bend up ahead, then drove straight at me.'

'And did you see anything odd? Someone jumping out, for instance?'

'No, Sarge – but it was dark. You could only see the slits in the headlights.' He tugged at his bottom lip, thinking. 'Come to think of it, I did hear something. Like a door slamming. Or, at least, I think I did.' He ran a finger round his collar. 'But it happened so fast, like.'

Tanner walked on down the road, taking out his torch. It gave off only a little light when the blue lens was in place but it was enough for him to see the verge. After a couple of hundred yards, he began to think his theory had been wrong and perhaps the Poles had been to blame, after all. The vegetation was apparently undisturbed, silvery cobwebs stretching across the abundant cow-parsley. But just before the corner he saw what he had been looking for: an area where the plants had been flattened and broken stems hung limply, clearly showing where something heavy had rolled across – something like a man's body. And on the road there were faint foot-prints where dew-sodden boots had trodden. *So there was a fourth man*, thought Tanner. How easy it must have been: the corner was almost at right angles; the bowser would have had to slow down almost to a stop to turn. Then, before it had built up speed again, the driver had simply jumped out. Ahead, to the roadblock and beyond, the road was dead straight so the lorry had thundered towards Ellis. Whoever had jumped from the cab would have had all the time in the world to make good his escape and, with the bowser full of fuel, the inevitable crash, when it came, would cause an explosion that should have killed the three men still in the cab. *Jesus*, thought Tanner, as he went back to the checkpoint. The Pole had been telling the truth.

When he reached the others, he was still deep in thought. He pulled out a cigarette, then heard the sound of screeching tyres from the direction of the hotel, followed by shouts and the gunning of a car engine. 'For God's sake, what now?' he said. He heard more shouts, then saw a car's dim headlights approaching.

'Bloody hell, this one's not going to stop either!' yelled McAllister.

'Yes, it bloody well is,' said Tanner, striding into the centre of the road and shining his torch directly at the vehicle.

It made no attempt to slow down or stop. Tanner took his rifle from his shoulder, pulled back the bolt and fired a warning shot into the air, but still the saloon came towards him.

'Watch out, Sarge!' said Hepworth. The driver swerved, but Tanner was forced to leap out of harm's way. He heard laughter as the car drove on and cursed to himself. Then, having regained his composure, he drew the rifle to his shoulder, aimed at the rear wheel, pulled back the bolt again and squeezed the trigger.

The shot cracked loudly in the still early-morning air. There was another report as the left rear tyre burst. The car lurched from side to side, ran off the road and eventually came to a halt in the hedge a hundred yards ahead.

'Blimey, Sarge, what have you done?' said Hepworth.

Tanner slung his rifle back on his shoulder. 'Hopefully taught them to respect checkpoints, Hep.' With McAllister and Hepworth, Tanner jogged down the road to the car. The men who had been inside were already staggering about beside it. One was being sick into the hedge.

An officer, clutching his forehead with his handkerchief, strode awkwardly towards them. 'What the bloody hell d'you think you're playing at?' He swayed; he could barely stand.

'We'll get the truck and take you home, sir,' said Tanner, noticing squadron leader's rings on his jacket cuffs.

'No, you'll bloody well tell me what the hell you were doing.' He had taken a step forward so Tanner could smell the alcohol on his breath and felt spittle spray his cheek. Wiping his face, he said, 'Mac, go and get the truck.'

'Sarge,' said McAllister, and hurried off.

'Is this the bastard who shot at us?' said another man, staggering towards Tanner.

'We'll be getting you home in a minute, sir,' said Tanner.

The man, a flight lieutenant, stood beside the squadron leader, and pushed Tanner in the chest. He took a step backwards, his anger rising.

'Who the bloody hell do you soldiers think you are?' said the flight lieutenant. He shoved Tanner again, then made to punch him, but Tanner saw it coming and stepped deftly to one side. The pilot lost balance and fell over onto the road. He heard Hepworth laugh.

'So you think it's funny, do you?' slurred the squadron leader. 'Let me tell you this, sonny, you won't be laughing tomorrow when your CO hears about it. You won't be laughing at all.' He stabbed a finger at Hepworth. 'And as for you, Sergeant,' he said, turning to Tanner, 'you're going to regret your men firing on us like that.' He tugged at the stripes on Tanner's sleeve. 'Think you might not be wearing those for much longer.'

Tanner knew there was no point in arguing with the man. He was drunk, and so were the six other pilots who had been crammed into the saloon. The squadron leader had a trickle of blood running down the side of his head, and another man was clutching at his arm, but otherwise no one appeared to be badly hurt. They had not been travelling particularly fast and the car's momentum had largely dissipated by the time it had stopped. Tanner thought about knocking them all to the ground, then simply piling them into the back of the truck, but no matter how drunk they were, he decided it was not worth the risk, should they remember it in the cold light of day. In Norway, he had knocked down a French officer and had regretted it ever since.

Instead, he merely stood his ground. 'The truck will be here in a minute, sir. Then you can get back to the airfield.'

One of the men tried to start the car, but the starter motor whined helplessly. In frustration, he got out again, kicked the wheel and yelled with pain. The squadron leader staggered, grabbed hold of Tanner for support, then stood upright. 'What's your name, Sergeant?'

'Tanner, sir.'

'Tanner. Tanner.' He looked around at the others, nearly losing his balance again. 'Chaps, this sharp-shooter's called Tanner. Sergeant Tanner. Remember that, will you? Want to be sure we don't forget so we can make life really unpleasant for him as pay-back for ruining our little night out.'

Tanner clenched his fists, but at that moment the truck drove up and, with a squeak of brakes, halted beside him. McAllister and Sykes stepped out.

'Stan,' said Tanner, 'you and Mac can get these men back to the airfield. I'll stay here with the others.'

'Don't take this the wrong way, Sarge,' said Sykes, in a low voice, 'but was that a good idea?'

'You heard Mr Peploe, Corporal,' Tanner snapped. 'Let no one through. These jokers didn't stop.' He sighed. 'Just get them out of here, Stan.'

He glanced at his watch – nearly four a.m. – then walked slowly back to the checkpoint. Another four hours before they were due to be relieved. Behind him, the first streak of light spread across the horizon, announcing the dawn of a new day.

When the truck had departed Tanner took two of the new men and went back to the coast, between Kingsgate and White Ness. The air was crisp, the scent of cow-parsley and grass heavy on the morning air. Birdsong filled his ears, busy and shrill from the trees and hedgerows. He and his men walked along the track in silence; he knew they wanted to talk to him about the night's events but he had given a curt growl in response to one question and since then they had not dared ask another.

Damn, damn. He wondered what would happen when he got back to Manston, although the sinking feeling in the pit of his stomach told him the answer. As far as he was concerned, he had obeyed orders, but he had not yet been with the company for twenty-four hours and knew little about the men and officers he had joined. Whatever respect he might have earned in Norway counted for little here – he would have to win it all over again. There was a strict hierarchy in the armed forces and class played a large part in that; in his experience, officers tended to stick together. Blackstone was an exception to the rule. NCOs who were perceived to be getting above their station were normally cut down swiftly to size. He just hoped Peploe would stick up for him.

And then there was the matter of the Poles' death. He was convinced Torwinski had spoken the truth, which meant that someone had committed murder. Admittedly, there were a lot of RAF personnel at Manston and even anti-aircraft gunners as well, yet Torwinski had been sure the men who had dragged him out of bed were soldiers – he had been quite specific about it. If he was right, that meant the chances were they were from within Training Company, which was not good – not good at all. Men who stole and committed murder had no respect for command or discipline. They could undermine an entire company. That was a bad enough prospect while they were idling in Kent, but would spell disaster if they were sent to France and found themselves in action. *Blackstone*, cursed Tanner, not for the first time that day. He had to be involved. *Had* to be. Nothing could happen without Blackstone knowing about it, without his approval. That was his way: complete control through a combination of charm and ruthlessness.

He needed to think. As he gazed out over the sea, the Channel seemed calm, deep and benign, twinkling as the first rays of sunlight spread across the water. Beyond, he could see the French coast, a hazy line on the horizon. He took out a cigarette, lit it and inhaled deeply. It was hard to imagine a more peaceful scene.

Just three hours after he had collapsed fully clothed into his bed, Squadron Leader Lyell had been woken. At first, his head did not hurt because he was still slightly drunk. Having quickly immersed himself under a cold shower, he dressed again and headed down to Dispersal on Northern Grass, with Granby and several of the other pilots in tow. No one spoke much as they stumbled across the grass.

Dennison was waiting for them at their dispersal tent.

'Anything up?' muttered Lyell, his eyes like slits.

'A flight patrol over the Channel,' Dennison told him.

Lyell yawned. As he heard the clang of an erk's spanner, his head began to throb. 'Right,' he said. 'I'll take A Flight up.'

It was a bit of a struggle hoisting himself onto the wing, then into the cockpit, but as he collapsed onto the bucket seat, he put his oxygen mask over his mouth, switched on the supply and breathed deeply. Almost immediately his headache vanished and his mind cleared, as he had known it would. By the time he was over the English coast and heading out to sea, he felt himself once more.

'This is Nimbus Leader,' he called, over the R/T. 'Keep close to me. We're going to climb to angels fourteen, then level out. Keep your eyes peeled. Over.'

He led them on a bearing of fifty degrees to avoid flying directly into the rising sun. It was a beautiful dawn, the sun climbing over France to the east, the Channel below a dark, glistening blue. He could see ships hugging the British coastline, fishing trawlers and merchantmen, white wakes behind them.

It had been a good night, he reflected – at least until that maniac sergeant had shot at them. Christ, he could have killed someone. And although Lyell had not had a chance to examine his car yet, he hated to think what the damage was. A new bumper and possibly even a wing, he guessed. *Bloody hell*. What had the man been thinking of? And how dare he stop them like that? Who did he think he was?

Off duty, Lyell was used to doing pretty much whatever he liked with his squadron; it was the fighter pilot's prerogative – an unwritten code. Yes, strictly speaking, Kingsgate Castle was out of bounds, but no one had ever worried about that before. *Bloody foot-soldiers*. And what was that sergeant's name? *Tanner*. Yes, he remembered that. Lyell thought about it for a moment, France stretching away off his starboard wing. He couldn't complain to the station commander because Wing Commander Jordan would only rollock him for visiting the castle. That was another unwritten rule: go there, but don't get caught. On the other hand, Lyell was damned if the upstart sergeant was going to get away with it. He decided that on their return to Manston he would pay Hector a visit and get him to tear Tanner off a strip or two. Lyell chuckled to himself. Old Hector would see to it that he got his car bill paid and his honour salvaged. All right, so they'd gone through a roadblock, but those Army boys couldn't go around taking pot-shots at pilots. It wasn't on. The man needed to be taught a lesson.

Much to his relief, when Tanner returned to the checkpoint just before eight that morning, Lieutenant Peploe did not admonish him for shooting the tyre of the squadron leader's car. 'Nothing more than they deserved, Sergeant. Bunch of arrogant bastards,' he told him, then added, 'Let's hope it wasn't the OC's brother-in-law.'

Tanner had forgotten the connection and winced. Peploe, however, was far more concerned about the earlier incident. Torwinski had been taken to hospital in Ramsgate, but the lieutenant was uncertain about what he should say to the OC. 'I've got to tell him, Tanner, but we could do with some hard evidence.'

'I've got proof that there was a fourth person in that truck, sir,' said Tanner, and explained his discovery of the flattened grass by the road.

Peploe insisted on seeing it for himself.

A short while later, as they stood by the verge, he whistled. 'Bloody hell. You're quite right, Sergeant,' he said. 'I can't think of another explanation. Rather clinches it, doesn't it?'

Tanner wondered whether he should say anything about his suspicions, then decided against it. The lieutenant knew what he thought of Blackstone and any finger-pointing would be unconvincing. Even so, it had occurred to him that once Barclay knew about Torwinski, Blackstone would inevitably be in the picture too. If he was right about the CSM's culpability, Torwinski's life would be in danger once more. It was a conundrum to which at present Tanner had no answer.

Peploe walked back to the checkpoint, shaking his head. 'Incredible, isn't it? I never thought the first deaths I witnessed would be deliberately caused by men on our own side. It's not why I joined up, Sergeant.'

'No, sir.'

Peploe sighed. 'Well, I'm not going to let this lie. Those men deserve justice. Christ, the condescending way everyone talks about the Poles, as though they're somehow to blame for the war in the first place. They're easy scapegoats, Tanner, but it's wrong – wholly wrong.'

Tanner agreed, but gut instinct told him that others would not be quite so keen to learn the truth as Mr Peploe. *Bloody hell.* It had been a long and depressing night.

The platoon had been relieved at eight a.m. and, to Tanner's surprise, they had driven back to Manston without any apparent orders for him to report to either the station commander or Captain Barclay. After breakfast, he had gone with the others back to the hut and had lain on his bed. He was tired, and despite a troubled mind, he had gone straight to sleep. It was a trick he had learned during his career in the Army: to sleep anywhere, any time, whenever the opportunity arose.

He had learned to wake up in an instant too. A hand on his shoulder, and he opened his eyes to see Blackstone standing over him. 'Wakey, wakey, Jack.'

Tanner gazed at the solid face, the slightly flattened nose and dark eyes. He saw the crooked teeth that grinned down at him and noticed now that one was almost entirely black. He looked at his watch – just after nine. Christ, he'd only been asleep ten minutes. 'What do you want?'

Blackstone continued to smirk, then tutted. 'What have you been playing at, Jack? Shooting at the OC's brother-in-law! I wouldn't want to be in your shoes right now.'

'Have you woken me just to tell me that or is there anything else?'

'Don't shoot the messenger, Jack,' said Blackstone, feigning indignation. 'I've been asked by Captain Barclay to fetch you.'

Tanner stood up and, without a word, stepped out of the hut into the bright morning sunshine. He strode towards the parade-ground quickly, so that Blackstone had to hurry to keep up with him.

'So, Jack,' said Blackstone, catching up, 'that must have been quite a shot of yours to hit the tyre like that. I'm not sure I'd be able to aim so carefully in the dark. I mean, just imagine if the shot had gone a bit wild. What if you'd hit one of those fighter boys? Could have killed him.'

'The only men dying last night were the Poles in that truck. But you'd know all about that, wouldn't you?'

There wasn't even a flicker on Blackstone's face. 'Yes, a sorry business, but didn't I tell you? I knew those Poles were behind the fuel trouble.'

They reached Barclay's office. 'Ready, Jack?' said Blackstone. 'I'm looking forward to this.'

Tanner stepped inside and saluted. Quite a crowd had assembled in Barclay's office and the room seemed smaller. The OC was behind his desk but on wooden chairs at either side sat three other officers, two RAF and one from the company. Blackstone had once again made himself at home on the armchair in the corner. Tanner eyed the men – he recognized the squadron leader and flight lieutenant from the previous night – and his heart sank. *Christ*, he thought, *it's a bloody court-martial*. And no Peploe. No wonder Blackstone had been gloating.

Barclay coughed in a manner that suggested the proceedings were to begin, then tersely introduced the other men in the room: Squadron Leader Lyell and Flight Lieutenant Granby from 632 Squadron; and Captain Wrightson, the T Company second-in-command.

'Now, Tanner,' said Barclay, his brow furrowed, 'what the devil do you think you were doing last night? You could have killed those pilots.'

'They crossed a checkpoint, sir. It was quite obvious we were there, even in the dark and with reduced headlights. I walked out into the middle of the road as they approached and held up my hand, signalling for them to stop. They ignored this, swerved and drove on so I shot out one of their tyres.'

'It was bloody dangerous,' said Lyell. 'There's no way you could have known you were going to hit the tyre. That bullet could have gone anywhere.'

'With respect, sir, I'm not a bad shot.' He lifted his arm to show his Skill in Shooting badge. 'I aimed at the left rear tyre and hit it.'

'Still a huge risk, Tanner,' said Barclay. 'They could easily have been badly injured or even killed when the car crashed.'

'I doubt it, sir. The car wasn't travelling fast and, in any case, as I discovered afterwards, they were so drunk they could barely stand, let alone drive.'

'That's absolute rubbish,' said Granby. 'We'd had a few beers, that's all.'

'One of you threw up,' said Tanner, 'and you, sir, took a swing at me and fell over.'

'I did no such thing.'

'Ludicrous exaggeration,' added Lyell.

'I remember it distinctly, sir. So, I'm sure, will the men who were with me at the time.'

'Are you saying I'm lying, Sergeant?'

Before Tanner could reply, Captain Wrightson intervened. 'Perhaps, sir, the drink affected your memory?' He chuckled.

'He's talking rot,' said Lyell. 'We'd had a few beers, and it was dark. I saw the checkpoint too late to stop, swerved to avoid the sergeant here and then he shot at us. Luckily no one was hurt but it could have been far more serious. As it is, my car's in a bad way and will cost a fortune to put right.'

Barclay sighed. 'Wasn't it damnably obvious, Tanner, that the car was full of pilots who'd had a few?'

'No, sir. I was told that Kingsgate was out of bounds to service-men. I wasn't expecting any pilots to come from that direction and, as I said, they didn't stop. I was following standard procedure.'

'Damned heavy-handed, though, Tanner.'

'They could have been Germans, sir.'

Barclay snorted. 'Swerving around in their car?'

'We were ordered to stop any vehicles that passed, sir. A lorry had already driven through the checkpoint and men had got themselves killed. I didn't want that to happen again.'

'I think what Sergeant Tanner is trying to say, sir,' interrupted Blackstone, 'is that he was thinking of the pilots' safety. I know it's not really an NCO's place to make such decisions, but I'm sure he felt that by shooting at them he would save them from further mishap.'

Tanner glanced at Blackstone and saw the sly smile on his face. *Damn him!* Tanner had believed the questioning had been going well until that point, but once again Blackstone had made him look a puffed-up fool.

Wrightson smiled again. 'So you were doing 'em a favour, eh, Tanner?'

'They still had a couple of miles to go to get back to Manston, sir. That's quite a long way to drive when you're drunk. But I stopped them because they were approaching from a direction that was out of bounds and because they failed to halt at the checkpoint.'

There was a knock at the door.

'Come!' called Barclay, and Lieutenant Peploe entered.

'Ah, Peploe,' said Barclay.

'Sir. I thought you said I would be present when you spoke with Sergeant Tanner.'

Barclay waved a hand. 'An oversight, Peploe. Anyway, you're here now.'

'Your sergeant has been telling us that it was primarily concern for our welfare that made him shoot at us,' said Lyell.

Tanner felt himself redden, his anger mounting. 'With respect, sir, that's not what I said.'

'Sergeant, you've said your piece,' snapped Barclay. 'You may have been within your rights but you clearly acted impulsively and without due consideration, putting the lives of several pilots at risk and severely damaging Squadron Leader Lyell's car in the process.'

'Sir,' interrupted Peploe, 'I gave Sergeant Tanner specific orders not to let anyone else through the checkpoint under any circumstances. If anyone is to blame for this it's me.'

Barclay sighed. 'I appreciate your loyalty to your platoon sergeant, Peploe, but I really think it's for Tanner here to defend himself.'

'An NCO in front of four officers, sir?'

Barclay shifted in his seat. 'We're just trying to get to the facts, Peploe. Any one of the pilots could have been seriously hurt, if not killed. And then there's Squadron Leader Lyell's car.'

'Then why don't we take this matter to the station commander, sir?'

Lyell glared at him.

'No need to do that just yet, Peploe,' said Barclay, glancing anxiously at his brother-in-law.

Tanner smiled to himself. *Good on you, Mr Peploe.*

'The fact is, sir,' continued Peploe, 'that, with due respect to Squadron Leader Lyell, a far more serious incident took place last night. Two men were killed and it was nothing less than murder.'

At this, Blackstone looked up and Tanner caught his eye. *So I was right,* thought Tanner. *He does know.* It was now his turn to smile.

'What do you mean, murder?' demanded Barclay.

'The third man survived,' said Peploe.

'Why didn't you tell me this earlier?'

'I was about to, sir, but you might recall that the telephone rang and you ordered me to leave.'

'Have you spoken to the Snowdrops?'

'No, sir. I took Torwinski straight to hospital and they hadn't arrived by that time. I haven't seen any civilian police and nor have they asked to see me. I assumed I should speak to you or the station commander first.'

Tanner watched Blackstone intently for any reaction to this

news. Was there alarm in his expression? He couldn't be sure.

'And this survivor claimed what, precisely?' asked Barclay.

Peploe told him.

'Good God, man!' The captain laughed. 'You believe that?'

'Yes, sir, I do,' said Peploe. 'It was also clear that a fourth had jumped from the cab a short distance before the checkpoint. From the driver's side, I should add. You could see where he'd landed on the verge.'

'It sounds most unlikely to me, Lieutenant,' said Squadron Leader Lyell.

'Why, sir? It doesn't seem so to me at all. It's a lot more probable than some recently arrived Poles trying to peddle black-market fuel in a country that's new to them and where they hardly speak the language.'

'Where is this fellow now?' asked Barclay.

'In Ramsgate Hospital,' Peploe told him.

Tanner had been keeping his eye on Blackstone, and at this revelation the CSM caught his gaze and, this time, held it. The threat was unmistakable.

'It seems to me, sir,' said Wrightson to Barclay, 'that we should at least talk to this man. How badly injured is he, Lieutenant?'

'He should make a full recovery, sir.'

At that moment, the telephone rang. With a look of pained exasperation, Barclay picked up the receiver. 'Yes?' he snapped.

Tanner watched the OC's expression change. The bluster and impatience drained from his face, replaced by stunned shock.

'Right,' he said. 'Right, sir. I understand, sir . . . Yes, sir.' Slowly he put the receiver down. 'It's happened,' he said. 'The Germans have invaded Belgium. And we're on standby to join the rest of the battalion. Twelve hours' notice. It seems we'll soon be going off to war.'

4

If he was completely honest with himself, Sturmbannführer Otto
Timpke had probably had too much to drink the previous night.
He prided himself on never losing control, but the news that the
division was at long last on standby to move to the front had been
worth celebrating. When the boss had suggested they might like to
dine out of the mess, he and the other officers in the Aufklärung
Abteilung, the division's reconnaissance battalion, had piled into
their cars and driven into Stuttgart.

There they had met up with some other officers from the 2nd
Regiment Brandenburg and it had turned out to be a particularly
enjoyable night: a good dinner, a few toasts, Rudolf Saalbach
singing 'Casanova-*lied*' – the adopted battalion song – which never
ceased to make him laugh, and then a few hours with an attractive
girl called Maria. He knew that several of his comrades had later
headed off to the city's fleshpots, but that was not his way. Timpke
had always believed that paying for it was an abomination. After all,
the seduction was half the fun. He was, he knew, a handsome
young man. He was tall and broad, with fair hair, a narrow nose and

a smile he had learned to use to good effect, and he had long ago realized that getting women to do what he wanted came rather easily to him.

His whole life had been rather like that. He was blessed with a good brain and a strong physique, and had made the most of both: school, sports, university – he had shone at them all. And when he had joined Brigadeführer Eicke's Totenkopfverbände, he had, naturally, been singled out quickly as officer material and packed off to SS-Junkerschule. It had pleased him to discover that most of his fellow cadets were less clever and educated than he: it ensured that he continued to stand out above the rest. Now, three years later and aged twenty-five, he was commander of the division's reconnaissance unit, the men who would lead the vanguard of any advance and, as such, about to be given the honour of leading the élite of the élite – as Eicke always liked to remind them they were – into battle.

That morning he had woken early. The early-summer sun had streamed through the closed window of his room, making him hot and restless. His mouth had felt dry and his head ached. He had drunk a litre of water, put on his black running shorts and white vest, with the SS runic symbol emblazoned on the front, then headed out of the garrison barracks, down Stuttgarterstrasse and into the baroque palace gardens of Ludwigsburg and the woods beyond. By the time he was running back through the palace gardens, his head had cleared and he felt alert and invigorated. He had drunk wine and schnapps at dinner, but he reflected that it was probably the *sekt* – that essential tool of seduction – that had made the difference. Maria had taken longer than some to succumb and had insisted he match her glass for glass. Still, it had been worth it. He had taken her in his open-top Adler Triumph to a hotel he had used several times before and, in bed, had found her most compliant. Eventually, leaving her asleep, he had crept out and driven back to the garrison. By half past two he had been in his room.

As he showered and changed into his uniform, he wondered

again when they would be moving. If he had one fault, it was impatience. Throughout his life, he had striven for the next goal only to find that once he had achieved it, the rewards were something of an anticlimax. He had been first drawn to the Totenkopf by Eicke's insistence on its élite status, but he had quickly tired of guarding the Reich's enemies. With the boss, he shared a desire for Totenkopf Division to become the finest military unit in all of Germany. With the outbreak of war, the reconnaissance battalion had been sent to Poland, a prospect that had excited Timpke. Once there, however, they had been left to carry out mopping-up operations, rounding up suspicious elements and Jews. Capturing and shooting these people had quickly ceased to give him any kind of thrill and Timpke had realized that this role, in support of the *Wehrmacht*, was unworthy of them.

Eicke had preached patience. Their time would come, he had assured them, but as far as Timpke was concerned, it couldn't come soon enough. Everyone knew that the war was far from over, that at some point the stalemate in the west would crack, and when it did, Timpke was determined to be a part of it. Over the winter, more and more equipment had been acquired. Eicke had sent Timpke and a number of other officers on several missions all over Germany to obtain guns, vehicles and ammunition. In Poland, Timpke had seen with his own eyes that the *Wehrmacht* infantry were poorly provided with vehicles and transport, and by spring had known that their *Waffen-SS* division was better equipped than any regular infantry unit. But still no move to the front had been ordered. It was, Timpke knew, a matter of perception. He had witnessed this first hand during a row with some *Wehrmacht* officers in Stuttgart, who had jeered at them for being concentration-camp guards rather than regular soldiers. Saalbach, and the others they were with, had wanted a fight, but Timpke had urged restraint. Instead he had secretly invited the *Wehrmacht* officers to a marksmanship contest at Ludwigsburg.

It had worked out exactly as Timpke had hoped. The *Wehrmacht* officers had been amazed by the massed vehicles and machinery the Totenkopf could boast, and in the shooting contest, Timpke and his fellows had won comfortably. Somehow, word had got back to Eicke. More importantly, word had also got back to Generaloberst von Weichs, commander of Second Army. In April von Weichs had paid a visit and had watched the division on exercise. Rumour had it that he had been duly impressed. Certainly, more guns had arrived soon after, and all leave had been cancelled. Something was brewing; Timpke had been feverish with anticipation. But the days had passed and no further word came. Every day Timpke trained his men, waiting, waiting, waiting for news that they would be deployed to the front.

Yesterday those orders had finally arrived. The relief had been overwhelming. Immediately trucks had been despatched to pick up sixty tonnes of rations and further ammunition from Kassel. Timpke had sent Oberscharführer Schramm from his own company. It had been an overnight round trip, but Schramm, his men and the rest of the convoy would be back that morning and then they would be ready. At a moment's notice, the division could be on the move, heading west to the front at long last.

After conferring with his company commanders, Timpke took himself off to the range, hoping that by firing a few rounds he would keep himself distracted. He took great pride in his marksmanship. Practice, he knew, was essential, that and an intimate knowledge and understanding of each and every weapon, whether it be a machine-gun, rifle or semi-automatic pistol.

On the rifle range he was joined by Hauptsturmführer Knöchlein, a company commander from the 2nd Regiment and one of those who had been with them in Stuttgart the previous evening.

'Beeck told me I'd find you here. How's your head, Herr Sturmbannführer?' Knöchlein asked.

'Fine, thank you, Fritz.' He aimed carefully at the paper target a hundred metres away, breathed out gently, made certain his head and hands were rock steady, then squeezed the trigger. He felt the rifle kick into his shoulder, his ears rang with the crack, and he turned to Knöchlein with deliberate jauntiness. 'And what about you? Don't tell me, it was light by the time you crawled back.'

Knöchlein looked sheepish. 'It wasn't quite,' he smiled, 'but not far off. Still, we had a good night, didn't we?' He grinned. 'I'm improving by the minute.'

He was older than Timpke by five or six years, with a square, unrefined face that Timpke had always felt betrayed his upbringing in the rougher suburbs of Munich. Timpke liked him well enough and considered him a friend, even though he knew Knöchlein looked up to him in a way that was, frankly, a bit embarrassing. As with so many of Knöchlein's age who had lived through the hard years of the 1920s, Timpke had detected resentment at his core. Poverty had forced him to abandon his schooling, and although he was no fool – and certainly had a streak of ruthless cunning – Timpke knew he was insecure about his lack of education. It was why the SS was so perfect for Knöchlein and others like him: an organization that gave its members a sense of purpose and unity, rewarding performance rather than social standing.

Timpke was peering through his binoculars at the target, and smiled to himself. *Not bad.*

'It's incredible news, isn't it?' said Knöchlein.

'What news?' said Timpke, immediately lowering them.

'Haven't you heard? We've attacked France and the Low Countries.'

'Without us! Damn them. What happened?'

'It's not entirely clear. The *Luftwaffe* have been busy, though.'

Timpke's heart quickened. So it had started! He glanced at his watch. 'Those supplies should be here soon.' He slung his rifle over his shoulder. 'How can you be so relaxed, Fritz? Let's get going. We might be ordered off at any moment.'

The trucks began arriving back at the *Kaserne* just before eleven that morning, filled with fresh supplies. Timpke sensed anticipation in the men, who were chattering and laughing loudly, a new spring in their step. Vehicles were soon lining up, engines rumbling, ready for the move. The courtyard of the barracks was crammed with trucks, troop-carriers, half-tracks, armoured cars and staff cars. Behind the *Kaserne* yet more vehicles waited, as well as the division's anti-aircraft guns, anti-tank guns and field guns, including a dozen 150mm heavy howitzers. Timpke and Knöchlein walked among them, marvelling with pride that the division would be heading to France with more than two thousand vehicles under its banner. A motorized infantry division about to move.

Timpke laughed and gripped Knöchlein's shoulder. 'We'll show those Army bastards, and we'll show those French and Tommy soldiers too.' Briefly he took off his cap, and admired the silver skull-and-crossbones insignia – the death's head – emblazoned upon it, then fitted it back on his well-groomed head. He smiled. 'We'll let them see what the Totenkopf is capable of.'

The news of the German offensive had made an immediate impact at Manston, too. In Captain Barclay's office, Tanner had been dismissed, albeit with a warning.

'All right, Tanner,' said Barclay, 'you can get back to your platoon. This matter will have to wait for the moment. There are more pressing things to attend to now.'

'And what about my car?' asked Lyell.

'For God's sake, Charlie,' Barclay snapped, 'how should I know? Get it to a garage and see what they say. Damn it, we've got a war to fight now.'

Lyell shoved back his chair angrily and made to leave with Granby. Tanner opened the door for them, but as Lyell passed him, he stopped and jabbed him in the chest with a finger. 'I'll be sending you the bill, Sergeant. You might have been saved for now, but I shan't forget about this.'

Not for the first time Tanner had to bite his tongue. Nothing would have given him greater pleasure than to wipe the arrogant snarl from the man's face and knock him out cold. He wouldn't forget the incident either, but he had long ago learned that patience was indeed a virtue. One day, he assured himself, his chance would come, and then he would teach the man a lesson.

He started to leave but Peploe stopped him. 'A moment, Sergeant,' he said, then turned back to Barclay. 'What about the murders, sir?'

Barclay sighed wearily. 'If they were murders, Peploe. What about them?'

'As the duty officer when the incident occurred, I wondered whether I should now contact the police.'

'No, Peploe. Leave it with me. I'll make sure it's looked into. No doubt they'll want to speak to you, but this should go through the proper channels.'

Peploe nodded, then he and Tanner walked out of the building. Ourside, the deep blue of the sky was broken by rolls of plump white cumulus. Tanner squinted in the glare. 'I'm not sure this can wait until Captain Barclay contacts the police, sir,' he told Peploe. 'I'm not saying he won't speak to them, but he's got other things on his mind.'

'You could be right.'

'I just don't think time's on our side, sir. I suppose we could always move him instead.'

Peploe eyed Tanner carefully. 'Is there something you're not telling me, Sergeant?'

Tanner sighed. 'I'm sure the CSM knows something about this, sir. And I'm not just saying that because I don't like the man. It's precisely the kind of stunt he used to pull in India.'

'Murder?'

'No – no, not murder. At least, I couldn't really say. Maybe he wasn't involved in that. Really, sir, I meant the fuel theft. Nothing happens in this company without him knowing about it, and who would dare to pull off something like this under his nose? I watched him, sir, in there. And I'm certain he knows something.'

Peploe took off his cap and ran a hand wearily through his hair.

'There's one way we'll know for sure,' continued Tanner, 'and that's if anyone turns up at the hospital asking for Torwinski. If they do, they've got to have been told by someone in that room a moment ago. Those RAF boys couldn't have been involved as they were getting drunk at the time, so that leaves you, me, Captain Wrightson, the OC and Blackstone. I think we can exclude ourselves, sir.'

Some Blenheims took off, their engines a roar. The two men watched three emerge into the sky on the far side of the office block, then head out towards the Channel.

'I don't know. Christ, I don't know what to think – but I'm not sure I'm convinced the CSM has anything to do with it,' said Peploe, 'but if he has, you're right. We need to protect Torwinski.' The lieutenant consulted his watch. 'We're not on duty again until three o'clock, and it's not ten yet. All right, Tanner. I'll go to the hospital now and see Torwinski. Maybe I can say something to the doctors there – perhaps they can ring the police.'

'I think that's best, sir.'

Peploe nodded. 'Good. I'll get off, then. I can drive down in my own car.'

'And, sir? Thank you for what you said in there.'

'I'm sorry I wasn't there at the beginning. I'm furious about it, to be honest,' he said. 'Stupid sods. Sorry, Tanner, shouldn't really be talking like this, but I'm afraid it's all because of Squadron Leader Lyell and his being the OC's brother-in-law and everything. Lyell knows perfectly well that he's in the wrong and that the station commander would give him short shrift. So he tries to get his revenge by nobbling Captain Barclay and reeling you in for a grilling – a grilling, I should add, to which he knew you couldn't answer freely because of your rank. It's nothing less than bullying – the sort of carry-on one used to have to put up with at school. I've always hated that kind of closing ranks, and I'm damned if I'm going to toe some line just to keep in favour with my fellow officers. I was brought up to do what I believe is right, Tanner.' He smiled sheepishly. 'Listen to me, ranting like some parson. Anyway, go and get some rest.'

Tanner set off for the hut. He felt exhausted and his body suddenly craved sleep. But despite that, the death of the Poles, and its significance, continued to circle in his mind. He was convinced more than ever that Blackstone had to have been involved. The man was like a cancer spreading through the company, corrupting and poisoning, turning good men to bad. *Jesus*. It didn't pay to go to war with men like him. Tanner passed another platoon going through their drill, the sergeant screaming his orders, boots heavy on the tarmac as the men tramped up and down, wheeled to the left, then halted almost as one. The sergeant admonished them for slovenliness. A miserable, useless lot, they were.

Tanner smiled to himself, momentarily distracted, only for darker thoughts to return. He wondered whether the lieutenant would reach Torwinski in time. Perhaps Barclay had already contacted the police. *Perhaps.* Tanner couldn't help believing that Torwinski was still in grave danger, yet catching any would-be murderer was, he knew, probably the only chance they would have of finding evidence that would nail anyone for this crime. The flattened verge would probably have recovered already. Neither Captain Barclay nor any of the other officers had shown much appetite for Peploe's claims. And would the police be any more interested? After all, who cared about a few Poles? If whoever had done this had any sense, they'd keep clear of Torwinski and leave him be.

Lying on his bed, Tanner smelled wafts of tobacco smoke, felt a cool breeze drift across his face and realized, to his annoyance, that he was awake. Opening his eyes, he saw Corporal Sykes standing in the doorway, his slicked-back hair shining in the sun, his field cap tucked into the epaulette of his battle-blouse. Between finger and thumb, he brought the cigarette to his mouth, then noticed Tanner was watching him.

'Oh, Sarge, you're awake.'

'No thanks to you, Corporal.' Tanner sat up.

'Sorry, Sarge. I was wondering whether or not I should wake you. Only I've something to tell you.'

'What? It'd better be good, that's all I can say.' He glanced round at the others, all still fast asleep. McAllister was snoring gently.

Sykes motioned him outside. Tanner buttoned his battle-blouse, grabbed his field cap, then stood up and stepped out of the hut. A glance at his watch – a quarter to one – and a fumble in his breast pocket for his cigarettes.

'What is it, then, Stan?' he asked, putting a cigarette between his lips.

'I woke up about midday and knew I wouldn't get back to sleep again so I got up and wandered around a bit. There's quite a lot of activity going on 'ere all of a sudden. Some ack-ack guns 'ave turned up and there's lorries going back and forth. I spoke to one bloke, and apparently a couple of batteries are moving in.'

'You haven't heard, then?'

'Heard what?'

'We're going to be out of here soon. Jerry's launched his attack. We're on twelve hours' notice to shift it over to Belgium and join the rest of the battalion.'

'Bloody 'ell! Well, that explains it.' He wiped a hand across his mouth. 'Frankly, Sarge, I'm glad. Don't like this place. Sooner we're out of here the better, far as I'm concerned.'

'I agree. Just wish we could leave a few people behind, that's all. Anyway, you didn't wake me up to tell me a few guns've arrived. At least you'd better not have done.'

'No, no – course not. No, what I was going to say was that I've seen the company quartermaster sergeant over by the stores. And guess what?'

'What?'

''E's got a big limp.'

'Has he now?' Tanner allowed himself a faint smile. 'Could have had it a while, though.'

'That's just it, Sarge. He hasn't. At least, he didn't have it yesterday cos I saw him and he was walking fine.'

'Interesting, Stan. Very interesting.'

'So, anyway, I was about to talk to him when the CSM comes over and starts talking to me instead. Friendly as anything, he was, asking me all about myself and handing out smokes. And all the while he was steering me away from CQS Slater and those stores. Eventually he said, "Well, you go and get some more rest while you've got the chance," and gave me a wink and a pat on the back. Said it very nice but I knew it was an order, so I came back and had another smoke, wondering whether I should say anything to you.'

'That's just like Blackstone. He's the biggest two-faced bastard I've ever known. Says one thing, means another.'

'Yes, but what I wasn't sure about was whether he was steering me away from Slater or the stores.'

'Or both.' Tanner scuffed the ground with the toe of his boot. 'I don't suppose you've seen Mr Peploe?'

'No, Sarge.' Sykes eyed him. 'What do you think? What should we do?'

'I'll see if I can find Slater and talk to him. What does he look like?'

'Quite a big bloke. A bit smaller than the CSM and his face looks like he's been a few rounds. Oh, and he's got a limp.'

Tanner grinned. 'Of course. Shouldn't be too hard to spot, then. Where are these stores?'

'Right down the back end of this place. There's a big hangar to the far side of all the huts. It's away to the left of that, on its own at the end of a long workshop.'

'I don't think we should poke around in the stores yet, though.'

'No. Too many people about. Have a look tonight, maybe. Didn't you say we're on airfield duty later?'

'I did. All right – we'll do that. I'll put money on there being something in that storeroom that shouldn't be.'

'Like stolen fuel?'

'Yes, Stan,' said Tanner. 'Like stolen fuel.'

Tanner found the store easily enough. It was a creosoted wooden structure with a corrugated-iron roof, tacked onto the end of a longer brick-built workshop. There were no windows, only a door that was double-padlocked. He wondered whether Sykes would have the means to break the lock – but that was expecting a lot. A small distance away, towards the pilots' accommodation blocks, a Bofors light anti-aircraft crew were manning their gun, but otherwise no one was about, and certainly no one answering CQS Slater's description. A truck rumbled onto the road that bisected the airfield, crunched through its gears and continued on its way. In the distance he heard someone yelling orders. A wasp buzzed near his face and, startled, he swished it away.

He walked round the building, the sun warm on his face. Damn it, he wanted to know what Slater and Blackstone had inside. Ammunition boxes principally, uniform, equipment spares, and what else? *Tonight*, he told himself. He and Sykes would have to get in somehow.

When he returned to the hut there was no sign of Sykes, but several of the others were now awake and playing cards.

'Mr Peploe was looking for you, Sarge,' said McAllister, his hand in front of his face.

'When?'

'Ten minutes back. Said he'll be in the office block.'

Tanner headed out again, across the parade-ground and into the now familiar building, and soon found Peploe's office, a small room that the lieutenant shared with the two other platoon commanders. Peploe was the only one there; the door was open and Tanner saw him leaning over his desk, his head resting in a hand. His brow knotted, he was apparently in deep thought. He didn't notice his sergeant. 'You wanted me, sir?'

Peploe looked up. 'Ah, Tanner, there you are. Come in.' He pushed back his chair, stood up and went to shut the door. 'Have a seat.'

'Thank you, sir,' said Tanner, sitting on a rickety folding chair. 'Did you see Torwinski?'

'Yes – he's all right. Well, physically at any rate. He's been placed under arrest and there's a – what did you call them? A Snowdrop standing by his bed.'

Tanner shook his head. 'At least he should be safe.'

'Well, yes, there is that. He was due to be discharged about now, handed over to the civilian police and taken to the station in Ramsgate.' Peploe sighed. Suddenly he looked very young. Tanner supposed he must be in his early twenties. 'I'm afraid it's all a bit bleak,' Peploe continued. 'They found documents this morning in the men's hut. Details of deliveries, that sort of thing. The OC told me that, as far as he's concerned, it's an open and shut case. And that, I'm afraid, has come from the RAFP and the police inspector working on the case. I protested, of course, but it seems no one's interested in hearing an alternative version of events. I mean, I can see it from Captain Barclay's point of view – he's got other things on his mind, like our departure for France, and he's obviously relieved to have had the whole matter taken out of his hands. But I would have thought the police might be a bit more open-minded. It's wrong, Tanner, very wrong.'

'Has anyone spoken with the other Poles? Who's in charge of them?'

'There's a Polish colonel and, yes, they have. According to the OC, they're being very co-operative. I went down there to see the colonel myself a short while ago and they're obviously a bit upset, but they seem to have accepted the official line without question.'

Tanner sat in silence, wondering whether to tell the lieutenant about Slater and the stores. *No. Best not.* Instead he said, 'Is there any news on when we'll be off, sir?'

'Could be any moment. And then we'll have to leave this sorry business unresolved. I don't mind telling you, Tanner, I still feel pretty bloody shocked about what's happened and, frankly, helpless to do anything about it. Whether the CSM had anything to do with it, I'm not sure, but the thought of a murderer getting away with it and for him possibly to be part of our company when it goes to France . . . Well, I can't say it thrills me.'

Tanner looked away. Uncomfortable memories were returning, memories from his childhood – or, rather, the end of his childhood. *But that was very different*, he thought. He frowned. 'Don't worry, sir. I'm sure the truth will out.'

'Do you believe that, Sergeant?'

'Yes, sir,' said Tanner. 'I do.'

It was around ten p.m. on Friday, 10 May, and Tanner and Sykes had kept their plans to themselves. The rest of the platoon were on airfield duty, which meant having sentries posted at the watch office, the fuel stores and the main office building, and manning the gates at the entrance to the airfield. Tanner had done several rounds, checking his men, but as dusk gave way to night, he called Sykes away from the watch office and together they crossed the southern end of the Northern Grass towards the company stores.

Rather than walking there directly, though, they doubled back, weaving a route through the rows of wooden huts until they emerged behind the building beside two accommodation huts that were visibly empty. Waiting in the shadows at the end of the last hut, Sykes felt in his pocket and pulled out a set of Bren-gun reamers. 'These should do the trick,' he whispered. 'Listen, Sarge, don't take this the wrong way, but I think it's better if I go there alone.'

'I don't – someone needs to watch your back.'

'Yes, Sarge, and no offence but you're quite a bit bigger than me and with two there's more to see than one. Let me sneak over there on my own, unlock the door and have a squint inside. If there's anything worth seein' and the coast's still clear, you come on over.'

Tanner thought about it. 'All right, Stan. Just be quick, all right?'

'A couple of minutes.' Sykes scampered lightly across the short distance to the stores and disappeared into the shadows.

Tanner strained his eyes but couldn't see him, then glanced to either side. Nothing. It was quiet. The sliver of moon was behind him, casting long shadows. *Good.* At least the door to the stores would be in shadow too.

Then something made him start. A kind of rustle, from the left-hand side of the hut. Tanner pressed himself to the end wall, and turned his head in the direction from where the sound had come. His heart thumped, but as the seconds passed and he heard no more, he began to relax. A rat or something, he told himself, even the breeze.

There it was again. Tanner strained his ears until a sixth sense made him turn. A dark shape and then, too late, he saw the silhouette of a rifle butt—

5

Sykes reached the door of the stores, paused and looked round. A couple of hundred yards away he could just distinguish the outline of the Bofors but he was sure he had been neither seen nor heard, especially from that distance. It was dark in the shadow of the building, but once he had found the first padlock he no longer needed his eyes. Picking a lock was about listening and feeling, not seeing. He selected a reamer but it was too big so he tried the smallest. *That's more like it.* Gently probing with the narrow metal pin, he felt for the mechanism. He crouched down, ear next to the padlock, turned the reamer and heard the locking mechanism spring open. With his hand already round the padlock, he slid it from the bolt. *One down.*

The second was even easier. It had, he reckoned, taken him about twenty seconds to undo both. Not bad, he told himself, especially considering he hadn't picked a lock in years. He drew back the bolt and prepared to open the door, praying its hinges wouldn't squeak. Slowly Sykes pulled it ajar and slipped inside. He pushed it to and got out his torch. He made sure the blackout was across the lens, then switched it on and opened the filter until he had a sliver of light.

The store was filled with rows of wooden shelving from floor to ceiling and smelled of dust, canvas, oil – and, yes, petrol. Immediately ahead he saw boxes of .303 ammunition, No. 36 grenades and Bren magazines stacked together. Slowly he walked past two more rows of shelving, turned down the third, and immediately smelled fuel. But there was nothing – no barrels, no four-gallon tins. For a moment, he paused, then squatted down and noticed circles in the dust, one of which had stained the floor. Circles caused by fuel barrels.

Sod it, he thought. It was evidence of sorts, but not enough. Then he went back, turned down the last row and his heart quickened. Halfway down, a stash of boxes blocked the passageway between the shelves. Sykes went up to them. They were light cardboard, filled with clothing and overalls, easily movable. He lifted down the top box, then others until he could see beyond. He shone his torch. There, double-stacked at the back of the storeroom, were a dozen barrels of aviation fuel.

He was about to head back to find Tanner when he heard a noise from the other side of the wall now facing him. Turning off his torch, he pressed himself against the shelving. A moment later, the door creaked open and he heard a man gasp. Then something heavy was dropped on the floor.

'There's got to be someone in here,' said a low voice.

Sykes froze. He heard muffled whispers, then a torch was turned on, throwing shadows. Sykes dared not move. Footsteps, careful, measured. Two steps, pause, two steps, pause, each time getting closer.

Now Sykes wished the sergeant was with him. He had no weapon on him, save his clasp knife. The sergeant had just seconds to rescue him. *Come on, Sarge. Where the bloody hell are you?*

Two more steps, then the man shone his torch straight into Sykes's eyes, momentarily blinding him.

Blinking, Sykes tried to see who it was but couldn't tell. All he saw was a dark figure behind the torch beam. He held up a hand to block the light, but as he did so, the man swung his fist into the side of his head. The force of the blow knocked Sykes backwards into the stack of clothing boxes, then onto the floor.

With his eyes closed, he lay as still as he could, despite the pain. The man took two more steps towards him and kicked him. Then, satisfied that Sykes was out cold, he turned and went back. More muffled voices, then the sound of tearing cloth and a fresh smell of fuel. *Jesus, no*, thought Sykes. A match being struck, a brief pause, then the whoosh of petrol igniting. He heard the door close and the keys turn in the padlocks.

The stores were darker now, but a faint orange glow came from near the door. He fumbled for his torch, switched it on and got to his feet groggily, staggered and half fell, then recovered and hurried back to the entrance. Flames were already licking up the first row of wooden shelving and at its foot lay a body – Tanner's.

For a split second, Sykes was paralysed by indecision. Then he stepped round the flames, shoved Tanner to one side and began frantically to pull ammunition boxes off the shelves. Already several were blackening, but he knew that the moment they caught he was dead. When he had given himself breathing space, he dragged Tanner to the next row and, to his relief, heard the sergeant groan.

'Sarge!' he said, slapping his face. 'Sarge! Wake up!' He slapped Tanner again and this time the sergeant opened his eyes.

'Stan?' he mumbled.

'Get up, Sarge! Quick!' He leaned round to check the flames. They were spreading fast. Soon they would reach other ammunition boxes and the stacks of grenades. Time was running out rapidly. He sped back to where the flames were now licking towards the roof and along the shelving. The storeroom was filling with smoke and he coughed, his chest tightening, his throat beginning to sear. He quickly tied his handkerchief around his face, held his breath and grabbed another box of grenades, then stumbled back to Tanner.

Tanner was shaking his head and blinking.

'Sarge!' said Sykes again. 'We've got to get out of here – quick!'

Tanner spluttered, then seemed to regain his senses. He looked around, then scrambled to the other end of the stores. 'Stan, bring your torch,' he called, his voice hoarse.

Sykes did so. The last row was filled with rifles and a couple of boxed Bren guns.

'Good – no ammo here.' Crouching, Tanner hurried away, grabbed one of the boxes of grenades and, with trembling fingers, undid the fastening. 'Thank God,' he said, when he saw that the weapons were not greased up. 'Quick, open these,' he told Sykes, passing him the tin of igniters in the centre of the box. Then he took out a grenade, unscrewed the base plug and grabbed an igniter from the now open tin.

They were lying on the floor away from the flames but already the smoke was choking.

'The torch, Stan – shine the bloody torch!' *Keep calm*, Tanner told himself as he struggled to feed the igniter. *Don't rush*. He was conscious of Sykes's frantic glances at the growing flames.

'They've reached the ammo boxes, Sarge. Are you nearly done?'

Tanner took the base plug, tried to screw it on, missed the thread, cursed, then got it right at the second attempt.

'Sarge, any second now those bullets are going to go!'

'Shut up, Stan,' said Tanner, snatching the base-plug tightener from the lid of the box. 'You're not helping.' He tightened the grenade, then scrambled to the end of the last row, pulled the pin and ran back, hurling himself to the ground.

There was a sudden surge of flames and the sound of bullets as strips of .303 rounds ignited and pinged furiously around the storeroom. A second later the grenade went off.

'Go!' shouted Tanner. 'Go!'

A draught from the far end of the storeroom told them the explosion had been successful. Sure enough, there was a jagged hole just big enough for them to squeeze through. 'Quick, Stan, out you go!' urged Tanner, and then it was his turn. The clear, fresh air hit him like a wall. 'Run!' he said. 'Iggery! Let's get the hell out of here!'

There were now cries and shouts from the other side of the storeroom. Tanner saw Sykes run ahead, past the first of the huts. First, though, he had something to retrieve. Pausing where he had stood not ten minutes before, he dropped to his knees and felt around the grass. *Good*, he thought, as he found the familiar wooden butt of his rifle. Then, just to make sure, he put his hand around the breech and his fingers touched the scope mounts he had had especially fixed to it. Clasping it, he ran on, until a loud whisper from Sykes called him into the shadows of the second hut along.

'I can't believe I'm alive,' gasped Sykes. At that moment there was a deafening explosion and the storeroom was engulfed in a mass of livid orange flame. Both men flung themselves flat on the ground, already damp with dew, as debris pattered around them.

'Come on, Stan,' said Tanner, hoarsely. 'We don't want to hang around here. Let's get to the hut, clean up and join the others.' He stood up and dusted himself down. 'You all right?'

'I think so, Sarge. What about you?'

'My head's felt better.' He put his hand to it and peered at his fingers. 'Damn.'

'Blood?'

'I'll have to think of some excuse. I tell you, Stan, we can't let those bastards frame us for this. We'll have to be bloody careful. Blackstone was always a right bastard in India but I wouldn't have said cold-blooded murder was his way.'

'You're sure it was him, then?'

'Aren't you?'

'I don't know. I couldn't see. Whoever it was always kept the torch shining on my face. Then he whacked me one and I pretended to be out cold so I didn't dare open my eyes. He never spoke. I heard another bloke, but it wasn't the CSM. What about you, Sarge?'

'I fell for the oldest trick in the book. I was distracted by a noise from one side of the hut and hit in the head from the other. And, no, I didn't see who it was, but I still know Blackstone's behind this. He's got to be.'

'Anyway, at the moment they think we're croakers, don't they? That gives us a bit of time.'

'So it does, Stan. Let's make the most of it.' He stumbled forward, then stopped. 'Thanks – back there.'

'Self-preservation, Sarge.' He grinned. 'I didn't think I'd get out without your help.'

'That's all right, then.'

The wash-house was empty – a stroke of luck. They cleaned the smoke from their hands and faces and Tanner swabbed the gash to his head. He needed stitches, he knew, but that would have to wait.

Cleaned up, they hurried back to their hut. Tanner dabbed his head again then covered it with petroleum jelly from a tin in his pack to stem the blood. Then quickly changing into their spare battle-dress, the two of them headed out into the night once more. It was now just twenty-two minutes past ten. They had been absent from the platoon for less than half an hour but, with the inferno raging at the company stores, both men were keenly aware that they had to get back to their men without delay.

They wove their way behind a row of buildings to the south of the parade-ground, reached the road in front of the office block, then headed back towards the burning stores to the west of the Northern Grass.

'OK, listen, Stan,' said Tanner. 'We've come from the direction of the watch office, all right? We've been keeping an eye on things at the far side of the airfield, and we hurried over as soon as we heard the explosion. Got it?'

'Right, Sarge.'

The fire-wagons were already at the scene, as were Lieutenant Peploe and most of the platoon.

'There you are, Tanner,' said Peploe, on seeing Tanner and

Sykes walking briskly towards him. 'Where have you been?' The light from the flames betrayed the tension in his face.

'Sorry, sir. Came as soon as we heard the explosion. How did it start?'

'Not sure. The ack-ack boys say they didn't see or hear a thing until it was too late. Apparently, one of them noticed flames and the next minute the place blew.'

'Well, all that ammo and so on,' said Tanner.

'Probably someone dropped a cigarette or a match or something, sir,' said Sykes.

'Probably,' agreed Peploe. 'An odd coincidence, though, two blazes in two nights. And have you heard the other news?'

'We're off to France, sir?' said Tanner.

'No – we've got a new prime minister, Churchill. It seems Chamberlain resigned yesterday, the day before the Germans decide to launch their attack. They announced it this afternoon.' He pinched the bridge of his nose. 'Winston Churchill – who'd have thought it?'

'Proves coincidences do happen, sir,' said Sykes.

'I suppose so.' He looked back at the fire. 'Incredible, really, that no one was hurt. God knows what the OC will say. We needed those stores for France.' He felt inside his battle-blouse and pulled out his silver hip-flask, unscrewed the top and took a swig. 'Chaps?' he said, offering it to Tanner and Sykes.

Tanner coughed. He could still feel the smoke in his throat. 'Thank you, sir. This time I will.' The whisky burned the back of his throat deliciously. Briefly he closed his eyes. *That's good.* 'Shall I get the men back to their posts, sir?' he said, as he passed the flask to Sykes. 'The fire-wagons and Snowdrops seem to have everything under control.'

Peploe nodded. 'I'm going to stay here in case the OC or the station commander shows up, but you get going, Sergeant.'

With the men sent back to their posts, Tanner paused. He had a raging thirst and unclipped his water-bottle from his belt. He drank freely, savouring the cool fluid as it soothed his throat. His head hurt like hell – a throbbing, stabbing pain that prevented him thinking clearly. Gingerly he put his hand to it again, felt the Vaseline and blood in his matted hair and tilted his helmet to hide the wound. The worst of it was that there was nothing he could do. Peploe might believe him, and Sykes, but no one else. Blackstone would see to that – and it would be easy. Tanner knew he was already a marked man. *Jesus.*

A car approached and drew up alongside the far end of the workshop. Tanner watched Wing Commander Jordan and Captain Barclay get out and stride towards the still-burning storeroom. Then Peploe hurried towards them, silhouetted against the flames. He was glad it was the lieutenant rather than himself facing the anger of the station commander and the OC.

Footsteps from the direction of the parade-ground made him turn. Tanner strained his eyes, but it was not until the figure was only a few yards from him that he realized it was Blackstone.

'CSM,' said Tanner.

'Jack?'

Tanner switched on his torch so that he could see the CSM's face but, to his astonishment, his expression betrayed no surprise.

'Shouldn't you be with the rest of the platoon?' Blackstone asked.

'I'm on my way,' said Tanner.

Blackstone looked past him towards the fire. 'Well, get on, then.'

It occurred to Tanner that it would be easy to kill Blackstone there and then. The distraction of the fire, the night darkness, an arm round his neck, then a yank of his head. All over in a trice. Yet he knew he would do no such thing – not even if he had been certain that the CSM had tried to burn him alive half an hour before. Tanner had killed several men but had never resorted to murder, no matter how well deserved.

Yet for the first time, doubt gnawed at the back of his mind. Perhaps he had been wrong about Blackstone; perhaps he was not behind the fuel theft and the deaths of the Poles, after all.

Without another word, Tanner stepped past him and went on his way.

*

The following morning, just before eight o'clock, T Company's movement order arrived from the War Office. It had not taken the hundred and four men long to get ready. Canvas kitbags had been packed the day before, after the movement warning had been issued, although Tanner had decided not to bother bringing his with him. His old uniform was scorched and soiled and he reckoned he would hardly need his thick wool greatcoat in France in summer. In any case, he had always found ways of getting extra clothing in the past whenever he had needed it, and saw no reason why it should be any different in France and Belgium. What kit he reckoned he would need – respirator, spare shirt, spare underwear, shaving kit, mess tin, towel, jerkin, gas cape, housewife and his few personal belongings – fitted easily into the pack, haversack and pouches of his field-service marching-order webbing, which each man had been ordered to wear. He had discarded other bits of kit that he had either never used or reckoned would be of limited value on the Continent, such as his brushes, canvas shoes and overalls.

At ten, the company were paraded and ready to begin the three-mile march to Ramsgate harbour. An hour later, they were being ticked off a list by the embarkation supervising officer and walking up the gangplank of the cargo ship. Tanner watched the men as they boarded the *Raglan Castle*, a four-thousand-ton vessel already laden with trucks, guns and munitions. Some chattered animatedly, excited at the prospect of heading over the Channel to war. Others were solemn, alone with their thoughts, their faces betraying apprehension and fear.

Tanner waited for all the men in the platoon to board before he went up the gangplank. As he stepped on deck, Ellis grinned. 'So this is it, then, Sarge. We're finally off. I can't believe we'll be in France in just a few hours.'

'Maybe a bit longer than that,' said Tanner.

Ellis looked at him quizzically. 'I thought it was only twenty miles or so across. That can't take very long.'

'Nor does it. But we haven't set off yet, have we? Trust me, Billy, there's always a lot of hanging around at port. We won't be going anywhere for hours.'

His prediction proved correct. Tanner made the most of the delay by catching up on his sleep, as did Sykes and some of the other more experienced men. He was glad of the chance. Not only was he tired, his head still throbbed. He had seen the MO that morning. The doctor had seemed to accept his story about having been hit as someone opened the door of a truck and merely warned him to wear his tin helmet more often. The wound had needed four stitches, all of which were neatly hidden by his thick dark hair.

When he awoke a couple of hours later, his headache had all but gone, but the ship was still tied firmly to the quayside. When they had not left by three thirty, frustration mounted, even in Tanner. The delay, it seemed, was caused by a missing convoy of Guy Ant fifteen-hundredweight general-service trucks. It was four o'clock when at last they arrived, and half an hour later the ship let go its moorings and inched out of Ramsgate harbour.

Tanner had few superstitions, but he liked to be out on deck when a ship left port and now he stood, the gulls circling, to watch the cliffs and the neat little streets shrink before him. A light, soothing breeze brushed his face.

England always looked so unmistakably English, he thought – the sheer, white cliffs, the rows of terraced houses, the patchwork of high-hedged fields. The quiet order.

'Looks pretty, don't it, Sarge?' said Sykes, appearing at his side. Then without waiting for a reply, he said, 'How's the head?'

'Not too bad. The stitches itch a bit.' He touched the hard scab and the loose end of the thread. 'You seen the CQS yet today?'

'He came down with the trucks. So no.'

Tanner thought for a moment. 'Tell me again, Stan, you did hear voices in the store last night, didn't you?'

'Yes, but it wasn't much and it was quite low. I'm not sure I could identify anyone from what I heard. But it did sound like a Yorkshire accent.'

'Could have been anyone from up north – there's probably Yorkshiremen in the ack-ack units and in the RAF as well as our lot.' Tanner felt for his cigarettes. 'Damn it, Stan. Damn those bloody bastards. We're never going to nail them, are we?'

Sykes shrugged. 'Don't know, Sarge. If we keep our wits about us . . .'

Tanner tapped one end of his packet of cigarettes. He offered one to Sykes, then placed another between his lips. Turning out of the breeze to cup a match, he had just successfully lit his cigarette when Lieutenant Peploe joined them.

'I suppose you two are old hands at this sort of thing.' He pulled out his own cigarettes.

'I wouldn't say that, sir,' said Sykes. 'Only the second time for me. That last trip was a bit hairy, wasn't it, Sarge? I hope we don't get another torpedo.'

'You were torpedoed?' said Peploe, bleakly.

'Not us, sir, no. A supply ship. We lost most of our kit, guns and transport. But we'll be all right. Be in Calais before you know it.'

Peploe gazed at the shrinking English coastline. 'I know people have been doing this for centuries, but it's quite a thing to find oneself a part of it – you know, leaving home and heading off to war. I don't mind admitting I feel apprehensive.'

'It would be strange if you didn't, sir,' said Tanner.

'Still,' Sykes put in, 'I'm glad to be getting away from Manston.'

'Yes,' said Peploe. He coughed. 'I'm sorry, Sykes, but would you mind giving me and Sergeant Tanner a moment?'

'Course, sir. Let me go and check how the lads are doing.' He raised his cigarette in acknowledgement and left them.

'Sorry about that, Tanner, but I feel we've barely spoken today, apart from to issue orders and so on.' He took off his cap and the breeze ruffled his unruly hair. 'I just wish we were leaving in better circumstances. This matter with the Poles, I promised we'd get to the bottom of it and I haven't been able to.'

'We couldn't have known we'd be sent to France so soon, sir.'

'Even so . . .'

'I know, it doesn't seem right, but we've got other things to worry about now and the platoon to look after.'

'It's the thought that those responsible are with us here, on this ship. It makes my blood boil.'

'Maybe they're still in Manston, though, sir. Perhaps they weren't from our company, after all. Could have been RAF or the ack-ack lads.'

'I thought you were convinced CSM Blackstone was behind it.'

'I'm not so sure. I might have been wrong about that.'

'Why the change of heart?'

'I can't explain. Just a hunch. But the point is, sir, we know it's definitely not anyone from this platoon. If we make sure our men go about their business in the right way, we'll be fine.'

Peploe smiled. 'Perhaps you're right, Sergeant.'

Tanner flicked his cigarette into the sea. He wished he could believe what he'd just told the lieutenant. Perhaps the killers really were back in Manston, and perhaps the platoon could look after itself. Yet the unease that had accompanied him almost from the moment he had arrived at Manston had not left him. Rather, it had grown. A hunch, he had told Peploe, a sixth sense, some instinct he couldn't really explain but that had saved his neck on a number of occasions. The problem was, it was only telling him one thing: that up ahead lay trouble.

6

Thursday, 16 May. At the ornate brick-walled, grey-roofed house in the quiet French village of Wahagnies that had become his command post, General Lord Gort was struggling to maintain his composure and ruminating that high command could be a lonely business, especially when one's French superiors repeatedly failed to communicate orders.

With exaggerated frustration, he pushed back his chair and, not for the first time that morning, stood up to peer at the large wall map that hung next to the simple trestle table that was his desk. The quarter of a million troops that comprised the British Expeditionary Force – and which were under his command – were sandwiched within a narrow finger that, at the front line, was no more than fifteen miles wide. To the north were the Belgians, to the south General Blanchard's French First Army – and both, it seemed, were crumbling.

Gort glanced at his watch – 10.25 a.m. – and then, as if doubting its veracity, he looked at the clock above the mantelpiece. It told him the same. It was six days since the Germans had launched their attack, yet twenty-five minutes earlier he had received orders to fall back fifteen miles to the river Senne. Retreat! It was incredible. His men were in good order and in good heart and had only just reached the apex of their advance. The enemy who had dared show their faces had been sent scuttling. He had seen the high spirits of his men for himself. Not so the French on the British right, it seemed. General Billotte had assured him that the North African division was one of the best in the Ninth Army, yet the previous day the Germans had blown a five-thousand-yard breach in their line. Gort had offered the immediate transfer of a brigade to help, but this had been turned down, dumbfounding him. Instead, he had had the gut-wrenching task of issuing orders for I Corps to swing back a few miles to keep in line with Blanchard's divisions. *And now this.*

Retreat. A terrible word. He knew the men wouldn't understand it. Why should they retreat when they were holding their own? He traced a line with his finger from Louvain to Brussels, then pointed towards III Corps, his reserve, who were still spread out along the river Escaut some forty miles behind the Senne. He cursed to himself. It was a shambles, a bloody shambles.

A knock at the door. Major-General Pownall came in. 'Rusty's back, my lord.'

'Well, send him in, Henry,' snapped Gort.

Major-General Eastwood strode in, a rigid expression of barely concealed anger on his face, and saluted sharply. Sensing there was only bad news to come, Gort sat down behind his makeshift desk. 'Spit it out, then, Rusty. Give me your best volley.'

'I'm sorry, my lord,' Eastwood began, 'but it's worse than we thought. They're like rabbits hypnotized by a damned stoat. No one has the first idea of what's really happening. There are no clear decisions being made, and Billotte's HQ is about to up sticks yet again. There were staff officers running hither and thither, trying to pack up and get going, and all the while no proper appreciation or plan being developed.'

'So Archdale wasn't exaggerating?'

Eastwood rubbed his eyes wearily. 'No, my lord. Billotte's falling to pieces. He burst into tears on me.'

'For God's sake,' muttered Pownall. 'That's all we need. First Blanchard and now the Army Group commander too.'

'But you did get to speak to him about the withdrawal?'

Eastwood nodded. 'Yes. He assured me he'd send orders right away – have you not received them?'

'Only that we're to fall back to the Senne,' said Pownall. 'Came through about half an hour ago.'

'Only then? But I left his HQ before nine.' He cleared his throat. 'That's only the first part of the retreat, my lord. We're going back to the Escaut.'

Gort groaned. 'The old Plan E.'

'Yes, sir,' said Eastwood. 'We're to fall back to the Senne tonight, pause there, and on the night of the eighteenth/nineteenth fall back again to the river Dendre and complete the withdrawal to the Escaut on the nineteenth. Those are the orders.'

'And did you speak to him about the roads?'

'Yes, my lord. He said there was nothing he could do about them.'

'Damn it!' Gort sat back in his chair, and stroked his silvery moustache. 'It took three and a half days to reach the Dyle after some very careful planning and when the roads were clear. They're now heaving with refugees and we'll have the Germans snapping at our heels all the way, with the *Luftwaffe* bombing us. How does he expect us to do it?'

'I asked him the same question, my lord. He said we'd have to find a way.'

'Imbecile,' muttered Gort.

'There's more, my lord,' added Eastwood.

Gort stared back at him. *Let's have it, then.*

'It's to the south. German mechanized columns have not only broken across the Meuse, they're pushing towards Laon and St Quentin.'

Gort stood up again to return to the map, and made rough

measurements with his fingers. 'If they do that they'll have gone more than forty miles in a day! It's impossible – surely the French Ninth and Second Armies can hold them? I hate to say this, but I'm beginning seriously to doubt the fighting qualities of our French allies. Not something I'd have said about them during the last show.'

For a moment, no one spoke. Gort's mind raced. To the north, the Dutch had already surrendered. The Belgians were struggling and the French Seventh Army had had to fall back to adjust for the collapse of the Dutch. But what struck him now was the terrible realization that the German thrust in the north had been nothing more than a feint. The main effort was to the south, through the Ardennes.

'We've been humbugged, by God,' he said, eyes glazed.

'Yes, my lord,' said Eastwood.

'And our entire plan has been based on Jerry making his main effort through the Low Countries.' He clutched the back of his chair as the shock of what was unfolding spread through him. 'All right, thank you, Rusty,' he said, in a voice of weary resignation. 'Issue the relevant orders right away.' Eastwood saluted and left.

When he had gone, Gort clenched one hand tightly on the back of his chair, then smacked the table, shock replaced by anger.

'This is not good enough, not good enough at all! One order is all I've had from Billotte in the past twenty-four hours. One order! I mean, for God's sake, would he ever have bothered to let me know the rest of the plan for withdrawal if I hadn't sent Rusty down there? Blubbing's no good. What's needed is decisiveness, clear thinking and attention to detail.' He snatched at the telephone. 'Here, Henry. Try to get through to Billotte now.'

Pownall took the phone while Gort paced the large and mostly unfurnished room. His chief of staff began to speak in French, calmly at first, then with increasing impatience. Eventually he replaced the receiver. 'Billotte's not available, my lord. Apparently neither he nor his chief of staff are at their headquarters any longer.'

'Then get me Gamelin, damn it.'

Pownall nodded. After several conversations he again replaced the receiver. 'It seems Gamelin is with Monsieur Reynaud and the Prime Minister in Paris.'

'Keep trying, Henry. I refuse to believe that the combined armies of France, Belgium and Great Britain can do nothing about this. A major counter-attack is needed – and fast – not retreat. Someone must be organizing this.'

'The problem is communication – or rather, I should say, lack of it. We simply don't have enough radios.'

'No, Henry, that's only part of it. The main problem is that these damned French generals won't make decisions. Keep trying Billotte. Somehow we have to put some spine into these bloody Frogs and get them to mount a serious counter-attack. I mean, for God's sake, what's Corap's army doing? Standing by and watching?'

'They're certainly not doing much fighting.'

'Then it's about bloody time they did!' shouted Gort, anger and frustration spilling into his words. He breathed deeply. He could barely believe what was happening – the incompetence, the lack of leadership, the bare-faced panic . . . Throughout his career in the Army, he had prided himself on his ability to make decisions and to lead men. In 1918 it had won him a Victoria Cross, and after the war had helped propel him to become the youngest ever chief of the Imperial General Staff. When Britain had sent an army to France at the outbreak of war, it had been Gort who was appointed to command it. Throughout his career, he had always gone forwards. Yet now he was going backwards. The unthinkable preyed on his mind: that despite their vast number of men and machines, the French could well lose the battle.

And if that happened, Britain might fall with them.

The column was halted at just after four o'clock that afternoon at a village called Quenast and the men dropped down onto the grassy verge at the side of the road. Sergeant Tanner had assumed they would travel at least part of the way by train or truck, but instead

T Company had been left to march all the way from Calais to Tournai, some eighty-six miles. Admittedly, their kitbags and large packs had been left with the two trucks that made up the company transport, but with a rifle, a stuffed haversack, rolled gas cape, respirator bag, full ammunition pouches, entrenching tool, bayonet and sundry other items in their pockets, each man still had to carry equipment that weighed the best part of forty pounds. Despite this, they had managed the march to Tournai in three and a half days, and there, they had finally met up with the rest of 1st Battalion, who, with much of 13th Brigade, had been moving north to Belgium from near Le Havre.

That had been early in the afternoon the day before, and since then they had tramped a further forty miles. It had been one of the hardest marches Tanner had ever done, not because of the distance but because of the traffic. The roads had been choked with troops, tanks, trucks, cars, motorbikes and thousand upon thousand of refugees. Some had simply been walking in what they were wearing, but others carried their lives in their hands, many struggling with the weight of suitcases and bags. Tanner saw horses, donkeys and even cattle with cases and belongings piled high on their backs. It had reminded him of refugee columns he had seen in Waziristan; they had been a pathetic bunch then, but he was sickened to see such scenes in Europe. Most were on foot, but a few had inched their way through the throng in cars. Tanner had lost sight of the number of vehicles he had seen ditched by the edge of the road, presumably having either overheated or run out of fuel. And the dust! Many of the roads had not been metalled and in the dry early-summer sun, with God only knew how many wheels, tracks and boots pounding down, the surface had turned to a fine powder that swirled and settled on clothes, found its way into socks and chafed feet, up nostrils and into the throat and eyes.

The further west they had travelled, the more they heard the sounds of battle ahead and in the sky above. That morning they had watched numerous enemy bombers fly over. Some miles away an anti-aircraft battery had opened fire, dull thuds resounding through the ground on which they walked. Tanner noticed that those new to war flinched and stopped to gaze in wonder as the shells exploded in black puffs. At one point, German bombers had been engaged by British fighters. One bomber had been hit and had dived out of the formation, trailing smoke. At this, the men had cheered.

An hour ago, Stukas had attacked a column some miles ahead. They had heard the sirens and the bombs. Refugees had fled to the side of the road, but Tanner had yelled at the men to keep their discipline. 'They're bloody miles away!' he had shouted. 'Keep going!'

He was as glad as the rest of them for the pause now, enjoying the lightness across his shoulders.

'Any idea where we are, sir?' he asked Lieutenant Peploe, as he unscrewed the lid of his water-bottle.

Peploe wiped his brow with a green spotted handkerchief, then took out a battered paper map. It was his own – the company had not been issued with any – and fifteen years old, but accurate enough.

'We're twenty miles or so south of Brussels, I think,' he said at length. 'A few miles ahead of us is the Brussels–Charleroi canal. I can't see the river Senne, though, which was where I thought we were heading.'

A staff car, making the most of the sudden clear stretch of road, thundered past, more clouds of dust swirling in its wake.

'Stupid sodding bastard,' cursed McAllister. 'Watch where you're bloody going!'

Sykes wandered over to stand in front of Tanner and Peploe. 'Any news, sir?'

Peploe shook his head. 'I'm sure we'll be here for the night, though – or close by, at any rate.'

'Good,' said Sykes, 'because my men are fed up. They're all moaning like mad. "Corp, me feet ache. Corp, I've got another blister." I've 'ad enough.' He grinned, then took out a comb from his top pocket and smoothed his hair. 'The village looks pretty empty.'

'They've all scarpered,' said Tanner. 'Should have stayed put. These refugees are a bloody nuisance.'

'It's a terrible sight,' said Peploe. 'What an awful thing to have to do – leave one's home. I mean, where are they heading anyway?'

'Can't help thinking they'd be better off at 'ome,' said Sykes. 'Didn't really see any in Norway, did we, Sarge?'

'No – they must have been made of sterner stuff.'

Suddenly a plaintive bellowing struck up somewhere close behind them.

'Christ! What the 'ell's that?' said Sykes.

Tanner got to his feet. 'Cows, Stan. There's a field of them here.'

'They need milking,' said Peploe, scrambling upright. 'Their udders are full and they're in pain.'

'I can see a dozen, sir,' said Tanner.

Peploe looked up and down the road. With no sign of any imminent movement, he said to Tanner, 'See if anyone knows how to milk a cow.'

'Bell was brought up on a farm, sir,' said Tanner, 'and I know what to do.'

'Good. Ask the others too.'

The only other man raised on a farm was Corporal Cooper of 2 Section, so the four men climbed over a gate a short way up the road and began to milk the cows, which had redoubled their agonized mooing.

Sykes had followed and stood beside Tanner as he knelt on the ground, stroked the side of a black and white Friesian and began to pull at the teats. 'We'd be better off putting bullets to their heads,' the sergeant muttered. 'We might be helping the pain now, but what about tomorrow morning – or evening?'

Sykes watched the milk squirting into the grass. 'Bit of a waste too.' He looked up. 'There's the farm over there.'

'Go and have a snoop. See if anyone's about.'

Tanner had moved on to another beast by the time Sykes returned.

'It's deserted,' said Sykes. 'There's chickens and geese

wandering about. Cats too, and a couple of dogs tied up on chains. They all look very sorry for themselves.'

'For God's sake,' muttered Tanner. When he had finished milking the second cow he went to the lieutenant.

'That place is empty, sir,' he said, jerking a thumb towards the farm, 'and there's two dogs chained up. Shall I set them free or shoot them?'

'Set them free. They'll probably eat the chickens but at least it'll give them a chance.'

Tanner and Sykes did so, then rejoined the others. The milking completed, they walked back to the road, where the remainder of the platoon was still resting.

'I found that more depressing than anything I've seen all day,' said Peploe. 'I know civilians are innocent but we humans are to blame for all this. The animals have no say at all, and to leave them like that, well, it's cruel.'

Just then two shots rang out, the second followed instantly by the yelp of a dog. A few moments later CSM Blackstone was walking purposefully down the road towards them. 'We're moving into the village, sir,' he said, as he approached Peploe. 'T Company are to billet in this farm here. Officers and senior NCOs in the house, junior NCOs and ORs in the outbuildings.'

'What was that shooting, CSM?' Peploe asked.

'Two stray dogs, sir.'

'On whose orders?'

'Colonel Corner's, sir, which presumably came down from Brigade. All dogs to be shot. Can't have them running astray and going feral on us.' He glanced down the road, then turned back to Peploe. 'There's an officers' meeting in fifteen minutes, sir, with the divisional OC. Battalion HQ is in the large house next to the church.'

There was a weary cheer from the men at the news they would be marching no further that night. Slowly they got to their feet, slung rifles over shoulders and hitched packs and haversacks back onto their webbing. Peploe headed off to Battalion Headquarters, leaving Tanner in charge of the platoon. When he saw 12 Platoon, ahead, set off through the village to the farm, Tanner led his men through the field and into the yard. As he had hoped, they were the first platoon in the company to reach their billet.

He scouted the buildings and chose a large, high-pitched barn for his men. Just outside in the yard there was a well, while inside, at one end there were old carts and farm equipment, and along one wall a series of wooden stalls. Above, he found a hay loft, in which there was still plenty of last year's hay and straw. He put his kit in one of the stalls, called the men in and ordered them to bring down some straw to sleep on.

He had just got his own makeshift bedding ready when there were shouts from across the yard. Hurrying out, he saw a number of men running to a small storehouse. Shouts and cheers floated out to him. Tanner strode over. The men had broken open a large vat of cider they had discovered in an outhouse off the yard. 'What the hell do you think you're doing?' he shouted. 'Get out now, all of you.'

'But, Sarge,' said one of the men, 'the CSM said we could take anything we found outside the house.'

'Come on, Sarge,' said another. 'You can't begrudge us a little drink.'

'I can and I do,' said Tanner. 'First, this is theft. Second, we might be fighting tomorrow and, believe me, you don't want a hangover then. All of you, get out. Now!'

Grumbling, and with angry glances of resentment, the men shuffled out. Tanner waited for the last to go, then went inside and did his best to put the room back in order.

A few minutes later, a shadow fell across the threshold. 'How dare you undermine my authority like that?' said Blackstone.

'That wasn't my intention,' said Tanner, facing him squarely. 'I didn't believe you'd have let the men drink freely when we're so close to the front, so I stopped them until I'd had a chance to speak to you and confirm that you'd given them permission.'

Blackstone smiled mirthlessly. 'Are you suggesting I don't know my own men?'

'I'm not suggesting anything, CSM. I'm saying that to let exhausted men drink the local Belgian hooch and get themselves puggled when we could be called on to fight the enemy at any moment is hardly sensible.'

Blackstone took a step towards Tanner, and pushed him in the chest. Tanner stiffened with anger. 'Always the bloody same with you, isn't it, Jack?' said Blackstone. 'Pushing your nose in where it's not wanted, thinking you know it all. The lads deserve a bit of grog. It won't harm them and I don't need you putting your sodding little paw in and telling me how to run the company.'

'I don't have to listen to this,' said Tanner, moving towards the door. But Blackstone blocked him.

'Oh no you don't, Jack. I haven't said you can leave.'

'For God's sake, you can't tell me you're thinking of the men. You're just currying favour – showing them what a good bloke you are. If you really worried about them, you'd make sure they got their heads down and were bright and fresh for tomorrow.'

At this, Blackstone grinned. 'Oh dear, Jack, you really don't get it, do you?' He leaned closer and hissed, 'I told you, I'm the one in charge around here and I mean it.'

'I ought to knock you down right now,' snarled Tanner.

'Go ahead and try, Jack.' He stepped aside and Tanner, his face taut with rage, pushed past him.

Damn it, damn it, damn it! He needed to calm down, he knew, because right now anger could get the better of him. He went across the yard, making for the field, hoping to find somewhere quiet to regain his composure.

'Ah, Tanner, there you are!'

Tanner turned to see Lieutenant Peploe emerge from the farm-house. Swallowing hard and taking a deep breath, Tanner walked towards him, saluting as he reached him.

'I've got good news,' said Peploe. 'That is, good news for you but rather disastrous for me.' He took off his cap, squinted, and put it back on again. 'We've now been officially absorbed into First Battalion. As of now, we're D Company, although we're going to lose our fourth platoon.'

'It's under strength anyway, sir, so that won't make much difference.'

'Yes, but it's going to join B Company and be brought up to two full sections. And this is where you come in. There aren't enough officers, so someone needs to be promoted to platoon sergeant-major and take command of that platoon. It's a WO III post.'

Tanner felt his mood lighten. 'And move across to B Company?'

'Yes. As you're the senior sergeant in the company it'll almost certainly be you.'

There was no denying he was the senior sergeant – and by some margin too.

'I see, sir,' he said. He wanted to laugh with relief. Of course, he'd be sorry to leave Sykes and the others, and even Lieutenant Peploe, but the chance to get well away from Blackstone was like the answer to his prayers.

'Bloody hard luck on me, though,' added Peploe, 'but I can see that you more than deserve your chance.'

'Thank you, sir.'

'And you've done a good job getting everyone settled in. I'm afraid it's still a bit unclear what's going on but it seems the French First Army have been getting into trouble to the south of here and so have the Belgians to the north ever since the Dutch surrender, so although our chaps have been doing well, we've all got to fall back to keep in line with the others. Tomorrow we're moving up not to the river Senne but to the Brussels–Charleroi canal. We're going to hold the line there while the rest of One and Two Corps fall back through our position. It wasn't clear to me at first which was the canal and which was the river, but I found them both on my map eventually.'

'At least you've got a map, sir. The lack of them seems to be a feature of this war.'

Tanner left Peploe and went back to the barn, where he lay

down on the straw and closed his eyes. He had joked with the lieutenant about the maps but, really, it was no laughing matter. He couldn't shake off the thought that, once again, the Army had been sent to fight a campaign without the right tools for the job. He reminded himself that at least this time they were better equipped. He had seen plenty of guns – heard them too – and there seemed to be transport on the roads, even if they had been made to march. Nonetheless, it had been a disquieting couple of days – today especially, with the refugees clogging the roads, and enemy aircraft appearing to dominate the skies. And the British Army was on the retreat – again.

Tanner chided himself. *Just get on with it, man.* There was no point in worrying about matters that were beyond his control. Instead he thought about the platoon he would soon be commanding. A life without Blackstone, now that was a prospect to lift the spirits. This evening, or perhaps the next day, he would be free of the man.

7

For Sturmbannführer Otto Timpke the past week had been one of deep frustration and mounting agitation. For two whole days the division had remained at Ludwigsburg, vehicles and kit at the ready, waiting for the signal to move. The order had finally come the previous Tuesday, 12 May, but having sped north of Cologne, then west through Aachen to the Belgian border, they had gone no further. In the meantime, Timpke and his colleagues had had to listen to wireless bulletins proclaiming the sweeping successes of the *Wehrmacht* and the *Luftwaffe*. In the north, crucial forts had been captured in Belgium; Rotterdam had been bombed and after four days the Dutch had capitulated. As if that was not galling enough, Army Group A had made even more dramatic and far-reaching progress. It seemed General Guderian's panzers had achieved total surprise as they had attacked through the thick forests of the Belgian Ardennes. The gutless French had crumbled, so that the tanks had managed to cross the river Meuse – a crucial obstacle to have overcome – and had swept all before them.

They had not been idle – Eicke had made sure of that, insisting that his commanders keep the men busy, something with which Timpke agreed entirely. None of his men had seen front-line action: most had been former camp guards and SS reservists, and although they had trained continually since the end of the Polish campaign, Timpke was determined that until they were in a position to draw on combat experience, they should fall back on rigid discipline instead. For four days, as they had waited in the rolling border country, Timpke had drilled them, sent them on long marches and given them rifle practice, as well as despatching them on manoeuvres and making them practise their codework and radio telegraphy. He had also made them clean, re-clean, then clean again their vehicles, weapons and uniforms. On two separate evenings, he had sat the men on the banks of a shallow hill over-looking the camp and had lectured them on one of his favourite subjects, National Socialist and SS ideology, reminding them that the German Reich was rising, phoenix-like, from the ashes of despair into the greatest nation the world had ever known. It was their destiny that they, the chosen ones, should be the élite of this new Aryan order.

Then had come the news that Rommel and Guderian had advanced as much as forty miles the previous day, Thursday, 16 May. Forty miles! An advance of that speed was unheard of. A strange anxiety had gripped Timpke. Surely it wouldn't all be over before the division had been thrown into the line. It couldn't be, yet as every day passed, with reports of outrageous gains made, Timpke became increasingly concerned that the *Waffen-SS* would be ignored once again by the *Wehrmacht*, left to idle out the campaign in their makeshift camp on the Belgian border.

Although he was not a man who had ever needed much sleep, he had slept particularly badly that night; outside, it had been warm and humid, but his mind had been unable to put aside the news of the day's fighting. Major-General Rommel's 7th Panzer Division had reached Avesnes, only thirty-five kilometres south of Mons. Timpke had never heard of the place before, and had been stunned when he had discovered just how far into northern France the town was. On the map, the French coast had seemed impossibly close to the leading panzers. The huge extent of the German thrust was astonishing, and he had been struck by a wave of despair. Soon the war would be over, and the *Wehrmacht* would take all the credit.

Unable to clear such thoughts, he had risen, washed and shaved, then turned to his desk, keeping himself busy by writing further company training exercises. As a consequence, he had already been up for several hours when the company clerk knocked at the door shortly after seven. Entering, he had handed Timpke a note.

Timpke read it, grinned, then crunched the paper into a ball and threw it away.

'Good news, Herr Sturmbannführer?' his orderly, Sturmann Reinz, asked.

'Most definitely,' Timpke replied, putting on his jacket. 'Very good news indeed.'

Downstairs, in the officers' dining room, he found his company commanders, Saalbach, Beeck and Hardieck, already there, drinking ersatz coffee.

'Look at his face,' laughed Saalbach. 'Our boss is happy at long last! I'd begun to think we'd never see you smile again, Herr Sturmbannführer.'

'Part of Army Group A! It couldn't be better. With luck we'll be at the van with von Rundstedt.' Timpke slapped Hardieck's back, then smacked a fist into his open hand. 'At last!'

A little under seventy miles away as the crow flew, Sergeant Tanner had also woken early. In contrast to Sturmbannführer Timpke, however, Tanner had slept well. After eight years in the Army, he had long ago become accustomed to the lack of a mattress or other home comforts; and a bed of straw in a warm barn in May was considerably more comfortable than countless other places where he had spent the night.

However, it was not long before he, too, was feeling increasingly agitated. By seven, orders had arrived for D Company to move up to the canal, on a line to the south of the village of Oisquercq, yet he had still heard nothing about his promotion and transfer to B Company. With mounting irritation, he had woken the rest of the platoon, chivvied them to their feet, made sure they had breakfast – and still there had been no word.

'An oversight, I'm sure,' said Lieutenant Peploe, as the platoon stood in the yard drinking their morning brew. 'Let me find out what's going on from Captain Barclay.'

Yet the lieutenant had been unable to speak with him before they had moved off, so twenty minutes later, when the platoon had begun the three-mile march to the canal, Tanner was still a platoon sergeant in D Company.

'I expect the appointment had to be approved by Colonel Corner,' said Sykes, as they marched through the village. 'Maybe even Brigadier Dempsey. And there are lots of troops to move and other things to do. You know 'ow it is, Sarge.'

Tanner scowled. 'Bollocks, Stan. They've changed their mind – I know they have.'

'Course they 'aven't,' said Sykes, then added, 'but if they 'ave, at least you've got some good men in your platoon here.'

Tanner glared at him.

'I'm not saying you're right, Sarge.'

'I am, though. I can feel it in my bones.'

'And you like Mr Peploe, don't you? He seems a good sort.'

'Look, just stop talking about it, will you?' snapped Tanner.

They were now almost through the village. Ahead, Tanner could hear a grinding rumble. High above, a flight of aircraft thrummed over to disappear into thick white cloud. Soon after, they crossed a railway line, then turned onto another road where they were un-expectedly confronted by a mass of British vehicles and troops heading towards them.

'Jesus – will you look at that?' muttered Sykes. 'What's going on here?'

'Must be One Corps falling back,' said Tanner. 'They were due to do it last night.'

'Then why are we heading in the opposite direction?' said Hepworth, from behind him.

'Why do you think, Hep?' said Tanner.

'Dunno, Sarge.'

Tanner sighed. 'Use your bloody loaf and stop asking stupid questions.'

'But, Sarge—' Hepworth protested, but Tanner cut him off.

'We've got to guard the canal and make sure Jerry doesn't get across too easily and harry those boys' retreat.' He knew he had sounded irritable but, really, he thought, Hepworth should know better by now.

The company was halted as a long column of fifteen-hundred-weight trucks trundled past, choking dust swirling into the air. The Rangers could see the soldiers through the open tarpaulins at the back of each truck. Most seemed sullen, faces long, cigarettes hanging from their mouths. Several carriers whirred past too.

'You're going the wrong way!' one man shouted at them. A few of his fellows laughed but, Tanner noticed, not many.

Eventually the column disappeared in a haze of dust. Coughing and spluttering, the platoon continued its march, dropping down a long, gentle slope into the village of Oisquercq, where they rejoined the rest of the battalion. More carriers and trucks were crammed along the roads that led into and out of the village. Troops milled around. NCOs shouted. Tanner wondered which group was from B Company, but then they moved on again, past the church and onto a tree-lined path that led out of the village between a single-track railway line and the banks of the broad waterway that was the Brussels–Charleroi canal.

'Some barrier this,' said Sykes. It was at least sixty yards wide, filled with dark, murky water. Opposite, fields rose away towards a long, thick wood, which dominated the horizon overlooking the canal.

Just south of the village, by a white-painted brick station house, the company was halted again, the runner appearing soon after. 'The men to stand easy, platoon commanders and sergeants for a

meeting with Captain Barclay,' he said, as he reached Peploe and
Tanner.

The two men followed him. Barclay, Captain Wrightson and
CSM Blackstone were standing in the shade of the station house,
examining a rough, hand-drawn map. Blackstone looked up briefly
at their arrival, then, once the others had arrived, turned to Barclay.
'Everyone's here, sir.'

Except Sergeant Wilkes, thought Tanner, with a stab of alarm.

'Good,' said the captain, then cleared his throat. 'We're going to
dig in along these banks from here to that farm up ahead on the
bend in the canal.' Set back from the water, it was some five
hundred yards away from where they were standing. Tanner
noticed there were troops there. 'That farm,' said Barclay, 'marks
the end of the BEF's line and the start of the French First Army.
It's currently occupied by a battalion of the Second North African
Infantry Division. Ten Platoon will dig in on our left, here, towards
the village, Eleven Platoon in the centre and Twelve between
them and the French.' He looked at Lieutenant Peploe. 'But try to
avoid the French. I know we're allies, but we do our thing and they
do theirs. What's more, their men are all bloody wogs, and
apparently even the officers are a shifty bunch, hardly to be relied
upon. Spoke to a chap back in the village – a major in A Company,
actually – who says the French First Army have been an absolute
bloody shower so far. One of the main reasons we're making a
general withdrawal is because their part of the line collapsed as
soon as Jerry showed up.' He tapped the side of his nose. 'But
that's strictly *entre nous*, all right?' He looked at the men then said,
'Good. All clear? Any questions?'

'Yes, sir,' said Peploe. 'How long are we expected to stay here?'

'Not long. We're not quite sure where Jerry is, so I can't say for
certain, but probably we'll fall back tonight. We'll be taking up the
rear once the rest of the corps are clear. Anything else?'

'Yes, sir,' said Peploe.

Barclay made little attempt to hide his impatience. 'Yes,
Lieutenant?'

'Last night, sir, you said that one of our sergeants would be joining B Company.'

'Yes, Lieutenant, and so they have.'

Tanner felt a hollowness in his stomach. *So I was right. The bloody bastards.*

'But, sir, Sergeant Tanner is the most experienced sergeant in the company by some margin. That posting should be his.'

'Careful, Peploe,' said Barclay. 'It's not your place to tell me who gets promoted from this company.' He shuffled his feet. 'There are a few question marks over Sergeant Tanner. That episode back at Manston, for example – shooting at Squadron Leader Lyell. And last night, I hear, he seriously undermined the authority of the CSM.'

Tanner groaned inwardly, saw Peploe glance at him – *what's this?* – and then, to his mounting fury, Blackstone grinning at him triumphantly. *Of course.* He should have known Blackstone would use that to his advantage.

'Now how would it look, Lieutenant, if I recommend a sergeant to join B Company as a newly promoted platoon sergeant-major and they find they've got a trouble-maker on their hands? Hm?'

Tanner watched Peploe's pale face redden with indignation. 'Very well, sir, but I'd like it made clear here and now that I do not believe Sergeant Tanner is a trouble-maker of any kind and that I, for one, am glad to have him in my platoon. I think he's been treated appallingly.'

Tanner looked at his feet, embarrassed by Peploe's impassioned outburst.

'That's enough, Peploe,' said Captain Wrightson.

'Yes,' added Barclay. 'I've made my decision and that's an end to it. Now, get to your men and start digging in right away.'

As they walked back, Peploe said, 'I'm sorry, Tanner. That's a bloody outrage.'

'Thank you for standing by me, sir. I appreciate it.'

'It's wrong, Tanner. Quite wrong. The man's a first-rate arse.' He tugged at his mop of thick hair. 'Shouldn't be saying things like that to you, I know, but it's true.'

Tanner could think of stronger words, but kept them to himself. Instead he said, 'We've got a platoon of good lads, sir.'

'That's true enough.' He looked at Tanner. 'Do you mind me asking what happened last night between you and the CSM?'

Tanner told him. Peploe listened. Then he said, 'Well, Sergeant, I'm sorry, and between you and me, I think you were probably right. I know I like the odd glass, but I'm sure the men would have got themselves drunk. If it's any consolation at all, though, I meant what I said back there. I'm glad you're still with us. I fancy we've got a testing time ahead.'

Tanner agreed. He had said nothing to the lieutenant but the scenes of retreat were horribly familiar to him. True, there were more vehicles than there had ever been in Norway, but the expressions on the faces of the men were those he had seen a few weeks before: fed up, resigned, exhausted. Men whose confidence in their commanders had been shaken.

A roar of aero-engines made him look up. Above, a dozen German bombers, no more than eight thousand feet high, were droning over, seemingly unchallenged. And that was another thing, thought Tanner. Once more the *Luftwaffe* appeared to rule the sky. He'd seen barely a French or British plane since they had arrived in France. He had never thought too much about air power, but he reckoned he had seen enough to know one thing: that whoever ruled the sky would probably win the battle on the ground. Sighing heavily, he pushed back his helmet and wiped his brow. The lieutenant was surely right. Things did not look good.

Although Tanner had seen few Allied aircraft, they had been operating in the skies above since the Germans had made their move a week before. In fact, together the RAF and French Army of the Air had many more aircraft than the *Luftwaffe*. However, most of these were either back in England or scattered over France, so that at the front, the Germans did have superior numbers, and especially in the northern sector operating over Flanders. Not only that, all too many French and British aircraft that had been available had already been shot down and even more destroyed on the ground; which was why at first light that morning, Squadron Leader Charlie Lyell had learned that 632 Squadron would, from now on, be one of six Hurricane squadrons that would fly daily to an airfield in France and there operate alongside what remained of the RAF's Air Component.

Lyell had led the squadron over to Vitry-en-Artois in northern France where 607 Squadron were already operating. Pandemonium had greeted them. Shortly before their arrival, the *Luftwaffe* had paid a call so that as the squadron circled over the battered airfield, plumes of thick smoke were still rising into the sky. The grass runway was pockmarked with bomb craters, full of soil and pulverized chalk. As Lyell turned in to land he could see the remains of a Hurricane still burning furiously, its blackening wings spread out against the ground, its fuselage nothing more than a fragile skeleton. He had hoped he had sounded confident and authoritative – nonchalant, even – when he warned the others to mind out for craters, but his heart had been pounding and his breathing had quickened. *Christ*, he had thought. It was not what he had imagined at all.

No sooner had they refuelled than they had been sent back into the air, ordered to patrol a line 'Louvain–Namur'. Armed only with a rough map, he had led the squadron of two flights north-east over Belgium, uncertain whether or not they were in the right place.

Nonetheless, having climbed to fourteen thousand feet he had spotted what he thought must be Mons and Charleroi, two grey stains among the green patchwork of Flanders, and had then turned due east. It was just as he was leading the squadron towards what he hoped was Namur that Sergeant Durnley had spotted a formation of two dozen Stukas emerging from a large bank of white cloud. The enemy formation was heading west, away from them, and several thousand feet below. It had been almost too good to be true and Lyell had immediately led the squadron round and into line astern, then ordered a Number One Attack.

The enemy dive-bombers spotted them too late, and although arcs of tracer fire curled up to meet Lyell as he led the attack, the aim had been wide and the bullets stuttered past harmlessly. The Stukas broke formation hurriedly, but they still provided rich pickings. Lyell was surprised by how slow and cumbersome they seemed. On his first pass he was certain he hit one and then, glancing behind to see the squadron still attacking in turn, spotted a lone Stuka banking hard to port so followed suit. His first burst of fire overshot, but on his second, now right behind it and closing faster than he had at first realized, the bullets struck home. Then, to his astonishment, the enemy machine exploded, disintegrating beside him as he sped past. Bits of aluminium clanged against his canopy, making him duck his head involuntarily.

And another surprise: in a trice the immaculate attack formations they had practised over and over again had broken up into a swirling mêlée of aircraft and individual battles. Gone, too, was radio discipline as his pilots whooped and cursed, shouted and chattered, deafening screeches reverberating through Lyell's headset. Aircraft tumbled from the sky, with trails of smoke following them but, to his surprise, it appeared to clear of aircraft as quickly as it had filled. As Lyell banked again and tried to bring himself back into the fight, he found the sky almost deserted. He tried to call his squadron back together but it was no use: several of his pilots were now miles away. Deciding that the patrol would have to be forgotten, he ordered the squadron to make their way back to Vitry instead.

He was one of the first to land. A sensation of intense exhilaration settled over him. That he had been responsible for the deaths of at least two people did not bother him, he was glad to discover, yet as he tried to light a cigarette on the way to Dispersal, he discovered his hands were shaking and his knees weak.

The others returned in dribs and drabs. Two had flown halfway to the German border, it seemed. Derek Durnley, who had spotted the formation in the first place, had not returned at all, last seen heading east; Robson had got completely lost and had eventually rung through from Lille-Seclin, some twenty miles away from Vitry. Most claimed to have shot down at least one Stuka, and although 607's intelligence officer eventually accepted claims of just six confirmed kills, this did little to dampen the pilots' buoyant spirits.

They had been due to fly back to Manston at noon, but with Durnley missing, Robson still grounded at Lille-Seclin and half of their Hurricanes still to be refuelled, rearmed and patched up, Lyell waited a while longer at the airfield. Robbo was finally back by half past two, but just as they were about to get going, a request reached Dispersal for another flight to provide top cover for a bombing mission on German positions east of Brussels. When Lyell was asked if 632 Squadron could help, he agreed immediately.

Half an hour later, at nearly half past three that afternoon, he was conscious that the exhilaration had gone, replaced by a wave of fatigue and irritation. Rendezvous with the bombers – a flight of Blenheims – over Brussels at 1520 hours. Well, he could see what he assumed must be Brussels, but there was no sign of any Blenheims or, indeed, any bombers at all.

'This is Nimbus Leader calling Bulldog Leader,' he said, over his R/T for the third time that minute. 'We're over RV at angels fourteen, over.' But still there was nothing. 'All right, boys,' he said to the others. 'This is Nimbus Leader. Make sure you keep your eyes peeled. Let's go round again. Over.'

He pushed the stick over to port, the horizon swivelling, then pulled back, his stomach lurching as the Hurricane banked and began its turn. Looking round, he was pleased to note both Walker and Nicholls tucked in close behind him. Then he glanced downwards again, hoping to see a sign of the bombers – the familiar outline of the Blenheims, or the sun glinting on a canopy. He cursed. Where the hell were they?

Lyell straightened and began to fly westwards again, the glare making him squint even through his tinted goggles. Looking back over his port wing, he glanced at the vic of Flying Officer Newton's

Blue Section, some forty yards behind, and spotted the last man in the formation, Sergeant Baird, peel off and dive out of the formation, smoke trailing. Stunned, he hardly heard Newton's screech over the R/T as he shouted after his friend.

A deafening crack, and despite the tightness of his Sutton harness, Lyell was pushed up out of his seat and smacked his head against the canopy. The choking smell of cordite filled the cockpit, as more cannon shells exploded. *Jesus!* He'd been hit, but where? Thrusting the stick to one side, he yanked it back into his stomach as a Messerschmitt 109 hurtled past.

'Jesus Christ!' shouted Lyell. His mind froze. *Christ, Christ, think!* Panic coursed through him, and then his brain cleared. Turning the stick to starboard, he half rolled the aircraft and tried to dive out of the fray, but then a second burst raked his machine. A large chunk of his port wing was punched out and the control column was nearly knocked from his hand. Lyell gasped. Clutching the stick firmly again, he heard the engine splutter, felt the Hurricane lurch, then begin to dive. The engine screamed, the airframe shook and more smoke poured into the cockpit. The altimeter spun anti-clockwise. Six thousand feet gone just like that! Grimacing into the rubber of his oxygen mask, Lyell gripped the stick with both hands, pressed hard on the rudder and dragged the stick back into his stomach until – *thank God* – the Hurricane levelled out.

He pulled back the canopy. As he did so, the smoke rushed out, sucked into the clear air. Frantically, he looked around him. Ahead, away to the west, he could see contrails and tiny dots as aircraft wove and tumbled around the sky – but it seemed no Messerschmitt had chased him down. With cold sweat trickling down his neck, he glanced at the dials in front of him. Oil pressure falling, manifold pressure dropping: confirmation of what he already knew – his aircraft was dying. A deep, grinding sound came from the engine in front of him. It was losing power fast. 'Jesus Christ, oh, Jesus bloody Christ,' he said, despair sweeping over him. He was not sure what to do – try to glide towards home until the engine completely died, or bale out now? But he didn't want to bale out. The idea of leaping from his stricken aircraft terrified him. What to do?

Lyell glanced in his mirror and jolted. A 109, like a giant hornet, flashed through his line of vision and, a second later, more bullets ripped through his fuselage, through the floor, between his legs, into the control panel and the underside of the engine cowling. With a loud crack, the engine gusted a new burst of black smoke and seized, the propeller whirring to a limp turn.

'Oh, my God!' he cried. For a moment his mind was blank. He couldn't think what he was supposed to do. Ahead, the Messerschmitt was banking, circling again. His heart was thudding, his whole body trembling. He looked below to the never-ending patchwork of fields, woods and snaking silver rivers, and thought how far away they looked. *I don't want to jump out*, he thought, *to plunge head first into an unknown sky.*

The aircraft was dropping. *I haven't long*, he thought, and glanced at his altimeter. Six thousand feet. He had to do it – he had to do it *now*. Trembling fingers. Radio leads, oxygen plugs, the clip on his Sutton harness. He closed his eyes, pushed the stick over and felt himself lift out of the seat, but as he began to slide out of the aircraft something caught and his head smashed against the gunsight. Now the Hurricane was diving, falling almost vertically. Frantically, Lyell felt behind him, heard something tear and then he was tumbling free, the ground hurtling towards him. *The ripcord, the ripcord.* He grabbed it with his gloved hand and yanked. *Please*, he prayed. The wind was knocked out of him and his arms almost pulled from their sockets as the parachute opened. *Thank God*, he thought. *Thank bloody God.* He could see his Hurricane plunging towards the ground, impossibly small already. *Any moment now*, he thought, and there it was – a burst of bright orange light and the dull crump of an explosion. His face was wet – *why?* – and the ground was rushing towards him now. There was a river, and he wondered whether he would fall into the water. But, no, he was drifting on the far side of it, to fields that rose towards a wood. Lyell braced himself for the impact.

*

The men of D Company, the King's Own Yorkshire Rangers, had watched the dogfight in the skies above them. Sergeant Tanner, sitting beside Corporal Sykes's freshly dug two-man slit trench, had looked up as soon as he had picked up the faint hum of aero-engines. Then, when he had heard the distant chatter of machine-guns and cannons, he had delved into his respirator bag and pulled out his binoculars, a pair of Zeiss brass Dienstglas 6x30, which he had taken from a German officer in Norway; it was about his only souvenir of that campaign. Admittedly they were a bit scratched, but he didn't mind too much about that; at least he no longer had to use his Aldis scope for this purpose.

Although the platoon had dug in behind a line of thick bushes between the canal, a narrow brook and the railway, the view above was clear enough. Tanner had been watching the sky carefully for most of the day. That morning he had seen a number of enemy air-craft, mostly lone twin-engine machines he had recognized as aerial reconnaissance. They were, he knew, the harbingers of a forth-coming attack; it would not be long before German ground forces appeared over the crest of the hill facing them. And the enemy would want the skies cleared – no wonder they were trying to drive off the Allied planes now flying overhead.

'Come on, get out . . . get out,' he muttered, as he followed a Hurricane spiralling from the sky. Near by some spent cartridge cases tinkled as they fell into the trees behind them.

'I reckon he's a croaker, Sarge,' said Sykes.

'Well, he's certainly not going to get out now,' said Tanner. They lost sight of the Hurricane but a few moments later they heard the crash – a sharp crack followed by a dull boom. 'I tell you, I'm bloody glad I'm not flying around in those,' he added.

He had then shifted his gaze back to the swirl of aircraft, and spotted another Hurricane diving out of the fray with a Messerschmitt swooping down on it from behind. 'Watch out, you dozy sod,' Tanner said. Then he heard the Hurricane's engine splutter and die and saw the aircraft begin to fall. 'Not another one – Jesus.' He trained his binoculars and fixed a bead as the Hurricane curved out of the sky. When the stricken aircraft was at no more than three or four thousand feet, he started. 'I remember those squadron markings.'

'What are they?' Sykes asked.

'LO. LO-Z.' He handed his binoculars to Sykes. 'Here, have a dekko.'

Lieutenant Peploe joined them, shielding his eyes as he gazed up at the Hurricane. 'That's 632 Squadron.'

Sykes whistled. 'Well, what do you know? You're right, sir. Can see them clear as day.'

'And that Hurricane up there is Lyell's,' Peploe added. 'LO-Z was his plane.'

'Look!' shouted McAllister, from the neighbouring slit trench. 'He's got out!'

They watched Lyell's deadweight figure plummet, then a white parachute balloon open.

'Thank God for that,' said Sykes.

'He's drifting,' said Tanner. 'Stupid bastard's going to end up the wrong side of the sodding canal.'

Wordlessly, they watched Lyell descend until he hit the ground about five hundred yards up the hill on the far side, directly opposite the French on the Rangers' right and a short distance from the line of thick wood. They watched breathlessly as the parachute silk flopped to the ground.

'Is he moving, Sarge?' said Sykes.

'I'm trying to see,' Tanner answered, as he peered through his binoculars. Lyell seemed to be lying lifelessly in the meadow. 'I can't tell whether he's alive or dead.'

They could all see him now.

'It looked like he'd come down all right,' said McAllister.

Tanner shrugged. 'Maybe he's concussed. Or broken his leg or something.'

'Should we shout to him or what?' said Sykes.

'We should go and see Captain Barclay,' said Peploe. 'Tanner, you come with me.'

Company Headquarters had been established in the white station house set back from the canal and beneath a high bank that overlooked the single-track railway. A field telephone had been set up but, Tanner noticed, as they went into the house, there was no sign of a radio transmitter.

'Where's Captain Barclay?' Peploe asked one of the men squatting by the field telephone.

'Out the back, sir. Him and Captain Wrightson.'

They found the two officers sitting at the foot of the bank. Both had mugs of tea, and Barclay had his Webley on his lap, an oily rag beside it.

'Peploe,' said Barclay, flicking away a fly from his face. 'All dug in?'

'Yes, sir. Sir, it's about the Hurricane that's just come down.'

'What Hurricane?'

'The dogfight, sir.' Peploe looked at Barclay as though he was mad. 'The one that's just been going on above us.'

Barclay faced Wrightson. 'Oh, yes, we heard that. Machine-guns going off and so on. I hadn't realized a plane had come down.'

'At least two, sir,' said Tanner.

Barclay glanced at him briefly – *you again* – then returned to Peploe. 'What about them?'

'A pilot's landed on the far bank, sir,' continued Peploe, 'opposite the French. We're not sure if he's alive, but the thing is, sir, I think he may be your brother-in-law.'

'What?' Barclay took his pipe from his mouth. 'What are you talking about? It can't be Charlie.'

'His plane had the same squadron markings, sir. LO–Z. That was Squadron Leader Lyell's personal aircraft.'

'But how on earth could you tell?'

'Sergeant Tanner was watching through binoculars, sir. He saw the markings on the fuselage.'

CSM Blackstone appeared in the doorway at the back of the house. 'What's going on, sir?' he asked.

'It seems my brother-in-law's been shot down and is lying on the far bank. Tanner saw the code on the Hurricane as it came down.'

Blackstone snorted. 'With respect, sir, I find it hard to believe that Sergeant Tanner could possibly see that from down here. Sure you're not just trying to get back into the OC's good books, Tanner?'

'I know what I saw,' said Tanner.

'Sir, who the pilot is – surely that's irrelevant,' said Peploe. 'I just wanted to let you know that it might be Squadron Leader Lyell and to ask your permission to send a team of men to fetch him. Since he's opposite the French I thought I should clear it with you and also ask their permission. There's a bridge just round the bend in the river,' he added. 'We could cross there – or even go over the one at Oisquercq.'

Barclay nodded. 'Yes,' he said. 'All right. You speak Frog, don't you, Peploe?'

'A little, sir.'

'Good. Then let's get the men ready and speak to the French commander at the farm.' He turned to Tanner. 'But I think it only fair that once we've cleared it with the Frogs you go and get Squadron Leader Lyell, Tanner. A chance to make amends for your indiscretion back at Manston, eh?'

Tanner swallowed hard, his face rigid with the effort of control-ling his irritation. 'Yes, sir,' he said. 'I'd be glad to.' He meant that, at least: it would give him an opportunity to gather his bearings. It was hard when you were travelling along roads with high hedgerows, through villages and woods, to get much of a picture of the land around. With the tree-lined fields and the woods behind them, Tanner had only a vague sense of how this part of the Belgian countryside fitted together. The slope on which Lyell had landed would, he guessed, give him a clear and far-reaching view back towards their own lines.

'How many men do you think you need?' Peploe asked.

'Three should do it, sir. Two to carry him, if necessary, and two to watch our backs.'

'All right. Who do you want to take?'

'Sykes, sir, with Hepworth and Ellis.'

'Why don't you take Lance-Corporal Smailes as well?'

'He's done the medic's course?'

'Yes.'

'Good thinking, sir. I don't think there's time to go to Battalion for stretcher-bearers.'

'Just get on with it, Sergeant,' snapped Barclay. 'The poor man could be dying in agony for all we know. I want to mount this rescue operation right away.'

When they reached the farm, they were stopped by North African troops who stared at them sullenly, with pointed rifles, until a young *sous-lieutenant* came over and ordered his men to lower their weapons. Apologizing, he led them to Battalion Headquarters at the main farmhouse.

'*Un moment,*' he said, leaving them to wait in the yard while he hurried inside.

Barclay clicked his tongue against his teeth. 'For God's sake,' he muttered.

Tanner looked around. Stacks of ammunition boxes stood near a shed across the yard; a staff car and a motorcycle were parked to one side. Coloured troops, in strange dark red woollen caps, double-breasted tunics and knee-high strapped leggings, walked past. The French mountain troops in Norway had had superb uniforms – far better than anything the British had been given – but Tanner was surprised by how old-fashioned these colonial troops were, as though they were from an earlier era. He moved back a few paces and saw a larger yard at the rear of the building where a number of vehicles – trucks, armoured cars and infantry tractors – were lined up. He was watching men loading boxes onto the back of a truck when his attention was caught by two men speaking animatedly, white Frenchmen, officers, wearing large khaki berets.

'What are they saying, Peploe?' said Barclay, softly.

Peploe listened, 'They're talking about the bridge, sir, that and the lock system by it. They must be sappers. They've laid charges but one thinks they haven't put down enough explosive.'

One of the officers, older than the other, turned now and saw them, shook his head in frustration and hurried off.

'They're expecting Jerry, then,' said Barclay. 'What do they know that we don't?'

For God's sake, thought Tanner. Couldn't the OC see the signs? Captain Barclay was clearly a bigger fool than he'd thought.

The *sous-lieutenant* now reappeared with a tall, good-looking officer in his late thirties. 'Commandant du Parc,' explained the lieutenant.

'I am second-in-command here,' he said, in heavily accented English. 'How can I be of assistance?'

Peploe explained in French. Du Parc replied.

'They were about to send a party out themselves,' Peploe translated to Barclay, then smiled, 'but they're only too happy to let us take on the task.'

'But your men must be quick, Captain,' said Commandant du Parc in English once more. '*Les Boches*,' he added, 'they are coming soon, I think.'

'Does he have intelligence of this?' Barclay asked Peploe.

Du Parc laughed as Peploe repeated the question. 'No, but the sky, the aeroplanes that come over to have a little spy on us . . . *la retraite* of our men across *le canal*. Of course *les Boches* will be coming.' He chuckled again. 'It is obvious.'

Course it bloody is, thought Tanner, and saw Barclay redden.

Commandant du Parc spoke to Peploe again.

'He says we should cross the bridge over the lock,' said Peploe, 'just round the bend in the river. His men can give us covering fire should it be necessary – as can our chaps, sir. He'll also send us an escort to the bridge.'

'*Merci, Commandant*,' said Barclay.

Du Parc bowed slightly, then spoke to the *sous-lieutenant*, who hurried back into the farmhouse. A moment later he reappeared with another junior subaltern, a thin-faced lad with a poorly grown moustache. Du Parc spoke to him, then the young French officer turned to Tanner.

'Shall we go?'

'*Bonne chance*,' said du Parc.

Barclay and Peploe saluted. Barclay looked at his watch. 'Right, Sergeant,' he said to Tanner. 'Get Squadron Leader Lyell back here and be sharp about it.'

Just then an aircraft roared over the building from behind them, making them all flinch and duck. It was so low that they could see the black crosses on the pale blue underside of the wings. Men shouted and a machine-gun began to chatter but the twin-engine Junkers 88 climbed lazily over the hill in front of them, banked along the ridge then disappeared.

'*Merde*,' muttered du Parc.

'Why didn't it drop any bombs?' asked Barclay.

Tanner's patience snapped. 'It's a reconnaissance plane, sir. They've been coming over all morning.' He turned his back on the captain and strode off. 'Come on, boys,' he said. 'Iggery. We need to get a move on.'

As they stepped out of the yard he looked up at the wooded ridge above them. It was still and peaceful, quiet in the warm early-summer afternoon. For how much longer?

8

They said little as they hurried towards the bridge. It was further than Tanner had appreciated – three-quarters of a mile, at least – and he wished he had asked whether there was a boat at the farm they could use. He also felt a stab of irritation that the Frenchmen had not offered one of their many vehicles to take them the short drive. Christ, they had enough of them. But they were twitchy, that had been clear. The Germans were pushing them back, and retreat sapped confidence – he'd seen it in Norway – like rot setting in. Reversing it was damnably hard.

Commandant du Parc had been expecting the Germans to attack at any moment and Tanner suspected the Frenchman was right. He hoped they still had time to fetch Lyell safely but it was best to be prepared so he had insisted that each of his small rescue party bring plenty of ammunition. Every man was now carrying four Bren magazines as well as at least half a dozen clips of rifle bullets. He had also shoved half a dozen Mills bombs into their haversacks and respirator bags.

'You don't need a sodding gas-mask, Billy,' he had told Ellis. 'Get rid of it and stuff the bag full of ammo instead.'

'I thought this was supposed to be a cinch,' Hepworth had grumbled.

'And so it will be, Hep,' Tanner had replied, patting him on the back. 'Just in case, hey?'

He now noticed that Hepworth, carrying the Bren on his shoulder, was lagging. He trotted back to him, took the machinegun and slung it over his own shoulder instead. 'Come on, Hep. Stop being such a bloody old woman.'

'I'm still knackered from a five-day march.'

'Did he grumble this much in Norway, Sarge?' asked Ellis.

'He was worse,' said Sykes, whose eyes were on the field where the pilot lay. 'The squadron leader's still up there, Sarge,' he added, as Tanner came alongside him. 'Look.'

Tanner used his spare hand to raise his binoculars. 'He's still lying down, too,' he said, pausing briefly to steady his view. 'Bastard better not be dead.'

At the bridge the French lieutenant ushered them past the sentries, then left them. The lock was deep, perhaps as much as forty feet. Under the bridge there was a kind of gallery from which observers could watch traffic approaching or moving in and out of the lock.

'This'll take some blowing,' said Sykes. 'It's a big old piece of engineering.'

'There's certainly nothing like this on the Rochdale canal,' said Hepworth, unable to resist peering over the rails to the viewing gallery and the water below.

'Move your arse, Hep,' said Tanner.

The five men hurried across. Just beyond the canal lay the original tributary of the river Senne – clearly the Belgian navvies had been unable to widen the river into the shipping canal it had become along the stretch towards Brussels.

They nipped down the bank to a track that ran beside the large turning circle in the canal below the lock, then hurried along it by the water's edge. Tanner led them up the bank and through a meadow to another track beside some farm-workers' cottages. As they reached a thick hedge on the far side, he paused.

'It's the field above, I'm sure,' said Sykes, reading his thoughts.

'Yes – but we need to find a way through this. It's denser than it looked from the other side.' To Tanner's right, the hedge seemed to thicken into a copse, so he led them to the left and, sure enough, at the field's corner found an open gate and a track that led up the side of the meadow. Feeling the sun behind him, he looked through his binoculars again and saw the prostrate pilot a couple of hundred yards ahead, the blue of his uniform trousers just visible through the grass.

'There he is,' he said.

'Is he moving?' asked Sykes.

'No. Come on. Let's go and get him, dead or alive.'

The meadow was already thick with wild flowers – a wet April and a warm first two weeks of May had seen to that. The grass was two foot high in places, Tanner noted, and caught at their feet, making it hard to walk through. It was no wonder they could hardly see Lyell now.

The men were no more than twenty yards from the immobile body when he moved suddenly, pushing himself up on his elbows.

'Jesus, you made me jump,' said Lyell. 'Thank God you're not Germans.'

So he wasn't dead or even dying, thought Tanner. 'Sorry, sir,' he said. 'We've come to rescue you.'

Lyell looked at the blood on his hand and his face twisted with obvious pain. 'I think I've been out cold,' he muttered. 'Only came to a few minutes ago. Christ, my bloody head hurts.'

'We'll get you back to our lines and then an MO can attend to you, sir,' said Tanner.

'How long have I been out?'

Tanner looked at his watch. 'It's just gone five now and we watched you come down about twenty past four. So, that's three-quarters of an hour.' Tanner now stepped up beside him. 'Squadron

Leader Lyell, is it just your head or are you hurt anywhere else?'

Lyell looked at him sharply. 'How the devil d'you know my name?'

Tanner pushed his helmet back. 'We met at Manston, sir.'

'You!' exclaimed Lyell. 'What the bloody hell are you doing here? Don't tell me I've survived only to be shot at again by a mad Tommy.'

Tanner couldn't help smiling. 'You're not drunk in charge of a vehicle this time, sir. We're with the rest of the battalion, dug in along the far side of the canal.'

Lyell struggled to suppress a cry of pain. There were beads of sweat and blood on his brow and a dark gash near the top of his forehead. 'My bloody head.'

'Lads, keep your eyes peeled,' said Tanner. Then, with Smailes, he squatted beside Lyell.

Lyell winced. 'I survive Christ knows how many bullets and cannon shells, then hit my head trying to bale out.'

Smailes placed his hands gently around the cut on the squadron leader's head. Immediately he yelled with pain. 'Christ, man! Jesus, aargh! Get your sodding hands off me.'

'I've got to determine what you've done, sir.'

'Isn't it bloody obvious? Just get me out of here.'

'Let me give you some morphine, sir. It'll relieve the pain.'

'Yes,' gasped Lyell, leaning his head back. 'Please do.'

As Smailes took a syringe and a phial from his medical bag, Tanner had a good look round. The meadow was, he guessed, about a dozen acres, lined with hedgerows of varying thickness. There were more meadows at either side and tracks, too, linking them. To the top was the wood they could see from the far bank. How deep it was, or what lay on the other side of the ridge, he had no idea.

Having eased off Lyell's Irvin, Smailes pushed up his sleeve and injected the morphine into his arm.

'Aah,' sighed Lyell.

'All right, Smiler,' said Tanner to Smailes. 'We should try to lift him now and get him to safety. Here, Billy, help Smiler with Squadron Leader Lyell.'

Ellis and Smailes each put an arm round his back and placed his on their shoulders.

'One, two—'

'What's that?' said Tanner, turning his ear to the woods above them.

'Just help me up, will you?' groaned Lyell.

'Sssh! Sorry, sir, but keep quiet a moment, will you?'

He listened again, and then they all heard it. Engines – several of them.

'Sounds like motorbikes to me,' said Sykes, in a hushed tone.

'Exactly,' said Tanner. 'Right. One, two, three – up.' Lyell's silk parachute lay on the ground. 'Leave that,' he said, seeing Lyell glance at it. 'Quick, get him to that hedge at the side of the meadow.'

They hurried over to it, then put Lyell back on the ground.

'Right,' said Tanner. 'Billy and Smiler, can you two carry him on your own?'

'I think so, sir,' said Smailes.

'Good, then give us your ammo and get going, quick as you can make it. If Jerry comes and you don't think you can get across the bridge safely, take cover and wait, but make sure you use the same route we took to get here. Iggery, OK? Stan, Hep, you come with me.'

'Where are we going, Sarge?' asked Hepworth, eyes wide.

'Just a little recce. Here, take the Bren – and no more grumbling.'

Crouching, he led them along the edge of the field. He could still hear the motorcycles, moving around on the hill above them. Instinct told him they were German – after all, the Belgian Army was on the left flank of the BEF, not here, and they'd seen few Belgian civilian motorcycles on the road. As they reached the edge of the wood, he still couldn't see them, but the sound was louder and coming from either side of them – several motorcycles seemed to be moving away to their left and more to their right. Indicating to Sykes and Hepworth to crouch behind an oak each, he paused to look back over the French and British lines. He could see Oisquercq clearly, the bridge intact. Some trucks trundled through the village, the mirror or windscreen of one glinting until it turned out of the direct line of the sun. And there were the farm and the lock. There was no sign of the other three. *Good. They're out of the meadow.*

'I want to get a better look,' he hissed. 'We'll move forward through these trees, but make sure you keep your ears sharp and your eyes open.'

They pushed on, half crouching, using the trees as cover. The wood floor was a carpet of bluebells. Shafts of sunlight poured through the canopy of oak, beech, birch and spruce. There were a few bushes here and there, bracken and rotten logs or fallen trunks, but otherwise it was easy to move, and, thankfully, soft underfoot.

Tanner now heard more vehicles moving forward, then a voice. It was too distant to make out clearly, but he sensed there was a road or track ahead to their right. He pointed to the direction of the engines, conscious that he could still hear a motorcycle moving away to their left and now almost behind them.

Suddenly he glimpsed something ahead, crouched lower and signalled to the other two to do the same.

'What is it?' whispered Sykes.

'I saw something – a large vehicle, I think,' hissed Tanner. 'There must be a road up there – or a track, at least. Let's move up a bit but make sure you keep your heads down. And no bloody noise.'

The ground ahead rose and then they could see a road bisecting the wood. Along it, engines running, stood a column of German armoured cars and motorbikes.

'Christ, Sarge!' whispered Hepworth. 'What the hell are they doing?'

'I'd say they must be the reconnaissance. Advance guard.' There were four armoured cars, squat four-wheeled vehicles; two had small cannons and machine-guns fitted to the turrets, but on the other two tubing extended from the hull and stretched round the turret.

'Any ideas what those two are about, Stan?' Tanner asked.

'I reckon they must be radio cars, Sarge. Yes, that'll be it.'

'Reporting back.' Tanner stroked his chin. He counted six motorcycles, all with sidecars and a machine-gun attached to them. Two more motorcycles appeared from away to their left, without sidecars. Tanner noticed their riders had rifles slung across their backs.

'Look,' said Tanner. 'See that fallen trunk? Let's try and get to it.' It was another fifty yards or so, thick with ivy. It offered cover and, underneath it, the perfect place from which to observe the enemy.

'Don't you think we've seen enough, Sarge?' said Hepworth, eyes still wide.

Tanner winked. 'No, Hep. We can have some fun here, I reckon.'

'Fun, Sarge?' Hepworth was clearly horror-stricken.

'Think about it, Hep. Our lads are falling back and so are the Frogs. Our job is to hold up Jerry as long as possible to give the rest of the boys as much time as we can to get back to wherever we're going to make a stand. These jokers here are obviously Jerry's advance guard. If Stan's right, they'll be sending radio transmissions back to the main bulk of the German advance, reporting on what they've seen and pinpointing targets, but they can't do that if we put them out of action, can they?'

'And how do we do that?' His face had drained of colour. 'There's only three of us.'

'Yes, but we've got the element of surprise. Look at them – they're having some kind of pow-wow. The last thing they're going to expect is an attack. And we've got the Bren, plenty of rounds, three rifles and a load of grenades. I'm sure we can think of something to do with that lot.'

'And a few other bits and bobs.' Sykes grinned.

Tanner smirked. 'Like what, you sly dog?'

'A couple of tins of safety fuse, two cartons of Nobel's finest, a tin of detonators, and something else I think you might appreciate, Sarge.' He delved into his respirator bag and pulled out a small tin about four inches long.

'What are those?' asked Tanner.

'Mark One time delay switches. You add a detonator to one end and put your detonator into a pack or more of Nobel's. There's a phial you snap that releases some kind of 'orrible corrosive and when it's burned through a thin tube of copper it releases a striker and a spring, and bang – off goes your gelignite.'

'What's the delay?'

'Depends on where you set the strip of copper. Ten minutes, half an hour, an hour and a half, and so on. They're new, apparently. I've only got five of them, mind. That's all you get in a tin.'

Tanner shook his head. 'Where on earth did you find this stuff?'

Sykes winked. 'Pinched it from Division sappers back in Tournai. I like having a few explosives about me, these days. Never know when they might come in handy.' He put away the tin. 'Norway taught me that much, Sarge.'

'Why didn't you tell me, Stan? We could have taken twice as much.'

Sykes looked sheepish. 'I thought you were probably in enough trouble, Sarge. No one's watching me particular, you see.'

'You're probably right.'

'I still don't know what we can do, though,' said Hepworth.

'Nor do I yet,' said Tanner. 'Let's get to that tree first. We'll think of something.'

They inched forward, the trees and some thicker foliage, with the engine noise of an armoured car, providing them with cover. At the fallen tree, they lay down on their stomachs. The enemy were about sixty yards away, still deep in conversation. Tanner brought his binoculars to his eyes. Immediately he spotted the officer in charge – different shoulder tabs, jacket, belt and breeches – standing in front of the leading armoured car, one with a gun turret. He didn't think much of the uniform. It was too stiff, too formal – impractical. Another officer's head was poking out of the radio car, headphones over his cap. The rest were other ranks – privates and NCOs – between twenty and thirty in all. He looked back in the direction from which the Germans had evidently come. He couldn't see far, but there was no sign of any others.

'We need some kind of distraction,' he whispered. 'Something to keep them busy while we get round the back and disable those armoured cars.'

'How about setting off a couple of packets of gelignite?' suggested Sykes. 'I could push round a bit, set them for ten minutes, then scarper back here. Then Hep can open up with the Bren and we'll hop in from behind with some grenades.'

Tanner nodded thoughtfully. 'Can't think of a better plan. All right. I'll try to pick off the officers when Hep opens up with the Bren.' He glanced through his binoculars again and saw that the senior officer was now peering towards the sky with his own. Others were also gazing upwards.

'Hello,' he whispered. 'What's going on here?'

Then he heard it. The faint, rhythmic thrum of aero-engines.

'Bombers,' he murmured. The sound of the approaching aircraft grew until it became a roar. Then, glancing up through the canopy, they glimpsed two dozen Stukas and a moment later the first aircraft began its dive, siren wailing, followed by another and another, as each hurtled down towards its target. Amid the screaming sirens and whine of the engines came the whistle of falling bombs and the rattle of machine-guns. The bombs detonated, cracking the air and rippling the ground so that Tanner could feel the vibrations even from where they were, nearly a mile behind. *Christ. I hope Smiler and Billy have got Lyell safe.*

Sykes nudged him. 'Couldn't have timed it better myself.'

'Get going now,' Tanner told him. 'I'll see you over there, by that big oak.' He pointed to a large tree roughly in line with their present position but behind the enemy column. 'Be as quick as you can.'

Sykes scampered off. Tanner unloaded his Bren magazines and laid them beside Hepworth. He put a hand on the private's shoulder. He liked the lad for all his bellyaching; they'd been through so much together in Norway and he hadn't let Tanner down yet. 'You'll be fine, Hep. When the explosions go off, wait a few seconds, then open fire. Just make sure you knock down as many as you can.'

'All right, Sarge.' He swallowed hard and Tanner saw that his hands were shaking as he moved the spare magazines.

Tanner patted Hepworth's back then set off, half crouching, half running, between the trees until he reached the large oak. There he stopped, put his binoculars in his haversack and took out his Aldis scope, carefully unwrapped it from its cloth, and fitted it to the pads on his rifle. He'd had it zeroed at four hundred yards, but the distance here was way less – maybe seventy. That meant adjusting the range drum and aiming a good deal lower than the main point of impact as indicated by the scope. He moved round the oak, found a cluster of brambles and positioned himself behind it but with enough of a view through the tangle of leaves and stems to pick out the two officers. Both were still watching the Stukas' attack. The bombs had been dropped, but Tanner heard the air-crafts' change of pitch and whine as they swooped and attacked with their machine-guns. He was certain they were targeting the French, rather than the British at Oisquercq and Tubize, but there was no doubt that D Company would be feeling the force of the attack. He hoped they were bearing up, and reminded himself that a soldier properly dug in had only a lucky direct hit to fear. And the enemy would want that bridge intact – they would have been care-ful where they dropped their loads.

Having reassured himself, he glanced at his watch, then saw Sykes coming towards him. 'How long have we got?'

'Two or three minutes.' He puffed out his cheeks. 'I hate the wait.'

'Got the grenades ready?'

Sykes patted his haversack – he'd undone the straps.

'Good,' said Tanner. 'There's only one way to do this.'

'Run?'

'Yes. There's plenty of trees and it's not far. We should be fine. Let's leave the motorcycles at the back alone, though. I'm going to make straight for those radio cars. You take the rear turreted one.'

'You don't think by sniping you'll make them realize we're behind them?'

'No – with the explosions and with Hep opening fire, they won't be able to tell what the hell's going on.'

The Stuka attack was lessening as aircraft flew away from the fray. The sound of machine-gun fire slackened. Tanner glanced at his watch again. 'Damn it, come on!' he muttered. Anxiety was etched across Sykes's face.

The first time-bomb exploded. Tanner saw the enemy soldiers flinch and brought his aim to the officer, whose head was still just visible among the swathe of men around him. He adjusted the distance, breathed in, held it and squeezed. The shot cracked loud and sharp among the trees, the butt of the rifle pressing back into his shoulder. The officer dropped, spraying blood. At that instant, Hepworth opened fire with the Bren. Sykes had already gone, but Tanner moved his aim to the second officer, who had initially ducked into the turret but had now poked his head out again. It was the last movement he made: Tanner pressed the trigger of his Lee-Enfield a second time.

Breathing out heavily, he took the rifle in his left hand and ran forward. Men were already scattered on the ground. Flitting between the trees, he sprinted forward. Ahead, Sykes was near the first armoured car. Movement – a soldier was hurrying back to the motorcycle and now grabbed the machine-gun. Tanner paused, pulled the rifle to his shoulder, drew back the bolt and fired as the German was swivelling the weapon towards Sykes.

Tanner sped forward. Sykes had clambered onto the back of the first armoured car. A crewman poked his head from the turret and Sykes brought down his rifle butt, jerking the man's head backwards against the circular steel rim. Then, with his teeth, Sykes pulled the pin from the grenade, dropped it inside and jumped away.

'Watch out!' yelled Tanner, as another soldier ran towards them, his pistol pointing from an outstretched arm. The grenade went off, knocking the German off-balance, and Tanner shot him at almost point-blank range, then ran on past, smashed another stunned soldier's head with a short, hard swing of his rifle butt, and leaped onto one of the radio cars as shells and bullets detonated inside the first vehicle. He dropped a grenade into the turret, then swung himself off the metal radio frame as the rear armoured car blew up.

'Bloody hell!' he said, as the blast swept over the radio car and shards of jagged metal clattered against it. Quickly, he scrambled to his feet and ran forward as the second grenade detonated, shrapnel rattling. Ahead, he saw dazed men getting to their feet, so he took another grenade, pulled the pin, hurled it towards them and leaped onto the next radio car. A driver raised his head and a pistol but Tanner ducked and the bullets fizzed uselessly over his head. Cocking his rifle, he stood up and fired, hitting the man in the neck. He went down amid a fountain of blood. As Tanner jumped onto the back of the vehicle, another German appeared round the side, aimed his rifle, then fell backwards with a cry as a rake of bullets from Hepworth's Bren hit him. Tanner threw another grenade into the car, jumped off and realized the Bren had stopped firing.

'Hep!' he shouted, as he crouched by the side of the fourth armoured vehicle. 'Hep! Why have you stopped firing?' With his rifle ready, pulled into his shoulder, he sprang out in front of the car only to meet Sykes with a German pistol in his hand. Ammunition inside the vehicle behind them was going off like fireworks, so they got down, waiting for the next blast.

'There's no one left to shoot, Sarge,' said Sykes. 'Look.'

Bodies were strewn across the road, blood seeping into the grit and dust. The smell, mixed with the pungent stench of explosives, petrol and burning rubber, was sickening, and Tanner's stomach tightened. The motorcycles were ruined. Two were burning, while the others stood awkwardly, riddled with bullet holes. Seven stunned Germans staggered in front of them, their arms raised in surrender. Bullets were still detonating in the armoured car behind them, whistling and pinging as they ricocheted around.

Tanner got to his feet. 'Right,' he said. 'We need to move. We can't be sure this lot were the only recce troops around here.'

'What about the prisoners?' asked Sykes, as Hepworth, eyes wide and disbelieving, came towards them.

Tanner tutted. 'We should probably take them with us.' The lead armoured car was still untouched, save for a few dents from Hepworth's bullets. The tyres were also undamaged. 'We could take this. Make them sit on the outside. One of us can drive, another watch them from the turret and the other ride one of their motorcycles. Check them for weapons, then get them to move this lot off the road. And give them some beadies. Poor bastards've just lost their mates.'

Tanner stepped around the bodies and walked a little way along the track until he could look down to the canal. A thick pall of smoke hung heavily over the French positions and was drifting in front of their own lines, but he could hear vehicles starting up. Then another explosion ripped through the air and he saw the bridge across the lock disappear in an eruption of smoke, dust and debris.

'Bollocks,' he muttered. Then he saw that the bridge at Oisquercq had been blown so that only its stone struts still stood, lonely columns jutting out of the water. Amid the fury of their small battle, he had not heard it go up. He reached for his binoculars. A hole had been blown in the bridge over which they had come; the iron fencing stood bent and twisted. But the gallery directly beneath it, which stood sentinel over the lock, remained intact. He realized that the charges under the structure must have failed and that the crater on the bridge must have been caused by a poorly aimed bomb. He reckoned that any vehicle would struggle to cross it, but they themselves would still get over. Now he let his eyes rest on the farm. The roof of the house had collapsed, rubble and broken tiles heaped in the yard. Behind, a number of vehicles stood burning and broken. There was no sign of life. He lowered his binoculars, then brought them back to his eyes. Yes, there could be no doubting it. Columns of men and vehicles were trailing west. The French were pulling back.

Tanner hurried to the others. 'Hep, work out how to drive this thing,' he said, pointing to the armoured car. 'Stan, get the prisoners onto the front.' He noticed Sykes still held a pistol. 'Got enough bullets for that?'

'Half a dozen clips, Sarge.'

'Good. I'm going to get the bike and have a quick look behind us. Then we'll go.'

He strode past the line of wrecked armoured cars and saw that, despite his intention to save both motorcycles at the back of the column, the first lay on its side, petrol still leaking from its tank. The second looked to be all right, so Tanner sat on it, knocked back the stand and kicked down hard on the starter. The BMW engine roared into life. He gunned the throttle, put it into gear, wheeled round and sped off.

Soon, he had cleared the wood. The road forked north and south, but although there was another large wood half a mile to the south, ahead, looking east, he had a clear line of vision. There was a village a couple of miles off and beyond it the countryside stretched away, softly undulating. He paused to peer through the binoculars. Ahead, in the far distance, he saw a cloud of dust rising. 'The German advance,' he muttered to himself. How far away was it? Ten miles? Fifteen? If he was right, they would reach the river in an hour, maybe two.

At the sound of vehicles he turned. Another column of German armoured cars and motorbikes was emerging from the wood to the south. He waved at them, turned the bike round and sped back.

Drawing up alongside the armoured car, he was relieved to hear the engine ticking over. Sykes was standing half out of the turret. 'There's another recce column half a mile away,' he said. 'Has Hep worked out how to drive that thing?'

'I think so.'

'Good. Head straight down this track – it leads to the canal – and make a lot of noise. We don't want any of our lot shooting at us.'

Sykes shouted at Hepworth. The gears ground noisily and then, with a jerk that nearly jolted several prisoners off the front, the armoured car lurched forward. Slowly – *too slowly*, thought Tanner – they rumbled out of the wood and down the slope towards the canal. The dust and smoke had now all but gone and Tanner saw ever more clearly the damage done by the Stukas. Craters dotted the far bank and the fields behind the farm. The buildings were more wrecked than he had first appreciated.

As they reached the track along the canal, a shot cracked out from the far bank, then another. Both were wide, but Tanner stopped and waved his arms frantically above his head. 'Don't shoot!' he shouted. 'We're Rangers!'

Then a burst of machine-gun fire came from behind, kicking a line of earth between him and the armoured car. Turning, he saw several motorcycles speeding out of the wood, manned machine-guns in the sidecars.

'Damn it!' said Tanner, and gunned the throttle as another burst of ill-directed fire hissed over his head. 'Stan!' he yelled. 'Get Hep to put his bloody foot down!'

Hepworth did so, and the armoured car was suddenly speeding forward. His steering was wild and as he swerved against the bank of the track, one of the prisoners fell. Tanner nearly lost control as he dodged round the man. He glanced back. For the moment, they had lost their pursuers. Dust and grit were getting into his eyes and he cursed himself for not taking a set of German goggles. On they sped, round the turning circle in the canal, and then they were climbing back up the bank towards the lock.

Hurtling past the armoured car, Tanner skidded to a halt, leaped off the motorcycle and quickly examined the bridge. The damage was far worse than he had originally thought. An ugly crater lay at one end, while large cracks ran down the side and across the gallery. Suddenly, he heard the structure creak as though it might collapse at any moment. If that happened while they were crossing they would all be dead.

'Stan, get Hep out quick!' he shouted.

Sykes motioned to the prisoners to jump off and, with his pistol, led them to the damaged bridge. 'Go on,' he said, waving his arms. 'Cross the bridge. *Geht!*'

They did as they were ordered, sidling past the crater, as Hepworth jumped down from the armoured car. The bridge groaned again, prompting anxious glances from the prisoners. Tanner looked back down the track. Where were the enemy? Perhaps they feared attack themselves. He turned to Hepworth. 'Go on, Hep!' he said. 'Bloody get your arse over that bridge.'

There were shouts now from the far side and Tanner turned to see Peploe emerge from the trees, urging them to hurry. A moment later a cannon shell whammed into the ground not ten yards from where Tanner was crouching.

'Jesus!' Looking round, he saw an armoured car and several motorcycles on the brow of the hill directly behind them. Another cannon shell hit the side of the armoured car, then a machine-gun sputtered and Tanner ran onto the bridge as bullets kicked into the ground.

'Come on, Sarge!' yelled Sykes, as a Bren opened up from the other bank. Tanner saw him sheltering behind a small brick hut on the far side of the bridge. The prisoners now ran across the open ground between the hut and the safety of the trees. Tanner saw one fall. Another burst of enemy machine-gun fire ripped through the centre of the bridge. *Bloody hell*, he thought, then took a deep breath and raced over the crater. Immediately another burst chattered, bullets pinging around him. A second Bren opened fire, and rifle shots cracked from the far bank too. Bullets whistled overhead and along the bridge, clattering into the metalwork and concrete and into the murky water in the lock. The bridge groaned again as he sprinted towards the hut, sliding behind it beside Sykes and Hepworth. But it was still another thirty yards to the trees.

'Come on, boys,' muttered Tanner, looking towards the Rangers hidden in the trees, 'keep bloody firing.' He glanced back and saw that the enemy armoured car and motorcycles were now pulling back. *Thank God.* Several more rifles cracked out and a Bren clattered.

'Looks like Jerry's had enough,' said Sykes. 'Reckon it's safe to make a dash for it?'

Tanner nodded. Sykes went first, then Hepworth, and when he had watched them scurry across the open ground, he made a run for it himself. As he did so, he felt something sear his side. Grimacing as he ran, he gazed up and saw Blackstone, kneeling by a tree towards the canal bank, lowering his rifle.

Anger welled as he ran the last few yards. Then he turned back towards Blackstone, his face set and fists clenched.

A hand on his shoulder. 'Tanner, what in God's name have you been doing?'

It was Peploe. 'We discovered a German reconnaissance unit, sir.' He glanced again to where Blackstone had been but there was no sign of him. 'We destroyed it, sir,' he added. 'Did Billy and Smiler get the squadron leader back all right?'

'Yes – just after the Stuka attack.'

'Good. Did we lose anyone?'

'Three wounded in Eleven Platoon, but otherwise no. Here,' he said, pulling out his hip-flask, 'have a nip of this. Then we need to get back quickly. The battalion's moving out.' As Tanner swigged, he said, 'Your side's bleeding. Christ, what have you done?'

Tanner hitched up his battle-blouse and shirt. The bullet had grazed him, carving a cut two inches long across his side. He had been lucky. 'It's nothing serious, sir,' he said.

'I'm amazed any of you are alive.'

'It was Blackstone who did this, not the Jerries,' said Tanner. 'It happened just now – as I was crossing the open ground between the bridge and the trees.'

'Blackstone? Are you sure?'

'I saw him lowering his rifle.'

'Are you absolutely sure it was him? There were bullets flying everywhere. Any one of them could have hit you.'

Tanner was in no mood to mind what he said to the lieutenant. He had been involved in a hard-fought engagement, had killed a number of men and very nearly been killed himself. Adrenalin still coursed through him. Had Peploe not confronted him, he was certain he would have knocked Blackstone down. Even now, his fists remained clenched and his jaw tight.

'I know it was him, sir,' he told Peploe. 'Oh, it won't stick and I'm sure Captain Barclay would back him to the hilt, but I'll have to watch that man like a bloody hawk.'

'And I'm watching him, too,' said Peploe. 'But my advice is to keep away from him. For both your sakes.'

They hurried through the trees that lined the canal and rejoined the track leading to the farm, past empty slit trenches and abandoned ammunition boxes. Tanner saw a dead North African, his leg twisted back on itself. Bomb craters pockmarked the ground and ripped branches littered it. The air was still thick with lingering smoke and the stench of cordite and burning rubber. It was only half past five – just twenty-five minutes since they had made their attack on the enemy.

Sykes and Hepworth were thirty yards in front and turned now to wait for him. Tanner raised a hand and felt another stab of anger as he spotted Blackstone ahead, with two other men and the prisoners. *Claiming them as his own. That bastard.* Just as he had feared, he was now fighting two enemies in Belgium – and right now, he knew which one was the more dangerous.

9

They made straight for the station house that for a day had been D Company Headquarters. The slit trenches dug that morning were still manned, but Tanner saw that the men were, once again, ready to march. Primus stoves had been packed away, entrenching tools and bayonets attached to belts and haversacks clipped back onto webbing. As soon as the order was given, the men would sling their rifles and Brens on their shoulders and move out.

Tanner wished he could sit down for a few moments, have a brew and a cigarette to calm himself, but as he paused by 12 Platoon's slit trenches, Peploe said, 'I'm sorry, Tanner, but the OC wants to see you right away. Sykes and Hepworth too.'

Tanner cursed to himself and scowled, unsure that he could trust himself when he next saw Blackstone. Peploe felt in his pocket and pulled out a pale green packet of Woodbines. 'All right,' he said. 'Perhaps there's time for a quick smoke.' He threw the packet to Tanner. 'Here, you chaps, have one of mine.'

'Thank you, sir,' said Tanner, taking one and passing it on to Sykes.

Peploe took a small silver matchbox from his pocket, and lit their cigarettes.

'Nice matchbox, sir,' said Sykes.

'Thank you, Sykes,' said Peploe. 'It was a twenty-first birthday present from my sister. It's damn useful, actually. Never have to worry about matches getting damp.'

Tanner inhaled deeply, then breathed out, a swirling cloud of blue-grey smoke rising into the thickening leaves of the chestnuts beside them. In the fields and woods on the opposite side of the canal, the enemy was no longer anywhere to be seen. He imagined the German reconnaissance troops radioing back the news that the British and French were in retreat again. He wondered whether their efforts in the wood opposite had made any difference. Although it was true that nearly thirty lay dead or wounded and would not fight them again, it was small fry. The main body of the German advance was presumably still ploughing its way towards them. *Christ.*

'Sergeant?' said Peploe.

Tanner pushed back his tin hat and rubbed his brow. 'Yes, sir,' he said. 'Thank you for that.'

Tanner had calmed considerably by the time they reached Headquarters. The violent rage he had felt towards Blackstone had been replaced by a more controlled anger, so that when he was ushered round the back of the station house to be grilled by Barclay, he was able to keep any murderous thoughts in check.

To his relief, there was no sign of Blackstone, but he was surprised to see Squadron Leader Lyell sitting beneath the oak tree behind the house, his head bound with a wad and bandage.

'Ah, my rescuer, the gallant sergeant,' said Lyell, his words slurred with morphine, 'or, rather, the man who buggered off and left us to be bombed to hell by Stukas.'

'I thought you'd been taken to the battalion MO, sir.'

'Well, he should have been, Sergeant,' said Captain Barclay, emerging from the house, 'but there's been a slight breakdown in communications. Ten Platoon have gone with the truck to Oisquercq. They're leaving slightly ahead of us with the rest of the battalion. Charlie – er, Squadron Leader Lyell was supposed to go with them.'

'I'm glad I'm not in the Army,' said Lyell. 'You lot always seem to be leaving each other behind.'

'It makes little odds,' snapped Barclay. 'We'll be rendezvousing with the rest of the battalion later tonight. We'll just have to carry you until then. It's not far.'

'Where is it, sir?'

Barclay pulled out a crumpled map. 'Er . . . here,' he said, holding it against the grassy bank beside the house and pointing to a wooded area some four miles west. 'Bois de Neppe. Orders from Battalion are for us to meet there at nineteen thirty hours.'

Tanner looked at his watch. It was nearly six o'clock already.

The OC read Tanner's thoughts. 'So we need to get going, smartish.'

'Yes, sir.' He saluted and made to leave, but Barclay stopped him.

'Hold on a moment, Sergeant. There's still time for you to tell me briefly what the bloody hell's been going on. Your orders were to rescue Squadron Leader Lyell yet you disappeared with two of your men and left Ellis and Smailes to get him back on their own. Lucky for you that they made it in one piece.'

'With respect, sir, the Stuka attack would have happened whether I was with them or not. I didn't leave Squadron Leader Lyell until I knew he was alive and that Smailes and Ellis could manage his injuries. But I heard enemy troops a short distance above us, sir, and was worried they might hinder our efforts to get the squadron leader back. I took Hepworth and Sykes with me to investigate.'

'Sergeant Tanner and his men discovered part of a German reconnaissance battalion, sir,' said Peploe.

'Four armoured cars and eight motorcycles. They were reporting our movements by radio and, I think, had been marking targets for the Stukas.'

'Sergeant Tanner and his two men destroyed them, sir,' added Peploe.

'Destroyed them? How on earth could three of you have done that?'

'We surprised them, sir. Surprise is a great advantage,' he said, then added hastily, 'as you know, sir. And they were distracted by the Stukas. Hepworth here cut most of them down with the Bren while Sykes and I crept behind them and disabled the armoured cars with grenades. We captured seven prisoners, but we lost one trying to make it back.'

'That was certainly good work, Sergeant. Captain Wrightson has taken them to Battalion HQ with Ten Platoon.'

'So you managed to get the prisoners to Battalion but not me,' muttered Lyell. 'Nice to know I'm lower in the pecking order than some bloody captured Huns.'

Barclay sighed. 'For God's sake,' he said, through gritted teeth, 'be thankful you're still alive and not being carted off to some German prison camp.' He turned back to Tanner. 'Go on, Sergeant.'

'I also took the chance to have a bit of a dekko, sir. I took one of the bikes to the far side of the ridge and saw the Germans in the distance. At the time, I reckoned they were twelve to fifteen miles away. They'll reach the canal by nightfall.'

Barclay swallowed. 'Right. I see.' He patted his pockets and took out his pipe.

'And, sir, I'd like you to know that Corporal Sykes and Private Hepworth performed well. Sykes alone destroyed an armoured car and Hepworth accounted for at least fifteen enemy.'

'Really? By Jove! All right, Tanner. Thank you. Duly noted. And, er, well done.'

Blackstone joined them from the back of the house. 'Sir, we really should be going. We've been held up long enough as it is.'

'Yes, all right, CSM,' said Barclay, without moving. 'Your old friend here has been performing heroics. How many dead was it, Sergeant?'

Tanner shrugged. 'Wouldn't like to say, sir.'

'About thirty, sir,' said Sykes.

Blackstone's eyes were unblinking. 'Well done, lads. Well done. We saw these boys hurtling down the hill, didn't we, Mr Peploe?' he said. 'At first we thought they were Jerries gone mad, then we heard your shouting and hurried to the bridge.'

'Another part of the enemy reconnaissance battalion opened fire on us, sir,' said Tanner.

'But you made it back,' said Barclay.

Blackstone grinned. 'Touch and go, though, wasn't it, sir?' he said, to Peploe. 'Bullets flying everywhere.'

'I was hit by one.' Tanner glared at Blackstone.

The CSM patted him on the back. 'But you're all right, aren't you, Jack?'

'I was lucky.'

'There!' exclaimed Blackstone. 'Haven't I always said so?' He smiled affably, took out a packet of cigarettes and held it open to them. Hepworth took one eagerly, but Tanner and Sykes ignored the offer. Instead, Tanner saluted Barclay again, then turned sharply and brushed past the CSM.

Soon after the company set off, two platoons and Company Headquarters – seventy-nine men in all. They marched, 12 Platoon following 11, along a dusty, unmetalled road, their backs now to the advancing enemy.

Lieutenant Peploe was walking beside Tanner. 'Still no sign. Hard to believe that less than an hour ago Germans were shooting at us down by the bridge.'

'They'll be up there somewhere,' said Tanner. 'All these woods make damn good cover. We've got a bit of time, though. Jerry can't get across the canal without bridges, so their sappers'll be busy tonight.'

'You think they'll be over by morning?'

Tanner shrugged. 'I reckon so.'

'We don't want to be long at the rendezvous, then.'

'No. I don't suppose we've been told where we'll make the next stand, but the sooner we get there the better. A bit of scoff in that wood and then a long night march, I reckon.'

'What about your wound?'

'Hardly a wound, sir. I've put a dressing on it. I'll have to get my housewife out, though, and sew up my shirt and battle-blouse. Don't suppose we'll be seeing too much of our kitbags in the next few days so what I've got has to last.'

They passed through another small village, as deserted as the others. In the fields, more cows lowed painfully, their udders swollen with milk. Tanner saw one cow already dead, its legs sticking up stiffly into the air, its body rigid and bloated. Two dogs barked and snarled as they passed until a soldier kicked one, and they scuttled away. An elderly woman was watching from a window. A few days before she would have seen British troops marching to the front, Tanner thought. Now they were marching back. What must she be thinking, left alone, her neighbours gone, the Germans just a few miles away?

He wondered whether they would really manage to reverse the retreat. All the momentum was with the enemy now – that was obvious – but he had also heard that the French Army was massive. Chevannes, a French officer in Norway, had boasted about that, and how they had more tanks and guns than the British and the Germans put together. The French had been caught off-guard but surely they would regroup, concentrate their forces, now that they knew the direction of the German advance, and fight back? He remembered his father telling him that something similar had happened at the beginning of the last war – a swift opening attack by the Germans that had taken everyone by surprise but was eventually halted.

Tanner stepped out of line to check his men were all still present and in good order. Company Headquarters led, followed by three sections of ten men, the last led by Corporal Sykes. He waited until the last two in Sykes's section – Hepworth and Rhodes – reached him, then continued alongside them. 'All right?' he asked.

'I suppose so, Sarge,' said Hepworth. 'I'm sick of all this marching, though. It's all we ever seem to do in the Army.'

'What are you talking about, Hep?' said Tanner. 'Wasn't that enough action for you this afternoon?'

'More than enough.'

'We'll be in that wood soon. Get some scoff. You'll feel better after that.'

The column crossed a railway line, the men climbing up the small embankment and over the rails.

'Sarge,' said Rhodes, as they cleared the line, 'is it true you used to know the CSM out in India?'

'Yes, it is. Why?'

'A few of the others had said so. Just thought I'd find out for myself.'

'Well, now you know.'

'Don't take this the wrong way, Sarge,' said Hepworth, 'but do you and the CSM not get on?'

'What makes you say that, Private?'

'You didn't have that smoke he offered you.'

'I'd had one a few minutes before. So had Corporal Sykes.'

'So had I,' said Hepworth.

'Well, you shouldn't have taken it, then. Doesn't do you any good, you know, smoking too much.'

'Well, I think he's all right, the CSM,' continued Hepworth. 'Seems like a good bloke.'

'Aye,' agreed Rhodes. 'He's certainly a lot better than the bastard we had at training. I hated him good and proper.'

'But am I right, Sarge?' persisted Hepworth. 'About you and Blackie not getting on?'

'It's CSM Blackstone to you,' said Tanner, 'and whatever I think of him is none of your bloody business.'

It was nearly eight o'clock by the time they reached the wood, and the light was fading. Eyes had adjusted to it out on the open road, but under the canopy of the trees, now almost in full leaf, it was suddenly dark – and quiet.

The track led straight through the wood, but a few hundred yards in, with no sign of the battalion, Tanner felt uneasy. He was not alone.

'Where the hell are they?' said Peploe, in a low voice. 'Surely we'd have seen something by now. This wood seems completely deserted.'

'You're right, sir. Even if it's a pretty big one, you'd expect sentries watching the road and looking out for any movement from the east.'

As they reached a fork in the road, Captain Barclay called a halt.

'Come on,' said Peploe. 'Let's find out what the bloody hell is going on.'

They found Captain Barclay with Blackstone and Lieutenant Bourne-Arton of 11 Platoon, studying tracks on the road. The compacted earth, under the canopy of the trees, was still damp rather than dry dust, and there were clear signs of carrier tracks, tyre marks and even footprints.

There was also a three-way signpost, pointing to Virginal-Samme in the direction they had come and, at the fork, to Oisquercq. Ahead, it pointed to Rebecq, just a kilometre away.

'Troops have passed through here, all right,' said Barclay.

The man was a genius, thought Tanner. He walked forward, down the track ahead of them.

'Where are you going, Sergeant?' Barclay called after him.

'I'm looking to see if these tracks move off the road, sir.' He trotted fifty yards, saw nothing, then hurried back. 'If we keep going through the wood towards Rebecq, we'll soon find out whether they've stopped or moved on.'

'State the bleeding obvious, Jack,' said Blackstone. Tanner could see he was seething.

'When did the message come through that this was the rendezvous, sir?' asked Peploe.

'CSM? When was it?' said Barclay.

'About seventeen thirty.'

'And when was the field telephone packed up?' asked Tanner.

Captain Barclay turned to Blackstone.

'Don't look at me, sir. I was at the bridge. But a runner would have been sent if the orders were changed – it's probably some cock-up at Battalion. It's eight o'clock, though, sir. Half an hour after we were supposed to meet them here. I did try and hurry up earlier.'

Captain Barclay seemed about to reply but instead he sighed. Smoothing his moustache, he said, 'Right, let's get moving. We head for Rebecq and hope we catch up with them soon.'

Tanner watched Blackstone go back to the men. He saw the CSM mutter something to several troops from Company Headquarters, then furtive glances at the OC. One of the men was the quartermaster sergeant, Ted Slater, a man Tanner had barely spoken to since Manston, but someone he had been keeping an eye on. Slater's limp had gone – in fact, there had been no sign of it ever since they had reached France – but Tanner had not forgotten Torwinski, or the other Poles, or that he and Sykes had nearly been burned alive. He was still not certain who had been responsible – the evidence was so maddeningly inconclusive. Damn it, if he was honest, now that he could think a little more calmly, he couldn't swear it had been Blackstone who had shot him on the bridge after all. Suspected it, yes, but the lieutenant had been right – there *had* been a lot of bullets flying. Nonetheless, Blackstone and Slater were friends, and as a consequence he neither liked nor trusted the quartermaster sergeant. Both men would have to be watched like hawks. *As if there isn't enough to think about*, he thought.

'What do you reckon has happened?' Peploe asked Tanner, as they rejoined the platoon.

'Orders probably changed.'

'And we didn't get them?'

'No, sir.'

'I suppose we just have to hope they're in Rebecq.'

'We need to stop whether the battalion's there or not, sir,' Tanner replied. 'The men need food.'

'Yes, of course,' said Peploe. 'I'd rather got used to B Echelon following us around.'

'If B Echelon isn't there, sir, we'll have to find something for ourselves.'

B Echelon was not in Rebecq, and neither were any other men of 1st Battalion, the Yorkshire Rangers. A large village, it was eerily quiet as D Company tramped down the main street. At the church they halted, and on Captain Barclay's instructions, Blackstone ordered the men to fall out. Immediately, the disciplined lines of three small columns crumpled as soldiers collapsed on the side of the road, some pulling out cigarettes, others taking thirsty swigs from their water-bottles.

'We'll hammer on the houses round about the church,' said Barclay, as the officers and senior NCOs gathered beside him. 'Peploe, we need your French again.'

While Peploe went across the street and started knocking on doors, Tanner ambled back to the platoon. Most of the men were now sitting beneath a wall by the side of the road. His side was hurting, an irritating, stinging pain, and his head had begun to throb. Too much smoke and cordite combined with fatigue.

He winced as he stood beside Sykes.

'How's the side, Sarge?' Sykes asked him.

'All right.'

'So where the hell is the rest of the battalion?'

'We're just trying to find out. Mr Peploe's putting that French of his to good use again.'

'When are we going to get some grub, Sarge?' said Bell. 'I'm starving.'

'Me an' all,' said Hepworth. 'I don't think I felt this hungry even in Norway.'

'Course you bloody did,' said Sykes. 'That was loads worse. Stop thinking about it, Hep. Think about lovely French and Belgian birds instead.'

'There's none here,' said Kershaw, another survivor of the 5th Battalion. 'They've all buggered off and I don't fancy that old dear over there.' He nodded in the direction of the elderly couple Lieutenant Peploe was now talking with on the other side of the square by the church.

'Use your imagination,' said Sykes. 'You have got one, ain't you, Hep?'

'That's what you do, is it, Corp?' said McAllister. 'Think about girls?'

'Always – that and how I can screw a few more quid out of you, Mac.'

They all laughed, Tanner too.

'We'll get some grub soon, I hope,' he told them. He saw Peploe striding back towards the church. 'Hang on. I'll try and find out now.' He turned towards Peploe as the lieutenant approached them. 'Sir?'

'They said they saw hundreds of men go through a short while ago,' said Peploe as he reached them, 'some in carriers and lorries, others on foot. The last went through a little over half an hour ago. Apparently they were heading towards Steenkerque.' He unfolded Captain Barclay's map and pointed to a small village a few miles to the south-west of Rebecq.

'South-west? Were they sure?' said Barclay.

'Positive,' said Peploe. 'I questioned that as well.'

'Well, that's just marvellous,' said Squadron Leader Lyell, sitting on the lychgate bench. 'Bravo, Hector. First class.'

'Put a bloody sock in it, Charlie,' said Barclay.

'For God's sake,' continued Lyell. 'All that time you were fannying about, listening to Tanner's tales of derring-do, when if you'd just got everyone going we would have reached the rendezvous on time and we wouldn't be in this mess.'

'Will you damn well be quiet?' said Barclay, turning on his brother-in-law. 'I will not have you undermine my authority. You're not with your squadron now, you're with us, and you'll bloody well keep quiet or else I'll leave you here by the side of the road and the Germans can have you instead.' His cheeks had flushed, Tanner noticed, and he was blinking rapidly, as he tried to regain his composure. 'In any case,' he said, now peering intently at the map, 'it's perfectly clear that the orders must have changed. I don't know why, but we didn't receive them.'

Lyell muttered in exasperation, then said, 'So what do you suggest we do?'

'They're only three-quarters of an hour ahead. It's getting dark, but there's light enough to march by. We'll keep going as quickly as we can. Hopefully, they've stopped for the night already and we'll catch them up. The men will just have to wait for their supper.'

But at Steenkerque there was no sign of the battalion; neither had the villagers seen any British troops passing through in the past few hours. There had been some French colonial troops, but that was all.

On the far side of the village, they halted at a farm. Several dogs stood a short distance away from them, barking protectively at the strange figures of the soldiers. It was now coming up to ten o'clock and completely dark, the only light coming from a half-moon and the stars that twinkled amid patchy cloud. And it was cool, now, too, the air damp and fragrant with the smell of uncut hay and dusty soil. Standing by the farm's entrance, Tanner breathed in deeply, remembering the sweet early-summer smell from his boyhood.

A voice yelled at the dogs, then a door opened releasing a thin shaft of light. A man called. Once again, it was left to Lieutenant Peploe to do the talking. He and Captain Barclay approached the farmer; a brief conversation ensued, then both men were ushered into the house.

Of course, the farmer had no choice in the matter – what could he do to stop two platoons of British soldiers who demanded to be fed? – but, as Peploe confided to Tanner a little later, Monsieur Selage was a fierce patriot, hated Germans and seemed only too happy to help his allies, the British, providing cheese, eggs and a number of chickens.

'You've done well, sir,' said Tanner, as they stood in the yard as men from each section collected their makeshift rations. 'That lot should fill a hole.'

'It's only one chicken per ten men, but better than nothing. Mind you, I hope they cook them properly in the dark. Last thing we need now is everyone getting sick from eating raw chicken.'

Someone coughed behind them, and they turned to see Corporal Wallis from Company Headquarters.

'Excuse me, sir,' he said, 'but the OC wants you and Sergeant Tanner in the house.'

'All right,' said Peploe.

They followed him into the kitchen where Captain Barclay, Blackstone, Lieutenant Bourne-Arton and Sergeant Seaton of 11 Platoon were already standing around an old pine table. Squadron Leader Lyell was resting on a cushioned window-seat, while the farmer and, Tanner assumed, his wife stood at the range, attending to some food.

'Ah, there you are,' said Barclay, as they entered. 'I've been thinking about what we should do.'

Tanner caught Peploe's attention, then nodded towards the farmer and his wife.

'Sir?' said Peploe. 'Don't you think we should have this conversation in private?'

'Eh?' said Barclay. 'It's all right – they don't understand English.'

'I speak a little,' said the woman.

'Oh,' said Barclay, straightening.

'For God's sake,' muttered Lyell.

Flustered, Barclay said to the woman, 'Er, would you mind awfully leaving us for a few minutes?'

She tugged at her husband's sleeve and the two left the room. Then, clearing his throat, Barclay spread the map upon the table.

'Right. God knows where the rest of Battalion have gone. Must have turned off somewhere along here, I suppose.' He pointed to the road between Rebecq and Steenkerque.

'Whatever, Hector,' said Lyell. 'We've lost them. That's the point.'

'Yes,' said Barclay. 'And, frankly, I don't think we can bank on finding them again now. Maybe we will – you never know – but from now on, we've got to think and act for ourselves.'

'Then we head due west, sir,' said Blackstone. 'If we don't bump into the rest of the battalion, we'll probably meet some other British troops. It's a general retreat, after all.'

'Yes, but we don't know where we're retreating to, CSM,' said Barclay. 'Could be south, could be north.' He cleared his throat again. 'But we do know where BEF Headquarters is.' He looked up at the others. 'Arras. I hardly think the Germans will overrun that before we can get there.'

'Arras? But how far's that?' said Blackstone.

'Hundred miles at the most.'

'Why don't we work it out on the map, sir?' suggested Peploe.

Barclay looked at them sheepishly. 'I haven't one – not of that area, at any rate. I'm afraid Captain Wrightson has the maps we used to get here.'

'Now I've heard it all,' said Lyell. He'd done nothing but whine ever since they'd picked him up, Tanner thought, and had they not bothered in the first place, they wouldn't have lost contact with the rest of the battalion. He couldn't understand why the captain wasn't firmer with the man.

'I thought we could ask the farmer if he had a map,' said Barclay, his unlit pipe sticking from the side of his mouth.

'Jesus wept,' said Lyell. 'I've got one.' He delved into the inside pocket of his tunic, took out a crumpled map of Belgium and northern France and handed it to Lieutenant Bourne-Arton.

Everyone gathered round as Barclay spread it out across the table. 'Less than a hundred miles,' said Barclay. 'More like seventy or so. We'll head towards Mons, then Douai and Arras. Agreed?'

For a moment, no one spoke. Then Blackstone said, 'If you say so, sir.'

'Good,' said Barclay, trying to brighten. 'We can't afford to stop for the night – we can rest up at some point tomorrow. I suggest we aim to be on the road again at, say, midnight. All right?'

Tanner left Peploe and the other officers in the farmhouse and went out into the yard to find the platoon. He only had to follow his nose, and headed through a gate at the end of the yard into a pasture that led to the river. Dim lights flickered ahead of him – from torches, from the low paraffin flames of stoves and the glowing red ends of cigarettes. The smell of chicken and eggs, frying in mess tins, wafted into the still night air, blending with the dewy damp of the meadow and the whiff of tobacco smoke.

He found Sykes's section standing or squatting around a Primus stove by an ageing willow on the riverbank.

'So what are we doing?' Sykes asked.

'Keep going tonight.'

'Thought as much. Where are we headed?'

'BEF Headquarters at Arras.'

'Jesus,' said McAllister. 'If you ask me, Sarge, that captain doesn't know his arse from his elbow.'

'That's enough, Mac.'

'It's true, though, sir.'

'I said, that's enough.'

'I'm only saying what everyone thinks. We had the whole battalion not half a mile away and we've managed to lose them.' Bell and Kershaw nodded in agreement. 'One of the lads in Company HQ said that the CSM told the captain we should have all gone to Oisquercq with Ten Platoon and those Jerry prisoners. If you ask me, Captain Barclay should have listened to him.'

Tanner leaned down, grabbed McAllister's collar and yanked him to his feet. 'I'm not asking you,' he said. 'Now listen to me, Mac, were you at Company Headquarters this afternoon? No. Did you hear the orders that were sent to us by Battalion? No, you didn't. Should you listen to idle tittle-tattle? No, you bloody well shouldn't. You're a sodding lance-corporal now, Mac. Start bloody well acting like one, and use your brain rather than your backside.'

Tanner dropped him back to the ground. 'And that goes for all of you,' he said, looking around the men. 'You're soldiers, not bloody schoolboys, so less of the mithering. What's happened has happened. We head in the direction of Arras. Hopefully we'll find some Tommies on the way and they can tell us whether we're supposed to be somewhere else. Now, let's get some grub inside us.'

There was, Tanner knew, something in what McAllister had said – Captain Barclay was a fool – but poisoning the rest of the company against the OC, as Blackstone was doing, was unforgivable. He had seen officers lose the respect and control of their men and it was painful to witness. But while in peacetime such a thing was unfortunate, in wartime it could be very dangerous indeed. Discipline, not dissent, was the best antidote to any crisis. *That sodding bastard*, he thought.

10

Saturday, 18 May, was a long day for the men of D Company, 1st Battalion, the Yorkshire Rangers, and one in which tempers had begun increasingly to fray; it had started shortly after midnight and had continued as dawn had given way to morning, and morning to midday. They had not seen a single British soldier, let alone the rest of the battalion, but their route had been dogged by people. Countless numbers of refugees – men, women and children, the elderly and even infirm – had appeared on the roads the moment the sun had risen and had seemingly increased with every passing hour. Their plaintive questions and appeals for help got on the nerves of the men and reminded them that they were heading backwards from the Germans too: running away from the enemy.

Above, aircraft had droned, mostly formations of enemy planes rather than British or French. Behind them, and to the south, they occasionally heard muffled explosions and the distant crump of guns. Around noon, they reached a crossroads in the middle of the flat, wide countryside just to the north of Mons, and were forced to watch as a French column turned onto the road, heading south towards France. The troops' progress was painfully slow. Carriers, guns, lorries and other trucks crammed with soldiers inched their way through the refugees, the men shouting at them to move out of the way. Tanner saw a woman on a bicycle hit by the wing mirror of one lorry – it only clipped her, but she tumbled into the side of the road. She got to her feet, waving a fist and cursing.

Their own small column was halted while the French troops passed on their way, the men moving off the road and collapsing onto their backsides in a field of green corn. The air was thick with dust, fumes and the misery of Belgian civilians struggling to escape the Germans. Away to the south, they heard the faint dull thud of explosions.

'Bombers?' Peploe asked Tanner.

'Must be.' Tanner gestured at the crawling French vehicles. 'Worth asking them for a ride, sir?'

'Nothing ventured,' said Peploe. In front of them, a staff car had ground to a halt while a man with a laden wooden cart battled to get his mule over the crossroads. The French officer was yelling at him, and Tanner smiled as Peploe interrupted. The response was an irate torrent of abuse.

'Nothing gained,' said Peploe, ruefully, as he rejoined Tanner and the rest of the platoon. 'They're heading to St Quentin any-way, which is too far south for us. Apparently every transport is already chock-full of men. He reckoned we'd be quicker on foot – although he didn't express it quite as politely as that.'

'Bloody Frogs,' said Tanner. 'I'll remember that next time one of them asks me for help.'

'Sir,' said Sykes as he came over to Peploe, 'surely we could ask the Frogs to take the squadron leader?'

'They didn't seem very keen to help, I'm afraid,' Peploe replied. 'I did ask.'

'But if Captain Barclay tried?' suggested Sykes. 'And perhaps a different Frog officer?

'It would certainly be good to offload him, sir,' said Tanner to

Peploe. 'It's not as if he's been particularly grateful. He's complained more than the men have.'

'All right,' said Peploe. 'I'll ask Captain Barclay.'

Tanner, Sykes and several others watched Peploe pick his way through to Barclay. They saw the captain shake his head, despite Peploe's best efforts to persuade him otherwise.

'Nothing doing, I'm afraid,' said Peploe as he rejoined them a few minutes later. 'The French have their hands full.'

'Bollocks, sir,' said Sykes. 'We saw him – he didn't even ask them.'

'I'm sure he has his reasons,' said Peploe.

At this point Tanner spotted McAllister muttering to Bell and Ellis, and gesticulating covertly at the OC. When he noticed his sergeant's eye on him, he stopped immediately.

Tanner turned back to Sykes and Peploe. 'The lads are fed up. We need to watch morale, I reckon.'

'They are, Sarge,' agreed Sykes, 'me an' all. The sooner we get to Arras the better.'

By afternoon, as they continued west of Mons, the numbers of refugees had thinned, but progress was no faster because the effort of marching for the best part of sixteen hours was taking its toll. Feet were sore, legs ached and stomachs were empty. To the east and south, more dull explosions ruffled the air.

'Some poor bastards are gettin' a pastin',' said Sykes, as Tanner tramped alongside him.

Tanner looked up to the sky. 'Nasty amount of bombers been going over.'

'Where's ours, Sarge? That's what I'd like to know.'

'You and me the same, Stan. Looks one-sided from down here, doesn't it?'

Just before four o'clock they stopped for their hourly ten-minute breather. They were on a low ridge of woods and open farmland, overlooking a river valley to the south. Tanner lit a cigarette and regarded the men, most of whom had lain down on the grassy verge. Several had their eyes closed, almost asleep already. He felt tired too, and hungry; his stomach groaned. All day they had had nothing but scraps they had scrounged on the way – a bit of bread and some cheese but nothing that could be considered a proper meal.

'Sarge.' Sykes quickly ran his comb through his hair and replaced his helmet. 'They're almost done in, Sarge. If you're worrying about morale, we need to lie up for a bit. It's one thing trekking on and on when you haven't got any choice in the matter, but the Jerries don't seem that close behind us, do they? I think that's what's getting to everyone a bit.'

'I know, Stan, and we need some bloody scoff, too. Mr Peploe's talking to the OC about it now. Hopefully this'll be almost it for a while.' He picked out a farm not far away. 'Don't see much wrong with trying there.'

When Peploe rejoined them, however, he told them the OC wanted to push on a bit further first.

Tanner sighed. 'Bloody hell, sir. How much further, exactly?'

'Not far. Can you see that village over there?' He pointed to a church tower that poked up through the trees a few miles away, on the far side of the river. 'He wants us to find food there, then lie up.' He turned to the men. 'Another hour, boys, that's all. Then we'll get food and you can all have a sleep.'

The men groaned. 'Another hour, sir?' said Hepworth. 'I'm going to need a stretcher soon.'

'It's all right for you, Hep,' muttered McAllister. 'You haven't had to carry a sodding great Bren.'

'Listen, Mac,' said Tanner, putting an arm round McAllister's shoulders, 'I know you're fed up. We all are – it's dispiriting, trudging backwards – but remember Norway? We had it tougher there, didn't we? And we had our fair share of arseholes to carry too.'

McAllister smiled ruefully. 'That Frog lieutenant, Chevannes. You're right, Sarge – he was worse than the squadron leader.'

'Come on. Another hour and we can put our feet up. That's not so long.'

'Suppose so, Sarge.' He got up. 'All right, then. Get it over and done with, eh?'

*

It was approaching five o'clock by the time they had dropped down into the valley and crossed the poplar-lined river that snaked its way sleepily through the Flanders countryside. They marched on beside a thick wood, then emerged into open country. Less than a mile ahead the village with the church spire was clearly visible. Before that, however, there was a farm, and Captain Barclay called a halt. As the men marched through an aged brick archway into the yard, chickens clucked and scurried about, a dog barked lazily, and a number of fat geese waddled towards them honking loudly.

While Lieutenant Peploe and Captain Barclay went to find the owner, Tanner had a look round. The farm and outbuildings were protected by a wall, while a rickety tower stood above the archway.

'Bloody nice old place this, Sarge,' said Sykes, beside him.

'It is, Stan. I might go and have a dekko from up that tower – looks like a damn good OP to me. I don't like being down in this valley – can't see much. It was better when we were on that ridge.'

'Good idea, Sarge. I'll come with you.'

There was a door beside the archway. They opened it and found a staircase. It led straight up to another door that then opened into the tower. It was dusty inside, old straw strewn across wooden floorboards.

'Christ,' Sykes whistled. Some pigeons fluttered from their perch, making the two men jump. Fifteen feet above them there was a wooden gallery, then the roof. Sunlight poured through holes where tiles had fallen away, highlighting a million dust motes swirling in the still, musty air. A ladder in the corner went up to the gallery.

'Careful, Sarge,' said Sykes, as Tanner began to climb. 'That ladder don't look too safe to me.'

'It'll be all right,' said Tanner. Despite the woodworm, he reached the gallery and peered through a hole in the roof. Away to the west, in the distance some dozen miles away, he could see Mons. Ahead of him lay the village and beyond, as the ground gently rose, a railway, then a road on which traffic appeared to be moving. *Good.* He tried to remember the map. The Mons–Cambrai road, it had to be, and from Cambrai it was no great distance to Arras. If they could get a ride to Cambrai that would be something. Delving into his respirator bag, he took out his binoculars and peered through them.

What he saw made his heart sink and his stomach lurch. 'Jesus,' he muttered. 'How the hell?' A long column of grey tanks was rolling through the Flanders countryside, with armoured cars and artillery pieces.

'Stan!' Tanner called down. 'Get yourself up here.'

'What is it?' asked Sykes.

'Come on up and you'll see.'

Sykes clambered gingerly up the ladder and stood beside Tanner, who passed him the binoculars.

'Look up on that ridge beyond the village. A mile or so away.'

'Blimey!' said Sykes. 'Sweet bloody Nora! It's the flamin' Jerries. How on earth did they get there?' He turned to Tanner. 'And how come there's that many of 'em just there?'

'Don't ask me, Stan.' More dull explosions rumbled from the south-west. 'Jesus,' he said. 'We've been thinking it's bombs we've been hearing, but what if it was fighting?'

'Perhaps that's where those Frogs was heading earlier.'

'Well, if Jerry's already taken the land to the south of here, they aren't going to get very far, are they?'

'Christ, Sarge, do you think we're surrounded?'

'I don't know. Let me think a moment.' He looked again, and then scanned to the north as well, from where they had just come. Nothing. 'No, I'm sure we're not,' he said at length. 'Think about it. We've not heard much fighting behind us, have we? I reckon those Jerries must have just punched a hole to the south. No wonder those French scarpered so bloody quickly yesterday. The whole of their line must have been collapsing. But we've not seen anyone today, have we? No, Stan, I'm sure we're not surrounded yet.'

'But I thought the Germans were attacking to the north and that was why we moved into Belgium.'

'Maybe they're doing both – a two-pronged attack.'

'Which means we're stuck in the middle.'

Tanner rubbed his chin. 'Christ, what a bloody mess. If only we had a radio. I can't believe they sent us out here without one. How can anyone possibly know what the bloody hell's going on?' He sighed, took off his helmet and ran his fingers through his dark hair. 'We should have a quick think about what to do.'

'Can't rely on Captain Barclay.'

'Or Blackstone.'

'The men won't be happy about moving again.'

'I'm not so sure we should move. If someone stays up here in the tower, we can hopefully get some scoff, then decamp to that wood. With the village between us and that ridge, they won't be able to see us and they don't seem very interested in heading this way. We get some kip in the wood and move on again at midnight, as the captain suggested. You stay here for the moment, Stan, and I'll go down and talk to Mr Peploe. Perhaps he can persuade the OC it's our best course of action.'

'All right, Sarge.' Sykes peered through the binoculars again. 'But I'll tell you what I'm thinking.'

'What?' said Tanner, as he began to descend the ladder.

'That we're going to have a hell of a job getting out of this mess. I told myself we wouldn't let Norway happen again but now I'm not so sure. Those bastards are whipping us good and proper.'

'We're not beaten yet, Stan,' said Tanner. 'Never say die.'

Where the SS Totenkopf were now concentrated to the west of Philippeville, south of Charleroi, there was no shortage of radio sets, telephones or even decoding machines. If anything, Brigadeführer Eicke and his staff had too much information; from what they were hearing, it sounded as though all of France and the Low Countries were folding up before the *Wehrmacht*'s panzers – and before the Totenkopf would have a chance to show the rest of the Reich and, indeed, the world what they were capable of.

For Sturmbannführer Otto Timpke, it had felt as though the

frustrations would never cease. A tantalizing promise of action would be dangled before them, only for them to discover it was still as far from their grasp as ever. Since leaving Aachen they had struggled across eastern Belgium, battling against endless refugees, pathetic citizens fleeing their homes. Timpke had tried to overcome the problem by sending his motorcycles on wide searches for better routes, but other than going cross-country – which the bulk of the division could not do – there was no alternative. He wondered where the mass of people thought they were heading. Why were they so terrified? Timpke wondered what Belgian and French propaganda had been like to prompt such a mass exodus. Of course, it was unfortunate for those caught up in the crossfire of fighting, but for the vast majority, if they had stayed in their homes, they would have been quite safe, and would soon find themselves peaceably absorbed into the Greater Reich, the lucky devils!

And it was not only refugees who had hindered their progress but *Wehrmacht* soldiers – troops on their way to the front. Timpke had personally seen Brigadeführer Eicke stand up in his command car and berate footsore German soldiers, yelling at them to clear off the road and let his superior, mechanized *Waffen-SS* division forge ahead. Timpke had smiled: Papa Eicke was an example to them all.

They had reached their concentration area at a village west of Philippeville earlier that afternoon and Eicke had immediately called together his staff officers and unit commanders in an orchard beside a river. There he had read out the sitrep that had just arrived. It had already proved a morning of dramatic advance for General von Rundstedt's Army Group A. General Guderian's 2nd Panzer Division had captured St Quentin earlier that morning, while just after midday, the 1st Panzer Division had reported having crossed the river Somme; 6th Panzer was engaging French armour at Le Catelet, while Major-General Rommel's 7th Panzer Division had recently taken Le Cateau and was now pushing towards Cambrai.

Timpke's heart sank, and he couldn't help turning away to rest his head despondently against the trunk of a gnarled apple tree. A breeze ruffled its leaves and the lengthening grass beneath them. Near by, wood pigeons cooed rhythmically, as though they hadn't a care in the world.

'Don't look so despondent, Otto,' said Eicke. 'It's not all bad news.'

Suddenly, Timpke was aware that the division's senior officers were all staring at him. He gazed at Eicke, at his cap with the death's head above the braid, the peak so low it almost covered those pale eyes of his. His thin-lipped mouth was turned up at one side – a half-smile that signalled to Timpke that he was a favoured son, *a man after my own heart*.

'Forgive me, Herr Brigadeführer,' said Timpke. 'I just want there to be something left for us to do.'

Eicke smiled. 'As do we all, Otto. And, as it happens, we have been asked to help Panzer Group Hoth who are concerned that Major-General Rommel is overreaching himself. In Seventh Panzer's rapid advance to Cambrai they have simply swept past a number of towns, and we are now to follow up behind and secure them. I want your reconnaissance battalion and Infantry Regiment 1 to carry out this role. Yes, it's a limited operation, but trust me, even the feeble-hearted *poilus* will counter-attack at some point. They've been knocked off balance, caught with their trousers down, but they'll get back on their feet. An army of that size has to. In a moment, I want you and Standartenführer Simon to sit down with the O4 and he will brief you about what I want your reconnaissance boys to do. The rest of us must be patient a short while longer. That's all, gentlemen.'

As Eicke strode towards the manor house that stood beyond the orchard, Timpke made his way to the division's O4 staff officer, Obersturmbannführer Geisler.

'Follow me,' said Geisler, leading Timpke and Standartenführer Simon towards the house. 'Hopefully, we've got an operations room set up by now.' They crossed the orchard and passed through an old door, half falling off its hinges, which led to a courtyard and the manor house. Trucks and other vehicles had been parked in the orchard and all along the road, but more trucks and staff cars were now crammed in front of the newly requisitioned house. Inside, Geisler showed Timpke and Simon into what, until an hour before, had been the dining room. Generations of the owners' family looked down on them, several soldiers from centuries past. One, in an eighteenth-century wig and blue velvet jacket, clutching the hilt of his sword, appeared to sneer, his lip curled with contempt. *Ha*, thought Timpke. *Well, we're here now.*

Geisler rolled out a large map across the table. 'We're here,' he said, pointing to the tiny village. 'Here's Avesnes, Le Cateau and St Quentin,' he added, placing a finger on each in turn. 'And here's the Somme. This is where General von Kleist's panzers are leading the charge. Up here are General Hoth's two panzer divisions. Rommel's is now here at Cambrai.' He turned to Simon. 'Herr Standartenführer, we need your Regiment 1 to clear these towns.' He pointed to the map. 'St Souplet, L'Arbre de Guise and Catillon. Enemy troops are still dug in around Mauberge, but you are to bypass them.'

Simon peered through his wire-framed round glasses at the map, then busily made notes.

'And the reconnaissance battalion?' asked Timpke.

'Also avoid Mauberge,' said Geisler, 'but probe north between Cambrai and Valenciennes and be on hand should the *Standartenführer* need you.'

Timpke nodded. 'So I'll spread out my companies.'

'Exactly,' said Geisler. 'Have a look around – get the lie of the land. See which bridges are still available, and what damage has been done. We need to know the best routes to the front. The boss wants us to move very quickly the moment we're ordered to do so.' He pulled out his pocket watch. 'It's not quite a hundred kilometres from here to Cambrai, so it would be best to move straight away. Get near to the front tonight, and the boss wants you to use your time well from the moment it's light enough tomorrow morning. Clear?'

'Perfectly, Herr Obersturmbannführer.'

Within half an hour, the Totenkopf's reconnaissance battalion was on the move, heading west in company formation, motorcycles and armoured scout cars leading, followed by motorized infantry, half-tracks towing their 37mm and 50mm anti-tank guns, and the Skoda tanks of the panzer squadrons.

It was with the 1st Company that Timpke now travelled in his staff car, following in the wake of the motorcycles as they sped north-west along the French-Belgian border, the roads, for once, blissfully free of refugees. He drummed his hand against his leg, bit at a nail, then glanced back at the column of armoured cars and trucks behind, swirling clouds of dust following in their wake. *I'm leading them into combat*, he thought, with satisfaction. At that moment, he felt invincible.

A young couple lived at the farm with their three small children and the farmer's mother. Although they were quick to sell the Rangers some food – cheese, bread and even two pigs – it was clear that the farmer and his wife were terrified, and within an hour of the Tommies' arrival they were gathering their family and a couple of suitcases into their truck.

Seeing this, Lieutenant Peploe went over to them. The farmer, with an agitated expression, casting anxious glances at the men now crowding the yard, spoke animatedly, then put the vehicle into gear and drove out through the archway.

'Scared, is he?' said Tanner, as he joined Peploe. Above, clouds were building and a cool breeze now blew across the yard.

'They saw the Germans earlier too,' Peploe told him, 'and they've heard the sound of battle for the past two days. They're going to keep out of the way until the storm passes. He said he didn't want any Germans finding out he'd helped the British.'

'Confident, the Belgians, aren't they?'

'I did tell him we weren't going to stay, but he wasn't having any of it.'

Tanner's idea to lie low in the wood – suggested to the OC by

Lieutenant Peploe – had been agreed by Captain Barclay, and the company now headed back down the road, leaving Tanner and Private Smailes in the tower to keep watch for any movement to the south.

They were relieved an hour later and, on reaching the wood, Tanner was pleased to see that sentries had been placed around the encampment and that their arrival was challenged. He gave the password, then heard his name called. He turned to see Slater, the company quartermaster sergeant, push through the bracken towards him. 'Tanner,' he said again, in a low, gravelly voice.

'What is it?'

'The CSM wants to see you.'

What about? 'Tell him I'll come and find him as soon as I've reported to Mr Peploe.'

'He said you were to come now.'

Tanner looked at the two young sentries, then at Smailes. 'All right,' he said. 'Smiler, tell Mr Peploe I'm with the CSM and I'll be back soon.' He was sure Blackstone wouldn't try anything now – not with so many witnesses to his whereabouts – but as he followed Slater, he unslung his rifle from his shoulder and carried it in his hand.

They found Blackstone sitting beneath an oak tree some way from the rest of the company. 'Ah, Jack,' he said, making no effort to get up.

'What do you want?' snapped Tanner. 'Make it quick, whatever it is.'

Blackstone smiled. 'Jack, don't be like that, please. I want us to make up. I've been too quick to antagonize you, I realize that, and I'm sorry.'

'For God's sake,' said Tanner, 'what do you want, Blackstone?'

'I want us to get along, Jack. I tried to put the past behind us when you first arrived in Manston but you wouldn't take the olive branch.'

'And why should I now, after all you've done?'

'What have I done, Jack?'

'You know damn well.'

Blackstone shook his head. 'All right, so maybe I've been a bit sharp towards you in front of the boss, but I can't have you undermining *my* authority, can I?'

'So who locked me in the storeroom?' He glared at Slater. 'And who took a shot at me on the bridge yesterday?'

Blackstone looked incredulous. 'You think *I* tried to kill you?' He laughed as Slater shook his head with equal disbelief. 'You're joking?'

'I saw you by the bridge. It had to be you who shot me.' He was conscious, suddenly, of how spurious the accusation now sounded.

'Jack, that's madness. There were bullets flying around everywhere. Anyone could have hit you. Yes, I fired off a few rounds, but I was trying to hit those Jerries on the ridge. Your mind's playing tricks, my friend.'

Tanner tightened his grip on his rifle.

'Trust me, Jack, the last thing I want is to see you out of the way.' He stood up now. 'I need you.'

'Jesus,' muttered Tanner.

'Hear me out, Jack. I know I've got the men eating out of my hand. They respect me and think I'm a good bloke. Most of them don't like you too much but they respect you as a soldier. And you're good, Jack, I'll give you that. Now, our problem is that the boss is an idiot who doesn't know his arse from his tit.'

Almost the same words Mac used. Tanner's heart sank.

'It's largely because of Captain Barclay,' Blackstone continued, 'that we're in this mess.'

'It wasn't his fault the rendezvous changed.'

'But it was his fault that we had to go and get his brother-in-law when the French were far closer, and it was certainly his fault that we took so long to move out of those positions. We were late for the rendezvous. We should have left with Captain Wrightson and Ten Platoon. And why we're heading to Arras when it's clear most of the BEF must be further north from here, God only knows.'

'I thought he did whatever you told him,' said Tanner.

'He did. But – dare I say it, Jack? – he hasn't been so keen on listening to me with you and Mr Peploe around. He's started to think for himself and look what's happened as a result.'

'That's bollocks,' said Tanner. He held Blackstone's eye. 'So what is it you're suggesting? Get to the bloody point.'

'I think we should split up. Let the boss and Lieutenant Bourne-Arton take Eleven Platoon and you, me and Lieutenant Peploe take Twelve Platoon. There are too many of us at the moment. It's hard to get food and transport. And that's what we need – vehicles, so we can get out of here and find the rest of the BEF.'

Tanner took out his cigarettes and realized he had only two left. *Damn*, he thought, lighting one. He had to admit, there was something in what Blackstone said; the idea had crossed his mind as well.

'I'm asking you to back me up on this, Jack, that's all. Try to persuade Mr Peploe.'

'I'm tired,' he said, 'and I'm going to have a kip. But I'll think about it.'

Leaning against the cobweb-hung brickwork of the tower, Corporal Sykes peered out of the hole in the roof, a cold breeze brushing his face. A cigarette was cupped in his hand between thumb and forefinger. Now, surreptitiously, he brought it to his mouth. He knew he shouldn't be smoking while on watch, especially not when he was standing in an OP that could be seen for quite a distance, but he had to do something to keep himself awake.

Smoke swirled into the night air as he exhaled. The countryside, so different at night, was swathed in a low creamy light. The horizon could easily be seen against the night sky, as could a line of trees away to the right of the village. A barn owl screeched, but otherwise the world beyond the tower was still and seemingly at peace.

On the other side of the rickety gallery, Private Bell strained his eyes towards the wood a couple of hundred yards away in which the remainder of the company were bedded down for the night. Sykes peered at his watch. Five past midnight – less than an hour before they were due to move off again. He yawned, and returned to staring at the unmoving night.

It was a faint rumble that first caught his attention, and then, as he brought Tanner's binoculars to his eyes, he saw, silhouetted against the horizon, a number of motorcycles heading west.

'What's that, Corp?' said Bell, hurrying across the gallery.

'Motorcycles,' said Sykes. 'And not ours neither.' He passed over the binoculars. 'They're like the ones we saw yesterday,' he said. 'Sidecar and machine-gun.' He took the binoculars back and saw the lead motorcycles turn off the main road and head straight for the village.

'Bugger it,' said Sykes. 'Tinker, we ought to get down from here. If we need to scarper in a hurry we don't want to have to muck around with rotten old ladders in the dark.'

'Too bloody right we don't, Corp,' agreed Bell.

'All right – you go first,' said Sykes. As Bell lowered himself onto the ladder, Sykes peered through the binoculars one last time and saw a larger column rumbling into view along the ridge beyond the village – armoured cars and trucks too. There they came to a halt, the low rumble of their engines audible on the still night air.

Bell was at the foot of the ladder and Sykes followed. As he reached the first floor he heard two motorcycles heading out of the village towards them.

'Come on, Tinker,' he said, groping for the stairs, 'we need to get out of here fast.'

In pitch darkness, not daring to turn on a torch, they scrambled down the stairs as quickly as they could, only for Bell to trip at the bottom and stumble into Sykes. 'Sorry, Corp,' he said.

At that moment, they heard the motorcycles slow, then turn into the farm, under the archway and into the yard, thin slits of light from their headlamps casting a dim glow. With the door onto the yard ajar, Sykes watched breathlessly. The first motorcycle stopped and he saw the rider jump off and approach the door of the farmhouse, the motorcycle's engine still ticking over.

You won't find anyone there, he thought.

The machine-gunner in the sidecar covered his comrade, weapon at the ready, while the second motorbike circled the yard, then also stopped. This time the man in the sidecar jumped out and, with a torch, looked at the outbuildings that lined the yard.

'Bugger it,' mouthed Sykes.

'What?' whispered Bell. 'What are they doing?'

'Shut your gob,' hissed Sykes. Carefully, he drew his rifle to his waist and, clutching the bolt, silently, slowly, drew it up and back, wincing as it clicked into place. The German was getting nearer, but he was out of sight. Doors were opened, boots clicked on stone, voices rang out. The man had had his weapon slung across his back, and Sykes prayed it had remained there. His heart pounded. Footsteps. Any moment now, the door would open. Sykes tightened his grip on his rifle and his finger caressed the cold metal trigger.

11

Around fifty miles away to the west, as the crow flew, Major-General Henry Pownall knocked on General Lord Gort's door at his command post at Wahagnies.

'Come!' called Gort from his desk. He had been studying a number of sitreps that had reached his tactical headquarters from his various liaison officers with the French Army; they had not made encouraging reading.

'General Billotte has just arrived, my lord,' said Pownall.

'At last, Henry.' Gort smiled. The British commander was a big man – more than six foot tall, barrel-chested, with a broad, full face and a trim, bristly moustache. 'This will be quite a novelty,' he said, with heavy irony, 'a rare opportunity to speak man to man with one's commanding officer.'

'Quite so,' agreed Pownall. 'Shall I bring him straight in?'

'Absolutely.'

A minute later Billotte entered with Major Archdale, his British liaison officer, limping behind him. Billotte removed his kepi and extended a hand to Gort. '*Mon cher général,*' he said.

He looked exhausted, Gort thought, and old. Why were all the French generals so aged? Billotte was – what? In his mid-sixties? And yet to look at him now, white-haired and with large bags under his eyes, he would pass for more than seventy. Gamelin was sixty-seven, he knew, while Georges was sixty-five. To command armies one needed experience, yes, but energy too. A commander in the field could expect long days and short nights, huge pressure and the difficult, frustrating responsibility of making decisions of great importance, often with insufficient information. Lack of sleep and the nature of the job were both exhausting, physically and mentally draining, which was why one needed a stout constitution and age on one's side. Gort, at not quite fifty-four, was fit and spry, but not so sure he would be able to say the same a dozen years on. It was no wonder the French were struggling. Generalship was not, Gort believed, a job for elderly men.

'*Eh bien, mon général,*' said Gort, smiling broadly and holding Billotte's gaze with his pale grey eyes. '*Qu'est-ce que vous avez à me dire?*' He pointed to a simple chair opposite his makeshift desk.

Billotte sat down with a heavy sigh. '*Je n'ai plus de réserves, pas de plan et peu d'espoir.*'

For a moment, Gort gazed at him blankly.

Major Archdale coughed. 'He says he has no reserves, no plan, and little hope, my lord.'

'I think we understood, thank you, Osmund,' said Pownall.

'Someone get the general a drink,' said Gort. 'Scotch, or some brandy, if he would prefer. Then perhaps, Archdale, the general could outline to us what is happening with the rest of his armies. And while I fancy my French isn't bad, it might be better if you do interpret, if you don't mind.'

'Yes, my lord,' said Archdale.

Gort listened as Billotte, slumped in his chair, a large glass of brandy in hand, recounted his day's events. He had sacked Corap, commander of the Ninth Army, and replaced him with Giraud; the new Ninth Army commander was now missing, however, and his headquarters at Le Catelet, near Cambrai, had been overrun.

Cambrai had fallen a few hours earlier. That thrust, south through the Ardennes, had broken the back of the Ninth Army and proved a devastating blow. '*Contre les panzers je ne peux rien faire,*' he said, over and over. *Against the Panzers, there is nothing I can do.* There were, he reckoned, nine or ten German panzer divisions in this thrust, against which he felt powerless. He now stood up and walked to the map hanging on the wall. With his finger, he etched a line to where the Germans had now advanced: thirty-two miles from Amiens and just twenty from Arras. He had ordered counter-measures, he told them, which, he hoped, would force the Germans back and enable French and British troops in the north to link up once more with French troops to the south of the German thrust. Just what his counter-measures were, Billotte did not explain.

Then, having said his piece and drained his glass, the army group commander shook Gort's hand once more, fixed his kepi back on his head and left.

Pownall made to leave too, but Gort pointed to the chair Billotte had just vacated. 'Sit down, sit down,' he said. Then, after a brief pause, he added, 'I think, Henry, we can safely conclude that General Billotte has shot his bolt. It's incomprehensible but the man really doesn't have a plan at all, does he?'

'As he himself admitted, my lord.'

'I hoped at first he hadn't meant it.'

'You've seen the reports from the liaison officers?' asked Pownall. He took out his pipe, deftly stuffed some tobacco into it and lit it, amid a swirling cloud of sweet-smelling smoke.

'Yes, I have. I was reading them before the general arrived. Not very encouraging.' He stood up and faced the map behind him. 'He's talking of counter-measures, by which I'm assuming he means a counter-attack to close the gap punched by the panzers. But I'm not at all sure he's got the reserves he needs – not where he wants them, at any rate.'

'You don't think it can be closed, my lord?'

'Do you, Henry?'

'I agree he didn't seem very confident.'

'An understatement.' Gort held his hands together and tapped his chin with them. 'I have to say, Henry, the situation is worse than I'd thought.'

'Our chaps have reached the Dendre in good order,' said Pownall, 'and they'll be at the Escaut tomorrow. But there's certainly a complete void on our right. Between us and the Boche there is nothing but a few disorganized fag-ends of French units, as far as I can make out.'

Gort was silent for a time, locked in deep thought. 'As I see it, Henry,' he said at length, 'we have three options. First, we can help Billotte counter-attack and try to push the Germans back. But, as we've discovered, he has apparently no plan whatsoever as to how we can achieve this, and we don't even know what troops he's got for such an operation. Second, we could swing all our forces back to the Somme, to the south, but that's assuming the Germans don't thrust any further and that we've got time to make such a move. It would have the advantage of enabling us to retreat on our lines of communication, but it would also mean deserting the Belgians.'

Pownall relit his pipe. 'You think neither option is practicable?'

'I don't see that they are.'

'And the third?'

Gort sighed. 'The third option, Henry, is to withdraw the BEF to the Channel ports as a preliminary to evacuation.'

'Evacuation?' Pownall took his pipe from his mouth. 'The entire BEF?'

Gort turned away from the map and began to pace the room. 'Yes, Henry – or as much of our force as possible. If the French don't buck up pretty damn quickly, the Germans *will* be victorious. Good God, look what they've achieved already! We can't do it alone here. Our boys have done all we've asked of them, but they can't work miracles. My responsibility is first and foremost to Britain and the men under my command. If France falls, who do you think will be next for Hitler? We're going to need every man available, so to send three hundred and fifty thousand to prison camps in Germany won't help our cause, will it?'

'No, but – good God, it'd mean leaving the battle at the time the French will most need us.'

'I can't help that. I need to speak to my corps commanders. Henry, tomorrow morning I want you to get Brookey, Barker and Adam over here, and convene a staff conference first thing to plan such a withdrawal. I still hope it may not come to this – the French may buck up, you never know – but we must be prepared. We have to have a plan, Henry, even if they do not.'

'By God, what a night,' said Pownall, now staring gloomily at the large wall map of northern France and the Low Countries. 'How awful it is to be allied to such a temperamental race.'

At the farm, Sykes held his breath, but his heart was hammering. Behind him, Bell moved and something chinked – his water-bottle against his bayonet, perhaps. It was a small noise but to Sykes, waiting by that partially open door, it had seemed horribly loud. The approaching German soldier was just yards away now.

Please, God. Sykes's whole body was tense.

Voices – orders. Then footsteps and, to his relief, Sykes saw both men go back to their motorcycles. *So maybe there is a God after all,* he thought. Gunning their throttles, the noise ripping apart the stillness of the night, the soldiers sped back through the archway and up the road towards the village.

'Quick!' said Sykes. They dashed out into the yard, ran between two outbuildings, and helped each other over the wall into the orchard.

They sprinted without stopping all the way to the wood, gave the right password – 'Churchill' – and, using the light of a filtered torch, made their way to 10 Platoon's bivouac area. There they found Tanner asleep on a patch of soft moss at the foot of a large oak, wrapped in his gas cape and leather jerkin.

'Sarge! Sarge!' hissed Sykes, shaking his shoulder.

Tanner opened his eyes immediately and sat up, pulling off his cape. 'What time is it?' he asked. 'And what are you two doing here? Who's at the tower?'

'It's twenty past midnight,' said Sykes. 'Germans came to the farm, Sarge, men on motorcycles, and there's a whole lot more in the village. I wondered whether you'd all heard them.'

'Not in these woods. Amazing how much trees deaden noise. Have you told anyone else?'

'No, Sarge.'

Tanner packed away his cape but kept on the jerkin, and grabbed his rifle. 'They must have been doing a quick recce of the place. I wouldn't be surprised if more of them come back. A big empty farm is always going to make a good billet. Let's find Mr Peploe.'

The lieutenant was woken and Sykes told him what they had seen.

'Sir, I'd like to go and have a look,' said Tanner. 'It may be that we can get some transport.'

'All right.' Peploe nodded.

'And I'd like to take Sykes with me, sir. He knows the way through the orchard.'

Peploe agreed. 'Just make sure you're back before one.'

The two men had not gone halfway across the field between the wood and the orchard before they heard more vehicles, and this time not just motorcycles.

'Good,' whispered Tanner.

They ran on through the orchard and up to the wall. The voices and clamour of several men mingled with the growl of engines until, one by one, the vehicles were turned off. They heard laughter from one of the stables, then two sets of footsteps just the other side of the wall. Then voices from the road and a flickering torch beam. Both men fell to the ground, barely daring to breathe. A match was struck; a man said something, then he and his companion walked away.

'We need to see what's in the yard,' whispered Tanner, his battle-blouse and jerkin damp with dew.

'Give it a few more minutes, Sarge.'

Tanner turned his watch face to the stars: 0040. They couldn't afford to wait long. A couple of minutes passed, then a couple more. The voices faded until the farm seemed quiet.

'All right,' whispered Tanner. 'I'm going for a look-see.' Taking off his helmet, he stood up and peeped cautiously over the wall. The yard was a place of shadows, not a single light to be seen. Above, cloud covered the moon, but there was a faint glow – enough for him to make out the dark shapes of vehicles parked in the yard. Tanner cursed and sat down again. 'It's too dark. Damn.' Then the half-moon began to slide from behind a cloud, and Tanner was on to his feet again. Now he could see more clearly: a staff car, half a dozen motorcycles with sidecars, two small infantry trucks, an armoured scout car and a half-track. He sat down beside Sykes. 'Not bad,' he whispered, 'but not enough for more than seventy men.'

'We should check the road,' suggested Sykes. 'Maybe there're vehicles parked there.'

'Good thinking.'

They crept along beside the farm wall until they reached the road. Then, Sykes on his stomach and Tanner squatting, they peered round. *Ha!* thought Tanner, and nudged Sykes triumphantly. Lined up along the road, to either side of the archway, there were four trucks, three of which looked like Opel troop carriers. They were uncovered, wooden-sided, and with ample room for twenty men in each. A fourth, at the far side of the archway, was smaller, with a sloping bonnet and, curiously, six wheels. It would be a squeeze, but the four would be enough.

'Come on, Stan,' whispered Tanner. 'Let's get back.'

As they hurried across the field in silence, Tanner thought about how best to take the vehicles. It had to be a simple operation, the emphasis, as ever, on surprise, but also speed. They needed to get in quick, steal the trucks and be gone again. *Yes. That could work.* He smiled to himself as the plan took shape in his mind.

Then his thoughts turned to Blackstone, who was proving more of an enigma than Tanner wanted to admit. There had been times since joining the company when he had been convinced that Blackstone was as evil a bastard as ever – and worse: that he was a murderer and wanted Tanner dead. He knew what he had seen on the bridge: Blackstone apparently aiming his rifle directly at him before lowering it. At that moment he had been as sure as a man could be that Blackstone had shot him. But now – well, now he wasn't so certain. The CSM had seemed so genuine in his denial when they'd talked earlier, and Tanner had to accept that the evidence he had built against him was circumstantial. There were no hard facts.

Tanner now wondered whether his knowledge of him in India – his intense dislike of him back then – had warped his view of the man these past ten days. Perhaps he had been too quick to see the worst in him, too ready to assume that Blackstone was at the heart of every bad deed he had witnessed. He still disliked the fellow, but was he himself guilty of trying to fit what scant evidence there was of these crimes around what he knew of Blackstone? Had he lost the ability to view matters objectively? All his life he had trusted his gut instinct, his sixth sense; it had saved his life a number of times. But now that gut instinct kept changing. By law a man was innocent until proven guilty; and Tanner could prove nothing. Not conclusively, at any rate.

Tanner sighed. And there was Blackstone's proposal, too. A few hours before he had been inclined to agree with the CSM's plan, but that was when the company had been without transport. If the vehicles could be successfully stolen, it would be better, he was certain, for them to stay together. But he doubted Blackstone would see it that way. No, the CSM would regard it as another deliberate act of defiance. *Bloody hell*, thought Tanner. It was hard enough fighting a war against the Germans without engaging in another among his own company. Perhaps, it now occurred to him, Blackstone didn't need to know – not for the time being, at any rate.

Past the sentries and back into the wood. The men were all

awake now, packed up and ready for another long, gruelling day's march. They were quiet, senses still dulled from sleep, their mood sombre.

'In the nick of time,' muttered Lieutenant Peploe, as they reported to him. 'The OC wants us to form up by the edge of the wood in five minutes.'

'Sir,' said Tanner, in a low voice, 'there's enough transport, but we need to wait another hour.'

'We don't have another hour, Sergeant. We're leaving now.'

'I've got an idea, sir.'

'Go on.'

'With your permission, I'd like to take Sykes's section. You go with the rest of the platoon, and once we've got the vehicles, we'll catch you up.'

'How will you know where to find us?'

'We'll come with you to the forming-up point and find out where Captain Barclay intends to lead us. Then we'll slip away.'

Peploe thought for a moment. 'I'm uneasy about it, Tanner. I've a feeling the OC would be against it, or else he'd want the whole company involved.'

'That would complicate things, sir. It has to be a small group acting quickly.'

'I see that, which means doing it behind the OC's back. Other grounds for concern? Well, I have a horrible feeling that if we part company in opposite directions in the middle of night, with Jerry lurking here, there and everywhere, it's the last we'll see of each other, which, frankly, would be a damn shame.' He took off his cap and tugged at his hair. 'On the other hand, it'd be madness to pass up such a golden opportunity. Does it have to wait an hour?'

'I was thinking that Jerry might be asleep by then . . . Sod it, sir. What if we go now? If we pull it off you'll have barely got over the bridge by the time we're finished. I'm presuming you'll be turning left down the road that runs alongside the river?'

'I'll make sure we do. In which case, all right, Sergeant. Go now.'

'You sure, sir?'

'Not a hundred per cent, no.' He held out his hand and Tanner took it. 'Good luck. Hopefully, I'll see you in a short while. Otherwise your absence will take some explaining.' He headed back to the rest of the platoon, waiting patiently for him in a nearby clearing.

Tanner clapped Sykes on the back. 'Right, Stan, get your section together and we'll be off.'

Sykes switched on his filtered torch, called over his men and brought them into a semi-circle. Tanner looked into their ghostly faces: McAllister, Hepworth, Bell and Kershaw – good men, who had all served with him and Sykes in Norway – and the new lads: Ellis, Chambers, Verity, Rhodes and Denning.

'What's this, Sarge?' said McAllister. 'Why aren't we going with the others?'

'We're going to get some transport,' said Tanner. He saw Hepworth's face fall. 'Don't worry, Hep, this'll be a cinch and it'll make our lives a lot easier. Not only that, it means our chances of getting out of this fix will be much higher too. So cheer up.'

'No more walking, then?' said Hepworth.

'No, all things being well.'

'In that case, Sarge . . .'

'Hold on, Hep,' said McAllister, 'we've still got to get it. This is about those Jerries Tinker and the Corp saw, isn't it, Sarge?'

'Yes,' said Tanner. 'A Jerry unit's moved into the village and, more specifically, into the farm. Now there are four vehicles parked up on the side of the road outside. Three look like those Opels we nabbed in Norway. The other's a bit different but it can't be that hard to start. We don't even need to go into the farm itself. We'll head across the fields, then into the orchard and come out at the road by the wall of the farm. I'll creep out and check the coast's clear. Then, Mac, you run forward with Ellis and set up the Bren on the other side of the road facing the archway into the yard. Stan, what have you still got in your bag of tricks? I'm wondering whether we can knock down that archway and block those other Jerry vehicles inside.'

'Not sure, Sarge. Might be tricky to get it in the right place. Could probably manage a trip-wire of some kind. Why don't we just throw some grenades at the vehicles?'

'Possibly. We'll see when we get there.'

'And what if there are guards or troops in the trucks?'

'If there are guards, we'll kill them silently. If there are troops, we'll just have to spray them with the Bren – Mac, make sure you don't fire near the engines. We need the trucks to work, all right?'

McAllister nodded.

'Right,' Tanner continued. 'Who remembers how to drive those Opels?'

'Think so, Sarge,' said Bell.

'I can,' added Kershaw.

'Good,' said Tanner. 'Kay – you take the last truck. Dusty – you go with him and give him cover.' Kershaw and Rhodes nodded. 'I'll take the smaller one with you, Hep. Stan, you're in the one next to the arch with Verity and, Tinker, you grab the first with Denning – all right, Dasher?'

'Yes, Sarge,' said Denning.

'Punter,' Tanner continued, turning to Chambers, 'you cover the corp. You'll all need a reamer.' He delved into his haversack and pulled out a set of five, standard issue with a Bren, but which Tanner kept for use on his rifle and as a spare should it be needed. The largest was too big, he remembered, but the rest were fine. He took four from the ring that held them together and handed them out.

'All right, listen. It's going to be dark and speed'll be everything. Remember, you'll be driving on the right, not the left. On the dashboard beside the steering-wheel is the ignition – there's a small metal plate underneath it. If there's no key, put the reamer into the ignition, then bend it upwards slightly to hold it in place. When you do this a red light should come on in the centre of the ignition button. Push the button to start the engine. Left foot clutch, top left for first on the gearstick. Handbrake is an ordinary ratchet lever to the right of the gearstick. Got that?'

The men nodded.

'Good, then let's go. There's a half-moon, but keep close.'

As they reached the orchard, Tanner raised his hand for them to halt. He was relieved to see them all safely there. 'Follow me to the wall,' he whispered. Half crouching, they made their way through the apple trees, then along the wall, Tanner wincing at every chink and audible footfall. At the road, he raised his hand again and stopped. At least the breeze had strengthened, dampening the noise and carrying any sound north-easterly away from the farm. Above, the moon shone palely through the cloud.

'Everyone ready?'

The men nodded silently.

'Good. Stan, cover me, will you?' He drew out his sword bayonet and, keeping to the softer grassy verge between the farm wall and the road, stepped forward towards the first truck. Reaching it, he glanced around and then peered into the cab, breathing a small sigh of relief that it was, as he had thought, an Opel. Slowly, he moved to the end of the truck and, seeing the tailgate was down, peered in. *Empty. Good.*

Suddenly he heard a cough just ahead and someone spoke. He squatted behind the front wing of the next truck. Two men were talking by the archway. *Guards.* He heard the strike of a match, then another and another. *Struggling to light a beadie in this breeze.* Pausing, he wondered what to do. One of the men laughed – *lit at last!* They spoke some more, then stepped out onto the road. Tanner dropped to his knees and bent his head to look under the truck. Yes, a guard was walking out into the road – he could just see the booted feet; a pause, then the man turned left towards the first truck. Where was the other? Tanner looked again. *Must be under the arch.*

Now was the moment. Deftly, he got to his feet, waited until he heard the guard walk almost level with him on the far side of the Opel, then moved towards the other end. He crouched, listened, then dashed from the last bit of verge to the edge of the arch and clicked his tongue against his teeth.

As he had hoped, he heard movement – boots on stone – and, a second later, a guard stepped out of the shadows. Tanner leaped at him, holding his right forearm tight against the front of the man's throat, preventing him making a sound, and with his left plunging the bayonet into the man's side and through his kidney, killing him instantly. He dragged him clear of the archway as the dead man's weapon clattered to the ground. He dropped him and grabbed the short-barrelled weapon, then heard the first guard walk back quickly.

'Hans?' called the guard. '*Sind Sie gut?*'

'*Ja, ja,*' Tanner replied, put the weapon back on the ground, took several quick paces to the end of the truck, waited for the man to pass, then stepped out into the road. The guard had barely time to realize someone was behind him before Tanner had yanked back his head, arm over his throat, and stuck his bayonet into the German's side. Noiselessly, the man went limp, and Tanner carried him to the grass verge and laid him down.

Now he edged back towards the arch and peered round it. The yard and farm seemed still. He waited a moment, straining his eyes. Thicker cloud had covered the moon and it was dark in there. He could only just discern the shape of the vehicles and buildings even though his eyes were fully adjusted to the night light. He wondered if anyone had been posted in the tower, although he guessed the trucks would be almost out of view for someone up there. Surely men would be in the stables and outbuildings, though. Had someone heard anything? It was time to get a move on.

He ran back to the others. 'We're clear for the time being,' he whispered. 'The trucks are empty. Mac and Billy – jump into the tail of the second rather than going to the far side of the road.'

'Sarge,' mouthed McAllister.

'And, Hedley, you come with me and Hepworth,' he whispered, tapping Verity. 'Hep, there's an MG on our vehicle. Get on it right away. All of you, get to your positions as quietly and quickly as possible. Go along the grass verge, not the road. And no one start their engine until I give the signal.' He turned to Sykes. 'What do you think?'

'I've got a packet of Nobels ready,' he murmured.

'All right,' said Tanner. 'Mac and Billy go first, then Kay and Dusty.'

He followed Sykes to the archway. His heart was pounding and his mouth tasted as dry as chalk, but his head was clear. Sykes looked at the doors, and both men pushed themselves back against the outer wall.

Tanner glanced round, saw McAllister and Ellis jumping on to the back of the truck, and Hepworth climbing into the six-wheeler. *Christ, the noise. They'll wake the whole sodding lot up.*

Sykes was now pulling one of the wooden doors. 'Get the other one, Sarge,' he hissed.

The ageing hinges creaked, causing Tanner's stomach to lurch and his heart to hammer even harder. Sykes now had the packet of explosives in his hands and was pulling out a length of fuse. Tanner watched for a moment, then hurried back to the two bodies. He liked the look of the weapon he had taken and rummaged through the first man's ammunition pouches. He found half a dozen narrow metal magazines. Then he patted the man's pockets, hoping he would feel what he was looking for – cigarettes – but when he tried to take them he realized the man was wearing a smock over his tunic and had to delve inside to reach the breast pocket. As he pulled out the cigarettes he noticed an embroidered skull and crossbones on the right-hand side of the collar. Glancing back, he saw Sykes motioning to him frantically to hurry to the truck.

Nodding, Tanner felt in his pocket for his reamer. Then, with one hand on the spare wheel at the side, he jumped up into the open cab and felt around the dashboard, trying desperately to find the ignition and starter.

Suddenly he heard voices from inside the yard and, at the same moment, as the moon emerged from behind the clouds once more, he found what he was sure was the ignition, down to the left of the steering-wheel. More voices. *Damn it, damn it, come on!* Fumbling with the reamer, he pushed it into the ignition and pressed the small round button above it. The engine burst into life as shouts rang out inside the yard. A moment later the gates were pushed violently open and several soldiers appeared. In the thin light, Tanner could see their surprise and horror. Behind him, the machine-gun now opened fire, the deafening noise making him jump. Then McAllister's Bren was spitting bullets from the truck in front, small stabs of orange fire blindingly bright in the dark night air. Immediately the men at the gates crumpled to the ground.

'Go!' Tanner shouted. 'Go! Go! Go!'

One engine started, then another. Behind him, he was conscious of Kershaw moving forward in the fourth truck, past his own vehicle. Shots cracked out – *where from?* Tanner sensed pandemonium now inside the farm as he felt down to his right for the handbrake. Where the hell was it? He fumbled blindly.

'Get moving, Sarge!' Hepworth was shouting. 'Get bloody moving.'

Another shot whizzed past his ear – *must be from the stables* – and pinged off the metal dashboard. *Sod the handbrake*, he thought, put his foot on the clutch, rammed the gearstick into first and lurched forward, inching out past Sykes's truck. Why hadn't the explosion gone off? And then he saw Sykes leap out of his cab, engine running, and dash to the gate. *Come on, Stan – get out of there* – and realized that the first truck hadn't moved.

'Bloody hell,' he muttered, moving alongside. 'What's the problem?' he yelled to Bell.

'I've dropped my reamer,' said Bell.

Damn! Tanner jumped from the cab as McAllister's Bren continued to rattle behind, leaped into Bell's truck and, taking his torch from his trouser pocket, shone it at the floor – there was no need for secrecy now. He saw the reamer almost immediately and, leaning against Bell, pushed it into the ignition, yanked it upwards and pressed the starter, just as Hepworth opened fire once more with the German machine-gun.

'Sarge!' shouted Hepworth. 'We've got to go – NOW!'

Tanner glanced back and saw Sykes moving out, arms waving, urging them forward.

'Bollocks,' said Tanner, dropped to the ground and, with one bound, leaped back into his stolen truck, thrust it into gear and sped forward. Bell was now moving in his truck too and, swivelling his head backwards, Tanner saw Sykes so close to his rear that the two trucks were almost touching. From the corner of his eye he saw enemy troops emerge from the archway and open fire, arcs of tracer from their machine-gun cutting across the night sky and following them along the road. A split-second later a blast of orange light erupted from the gateway, enveloping the Germans and spewing broken brick, wood and iron. Tanner felt its draught on his neck and looked back to see Hepworth drop into the seat behind. At the same time, above the throaty roar of the truck's engine, he heard falling masonry.

'Hep?' he shouted. 'Are you all right?'

'Just about,' came the reply.

'Can you see anything?'

'I can't now but I could a moment ago. The tower collapsed all right, Sarge.'

Tanner laughed. *Perfect*.

His plan had worked. The company had its transport.

12

Sturmbannführer Otto Timpke had been fast asleep in the farmhouse when he was woken by the commotion. He had flung on his
shirt, breeches and boots and had been about to hurry downstairs
when the explosion had occurred. The bright glare had lit up the
house and yard and he had stopped, frozen momentarily to the
spot. Shards of stone, brick and grit peppered the farmhouse,
tinkling on the roof and against the walls; a window-pane smashed,
then another, while outside in the yard, the deafening thunder of
collapsing masonry seemed to engulf the farm, shaking the house
to its foundations.

By the time Timpke had grabbed his belt and holster, then run
downstairs with a hurricane lamp and out into the yard, a choking
cloud of dust filled the air, trapped, so it seemed, by the surrounding buildings and walls. Men were racing from the house and barns;
some were coughing and spluttering, others crying out in agony.

It was hard to see what damage had been done or how, but he
strode forward, clutching his lamp, and nearly tripped over a
damaged motorcycle. Cursing, he stepped aside. Torches – electric

and flame – now glowed through the swirling dust. Timpke put a handkerchief to his mouth and, reaching the entrance, paused, aghast. The archway, tower and parts of the adjoining stable blocks had been completely destroyed. All that was left was a jagged pile of rubble, wood and brick. A motorcycle and sidecar lay near by, bent and skewed, almost completely covered with fallen brickwork.

'Herr Sturmbannführer,' said a voice next to him.

Timpke neither spoke nor moved, his face rigid with fury.

'Herr Sturmbannführer,' said the voice again, and this time Timpke turned towards his adjutant, Hauptsturmführer Kemmetmüler.

'What happened?' He spoke quietly, slowly.

'Sabotage, Herr Sturmbannführer. And the men who did this stole the trucks left outside the farm. I've radioed to One Company and they'll give chase.'

'Stop them, Kemmetmüler. It's dark and they won't be able to catch them. We don't want to lose any more men or vehicles.'

He punched a fist into the other hand. 'Whose platoon was on guard duty this evening?'

'Untersturmführer Reichmann's, Herr Sturmbannführer.'

'Bring him to me. We'll do what we can now for the injured, but we'll clear up this mess at first light. I shall be in the farmhouse. And post more guards.'

By the time he was back in his temporary battalion headquarters inside the farmhouse, Timpke was still numb. He sat down at a dark oak dining-table, took out his silver cigarette case and, tapping the end of a Turkish cigarette, realized his hands were shaking – so much so that he struggled to light it. *How could this have happened? How?* It was not possible: the area was clear of enemy – this part of southern Belgium was in German hands now. And, in any case, there had been guards posted around the farm. How could any saboteurs have got through such a cordon? He smashed his fist on the table.

There was a knock and Kemmetmüler came into the room. He

had brought Untersturmführer Reichmann with him. The young platoon commander clicked his boots together and saluted. He looked clean, Timpke thought – too clean. Apart from a smear of dust on one sleeve of his tunic and a smudge of dirt across his cheek, he was unblemished.

Timpke sat back in his chair, leaving Reichmann standing stiffly to attention.

'I've been wondering,' said Timpke slowly, his voice betraying his anger, 'how any saboteurs could get to this farm, steal four trucks, then blow up an entire tower and half of two buildings undetected. How can this be, when I gave express orders for there to be a guard on this entire compound?' He stood up and walked towards Reichmann. 'Perhaps, Reichmann, you could tell me how you had your men deployed.'

Reichmann was shorter than Timpke, a thick-set young man with dark eyebrows and a heavy forehead. His hair was shaved at the sides but slicked back with pomade underneath his field cap. Timpke smelled sour alcohol on his breath.

'I used Unterscharführer Liebmann's group, Herr Sturmbannführer.'

'Just one group?'

'Yes, Herr Sturmbannführer. With my approval, he placed two men in the tower, two men by the archway, two men at the front and three others watching elsewhere.'

'Where exactly?' said Timpke.

Reichmann swallowed hard. 'Around the farm, Herr Sturmbannführer.'

'Where they cannot have been watching very closely, can they?' He leaned over the table a moment, clutching the edge with both hands. 'One group,' he said, louder now, 'of which I am beginning to think half must have been sleeping.'

'It was dark, sir. The men were watching, but it was night.'

'Not good enough, Reichmann. Good God, your men have ears, do they not?'

'Yes, Herr Sturmbannführer, but—'

'Be quiet, Reichmann! This is the battalion headquarters and, quite apart from the personnel, we have important equipment and vehicles here. Do you have any idea how hard Brigadeführer Eicke had to work to get our vehicles? Most of the *Wehrmacht* troops still use horses and their own two feet. Do you understand how fortunate we are to have these vehicles? And you go and lose not one but *four*! And that does not include those damaged here.'

He had tried to contain his rage, to speak with a controlled calm, but standing in front of him was this disgrace of an officer – an ugly brute with a bad accent and the stench of wine on his breath. Had all that training, and all those lectures, been for nothing?

Timpke clenched his fist and drove it into Reichmann's stomach. The man gasped and staggered backwards.

'Has it not entered your thick skull, Reichmann, that we are in only recently captured enemy territory? How could it not? And yet you have the stupidity and nerve to deploy a mere group of ten men. And you have been drinking. It is unbelievable – you, an officer, a man supposed to set an example.' He punched Reichmann again, then took out his pistol, a wooden-gripped Luger P08, and pointed it at Reichmann's forehead.

'It was j-just some wine, Herr Sturmbannführer,' gasped Reichmann. 'I'm not drunk, I swear.' His eyes were wide with fear.

Timpke eyed him with disgust. 'Give me one good reason why I should not shoot you here and now.'

Beads of sweat had formed on Reichmann's forehead. 'I – I – I thought a group would be enough.'

Timpke lowered the pistol, saw the relief cross Reichmann's face, then whipped the barrel hard down on the side of his head. Reichmann cried out with pain and shock and collapsed on to the floor, blood pouring from a long gash.

'Idiot Swabian,' said Timpke. 'Where did you come from, Reichmann? How do people like you manage to be officers? A thick-skulled imbecilic camp guard and a poor one at that.' He kicked him in the ribs, and then again as Reichmann writhed in pain. Timpke looked up at Kemmetmüler. 'Ask Division to transfer this man. I have no use for him. Send him back to the camps.' He turned back to Reichmann. 'Get up,' he said, 'or I swear I'll shoot you.'

With blood pouring down his face, Reichmann staggered to his feet and clutched the table for support.

'Now,' said Timpke, 'you will take me to Unterscharführer Liebmann. He is still alive, I take it?'

Reichmann clutched his wound. 'Yes, Herr Sturmbannführer.' Wincing, he led Timpke and Kemmetmüler from the house to the yard, where men were trying to clear rubble under the light of a few torches and lamps. Passing his staff car, Timpke noticed, with renewed anger, that the Audi had a dent in the front wing and the windscreen was smashed.

Reichmann tried to call Liebmann, but his throat caught and he began to cough.

'Unterscharführer Liebmann!' shouted Kemmetmüler. 'Liebmann!'

They waited a moment, straining their eyes at the throng of men moving around the yard. A tall man stumbled forward, his uniform grey with dust. Seeing Timpke and Kemmetmüler, he stopped and saluted. His eyes turned to the half-crouching figure of Untersturmführer Reichmann. Timpke saw him blink anxiously.

'Come closer, Liebmann,' said Timpke.

Liebmann took a step forward. Timpke leaned towards him and sniffed. There was wine on this man's breath too.

'So you have been drinking?' said Timpke, his voice quiet once more.

Liebmann glanced again at Reichmann. 'Just a little earlier on, Herr Sturmbannführer.'

'I think it must have clouded your judgement.'

'No, sir, I swear, I—'

'Then why were four vehicles stolen from under your nose, Liebmann? Why was the enemy able to take four vehicles *and* blow up the tower? Four vehicles and how many dead?'

'At least eight, Herr Sturmbannführer,' said Kemmetmüler.

'Well, make that nine. Reichmann, you will now shoot this man.'

Liebmann's eyes darted between Timpke and Reichmann, panic etched across his face. 'No,' he said, 'please, no.'

Reichmann turned his bloodied face to Timpke. 'Shoot him?'

'Yes, Reichmann, shoot him. He has been drinking and he has failed not only me but the entire battalion. I am court-martialling him and passing instant judgement. And, as punishment, you will carry out his execution. Now.'

'But – but he's one of my men, Herr Sturmbannführer!'

'Precisely. Let this be a lesson to you. Now do it.'

'No,' said Liebmann again. 'Please, Herr Sturmbannführer, I implore you.'

'Reichmann – now! Or I'll shoot you too.'

With fumbling fingers, Reichmann tugged at his leather holster and pulled out his P38. His hand shook as he held the pistol, then he convulsed and began to sob.

'Oh, for God's sake,' snapped Timpke. 'You had no such qualms in Poland. You were happy enough to shoot people there.'

'Please,' said Liebmann, falling to his knees.

'Last chance, Reichmann,' said Timpke. 'One, two—'

'I'm sorry, Hans,' sobbed Reichmann, blood and tears running down his face. Shakily, he raised the gun to the side of Liebmann's head.

'Three,' said Timpke. Liebmann was staring at him numbly. A single pistol shot rang out, the report echoing around the yard. The side of Liebmann's head flew into the air. Eyes still staring at Timpke, Liebmann toppled over on to the ground.

There was silence, except for Reichmann's now uncontrollable sobbing.

Timpke looked around at the men, their taut faces outlined in the glow of the lamps. They had all stopped working and were staring mutely at the scene before them.

'Let that be a lesson to all of you,' said Timpke. 'Orders are to be obeyed. No more drinking and no more shirking. Is that understood?' He glared at them, then strode back into the house.

*

Across the bridge Kershaw, who had been leading, had pulled over and let Tanner pass. Turning left down the track that led along the riverbank, Tanner had initially seen no sign of the rest of the platoon and had just begun to worry that Peploe's prediction had been right when, up ahead, he had spotted dim figures scuttling into the side of the road.

Moments later he drew up alongside the head of the line of prostrate men taking cover either side of the road.

'Good morning, sir,' he said, shining his torch at Captain Barclay, who was trying to shield his eyes.

'Tanner?' said Barclay, dumbfounded. 'Good God, man, what the devil are you doing?'

'We've got some transport, sir,' said Tanner.

Barclay got to his feet and stared open-mouthed at the line of four trucks, their engines ticking over in the quiet night air.

'We should load everyone up quickly, sir. I suggest that for the moment, sir, everyone piles onto the truck nearest them. It'll be a bit of a squeeze, I'm afraid.'

Barclay nodded dumbly.

Now Blackstone pushed past the OC and stood beside the cab of Tanner's lead truck. 'Quite a haul, Jack,' he said. 'Good of you to keep me informed.' He glowered at him, then hurried on down the line, helping men up from the bank and ordering them onto the trucks.

Tanner knew what Blackstone was saying: *You still don't trust me.* Well, no, he didn't. He sighed, then stood up and peered into the back. 'All right, Hep?' he said.

'Yes, Sarge,' said Hepworth, 'although these Jerry MGs don't half get hot quick. I can still feel the heat from the barrel.'

Tanner switched on his torch and flashed it around the vehicle. There were two bench seats on either side, which, he guessed, could take eight or ten men in all. Then he sat down again and shone the torch at the dashboard. It was simple, with an explanation of the gears and different drive options on a plate. Further along was another plate. *So it's a Krupp.* Next to him he saw a flat leather case, picked it up and opened it. Inside, he discovered some maps. He smiled to himself as he opened the first. *Jesus, those Jerries were careless bastards.* There was Mons and, to the south, Mauberge. Further to the west Le Cateau, Cambrai and St Quentin were all circled. Between Cambrai and Le Cateau a line had been drawn in thick pencil and beside it the number seven, written with a line across the stem of the figure, and then 'Pz'. 'Seventh Panzer,' he mouthed to himself. 7th Panzer what? Division, brigade? Corps? His eyes rested briefly on Mons again and then he scanned the map immediately to the west of the town. Where the hell were they? There was the river, and the road they had been on the previous afternoon. Then he found two possible roads that led south across the river, but only one showed woodland in the right place. Just below a village was marked as Hainin.

'Sergeant Tanner,' said a breathless voice beside him, 'how very splendid it is to see you again.'

Tanner turned to see Lieutenant Peploe climbing up beside him. 'Morning, sir.' He grinned. 'Are we ready to go?'

'Almost. Just setting up the other Bren and making sure the squadron leader's safely aboard. Captain Barclay's going to join us.'

'And Blackstone?'

'He's at the rear with McAllister, Ellis and the rest of Company Headquarters.'

Other men were now clambering into the back, the truck rolling slightly as they did so.

'Where did you find that?' said Peploe, spotting the map.

'Kindly left by Jerry. Look, sir,' he said, pointing to the tiny circle made by the closed beam of his torch, 'we're here. There's the village, and there's the road on which Sykes and I saw the German convoy yesterday.'

Peploe peered at it. 'Ye-es,' he said. 'So this is the river Haine.'

'We need to keep a wide berth around Hainin, sir,' said Tanner. 'I suggest we follow the road along the river, then cross here at Montroeul-sur-Haine. That's – what? – five miles or so, and then we can head south and rejoin the main road to Valenciennes at Quiévrain.'

'Isn't that a bit risky? The enemy's already been seen on that road.'

'But it's quick, sir, and it's dark. Jerry might have changed his habits, but in Norway he liked to knock off during the night. If we do see any enemy, I reckon we'll get through – especially if we tell everyone to wear field caps and not helmets. German field caps look much the same as ours. Why would they suspect anything?'

'You don't think the word would be out?'

'Maybe. But it's a bit embarrassing for whoever's in charge. If I'd had four trucks nicked from under my nose, I know what I'd do. I'd keep quiet about it.' He pointed at the pencil markings on the map. 'If these are correct, sir, then Jerry's not at Valenciennes yet. He was just using this road as a means of getting near the front, which from this map seems to be further south. I reckon we can get through Valenciennes, then push on through this place – Denain – on to Douai and then to Arras.' He measured the distance with his finger and thumb. 'About sixty or so kilometres – what's that? Forty-odd miles. With clear roads we'll do it in a couple of hours.' He glanced at his watch. It was now just after two in the morning. 'We could be in Arras before the war starts again, sir.'

'All right, Tanner,' said Peploe, as Tanner took off his pack and set it beside him on the seat. 'You've convinced me. I'll suggest it to the OC.'

A moment later, Captain Barclay joined them. 'Damn me, Tanner, I take my hat off to you,' he muttered, shaking his head in wonderment.

'Sir, the previous owners very decently left us their map,' said Peploe. He held it open on his lap. 'I'd like to suggest this route – here.'

Barclay peered over as Peploe explained the plan, fingers tracing lines on the map. The captain followed, wearing a glazed expression.

'Good,' he said. 'Carry on, then.'

Peploe leaned behind him and said to the men in the back, 'Make sure you keep watching the truck behind, all right?'

'Well said, Peploe,' muttered Captain Barclay.

Tanner put his foot on the clutch, shoved the stick into first gear, took his other foot off the brake and the truck rumbled on into the Belgian night.

It soon began to rain, only lightly at first, then rather more heavily. Those in the Opels were under cover, but Tanner's Krupp had no covered cab or canvas tarpaulin to strap over the back. There was a single wiper on the driver's side of the windscreen, which Tanner soon discovered how to switch on, but although it worked well enough, it hardly helped make driving along dark, narrow roads any easier; as it was, the narrow slits of light from the blinkered headlamps cast only a small amount of light on the road ahead.

Tanner lifted his collar and temporarily swapped his field cap for his rimmed helmet, and then asked Peploe to take out his leather jerkin.

'Damn this rain,' muttered Captain Barclay.

'I reckon it's doing us a favour, sir,' said Tanner, as Peploe handed him the serge-lined jerkin. 'Even more likely to keep the Germans indoors.'

'Let's hope you're right, Sergeant.' The captain had been so quiet that Peploe had asked if he was feeling all right. Barclay had snapped that he was fine, then fallen back into deep thought. Now, however, he seemed to be rediscovering his voice. 'Where are we now, Peploe?' he asked. 'I can see something ahead.'

'Here, sir,' said Peploe. He switched on his torch directly over the map and pointed. 'That's the village of Montroeul-sur-Haine. In a few miles we join the main road.'

'Should be easier driving then, sir,' said Tanner.

'All right. I'll take the map from now on,' said the captain, snatching it.

'Of course, sir,' said Peploe.

'And, Tanner, grateful though I am, I don't want you going off on your own again. Is that clear?'

'Yes, sir,' said Tanner.

'Actually, I gave them permission, sir,' said Peploe.

'Yes, well, even so,' said Barclay. 'Remember that I'm in charge, not either of you. I don't like being kept in the dark. Makes me look foolish in front of the men.'

'Yes, sir. Sorry, sir,' said Tanner, mechanically, then cleared his throat. 'They were SS, sir.'

'SS? Are you sure?'

'Yes, sir. There are SS symbols on the numberplate and the men had a skull and crossbones on their collar.'

'Typical bloody Nazis,' muttered Barclay. 'Christ, that's all we need.'

'They didn't seem much to worry about, sir. We got in and out of there with barely a fight. They had good kit, mind you. The two I saw wore a kind of speckled camouflage smock and helmet liner. And I took this off one of them too.' He unslung the stubby firearm and passed it across Peploe to Captain Barclay.

'What is it?' said Barclay, handling it.

'It's a sub-machine-gun, sir,' said Tanner. 'It's got a perforated air-cooled barrel, like the other MGs, and a magazine that must take thirty rounds or so.'

'Did you get any ammunition?' asked Peploe.

'I took what was on him.'

'Good,' said Barclay. 'I'll hang on to it. Might come in useful.'

'You don't think Tanner should keep it, sir?' said Peploe. 'Spoils of war and all that?'

'No, I don't,' said Barclay. 'Really, I hope you're not questioning my authority, Peploe.'

'Of course not, sir.'

Damn, thought Tanner. He'd been looking forward to trying it out.

They passed through the village, Tanner once more replacing his helmet with his field cap. The place seemed deserted; not a light showed. An owl looped in front of them, making Tanner start while Captain Barclay cursed and put a hand to his heart.

They were travelling slowly, only fifteen miles an hour at times, but it was better to drive carefully than crash off the road and damage one or more of the vehicles, yet the slow-going was frustrating. Tanner stared ahead into the night, his eyes strained, and suddenly felt tired. It was always the same: once the excitement of combat had worn off, exhaustion swept over him. And the wiper was doing him no favours with that rhythmic swipe of rubber, back and forth, and a mesmerizing squeak. He shook his head, pinched his leg, and breathed in deeply. The air smelled so fresh: rain on dry soil, an evocative aroma that reminded him of his childhood, a summer storm, running for the shelter of the woods and the comforting sound of rain pattering against the leaf canopy.

A few miles on, they crossed a railway line, then reached the small town of Quiévrain. It, too, was quiet, but in the town square there were several vehicles: an armoured car and several half-tracks, the black crosses on their sides just visible.

'Christ,' mumbled Barclay. 'What do we do now?'

'Nothing, sir,' said Tanner. As they drove past they saw two men, shoulders hunched under their greatcoats, smoking cigarettes. Tanner waved and they waved back.

'Fortune favours the bold, eh, Tanner?' grinned Peploe.

'More often than not, sir.'

Once through the town, they joined the main road to Valenciennes and, as Tanner had hoped, the going immediately became easier. Soon after, they reached the French border. There was a border post, but it was deserted. Tanner jumped out, lifted the barrier, and they drove on, through quiet and villages. As they passed through another village, Tanner was forced to swerve violently to avoid a refugee family and their loaded cart, but for the most part it seemed that, with the onset of darkness and the arrival of rain, the war had shrunk away. Soldiers had crept into their billets, and refugees had sought shelter, halting their aimless wandering.

Nearing Onnaing, the rain relented and the moon emerged once more, bathing the surrounding countryside in a faint milky monochrome. Tanner saw a garage, white petrol pumps glowing luminously in the dark. Pulling off the road, he drew up alongside them.

'What on earth are you doing, Tanner?' said Barclay. 'Christ, man, we don't want to be stopping.'

'Fuel, sir. We should fill up while we can.' He jumped out of the cab as the others drew up behind him.

'Fuel? We can't just take it,' said Barclay. 'Those pumps will be locked or switched off, surely?'

Tanner walked round the front of the truck to examine them. They were electric rather than manual, but the nozzles were padlocked.

'There,' said Barclay, now out of the truck with Peploe beside him, 'what did I tell you? Come on, we're wasting time and unnecessarily exposing ourselves.'

'Sir, just give me a minute.' Before Barclay could reply, he ran off towards the last truck in the line.

'What's up, Sarge?' said Sykes, as Tanner reached the cab.

'I need you for a moment.'

Sykes followed him back to the pumps where Captain Barclay was still pacing impatiently.

'Come on, Tanner,' said the OC, 'let's get going.'

'Please, sir, just a moment more.' He turned to Sykes. 'Get these padlocks off, will you, Stan?'

'Certainly, Sarge,' said Sykes, casting an apprehensive glance at the captain. Delving into his breast pocket, he pulled out his skeleton key and, in moments, had the first padlock undone. Grinning at Lieutenant Peploe, Tanner took the nozzle and pulled it over to the barrel tank under the seat while Sykes undid the second padlock. The pump rumbled and fuel ran into the tank.

'How the devil did you do that, Corporal?' asked Barclay, clearly baffled.

'An old trick, sir,' said Sykes, then returned to his truck.

'Look, Tanner,' said Peploe, beside him, 'that window up there.' He pointed to the quarters above the garage.

Tanner saw a face peering out nervously through a narrow gap between the curtains. 'He thinks we're Jerries,' he said, as Kershaw drove his truck along the other side of the pumps. 'No wonder the Germans are finding it so easy to roll everyone over. You've only got to mention Stukas or see a black cross and everyone makes a run for it.'

'You have to admit they do seem rather good, though,' said Peploe. 'I mean, look at Poland and Norway.'

'I've seen the newsreels from Poland, sir,' said Tanner, as he replaced the nozzle and stepped back into the cab, Peploe clambering in beside him. He started the Krupp and rolled it forward to allow the next truck to fill up. 'Lots of Stukas and tanks and so on. And I saw pictures of the Polish cavalry too. They were on horseback, waving swords. I reckon any modern army could have beaten them.'

'What about Norway, though?'

'The Norwegians were rather like the Poles only they had even less kit,' Tanner replied. 'We hardly had any guns, any armour and almost no air force. It was easy for the Germans – just a skip across the Baltic. They could keep themselves better supplied. But don't forget it's still going on, sir.'

'We're going to lose there, though, aren't we?'

Tanner took out his packet of German cigarettes, offered one to Peploe, then helped himself. 'All I'm saying, sir,' he said, as Peploe struck a match, 'is that everyone seems to have got it into their heads that the Germans are somehow better than everyone else. But I don't believe it. I reckon if our boys and the Frogs stood still for a bit, rather than scarpering back to the next line at the first sign of trouble, we'd soon give them something to worry about. I thought the French had the biggest army in the world – at least, that's what a French officer once told me.'

'You may be right, Sergeant, and hopefully, if we find the battalion again, we can do exactly as you suggest.'

Tanner grinned. 'We've just got to find them, haven't we, sir?'

Captain Barclay stepped up into the cab. 'Right, Sergeant,' he said. 'You've got what you wanted – full tanks all round. Now let's get a bloody move on.'

It was now nearly half past three on the morning of Monday, 20 May. The town of Valenciennes lay a couple of miles ahead.

'Strange smell,' said Peploe, sniffing.

'Burning, sir,' said Tanner. 'There's been a fire near by, I'd say.'

'Damn great river running through this place,' said Barclay, 'by the look of it on the map, at any rate, and the road south follows its course pretty much. I'm afraid it's not a part of France I know – but the name's ringing a bell for some reason. Have a feeling our chaps may have been here in the last war.'

'The river – what's it called?' asked Peploe.

Barclay peered more closely. 'The Escaut. Hang on a minute – we crossed it further north on our way to the front.'

'I remember it, sir,' said Peploe. 'And I remember thinking it was quite a major natural barrier then.'

A *natural barrier*. Tanner cursed himself. *Of course!* He thought of the map again – where had that line been marked? Between Le Cateau and Cambrai, and Cambrai was not far south from where they were now. His mind raced: if Cambrai was the limit of the enemy's advance so far then the town must either be almost or already in German hands. *Think*, he told himself. *Think*. They had heard fighting the previous afternoon and had *seen* enemy troops – yet it was at least fifteen miles back that they had last glimpsed any sign of Germans. But neither had they met any French. None – no night-time leaguers, no troop movements, no army vehicles. Nothing at all. Because they had already fallen back.

'Sir,' he said, to Captain Barclay, 'I'm sorry – I should have thought of this earlier – but I think we might run into French troops at any moment.' He slowed and brought the Krupp to a halt.

'How can you possibly know that, Tanner?'

'Because we heard fighting earlier – yesterday afternoon, sir –

and we've seen no sign of either enemy or Allied troops since Quiévrain. The French must have gone somewhere and the most obvious place is behind a natural barrier like the Escaut. But Valenciennes is quite a big town, and you said the river runs right through it. That means they'll almost certainly defend it – or, at least, the approaches to the river.'

'And we need to cross the Escaut to get to Arras,' added Peploe. 'Yes, sir.'

'So when they see a column of four German trucks they'll think the enemy's trying a stealthy night-time attack.'

'Exactly, sir.'

'You have to admit, sir,' added Peploe, 'that it would be a bit annoying to have come this far only to get mown down by our own side.'

Barclay looked down at the map again in silence, his brow furrowed.

He doesn't know what to do, thought Tanner. 'Sir, I have a suggestion.'

Barclay sighed. 'What is it?'

'We avoid Valenciennes, sir. My guess is that it may well be thick with French forces but also refugees. We haven't seen any in the countryside but I'd have thought a big town is the first place they'll all have headed. Surely we can turn south, avoiding the town, then cut west towards Denain?'

Barclay nodded. 'Yes. Might take a bit more time, but there are certainly the roads to it.'

'Then when we reach the river we'll park the trucks and approach a bridge on foot. Hopefully it won't have been destroyed yet.'

'And then?' said Barclay.

'We shout across, asking for safe passage.'

Barclay was silent a moment, then sighed heavily. 'Yes. I was, er, going to suggest much the same. All right, Tanner. Let's get moving again.'

It was almost light by the time they reached the edge of the village of Neuville, a mile or so south of Denain. Behind, the sun was rising once more, spreading its golden rays across the flat countryside, the air sharp and fresh. Dew and the night's rain glistened on the grass and in the hedgerows, but ahead, to either side of the village, they could see a thin mist rising from the river.

Tanner drove slowly into the village, then stopped by a tall-spired church, the other three trucks pulling to a halt behind him.

'Right, sir,' he said. 'If Mr Peploe would accompany me, we'll head towards the bridge.'

'Very well,' said Barclay. 'I'll tell the rest of the men.'

'Ready, sir?' Tanner asked Peploe.

The lieutenant nodded. The village was quiet, although in the trees the birds were in full song. Tanner listened and his heart lifted. He hadn't heard a May dawn chorus since he'd left England eight years before, yet the sounds were as familiar to him now as they had been when he was a boy. He wished he could return to that life – a life that seemed so completely apart from the one he had led ever since. Yet, even so, he knew that his childhood – those precious years in Alvesdon with his father – had moulded him into the man he had become. A lifetime ago now, and it only needed the sound of a blackbird singing at dawn to carry him back, bringing to his mind a thousand details as fresh and vivid as ever. *One day perhaps.*

A sweet smell filled the air.

'Delicious,' murmured Peploe. 'Someone's baking. I've been to France a few times and the fresh bread and croissants first thing in the morning are one of the best things about it. I'm tempted to forget Arras and spend the rest of the day in that bakery.'

Tanner smiled. 'It's reminding me how hungry I am.'

'Well, perhaps after we've cleared our passage across the river, we can come back and pay it a quick visit.'

They had walked around a shallow bend in the road and now saw the river directly ahead at the end of the main village road. On the far side a single house loomed spectrally out of the mist.

'Hang on a minute, sir,' said Tanner. He delved into his pocket and pulled out a white handkerchief, which he tied to the end of his rifle.

Holding it high, they moved towards the bridge. A road ran either side of the river, which they now saw was not as wide as they had first thought. Barges were moored along the bank. The bridge, it seemed, was part of a lock system. The Escaut had been turned into a canal.

'Not at all what I was expecting,' said Peploe. He cupped his hands around his mouth, about to holler across the river, then Tanner saw vague figures on the far side and, a moment later, a spurt of orange flame. Two bullets flew over his head as he dived to the ground, pulling Peploe with him, then two more. He heard Peploe gasp and felt the lieutenant's body go limp. *Oh, no. Damn it all, no.*

13

Another short burst of machine-gun fire spat out, the bullets zipping over Tanner's head as he crouched next to Lieutenant Peploe, the report echoing off the buildings along the village street.

'Stop!' shouted Tanner. Then, trying frantically to remember the phrase card he had been given, he added, '*Nous sommes anglais! Nous sommes anglais!*' He raised his rifle with its white handkerchief into the air and waved it from side to side.

The firing stopped and now he heard voices – *French?* – from the far side of the river, then from behind him.

Still hidden behind the bend in the road, Captain Barclay called, 'Peploe, Tanner, are you all right?'

'Lieutenant Peploe's hit, sir,' Tanner yelled back. The lieutenant's face was ashen and a trickle of blood ran down the side of his right temple. At the side of the helmet there was a hole where a bullet had entered – a glancing blow, but enough to penetrate the steel. Tanner put his ear to Peploe's mouth, heard shallow breathing, then felt for a pulse. *Thank God.*

'Tanner?' It was Barclay's voice again.

To his right, a man was now emerging from a house – thick white moustache, black jacket and cap. He held up his arms. '*Arrêtez! Arrêtez votre fusillade!*'

Carefully Tanner eased off Peploe's helmet and heard something drop. On the cobbles beside him he found a spent bullet. Quickly he parted Peploe's thick flaxen hair and saw, to his relief, that the bullet had only cut his head, not penetrated.

The Frenchman was now beside him, crouching. His face was deeply tanned and lined, a two-day grey beard flecking his cheeks. The soldiers were across the bridge now, hurrying towards them.

'*Imbéciles!*' said the man. '*Ils sont nos alliés.*'

Tanner stood up. '*Nous sommes anglais,*' he said again, to a young clean-shaven French lieutenant.

The lieutenant took out his pistol, stepped forward and pointed it at Tanner's stomach. 'There are no British here,' he said, in heavily accented English. 'They are to the north and west.'

'We are, sir,' said Tanner. 'We got detached from the rest of our battalion on the Brussels–Charleroi canal a couple of days ago.'

'And you made it here? Nonsense! You are lying.'

'It's true, sir. Yesterday evening we discovered some Germans between Mons and Valenciennes and managed to take some of their vehicles.'

The French officer laughed. 'You expect me to believe that? What do you take me for? No, you are Germans – fifth columnists.' There was triumph on his face. Tanner groaned to himself. *Hell*, he thought. *That's all we need.*

'Tanner? Tanner!' Barclay again. Tanner turned and saw Captain Barclay with Blackstone, McAllister, Ellis and several others advancing cautiously down the street.

'Tanner!' called Captain Barclay again, as half a dozen French soldiers raised their rifles.

The French lieutenant followed their gaze and, at that moment, Tanner thrust forward with his left forearm, knocking the officer's gun away from his stomach. Then, with his right, he grabbed the pistol. The startled lieutenant had no time to react before Tanner had brought his left arm tight round the Frenchman's throat and dug the pistol into his side.

'Tell your men to drop their weapons,' hissed Tanner, fractionally lessening his grip around the man's throat to enable him to speak. 'Now!'

'*Jetez vos armes!*' he gasped. The men did as they were ordered, a mixture of fear and anger in their eyes.

'And tell your men on the other side of the bridge to cease firing.'

Tanner loosened his grip a fraction more, but pressed the barrel of the pistol more firmly into the Frenchman's side.

'I'm sorry, sir, but I swear we are who we say we are,' said Tanner in his ear. 'British soldiers from the First Battalion, the King's Own Yorkshire Rangers, Thirteen Brigade, Fifth Division, British Expeditionary Force. We are trying to reach British Headquarters in Arras and want safe passage across the Escaut.'

'Don't shoot, please,' said the lieutenant.

'I won't,' said Tanner.

'*Monsieur, s'il vous plaît,*' said the older man, looking up at Tanner with an appalled expression, '*votre ami . . .*' He swept his hand downwards and Tanner saw that Peploe had opened his eyes and was clutching the side of his head.

'Tanner, what the devil's going on? What's happened to Peploe?' said Captain Barclay, now hurrying up to them, anger and indignation etched across his face.

'Our allies opened fire on us, sir,' said Tanner, 'and Lieutenant Peploe was hit in the head.'

'Good God!' Barclay knelt down beside the still prostrate lieutenant.

'I reckon he'll be all right, sir,' added Tanner. 'This French officer thinks we're German fifth columnists. He was going to shoot, so I'm afraid I was forced to disarm him and order the others to lower their weapons.'

'Fifth columnists!' snorted Barclay. 'What absolute rot!' He stood up again and faced the French lieutenant. 'Now look here,' he said, 'we're who we say we are. British soldiers. Please take us to your superior officer.' He pointed down to Peploe. 'This man needs attention.'

'Sir,' said Tanner, loosening his grip and allowing the Frenchman to stumble free, 'perhaps show him some documents.'

His face reddening, Barclay said, 'Very well.' From the breast pocket of his battle-blouse, he produced his identity card, dog-tags and a letter from his wife. 'Here. Will this convince you?' He pointed to the address in Pateley Bridge. 'There. Do you think I'd have all this lot if I was a bloody Hun spy?'

The French *sous-lieutenant* peered at the letter, then at the pale pink military identity card with its different types of ink, its Leeds stamp and photograph. Tanner then showed him his own AB64 paybook, careful not to reveal the German packet of cigarettes as he delved in his pocket.

The Frenchman's face now flushed. 'Er, sir, *pardon*. It seems I was mistaken.' Triumph had been replaced by contrition. 'I am very sorry, but we have been warned repeatedly to keep a watch for fifth columnists and we have seen no other British troops.' He now stood up straight and saluted. 'Sous-Lieutenant Marais, Tenth Pioneer Company of the Fourth Infantry Regiment, Fifteenth Division, Four Army Corps.' He turned briskly and snapped some orders to the men behind, who, with an eye on Tanner, gingerly picked up their rifles, then bent over Peploe and lifted him carefully.

'What happened?' mumbled Peploe. Then his eyes opened and he saw the French soldiers. 'Who are you?'

'Don't worry, sir,' said Tanner. 'You took a blow to the head but you'll be fine.'

'Follow me,' said Marais. Then he turned to Tanner and held out his hand. 'My pistol, Sergeant, if I may.'

Tanner handed it to him, holding his gaze – *I would have killed you* – then turned to the old man, now standing beside the road watching the troops head over the river. '*Merci, Monsieur*,' he said, offering his hand. The old man took it, then heaved a big sigh.

'J'ai fait partie de la dernière guerre. A Verdun. C'était terrible. La guerre est monstrueuse.' He shook his head and turned sadly away.

Marais's company commander, Capitaine Marmier, an apparently less impetuous man, brushed aside concerns about fifth columnists, apologized profusely and insisted Marais drive Peploe to the 4th Infantry Regiment field dressing station. In the meantime, he urged Captain Barclay to bring the vehicles and the rest of D Company across the bridge and to wait at his command post, a roadside house a short distance from the river on the western side.

Tanner left Barclay and Blackstone with him, then walked back to fetch the vehicles. Ten minutes later, having fended off numerous questions about what had happened, he brought the Krupp to a standstill outside the French company headquarters, jumped down from the cab, crossed the road and went into the house.

'Ah, Tanner,' said Barclay, as he was led into Marmier's makeshift office. He was sitting in an old high-backed wooden chair across the desk from Capitaine Marmier. Both men were smoking cigars, with small cups of coffee in front of them. 'Our hosts are kindly going to feed us. As soon as Peploe's back, we'll be on our way.'

Tanner nodded. *'Merci, Capitaine.'*

'You're very welcome, Sergeant.' Tanner guessed he was, like Barclay, about thirty. He had a lean, clean-shaven face, with dark skin and intelligent eyes, although he had yet to put on his jacket; instead he sat in his breeches, shirt and braces – *It is only five o'clock, though.*

'We've been swapping intelligence,' said Barclay, his mood clearly much improved. 'Capitaine Marmier is most interested to learn there are SS units in the area. Apparently there is still fighting to the south, but Four Corps have been told that the Escaut is the front line now in this area. French Five Corps holds the line to Douai and then our chaps are along the river Scarpe to Arras.'

The Scarpe. The name rang a bell in Tanner's mind. Yes, he remembered now. It was there, near Arras, that his father had once fought, back in the last war, with the Wiltshires. Tanner cleared his throat. 'I was wondering, sir, whether they might have some paint – white preferably.'

'Paint, Tanner? What in God's name for?'

'For the trucks, sir. To cover up the German markings on the numberplates and write our own name on the bodywork. We're back behind Allied lines now, sir. We don't want people thinking we're Jerries.'

'Yes, of course,' said Marmier, before Barclay could reply. He called, and a moment later an NCO appeared. Marmier spoke with him, then turned back to Tanner. 'Follow him. He's the company quartermaster. He has some paint.'

When Tanner returned to the trucks armed with a brush and a tin of white paint, a number of French troops were examining them. He noticed several pointing at him as he approached. Ignoring them, he walked over to the Krupp, where he found Hepworth and Verity both fast asleep despite the hubbub around them. *Good.* It was important to sleep whenever possible. Ten minutes here, half an hour there: it could make all the difference.

He painted over the two SS runes on the numberplate beneath the radiator, then daubed 'Yorks Rangers' on the bonnet and, in even larger letters, 'BEF' beneath it. Then he did the same on the wooden side boards before turning his attention to the truck behind.

Squadron Leader Lyell still sat in the Opel's cab. 'Sergeant,' he called, as Tanner painted new markings on the bonnet.

Tanner stopped, then went to the window.

'So we're back behind Allied lines,' said Lyell. 'We've almost made it.'

'A little way to go yet but, yes, hopefully, sir.'

Lyell eyed him thoughtfully. 'Do you know why I chose to become a pilot, Tanner?'

'No, sir.'

'I'll tell you. It was because I wanted to fly, of course, but not just so I could see the world from the sky or even because of the thrill of it – though it is a thrill. It was also because I was damned if I wanted to bother with the spit and polish and crap that comes from being in the other services. I know I have men under my command, but it's not like old Hector and his company of infantrymen. We're a team, all right, but we're individuals too. We pilots live by different laws, different codes of conduct. Not quite so much yes-sir, no-sir, or cap-doffing, if you know what I mean.'

Tanner wondered why he was telling him all this. 'I see, sir,' he said.

Lyell hadn't finished. 'When you shot my tyre out back at Manston, I decided you must be just like all those other bloody hare-brained infantry types – following orders to the letter, with no imagination, no ability to think for yourself.'

'I'm sorry you thought so, sir,' said Tanner.

'Well, I don't any more. You're a rare bird – a bloody competent soldier. My brother-in-law . . .' He shook his head. 'You know, I've always thought he was a bit of a prig, albeit a good-natured one, but he's harmless enough in day-to-day life. Worked quite well for his father – they've a family business in Harrogate, you know – but hopeless as a soldier. Doesn't have a clue.'

'It's new to a lot of the men, sir,' said Tanner. 'There's a big difference between training and doing it for real. It takes time to learn.'

Lyell chuckled. 'Certainly a bit different from the weekend soldiering he was doing before the war. A few drills, a few marches and a few shots on the firing range, plus a two-week camp every summer. And now this.'

'He's got us here in one piece, hasn't he?' said Tanner.

'Now you're being disingenuous, Sergeant. No, I've learned something these past couple of days, which is what I wanted to say to you in this rather long-winded way – that is, I now realize I shouldn't tar you all with the same brush. Some of you do actually think for yourselves – you especially. That I'm not in some Jerry bag is down to you, Sergeant. And if I get safely to Arras, that will also be largely down to you. I've been an ass and, I suspect, a pain in the arse to you all. Frustration, I'm afraid, and exasperation. Shouldn't ever have allowed myself to be knocked out of the sky. Fed up with all the dithering, and angry that I'm not leading my squadron. No excuse, but an explanation – of sorts, at any rate.'

'Don't mention it, sir.'

'And one other thing, Tanner.'

'Sir?'

'We can forget about the car.'

'I already had, sir.'

They were on their way again before eight. They had been delayed for several hours but, if he was honest, Tanner had been glad of the pause. He'd been fed – French Army rations, but a lot better than some of the food he'd eaten in his time – and had even managed to get some sleep, stretching out in the back of the Krupp while they waited for Lieutenant Peploe's return. Moreover, it had given them a chance to reorganize themselves. Captain Barclay, Blackstone and the rest of Company Headquarters had taken command of the Krupp, while the two platoons had been split between the three Opels, with Sykes, Tanner and Lieutenant Peploe up front in the cab of the truck following the Krupp.

Peploe had come back to them in good shape, all things considered: he'd been shot in the head but all he had to show for it were a bad headache, mild grogginess, four stitches and a bandage. 'The French MO reckoned the bullet had lost a lot of velocity by hitting the helmet at the side,' Peploe told Tanner and Sykes, as they drove off towards Douai. 'He thinks it spun round the lining where it eventually ran out of puff and fell out.'

'It didn't fall out, sir. At least, not straight away.' Tanner reached into his pocket and took out the squashed bullet. 'Here you are, sir. A little memento.'

'Well, what do you know? Thank you, Sergeant.'

'You're a lucky man, sir. Maybe you're one of the charmed ones. What do you reckon, Stan?'

'Oh, definitely, sir,' agreed Sykes, winking. 'Some people have it – the Luck – and others don't. Just one of those things.'

'Oh, I'm not so sure about that.' He chuckled. 'But it's certainly a comforting thought.'

Soon after, the lieutenant was asleep, his head resting against the door, snoring lightly.

Tanner took out the German cigarettes, lit two and passed one to Sykes.

'Cheers, Sarge.'

Tanner stared out at the softly rolling Flanders countryside. Away from the road, on a shallow crest, he could see a couple of villages – a knot of houses and a church spire sticking out above the roofs; small, tight communities not so very different, he supposed, from the village where he had grown up. And now the war was cutting a swathe through them and people were leaving their homes in droves. He wondered what the inhabitants of Alvesdon would do if the Germans ever reached Britain. Would they run? He hoped not.

'Sarge?' said Sykes. 'I've been meaning to ask. How did you get those two guards last night? I never heard a sound.'

Tanner smiled. 'It was pretty straightforward, actually,' he said. 'I knew we had surprise on our side. They weren't expecting any-thing and they made it easier for me by splitting up so I could confront each in turn. Forearm tight round the neck to smother the voicebox, then a short sharp stab in the kidney. They were both dead before they knew what was happening. I learned a long time ago that the kidneys are the place to go for if possible.'

'Why's that?'

'Ever been hit there?'

'Yes.'

'And it hurt, right?'

'Like hell.'

'Exactly. Shove a bayonet in one and the pain is so intense the body packs it all in immediately. The brain can't take it and neither can the heart. And it's not particularly messy.'

Sykes nodded. 'I'll remember that, Sarge.' He was quiet for a

moment. 'By the way, did you smell burning near Valenciennes?'
'Yes – why?'

'Seems the population fled just after the balloon went up and
then the French Army moved in. Anyway, they weren't best
behaved and managed to set alight a huge fuel dump that caused a
massive fire in the centre of the town. So we could have gone
through there after all.'

'Bloody Frogs,' muttered Tanner.

The road was soon filled with refugees again, the same trail of
wretched civilians traipsing along, some on foot, others on carts, a
few in vehicles. The road had clearly been busy for some time now.
All along it there was human detritus: bags, suitcases – some flung
open – paper, even books lined the verges. Here and there a shirt
or dress was caught in a bush or on a branch and flapped helplessly
in the breeze. There were cars and other vehicles too, run off the
road and abandoned. Those too exhausted sat or lay on the grass –
mostly the elderly and children, the former gazing outwards with
blank disbelieving expressions, the latter often crying, tears
streaming down grubby cheeks, anxious parents trying vainly to
comfort them.

A few miles short of Douai, a Citroën in front of them, laden too
high with cases and bags, swerved to avoid a mule that had
wandered into the middle of the road. The string holding the load
snapped and everything tumbled down across the road. A flustered
middle-aged man wearing spectacles and a Homburg got out to
collect his cases and put them back.

'Bloody sensible that,' said Sykes. 'Why the hell doesn't he pull
off the road and sort himself out there?'

Captain Barclay was now standing up in the Krupp yelling at the
hapless man. 'Come on, Stan, let's give the poor sod a hand,' said
Tanner.

They jumped down from the cab, collected the remaining cases,
and put them on the verge.

'*Merci, messieurs*,' said the man, pushing his spectacles back up
his nose.

Tanner pointed to his car and motioned to him to move it.

'*Ah, oui, oui*,' said the man, tapping his head apologetically, and got in.

The aircraft was upon them almost before anyone had a chance to react – a faint whirr and then a deep-throated roar as it sped towards them.

'Get down!' yelled Tanner, diving to the ground. For a split second he thought the aircraft might pass without firing. But as it thundered overhead, no more than a hundred feet above them, the Messerschmitt's machine-guns opened up, two lines of bullets scything along the road ahead, the first just inches from him. A splinter of stone clattered against his helmet and nicked the edge of his ear. Then the fighter flew on, climbing slightly, and disappeared over a line of trees.

'So that's a 109,' said Sykes, as he and Tanner dusted themselves down.

'You two all right?' asked Captain Barclay, fifteen yards behind them in the Krupp.

'Fine, sir,' said Tanner, dabbing at the blood from his ear. 'Bloody close, though, eh, Stan?'

'Reckon he was aiming for our lot, don't you?'

Tanner shrugged. 'Maybe – and just overflew slightly.'

A curious smell now hung heavy in the air: a cloying stench of oil, petrol, dirt and blood. Ahead they heard wailing. The mule that had caused the hold-up in the first place lay sprawled across the road, its owner bent over it sobbing. Further on there were more dead, and a boy was screaming, the sound jarring Tanner's head. 'Jesus,' he muttered.

Then Sykes saw the Citroën. 'Bloody hell,' he said. 'Look, Sarge. The bastard.'

Following his gaze, Tanner saw a line of bullet holes across the car. The driver was slumped, lifeless, across the steering-wheel. Blood ran down the bonnet in front of him.

Poor sod. Tanner was vaguely aware of Blackstone barking orders to the men.

The men of D Company did what they could. They handed out field dressings to the wounded and put the worst injured into the backs of the trucks to take them to hospital in Douai. The Krupp shunted the car, mule and cart off the road, with the stray cases and other belongings.

Before the German pilot's attack the men's mood had been good, buoyed by food and rest, and by the knowledge that they were nearing British forces. Now, however, they cleared away debris, wreckage and broken bodies sombrely, speaking little. It was the boy that got to Tanner most. Repelled by his screams yet compelled to go to him, Tanner had found him – no more than ten years old, he guessed – with his leg nearly severed. His parents were crouched beside him, almost demented with grief and by their inability to help him.

'Smiler!' shouted Tanner, as the platoon medic tended an elderly lady further back. 'I need you here now!'

Smailes hurried over and put his hand to his mouth as he saw the boy. 'He – he's not going to make it, Sarge,' he stuttered. 'He's lost too much blood already.' A dark stain covered the grass beneath him.

'Just do something,' snapped Tanner. 'You've got morphine, haven't you?'

Smailes nodded.

Wide frightened eyes stared up at the two soldiers. Smailes drew the morphine, flicked the end of the needle, then stuck it into the boy's arm. A few moments later, the child's eyes flickered and finally closed.

Tanner walked back towards the truck, the convulsive sobbing of the boy's parents ringing in his ears.

'Come on, Tanner, chop, chop!' said Captain Barclay, as he walked past the Krupp. 'The road's clear. We need to get a move on.'

'Yes, sir,' he replied, making no effort to hurry.

'Come on, Sergeant,' called Blackstone. 'Didn't you hear the captain? Run!'

To hell with him. Tanner ignored him.

'Tanner!' called Blackstone.

He looked up and saw that Lieutenant Peploe, Sykes and the men behind were watching him and this sudden altercation with Blackstone. *Damn!* He turned slowly to face Captain Barclay and the CSM.

'Oh, for God's sake,' muttered Lyell from the front of Barclay's vehicle, 'you're acting like bloody kids.'

'Sergeant Tanner, did you not hear what the captain said?'

Tanner sighed. 'Yes, Sergeant-Major.'

'And you thought you'd ignore what Captain Barclay ordered you to do?'

Tanner said nothing. He knew he was trapped. No matter what he said, Blackstone would use it to humiliate him further.

'What was that? I didn't quite hear it, Sergeant,' said Blackstone.

'I apologize, sir,' he said to Captain Barclay.

'No respect, Tanner, that's your problem,' said Barclay. 'Think you can do it all on your own. Now apologize to the CSM here, and then I want you to *run* to your truck. We're wasting valuable time.'

Tanner clenched and unclenched his fists, swallowed, then turned his face up to Blackstone and forced himself to say, 'Sorry, Sergeant-Major.'

'Get back to your truck, Sergeant,' Blackstone said, in a voice loud enough for all those in the truck behind to hear, 'at the double!'

'I'm sorry about that,' said Peploe, as Tanner got back into the cab. 'That was completely unnecessary.'

'They're just flexing their muscles, Sarge,' added Sykes.

Tanner took out a German cigarette and lit it. 'Let's just get to Arras,' he said.

At the BEF command post at Wahagnies, twenty miles north-east of Arras, General Lord Gort left his spartan office, went down the stairs and into the large drawing room, now busy with numerous staff officers, liaison officers and clerks working from makeshift trestle-table desks. The clatter of typewriters and the collective hubbub of different conversations filled the room. Dust particles hung faintly in the air, illuminated in the sunlight that shone through the tall french windows; cleaning the building after requisitioning it from the owners had not been a high priority and, in any case, Gort's large command post staff had brought their own dust and dirt with them.

Careful to make sure he looked as fit and energetic as ever, he strode purposefully towards one of his aides-de-camp and said, 'Get someone to bring a bite of lunch out to me in the garden, will you?'

'Right away, sir,' the ADC replied, getting to his feet.

'Good man.' Gort nodded to the others, said, 'Carry on, carry on,' then walked briskly to the glass doors, stepped out onto the terrace and trotted across the lawn to the bottom of the garden where, beneath a large cedar and out of sight of the house, there stood a wooden bench. Sitting down, he rubbed his hands over his face and allowed himself a wide yawn. For a moment, he gazed at the small pond in front of him. At its centre stood a stone cherub, discoloured with age, whose mouth emitted a trickle of water. In the murky pond, goldfish showed intermittent flashes of golden-orange. Somewhere near by a wood pigeon cooed soothingly.

Lord Gort sighed and yawned again, then briefly closed his eyes. Damn it, he was exhausted. He reckoned he'd had about two hours' sleep last night, and not much more the night before. But that was only the half of it: since 10 May, from the moment he had been awake to the moment he had gone to bed, he had been on the go constantly, trying to organize his forces, attempting to get some sense from Gamelin, Georges, Billotte and the rest of the French high command, sending missives and orders, meeting with commanders and liaison officers, seeing the troops, and trying to keep London informed of increasingly confused events.

A bee hummed lazily in front of him and he followed its path enviously. It had been a devil of a morning. Up at five with the news that the chief of the Imperial General Staff himself, General

Ironside, was about to visit. At six o'clock on the nose, Tiny Ironside had walked in, blustering as usual, to hand-deliver a personal message from the war cabinet. At the conference soon after he had pointed to the map hanging in Gort's office and announced that the entire BEF should withdraw south-west to Amiens, closer to their lines of supply. 'We've all agreed this plan,' he had announced. 'Churchill and the cabinet were unanimous.'

Gort had patiently pointed out that it was not the war cabinet who were commanding the BEF and explained that to leave their positions on the Escaut *en masse* and move the best part of a hundred miles directly across the flanks of the German panzers' advance was not merely impossible but plain suicide. Of course, the CIGS had quickly come round to his point of view, but this, Gort felt, should have been perfectly clear to him back in London. What Gort had offered to do, however – and he'd been thinking about it since his meeting with Billotte the previous night – was use his two reserve divisions, the 5th and 50th, for a counter-attack south of Arras and the river Scarpe to the east of the town. If the French mounted a similar attack from the south, Gort had suggested to the CIGS, it might be possible to close the gap that had been punched by the German panzer divisions between the Allied armies north of Arras and the Scarpe, and those south of the river Somme.

It was a positive plan at least – one that promised aggressive action rather than passive defence, and Ironside had seized it wholeheartedly, just as Gort had known he would. The CIGS had immediately headed straight off to see Billotte and Blanchard, taking Pownall with him, determined to put some resolve into the French commanders and persuade them to join in Gort's proposed attack.

Gort took off his cap with its red band and laid it on the bench beside him, ran his hand over his largely bald head, then closed his eyes, letting the May sunshine warm his face. He wondered how Ironside and Pownall were getting on. It was essential that the French should play ball but his conversation with Billotte the previous evening had left a deeply unfavourable impression. Perhaps they could yet turn it around but all morning he had been unable to banish the niggling suspicion that the French had shot their bolt completely. Once again, he found his thoughts returning to what now seemed a horrible inevitability: evacuation of as much of the BEF as possible.

A cough brought him from his thoughts and he opened his eyes to see a young RASC lance-corporal holding a metal tray on which there was a bottle of beer and a plate of bread, cheese and chocolate. 'Your lunch, sir.'

'Thank you,' Gort replied. He indicated the bench. 'Just put it down there, will you?'

The orderly left him and Gort continued to sit where he was, drinking his beer and eating the cheese and bread. This end of the garden was a peaceful haven: warm, softly scented and alive with the calming sounds of early summer. Nonetheless, the soothing ambience could do nothing to relieve the gloom that swirled in the British commander-in-chief's head – a gloom that would only deepen as the afternoon wore on.

14

Around the time that General Lord Gort was eating his lunch, D Company, 1st Battalion, the King's Own Yorkshire Rangers, finally reached BEF Headquarters. It was not, as Captain Barclay had assumed, in Arras itself, but centred around a château in the small village of Habarcq, some seven miles to the west.

They had learned as much on entering the city where, in the town hall, they had found the headquarters of the town's garrison. A Welsh Guardsman had redirected them, having confessed he had no idea where 13th Brigade were, or 5th Division, and least of all the 1st Battalion, the Yorkshire Rangers. Captain Barclay had cursed irritably, but Lieutenant Peploe, who had woken as the truck rumbled over the broad cobbles of the Grande Place, had been glad of the brief detour into the town. Despite a splitting headache and light-headedness, he had been sufficiently *compos mentis* to wonder at the reconstructed beauty of an ancient town that he had seen before only in a selection of picture postcards taken soon after the last war – which his mother had brought back after a visit to find his uncle George's grave. He remembered them well: the squares of broken buildings, the piles of rubble and, not least, the skeletal town hall and its damaged belfry. Now, however, it was as though the postcards had depicted a lie. Arras had emerged, phoenix-like, from the wreckage, as splendid and opulent as it must have been a hundred or more years before.

Peploe followed Captain Barclay and Lieutenant Bourne-Arton unsteadily through some impressively ornate iron gates to the side of the château, then along a gravel pathway to the main entrance of the white-stone building. The place seemed a hive of activity. Doors opened and closed, staff officers hurrying to and fro with an air of grave intent. Phones rang, typewriters clacked, orders were barked. The three men were told to wait in the hall and did so in silence, watching the comings and goings until, after about a quarter of an hour, Captain Barclay stood up and began to pace.

'Now look here,' he said eventually, accosting a pale subaltern, 'how much longer are we going to have to wait? We've got an injured pilot who needs proper medical care and we need to know where we can find the rest of our battalion. Damn it, surely someone here can point us in the right direction.'

'What unit are you, sir?' asked the subaltern.

Barclay sighed. 'D Company, First Battalion, King's Own Yorkshire Rangers.'

'All right,' said the subaltern. 'I'll send an MO.'

'And what about the rest of First Battalion?' said Barclay, his mounting frustration showing in his tone.

'Just a moment, sir,' said the subaltern, and disappeared.

'For God's sake,' muttered Barclay.

It was a further twenty minutes before the medical officer arrived, apologizing for keeping them waiting.

'Take the MO to Lyell, will you, Lieutenant?' said Barclay, to Bourne-Arton.

'Right away, sir.' Bourne-Arton led the doctor outside to the trucks.

'Let's hope that's the last we've seen of him,' muttered Barclay.

'Your brother-in-law, you mean, sir?' said Peploe.

'Yes. Bloody pain in the arse. Wish I'd left him in that damned field. The CSM was right.'

'You couldn't have left him there, sir.'

Barclay tapped a foot on the stone floor. 'Hm. Did it for my sister, not for him. Put men's lives at risk. Held everything up.' He began to knead his hands together. 'I put my family before the needs of the men and what thanks did I get? None.'

'I think you're being a bit hard on yourself, sir,' said Peploe. 'After all, we've made it here in one piece.'

Barclay said nothing, instead pacing the hall, his boots clicking on the bare stone floor. Peploe wished he would stop. His head throbbed and pulses of pain coursed down his neck. What he needed was quiet, not the frenetic pacings of his OC.

At the point when he thought he could bear it no longer, a tall, slim man in his late thirties, with an immaculately groomed appearance, trotted down the main staircase and said, 'Sorry to keep you, gentlemen.' He held out a hand to Barclay. 'Lieutenant-Colonel Rainsby. Do follow me.'

He led them back up the stairs, along a short corridor and into a room with a large window. Peploe peered out and saw their German trucks parked beneath the horse-chestnuts on the far side of the road. The men were chatting and smoking, others making the most of the pause to snatch some sleep. Beyond, the avenue of trees continued, sloping down through undulating lush pasture.

Barclay cleared his throat and Peploe turned to the half-colonel standing in front of them behind a makeshift desk.

Waving them towards two mismatching chairs, Rainsby offered cigarettes, then sat down behind his desk. 'Sorry to keep you.' He smiled genially. 'As you can see, it's pretty busy here – Jerry's probing not far to the south and it may be that we have to ship out at any moment.'

'Surely not, sir,' said Barclay, startled.

Rainsby steepled his fingers. 'Hopefully not. One of the problems is that the picture is so confused. But Cambrai has fallen and the enemy has now punched a wedge of about twenty-five miles between us here in the north and the French forces to the south.'

'Surely some kind of pincer movement is what's needed,' put in Peploe. 'A joint counter-attack from north and south.'

Rainsby smiled. 'Exactly, and that's precisely what we're hoping to do. This place is still home to GHQ, but also Frankforce, created by the C-in-C as of this morning under Major-General Franklyn – the best part of two divisions, plus tanks from First RTR and various other units. I'm GSO3 Operations – planning tomorrow's little show.' He paused. 'We've been admiring your haul of German trucks.'

'We're trying to find the rest of our battalion, sir,' said Barclay. 'We lost them as we pulled back from the Brussels–Charleroi canal. We had a bit of a ding-dong with the enemy, which held up our retreat rather. By the time we'd forced them back, the rest of the battalion had already moved out.'

Lieutenant Peploe smiled to himself.

Rainsby raised a hand – *say no more* – and unfolded a map. 'Easily done,' he said, 'and you're hardly the only ones to have become separated from their units.' He put down the map and picked up another sheet of paper. 'Yorkshire Rangers, Yorkshire Rangers,' he mumbled, running his hand down the page. 'Yes, here we are. Thirteenth Brigade have been ordered to the Scarpe. Not so very far from here, actually. They're on their way there now. They're to hold the line at Vitry-en-Artois.'

'That's excellent news, sir, thank you,' said Barclay, pushing back his chair.

Rainsby chuckled. 'Not so fast, Barclay. I'm afraid you're not going to rejoin them just yet.'

'Whyever not, sir?'

'Because tomorrow we'll be launching a counter-attack west and south of Arras. Enemy panzers are now pressing to the south. Our task is to push them back. Fifth Div are going to stay put on the Scarpe, but the main attack will come from Fiftieth Div, plus tanks of First RTR.'

'Then surely we should head to Vitry-on-whatever-it-was, sir.'

'The thing is, Barclay, the job on the Scarpe is mostly static, but you chaps have turned up with your four very decent trucks. We could, of course, simply take them from you, but I rather think it would be better to attach you to the 151st Brigade for this operation. We want our infantry to be able to keep up with the tanks, you see.'

'And what infantry will there be, sir?'

'Two attacking battalions – Eighth and Sixth DLI.'

'The Durham Light Infantry, sir?' Barclay looked appalled.

'Yes. A damn good regiment.' Rainsby smiled. 'Look, it's the most marvellous opportunity for you to show us what you chaps can do. A successful counter-attack like this will do wonders for the name of the regiment. And for you, too, Captain.'

Peploe smiled to himself again. Rainsby had certainly got the measure of Barclay.

'Very well, sir,' said Barclay, his back stiffening. 'If those are our orders, then of course we'll carry them out to the best of our abilities.'

'Good man,' said Rainsby, rising from his seat. 'Here are your instructions.' He handed over a sheet of paper. 'Make your way to Vimy – a smallish village a few miles north-east of here. General Franklyn's setting up his command post there. In fact, I'll be heading there myself shortly. You should ask for the brigade-major. Fellow called Clive. Any questions?'

'We'll rejoin the battalion after this battle?'

'Absolutely.'

Rainsby took them back to the hall, shook their hands and wished them luck, then skipped up the stairs again.

So, thought Peploe, as they headed to the waiting men and trucks, *we go into action tomorrow.* So far he had not felt particularly frightened, but that was because the two small pieces of action he had taken part in had happened suddenly; he hadn't had time to think about what was happening. Now, however, there was most of the afternoon and the night to wait – and this time it would be a proper attack, not a light skirmish or brief exchange of fire. His stomach churned and his throat felt tight.

Tanner and Sykes were asleep when Peploe stepped up into the cab of the Opel, but both men woke instantly.

'How's the head, sir?' asked Sykes.

'Not too bad, thank you, Corporal.' He cleared his throat. 'We've been temporarily assigned to join the Eighth DLI.'

Tanner raised an eyebrow.

Peploe found himself sighing heavily. 'We're going to be part of a major counter-attack tomorrow.'

Tanner nodded. 'Good. About time. Perhaps I'll be able to get my hands on another Jerry sub-machine-gun.' He grinned at Sykes.

A few minutes later they rumbled off. Peploe stared out at the rolling countryside, the fields green with young corn. Where was his uncle buried? Somewhere near Arras – the scene of such bitter fighting more than twenty years before. They drove past a cemetery, not British but French, row upon row of white crosses stretching away from the road. Peploe swallowed, then glanced at Tanner, who was smoking a cigarette and gazing at the thousands of graves too. What he was thinking, Peploe couldn't tell. Tanner was a difficult man to read. Was he scared? He had barely batted an eyelid at the news that they would soon be going into battle. If any-thing, he seemed to relish the chance – Sykes too. *Extraordinary.* He was glad that the sergeant would be alongside him tomorrow. Damned glad.

At four twenty p.m. on 20 May, General Lord Gort fixed his pale eyes on General Billotte's liaison officer from Army Group 1 in Lens, Capitaine Melchior de Voguë. Outside, the afternoon had grown grey, a gathering blanket of cloud now blocking out the sun and all but a few faint patches of summery blue so that, despite the tall windows, the room was quite dark. A cool breeze ruffled some of the papers on Gort's desk.

'Capitaine,' said Gort, 'thank you for coming.' He picked up a sheet of paper and waved it at de Voguë. 'Do you know what this is?'

'No, my lord,' replied de Voguë.

'It's a sitrep informing me that a handful of German advance tanks and infantry have taken Cambrai without a fight. Tell me it's not true.'

De Voguë shifted his feet uneasily. 'I am afraid it is, my lord.'

Gort sighed. 'But how can that be? All the garrison had to do was stand firm and they would have driven off the enemy.'

'It was the dust, my lord.'

'Dust?' Gort spluttered.

'Er, yes, my lord,' said de Voguë. 'The enemy advanced on a broad front causing a huge cloud of dust. The garrison there thought the attackers were part of a far larger force than was reality.'

Gort could hardly believe what he had heard. 'And is the French Army now refusing to fight?' he asked.

'No, my lord, of course not.'

'Capitaine de Voguë,' said Gort, 'when I tell British soldiers to attack, they attack. So why haven't French forces counter-attacked and retaken Cambrai?'

De Voguë cleared his throat, then said quietly, 'There has been no order to counter-attack.'

'Good God, man, why the devil not?' said Gort, bringing his hand down hard on the table. His voice rose. 'In the last war, the French Army was proud and fearless. Any one of the commanders would have taken it upon themselves to throw out a weak advance guard like the one that took Cambrai yesterday. When is the French Army of old going to stand up and fight? When? Because if they don't start doing so, Capitaine, the Germans will get to Abbeville and Calais and then I will have no choice but to fall back on Dunkirk and sail my men back to England. I'm not prepared to lose my forces trying to defend a country that's already given up. Do I make myself clear?'

'Yes, my lord.'

'Now, go back to General Billotte and tell him we need Blanchard's First Army to attack simultaneously tomorrow. Much as it pains me to say this, I think it's probably our last chance.'

When de Voguë had gone, he picked up his telephone and had

himself connected to Captain Reid, his liaison officer at Blanchard's First Army Headquarters. He drummed his fingers impatiently.

'Hello, sir,' said a voice eventually, the line crackling with static.

'Reid?' said Gort. 'I want you to take down a message.'

'Of course, sir.'

'Ready? It runs as follows: "If this attack – i.e. the counter-attack tomorrow – is unsuccessful, we cannot remain longer in a position with our flank turned and German penetration proceeding towards the coast. Stop." Have you got that?'

'Yes, sir,' said Reid.

'Good. Relay it to Blanchard, and make sure that Billotte and Weygand see it too.'

'Yes, sir.'

Gort hung up the receiver and breathed out heavily. Ironside and Pownall had gone to stiffen the French commanders' resolve in person; he had spoken more than plainly to de Voguë; now he had sent a further message that he hoped would jolt them into action. He could do no more. But if the French failed them tomorrow, he would have to start preparing the evacuation. He had told de Voguë it was their last chance – and that had been nothing less than the truth.

Sturmbannführer Otto Timpke had woken at first light to find his command post still in disarray. The tower had completely collapsed, as had half of the barns at either side, and there were no fewer than twenty-six casualties. Yet although his command car had been badly damaged by falling masonry, three of the motorcycles and the two armoured cars inside the yard were largely unscathed and, it seemed, in running order. Furthermore, in the cool light of dawn, a route was quickly established through a gate at the back of the yard, leading out onto a pasture and around the walled confines of the farmstead to the road. Leaving the dead and wounded at the farm, with a small burial detail, he had then marched the remainder into the village where they had rendezvoused with the rest of

1 Company and the panzer squadron, in the square by the church, just after five.

Scouting the area in the fresh first hours of daylight, with Timpke in the radio scout car, they had found a largely deserted stretch of countryside. Timpke's mood had begun to improve. With his head clear of the turret and the breeze in his face, he had enjoyed the chance of activity; he felt like a warrior of old, looking down from his high position, a hunter sniffing out the enemy.

They had spotted a stranded unit of French colonial troops in the small town of Solesmes. Calling in 2 and 3 Companies, they had stealthily approached like lions stalking their prey. With the bridge and routes from the town blocked, they had rushed upon the Frenchmen in the square and captured them with barely a shot fired. It had been almost ridiculously easy, as though the French had been waiting to be taken. More than seventy Moroccans had been captured – but a far more important booty had been the three Citroën troop trucks.

Late in the morning, a signal had come through informing him that the whole division was now moving west, while his own orders had been to push on through Cambrai, cross the Escaut and, in direct support of Major-General Rommel's 7th Panzer Division, to probe west towards St Pol, some thirty-five kilometres west of Arras. Shattered vehicles had littered the countryside near Cambrai – some civilian, others military. The roads had been busy, too, with both refugees and retreating French troops. Timpke had driven on – several motorcycles in front, another two armoured cars and three half-tracks behind – past one long column of French and North African soldiers, as many as eighty strong. What a pathetic bunch of men they had been: exhausted and demoralized, with sagging shoulders and leaden feet. Timpke had been disgusted. They were a disgrace to their country. Not one man had so much as aimed his rifle at them as they had rolled past.

Progress had been swift. By early afternoon they had been south-west of Arras and had passed some of 7th Panzer's lead units. It had been a proud moment for Timpke. At last his men – men of the SS-Totenkopf – were in the van of the German advance. Not long after, as they pushed north towards Aubigny, they saw, ahead, a large formation of French forces in retreat. The road to Abbeville was dense with horse-drawn and motorized columns heading west. Watching the procession, Timpke's contempt grew. The lead motorcycle now turned and slowly rolled up to the radio car.

'How are we going to get across, boss?' asked Untersturmführer Ganz.

'We push straight through them,' Timpke replied. 'Let's get the panzers to help. Two Group is only a few kilometres away. They can bulldoze their way through and the rest of us will follow.'

Ganz grinned. 'Good idea, Herr Sturmbannführer.'

The four fast-moving Czech-built Panzer 38s of II Armoured Pursuit Group were quick to join them and, rattling and squeaking, made their way noisily to the front of Timpke's leading reconnaissance column. Advancing in line abreast, two on the road, and two on the grassy verge at either side, in full view of the trudging French forces ahead, they opened fire with their twin MG37 machine-guns and 37mm cannon, raking the French column with bullets and shells. The sound of the firing ripped through the air. Startled soldiers yelled, horses whinnied; a truck ploughed off the road and caught fire; a group of frightened horses bolted across a field near Timpke's relentlessly advancing panzers. A few men fired shots towards them, but the bullets pinged off the tanks' armour harmlessly.

Calmly, steadfastly, the tanks reached the road, and then, tracks clanking, they turned to face the mangled ends of the severed French column, crushing several carts and fallen Frenchmen as they did so. Watching this scene of carnage with satisfaction, Timpke then gave the order for the rest of his column to follow. There was barely any sign of resistance from the French – perhaps they were too stunned and devastated by what was happening to them to respond – and so, calmly, the SS men rumbled on over the debris. Timpke saw blood spreading across the road, and the mashed remains of what, a few minutes before, had been a horse and living soldiers. Stupefied, disbelieving faces stared up at him amid the cries and wails of the dying and wounded. Then a Frenchman cursed and raised a rifle, aiming towards him. The man's defiant shout had acted as a warning, though, and Timpke quickly drew out his Luger, aimed, then squeezed the trigger. A shot of no more than ten metres, and even though the scout car had been moving, the single bullet hit the man square in the forehead and he collapsed, bulging eyes glaring back angrily at his killer. Timpke felt a wave of renewed exhilaration sweep over him.

As they neared Aubigny, they drew some enemy fire – a few machine-guns chattered as they crested a ridge overlooking the shallow valley, but it was wildly inaccurate. By the time shells were being fired towards them, Timpke had withdrawn his men to a safe distance; his instructions were to reconnoitre only. *Enemy north of Scarpe, but in disarray and retreating to south of Aubigny*, he signalled back to Division.

Having sent the message from his radio car, he was about to push west towards St Pol when another signal arrived, recalling his entire reconnaissance battalion back to the southern Arras area, where they were to screen the roads and villages south of the city. At the same time, the rest of the Totenkopf would be moving up from Cambrai that evening. More refugees and troop stragglers flooded the roads, and although at times they dogged their progress, the open countryside allowed them, for the most part, a long view ahead, enabling them to avoid the more congested roads. Once again progress had been rapid.

'Boss,' called Schultz, Timpke's radio operator, as they reached the rail stop at Beaumetz, twelve kilometres south-west of Arras, 'another signal for you.'

Timpke lowered himself from his standing position in the turret to the hot belly of the scout car. 'What is it?' Immediately sweat was running down his neck; even with the vents open, it was warm and clammy down there and the air smelled strongly of oil, metal and body odour.

'It's from Obersturmbannführer Geisler, sir,' said Schultz, passing him a hastily scrawled note.

Timpke snatched it and stood up, the evening breeze refreshingly cool on his face. *Rec. Bn. to remain screening south of Arras. Stubaf Timpke to report to 7 Pz Div CP Vis-en-Artois 1900 hrs. O4 Geisler.*

Timpke glanced at his watch. Nearly 1810 – less than an hour to make his way through too many villages and along too many winding country roads to reach Rommel's command post almost halfway along the Arras–Cambrai road. But it had to be done. Leaving Kemmetmüler in charge, he took his scout car and two machine-gun-carrying motorcycle outriders, and set off, speeding along the country lanes of Artois through seemingly deserted villages – Rivière, Ficheux and Mercatel. Only when they reached Neuville-Vitesse, where they found the centre of the village clogged with refugees, was their progress slowed.

The irony of the village's name was not lost on Timpke, but he failed to find any humour in it. 'Get out of the way!' he shouted. '*Vite vite!*' Frightened and angry people scuttled clear of the motorcycles as the riders gunned the throttles. As the vehicles inched forward through the village, their path began to clear, but up ahead, as the road narrowed past the church, a rickety cart, piled high with belongings, blocked the route.

Timpke yelled at the occupant. The old man, wearing a battered felt hat, shrugged – *I'm going as fast as I can*. Again Timpke ordered him to hurry, but the old man just shook his head.

'Not good enough,' Timpke told him. 'I haven't time for this. Sturmmann Reigel,' he called, to the lance-corporal manning the machine-gun in the sidecar of the motorcycle in front of the scout car, 'shoot the man and his horse.'

Reigel drew back the bolt on his MG34, then opened fire with a three-second burst. Around fifty bullets, at a velocity of 755 metres per second, sliced across the horse and cart, then raked the man. Neither beast nor man knew a thing about what was happening to them; in the first second of fire both were dead, the man almost cut in half by the power of the bullets. There was a dull thud as the horse collapsed onto the road, followed by a loud crash as the movement caused the cart to yaw, a wheel to buckle and break and the entire wagon to tumble over.

While the onlookers were stunned into horrified silence, Timpke ordered Reigel and his rider to grab the thick tow-rope wound around the front of the scout car and loop it onto the cart. That done, the vehicle reversed, the rope grew taut and then, with a jarring, scraping sound, the horse and cart were dragged clear of the road to the side of the square, the corpse of the man rolled and pummelled among the bloody remains.

'Good,' said Timpke. 'Let's move.' He lowered himself back into the scout car and studied his map, away from the breeze.

'Why did we open fire, boss?' asked Schultz. 'I didn't see. Trouble with the locals?'

'A foolish old man was in our way and wouldn't move,' replied Timpke. He wiped his brow and neck with a handkerchief, and took off his field cap. 'He was nothing – a nobody. What are the lives of one old man and an ageing horse, Schultz? We are at war, and the sooner it's over, the sooner our own men will stop being killed. If shooting an ancient Frenchman saves the life of a young German, I'll do it.'

They reached the long, straight road to Cambrai, found it largely clear of traffic, and arrived in Vitry with time to spare. At a fork in the road a number of vehicles were parked. There was a large café-bar, outside which stood a half-track and an eight-wheel armoured car. More half-tracks – most towing artillery pieces – armoured cars, trucks and motorcycles lined both sides of the road through the village. Timpke paused in his scout car, then spotted Brigadeführer Eicke's Adler, with its distinctive SS numberplate.

He clambered out and strode towards the bar. The end of the building was painted with a giant advertisement for Stella Artois beer and Timpke realized how thirsty he was. Opposite, he noticed, at the fork in the road, stood a memorial to the dead of the last war, crested by a statue of a dying soldier clutching a French flag. He was gazing at it when he heard his name called and turned. Standartenführer von Montigny, the division chief-of-staff and Ia, was standing at the entrance to the bar.

'Good evening, Herr Standartenführer,' said Timpke, raising his arm in salute. Von Montigny stepped towards him and they shook hands. 'We've seen a few more dying *poilus* today,' he went on, nodding towards the memorial. 'It seems the French are on the run.'

Von Montigny smiled. 'You've done well today, Otto. Papa Eicke's pleased.'

Good, thought Timpke. *They don't know about the loss of the trucks at Hainin.*

'But tomorrow we fight the British,' said von Montigny, 'and they might be a tougher nut to crack.'

As they passed the half-track, Timpke peered into the open back where several men were tapping away at encoding machines, wearing headphones. Leaning over the signals men, however, stood a man wearing the red-striped breeches, plaited triple cord shoulder straps, and red and gold collar tabs of a major-general. As he looked up, Timpke saw that an award hung close to his collar: the blue and gold Maltese cross of the Pour le Mérite – the 'Blue Max', Germany's highest award for valour in the last war. He had a handsome face – a square, resolute jaw, full lips and grey eyes that seemed both determined and intelligent. Timpke knew immediately who he was.

'Von Montigny,' said the general, his lips breaking into a smile. 'I'll be inside in a few moments.' His eyes turned to Timpke, who saluted. Major-General Rommel nodded in acknowledgement.

Inside the bar there were only a few staff officers, their faces grimy with dust and oil. Friedling and Goetze, commanders of the Totenkopf Regiments 2 and 3, were drinking beer with Brigadeführer Eicke. They greeted Timpke warmly and put a bottle into his hand. Cigarette smoke swirled about the room, mixing with the smell of beer and sweat. Regiment 1, it seemed, had had a busy day, and although the division had suffered its first combat losses, many more Frenchmen had been killed and captured. Eicke was pleased.

Soon after, Rommel swept in and asked the officers to gather round an old table on which he spread a map of Arras and the surrounding countryside. Taking off his cap, he followed a few imaginary lines with his finger.

'My plan, gentlemen, is now to thrust northwards, towards Lille. The bulk of both our divisions have caught up at long last, we have received new supplies of fuel and ammunition and we can afford to launch this next thrust with far more men than we have done so far.' There were a few amused glances. 'Tomorrow Seventh Panzer, led by Oberst Rothenburg's Twenty-fifth Panzer Regiment, will push west of Arras and try to capture the bridges over the river Scarpe at Acq – here.' He pointed to the village, some ten kilometres north-west of Arras. 'Two rifle regiments, the Sixth and Seventh, will follow, while the Totenkopf will thrust on our left flank and take the bridges at Aubigny.' He turned to Timpke. 'I understand you reached Aubigny this afternoon, Major?'

Ignoring Rommel's use of *Wehrmacht* rank rather than *Waffen-SS*, Timpke cleared his throat and said, 'Yes, Herr General. We came under some inaccurate machine-gun fire, followed by a few howitzer shells, but nothing much. The river looked narrow there, too. Fordable in places, I'd say.'

'In any case,' said Rommel, 'the Scarpe to the north-west of Arras is far smaller than it is east of the city – and considerably less well defended. We will encircle the city from the west and sever the British lines of communication.'

'What about aerial support?' asked Eicke.

'The *Luftwaffe* has been bombing the area and will continue to do so this afternoon and tomorrow morning.' He stood up. 'Any more questions?' He looked at Eicke. 'Thank you, Brigadeführer, for joining us. How you deploy your men is, of course, entirely up to you.' Briefly, he was silent. 'We have yet to come up against the British so do not underestimate them. But we have achieved great things so far. Fortune, momentum and, of course, experience are

now with us. They are formidable attributes, especially when combined.' He smiled and his face, stern and patrician a moment
before, now softened. 'Good luck, gentlemen. Tomorrow will be an
exciting day.'

As Rommel left the bar, Timpke drank from his bottle of beer. The
general's men might not have come up against the British, but
Timpke had – those swine had taken four of his vehicles from under
his nose, and had killed and wounded a number of his men. A
renewed flash of anger swept over him as he recalled the events of the
previous night. Well, he would have his revenge. No *Englander* would
enjoy such success against him or his men again, he promised himself.

D Company, 1st Battalion, the Yorkshire Rangers, had made it to
Vimy, had found the brigade-major and been sent promptly to the
nearby village of Givenchy, near the base of Vimy Ridge, where
they were told to lie up. At dawn the following morning they were
to form up back in Vimy, where they would join the right-hand column attacking south.

It meant the men had a long afternoon and evening to kill.
Tanner had seen they were nervous, jittery, even – Christ, he felt
nervous himself. The feverish atmosphere that consumed the
village hadn't helped. There were apprehensive locals – the parish
priest among them – and exhausted, frightened refugees with their
sad collection of worldly belongings, and not all were pleased to see
British soldiers around the church and *mairie*, or to find army trucks
parked between the lime trees in the square. Above, enemy aircraft
had buzzed and swirled, prompting panic among the civilians.
When, that evening, several Junkers 88s had swept over low,
dropping their bombs on the village, pandemonium had erupted.
No one had been hurt, but the hysterical sobbing from one young
woman in particular had been unsettling.

'Can't someone shut that silly bitch up?' muttered McAllister,
casting resentful glances in her direction. They were spread out in
a corner of the church, some cleaning their weapons, some playing
cards, others trying to sleep on the hard wooden pews.

'Poor girl's probably lost everything,' said Sykes. 'Come on, Mac, how would you feel if your home was bombed?'

'I'd write the Hun what did it a thank-you note,' said McAllister. 'Bloody hovel, my place is.'

They laughed.

'Actually, now you mention it, I wouldn't mind them flattening my old place either,' Sykes grinned.

'I've just remembered, Mac,' said Tanner. 'You're saving up for that house in Harrogate, aren't you?'

'I am, Sarge. I'm not going back to Bradford. I've got two pounds six and six so far.'

'You'd better stop playing Stan at cards, then.'

Blackstone was standing beside them. 'All right, boys?'

'No, Sergeant-Major,' said McAllister. 'That woman crying – it's getting on our nerves.'

'Leave it to me, Mac,' he said, and walked up to the front of the church where several other civilians were crouched around her.

'What's he up to?' said McAllister.

Tanner now got up from the pew on which he was lying and watched Blackstone squat beside the woman. His back was towards them so it was hard to tell what he was doing, but almost immediately the sobbing stopped, and a few minutes later the woman, surrounded by several others, stood up and walked out of the church.

'Well, I'm damned,' muttered Sykes.

''Ere, sir!' McAllister called to Blackstone, who was following the procession. 'What did you say to her?'

Blackstone came over. 'Told her it was her lucky day and that I'd see her behind the church in ten minutes.' The men laughed. 'Actually, I gave her a slug of cognac and a few francs. Booze and money, lads – it's what makes the world go round.' He grinned. 'Ready for some heroics tomorrow, Jack?'

Tanner said nothing, so Blackstone turned back to the others, shrugged – *what's his problem?* – winked and sauntered outside.

'He's a funny bloke, isn't he?' said Hepworth.

Ha bloody ha, thought Tanner. He wondered where Blackstone had got the cognac and francs from – knowing him, they'd probably been stolen. He lay down again on the pew and closed his eyes.

He was awake the moment Hepworth shook his shoulder, although momentarily disoriented. It was dark now in the church, the only light cast by several rows of candles beneath the pulpit. He sat up and looked at his watch – 2215. 'What is it?'

'The OC wants to see you, Sarge.'

'Where is he?'

'In the bar across the far side of the square.'

Tanner stood up, slung his rifle over his shoulder, then went out of the church, round the front of the building and into the square. It was quiet now. Tanner wondered where all the refugees had gone – he supposed they had either moved on or taken shelter somewhere in the village; in the *mairie*, perhaps, or in some of the abandoned houses. *Christ knows*. He walked across the road and to the bar. But there was no sign of Captain Barclay so he stepped back outside and began to walk back across the road towards the trucks.

He was conscious of movement at either side of him, but before he could react, three men had leaped at him, the first hitting him hard with a wooden cudgel across the stomach. He gasped as the breath was knocked out of him and doubled up, only for a second man to knock him to the ground, where his head was saved from slamming against the gravel by the rim of his tin hat. He grabbed one man's legs, yanked hard and pulled him over. Then he swung his fist into the man's jaw, momentarily surprised to see, in the dim light, that the fellow wore civilian clothes. Hands clasped his neck and hauled him away. He thrust his arm backwards, heard the man gasp, but the third figure punched him in the stomach, then again across the face. Tanner tasted blood and pain coursed through him. His rifle had fallen from his shoulder and now he kicked out in front of him as, with his left hand, he felt for his sword bayonet. The man behind still had him tightly by the neck, then a blow connected with his kidney, making him cry out in pain.

'Oi, stop that!' said a voice, followed by a single revolver shot into the air. The effect was immediate: his neck was released, Tanner fell back on to the ground, and two assailants ran off down the street, their footsteps ringing out in the evening quiet. The third got to his feet groggily and ran off too.

'Good job I turned up, Jack.'

Tanner's spirits fell further. *Bloody Blackstone.* 'Thanks,' he muttered, getting slowly to his feet. He leaned back against one of the Opels and felt his face. His cheekbone was cut and his lip was bleeding. His stomach and side were bruised, too, but the damage might have been worse. He had survived harsher beatings than this one.

'What the bloody hell was all that about?' asked Blackstone, now beside him.

'God knows,' muttered Tanner. 'They just jumped on me.'

'Here,' said Blackstone. 'Have a swig of this.' He passed Tanner a bottle of cognac and Tanner drank, the liquid stinging his mouth and burning his throat.

'Thanks,' he said again.

'Don't know what would have happened if I hadn't shown up,' said Blackstone. 'Three against one. Could have been nasty.' He struck a match, whistled, then lit a cigarette. 'Whoah! You're a pretty sight, Jack.'

'I'll live,' said Tanner.

'Reckon you owe me one now, though.'

'Oh, here we go,' snapped Tanner. 'What do you want?'

'No need to be so touchy. Christ, I save your bloody life and you're having a go at me already.'

'Just spit it out.'

Blackstone chuckled. 'It's a simple thing, really, Jack.' He moved a step closer. Tanner smelt the mixture of tobacco and brandy on his breath. 'Start being a bit friendly, like. As I said to you the other night, I run this company, all right? We do things my way, not yours and Mr Peploe's.'

'Jesus,' said Tanner, 'is that what this is about? You and your sodding little fiefdom?' He laughed croakily.

'Will you start being a good boy, Jack?' said Blackstone. 'You're causing me all manner of trouble.'

Tanner's fists clenched and he stiffened. 'You set this up, didn't you?'

Blackstone moved even closer to him. 'I've tried, Jack, tried to be nice, tried to be friendly. Offered olive branch after olive branch. I'm telling you now. Do as I ask, Jack. Life will be better for everyone if you do.'

Tanner pushed him away. 'Bugger off, Blackstone, will you?'

'I'm not warning you again.'

Tanner straightened, then pushed past him.

'Very well, Jack,' said Blackstone, after him. 'On your head be it.'

15

It was not until around seven the following morning, Tuesday, 21 May, that General Lord Gort learned that the French would not be attacking simultaneously with Frankforce. It was Captain de Voguë who rang Major-General Pownall to break the news. Shortly afterwards the liaison officer at General Billotte's headquarters, Major Archdale, confirmed the French decision.

'I'm sorry, my lord, but all they can spare is Third DLM and a few Somua tanks,' said Pownall, from the uncomfortable wooden chair in front of the commander-in-chief's desk that he had spent so many hours on since their move to Wahagnies. He yawned. 'Excuse me,' he muttered. Outside, it was warm already. The morning mist was lifting, the haze in the garden suffused with a promising brightness.

'Here,' said Gort, irritation in his voice. 'Have some coffee.' He stood up and leaned across his desk to the wooden tray on which stood a coffee pot and the remains of a light breakfast. He poured his chief-of-staff a cup, then said, 'So Altmayer's cracking up, too, is he?'

'Says his men are exhausted and in no position to fight today. Tomorrow is the earliest they could join us.'

'It'll be too damn late by then. You've read the latest sitrep?'

Pownall nodded. 'The Germans have reached Abbeville.'

'And Billotte agrees with Blanchard and Altmayer?'

'According to Archdale, Billotte's been spending his time agonizing over whether a fuel dump should be blown up rather than organizing any counter-attack. And he's moved his HQ to Béthune, which has taken time and caused communication problems. Archdale thinks Billotte's losing his marbles entirely.'

'The devil!' Gort thumped his fist on the table. 'Now's the time to strike – now! It's only the Hun cavalry that's been sending us reeling. The main bulk of the German Army is still miles behind. A big effort today and we slice the head of the German advance from the body. Delay, and the rest will catch up. Then it'll be too late.' He shook his head. 'At least One and Three Corps are holding their line, but let's face it, Henry, if the Germans reach the coast, our lines of supply are going to be buggered. What's the food and ammunition situation?'

'Ammunition isn't critical yet, but food's getting short. We've only another two and a half days at current rates.'

'It's impossible,' he muttered, then added, 'Let's hope General Weygand's got a good plan up his sleeve. How are we getting to Ypres this morning?'

'By car, my lord. I just pray the roads are clear enough.'

'God willing. I want to meet Weygand. I want to see whether he's got what it takes and I want to damn well impress upon him the importance of quick decision-making. I've heard he's good, but he's dashed old – seventy-odd, isn't he? Like all these French generals.'

'And too rooted in the last war, perhaps.' Pownall gulped his tepid coffee. 'And what about Frankforce, my lord? Do we cancel the attack today?'

'No, Henry. No. We've got to be seen to be acting on our promises. In any case, it might achieve something. I can't say this is a great surprise. It's why I didn't tell Franklyn we were hoping the French would join us. He still thinks it's an operation to clear our southern flank.'

'And surely that's what it is, my lord.'

'Yes, that's exactly what it is,' Gort concurred. 'The threats of evacuation have had no effect at all. Tell me, Henry, am I going to have to call in the Navy and move the BEF to Dunkirk before the French wake up?'

Tanner was in a filthy mood. He had stumbled back into the church and, in the near-darkness, had found a corner and got his head down, but the cover of night would only delay the inevitable. The men had been up at first light and, of course, had seen the cut on his cheek, the bloodied, swollen lip, and he'd been unable to hide the pain in his side. His head throbbed and his body hurt like hell. What was more, the wound he had received at the lock a few days ago had opened again and stung sharply every time he moved.

In many ways, however, the pain was the least of it. Worse were the comments, the looks, the seemingly endless questions. First Sykes, then the others. 'What happened to you, Sarge?' 'You look terrible, Sarge.' And what could he say? That, for no apparent reason, three Frenchmen had jumped on him and given him a going-over? It was so bloody humiliating. And Blackstone had let slip that he'd rescued him, saved his life, even. The bastard. Tanner had known he was making a bad show of hiding his feelings. When Hepworth said, 'I told you old Blackie was a good bloke,' Tanner had nearly knocked him cold there and then. It had taken much willpower to ignore the comment and walk away.

If only they could get on with the battle, everyone would forget about it, but six o'clock came and went, then seven and still they had received no orders. Lieutenant Bourne-Arton was sent to liaise with Brigade; soon after he had gone, a swarm of Junkers 88s had flown over and pasted Vimy, but the lieutenant had returned unscathed a short while later, with news that they would be forming up at ten a.m., and that the company was to rendezvous with the rest of the right-hand attack column at eleven a.m. in Neuville-St-Vaast, a village a mile or so on the far side of Vimy Ridge. That meant a further two hours of sitting around, re-cleaning weapons, and suffering the nudges and comments of the men.

'Come on, Sarge,' said Sykes, as they waited out on the village square. 'Have a tab and cheer up a bit.' He lit Tanner a cigarette and passed it to him.

Tanner took it and grunted his thanks. He hadn't really spoken to Sykes about it, but now he felt more inclined to do so. 'It was Blackstone, Stan.'

'I might have known,' said Sykes. 'What did happen between you two? In India, I mean.'

'It was a bit like now. Him trying to run the show. He had everyone in his pocket – not just the platoon but others too.'

'Not you, though?'

Tanner smiled. 'No. I don't know why but I instinctively mistrusted him. I think he sensed it. Anyway, he went out of his way to make life difficult.' Tanner paused to draw on his cigarette.

'I see,' said Sykes.

'I began to realize he was a coward,' Tanner continued. 'Throughout the Loe Agra campaign he'd do anything to avoid a scrap. Anyway, one day I told him what I thought.'

'And it wasn't appreciated.'

'No. Anyway, he also had this racket going – opium. He was trading with the Wazirs. I'm not quite sure how he did it, but I think he was nicking arms and handing them over in return for the stuff, then selling it on.'

'Jesus – and them guns was being used against our own chaps?'

'To be fair, I couldn't swear to it. But, yes, I think so. At any rate, those Wazirs always seemed to have a fair amount of British kit. Anyway, next thing I know, I'm being accused of trading opium and I'm in choky awaiting the firing squad.'

'So what happened?'

'I had an alibi. And I'd just been put up for this.' He touched the ribbon on his battle-blouse. 'My record was pretty good and the intelligence officer was a decent bloke. He didn't like Blackstone either and stuck his neck out for me. I got off, but I couldn't nail anything on Blackstone. The bastard.'

'So that's why you 'ate 'is guts.'

'That's why. And nothing I've seen of him since joining this mob has made me think he's changed.'

'Blokes like that never do.'

'No.'

He looked up as footsteps approached and saw CQS Slater. 'Here's trouble,' he muttered.

'Tanner,' said Slater, 'the OC wants you.' He glared at Sykes. 'Now.'

Tanner followed him in silence to the low brick house a short distance beyond the church that Barclay had made his company headquarters. It had been abandoned by its owner, but most of the belongings were still there, and as Tanner entered he saw pictures on the wall, florid wallpaper running up the staircase, a crucifix and shelves full of books. To one side of the entrance there was a living room, to the other a kitchen. It was startlingly unmilitary in appearance.

'In there,' said Slater.

Tanner entered to find Captain Barclay sitting at the head of an old pine table. Behind him, leaning against an unlit range, stood Blackstone. A girl sat beside Barclay at the table. At first, Tanner didn't recognize her, and then it dawned on him that it was she who had been wailing in the church the previous evening – the one Blackstone had managed to silence.

Tanner saluted. 'You wanted to see me, sir.'

'Christ, man, look at you!' snapped Barclay. 'You're an absolute disgrace.'

'I'm sorry, sir,' Tanner replied. 'I was set upon last night.'

'By three Frenchmen – yes, I've heard, and I'm not surprised after what you did.'

What's this? Alarm bells rang. 'I'm sorry, sir, I don't understand.'

'No? Are you sure?' He indicated the girl. 'Are you telling me she's lying?'

'I don't know what you're talking about, sir.' He looked at the girl, who avoided his gaze.

'Mademoiselle Lafoy here claims you raped her last night.'

'*What?* But that's absurd!' Tanner's heart quickened and a dull veil of intense dread swept over him. His legs felt unsteady.

'It was him,' said the girl, her accent heavy. 'He – he raped me!'

'I did nothing of the sort,' said Tanner. 'I swear it, sir. She was crying in the church last night. The CSM calmed her down and then she left. That is the only time I've ever seen her in my life.'

'And you think a French girl you claim you've never seen before would make such an allegation if it wasn't true?' said Blackstone. 'Give over, Sergeant.'

Tanner glared at him. 'I don't know what her motives are, sir,' he said to Barclay, 'but I tell you she's lying.' He turned to Blackstone again. 'Someone with a grudge against me must have put her up to it.' And then he saw the girl glance at Blackstone – a brief flicker, but unmistakable. It was all the proof he needed. *I'll bloody kill him.*

'Well, I'm sorry, Tanner, but I don't believe you,' said Barclay. 'You're a good soldier, I'll admit that, but you're trouble. You have been from the moment you joined this company and I can't help having a dim view of your character.'

'Based on what, sir?'

'Don't answer back, Tanner.'

'This is ridiculous,' snarled Tanner. 'I know who's behind it, sir.' He nodded at Blackstone. 'And I'll prove it too – one way or another.' He turned to Mademoiselle Lafoy. 'How much did he pay you, eh?' The girl flinched, frightened by his anger.

'That will do, Tanner!' shouted Barclay. His face had reddened, and then, as though recognizing the need to compose himself, he placed his hands carefully on the table in front of him and said, in a slow, measured voice, 'You'll have a chance to defend yourself, but for now you're relieved of your duties. You'll wait here until the MPs arrive.'

Tanner stared at Barclay, barely able to take in what the OC had said.

'And you're demoted to the ranks,' said Blackstone, unable to hide the triumph in his voice. He walked to Tanner, took out a clasp knife and grasped Tanner's arm.

Tanner grabbed the CSM's wrist. 'You'll pay for this,' he whispered to Blackstone, 'and that's not a warning. It's a statement of fact.'

'Let go of my hand, Private,' said Blackstone, and then, out of view of Barclay, he winked. Stitch by stitch, Tanner's sergeant stripes were unpicked, first on one arm, then the other, until all that was left were the loose khaki threads still hanging from his serge battle-blouse.

Corporal Sykes was worried about Tanner, but he was also worried for himself and the rest of the lads. They were about to go into battle, and Sykes, for one, knew there was no one else he would rather have at his side than their sergeant. The other lads needed him too – they all did. Yet Tanner was in a bad way – clouted the previous evening and in a black mood like he'd never seen before. And that was before Slater had turned up. Something was wrong, he was sure of it. Tanner had been gone an hour, and they were due to form up shortly.

Sykes paced up and down the square, the scent of the lime trees heavy on the morning air, smoked a cigarette, then decided to find Mr Peploe. They'd barely seen the lieutenant since the previous afternoon – he'd been found digs in the village where he'd been resting and giving himself a chance to recover from his wound. Well, to hell with it, thought Sykes. He'd have to disturb him now.

The house was a short way up the road to Vimy Ridge – a brick affair with curious limestone blocks along the foundations and at the corners. Sykes knocked on the door, which was answered by Private Smailes.

'Smiler,' said Sykes, 'is Mr Peploe about?'

'Good morning, Corporal,' he heard the lieutenant say from inside. He appeared, already wearing his webbing, kitbag and holster.

'How are you feeling, sir?' Sykes asked.

'Better, thank you. Head's still a bit sore, but I have deep reserves of courage and I think I can now resume full duties as platoon commander.' He grinned.

'Glad to hear it, sir.'

'Shall we get going, then?' said Peploe.

'Er, sir,' said Sykes, 'it's Sergeant Tanner, sir.'

'What about him?' said Peploe, anxiety clouding his face. 'What's happened?'

Sykes explained. 'I thought maybe you could check with the OC what's going on,' he added.

'Absolutely, Corporal,' said Peploe, clapping his damaged tin hat back on his head. 'Come with me. We'll see him right away.'

It was a grim-faced Captain Barclay who informed them that Tanner was under arrest on a charge of rape.

'What absolute rubbish!' said Peploe. 'What proof have you got? I've never heard such poppycock in all my life.'

'Lieutenant!' said Captain Barclay. 'I will not have you speak to me like that. Why on earth would the girl make it up? She's clearly distressed, she has identified Tanner quite specifically and, apart from anything else, we can't have our troops raping and pillaging our allies. I'm merely observing the proper procedures.'

Peploe snorted derisively. 'Let me see him, sir. He's my platoon sergeant. I demand to be allowed to speak to him.'

'I'm not sure that's advisable, sir,' began Blackstone, but Barclay cut him off.

'Yes, all right, Peploe. Blackstone, take Lieutenant Peploe to see Tanner.'

Tanner was sitting on a stool in the scullery at the back of the house. He stood up as Peploe and Sykes entered. 'It's not true, sir. I don't know that girl at all. I've been put on the peg for nothing.'

'I believe you, Tanner, don't worry,' said Peploe. Then, seeing his sleeves, he asked, 'What's happened to your stripes?'

'I've been demoted, sir.'

'But that's monstrous!'

'Sir, Blackstone's behind this. He set me up last night – as much as admitted it – and I'm sure he's paid that girl to make the charge. But it's rubbish, a lie – he wants me out of the way.'

'But why, Tanner? What has he got against you?'

'I won't dance to his tune, sir. He likes being in control. He thinks he runs this company, not the OC, and I reckon that, for the most part, he's right. The OC's putty in his hands. The CSM thinks I undermine his authority and his influence on the others. And he's a coward, sir. He always was and he always will be. He'll want to hold back today, sir, keep a low profile, and avoid too much fighting. I reckon he's worried I'll show him up.'

Peploe was thoughtful for a while. 'Let me talk to the girl, and I'll speak with Captain Barclay again. I mean, for God's sake, when were you supposed to have done this?'

'When I went to look for Captain Barclay last night. Apparently I jumped on her and the three Frenchmen who jumped on me had seen me do it.'

'And who are they?'

Tanner shrugged. 'They were wearing civvies but I never saw their faces.'

'And 'ave you asked whether the OC did want to see you, Sarge?' asked Sykes.

'No – I hadn't thought of that,' Tanner admitted. 'Christ,' he added, running his hands through his dark hair.

It seemed that Captain Barclay had asked to see Tanner the previous evening, but in the house, not the bar. Tanner had never shown up, he told Peploe, another reason why he was inclined to believe the accusation. Blackstone had passed the message to Slater, Slater had passed it to Private Hepworth. Slater told Peploe that he had been quite specific to Hepworth that the OC wanted to see Tanner at Company Headquarters.

'Has Hepworth verified this?' asked Peploe.

'We haven't spoken to him yet,' said Barclay.

'There's no real need to, sir,' added Blackstone. 'Slater knows what he told him. Why would Hepworth tell Tanner any different?'

Peploe eyed Blackstone for a moment, then said, 'And where's the girl? This Mademoiselle Lafoy? I'd like to speak to her.'

Suddenly Barclay seemed flustered. 'Actually,' he said, 'I don't know. She was a refugee. But she made the charge and I acted on it. We took a statement from her and she left.'

'How can you charge Tanner without the key witness?' asked Peploe, his exasperation evident.

Barclay looked at his watch. 'Look, Peploe, we've got to form up shortly. This will have to wait until later.'

'Sir,' said Peploe, 'you cannot detain Tanner on the basis of a statement from an unknown and, frankly, emotionally suspect witness who has since disappeared.'

'Tanner has been placed under arrest, sir,' said Blackstone, 'and the MPs will be here at any moment. The captain is merely following correct military legal procedure in such cases.'

'And I suppose you had nothing to do with any of this, CSM?'

'Me, sir?' said Blackstone. 'No, sir. What makes you think that? Has Tanner been trying to pass the blame on to me?' He shook his head. 'He's unbelievable, that man. And to think I saved his life last night. I wouldn't have bothered if I'd known what he'd done. He's a disgrace to the regiment.'

'Well, I don't believe a word of it,' said Peploe. 'He's my best soldier and I want him in my platoon when we go into battle today.'

'I'm sorry, Lieutenant,' said Barclay, 'but he's being handed over to the police and that's all there is to it. Whatever his merits as a soldier, we cannot have rapists among our number.'

'That's bollocks, sir, and you know it. Throughout its history, the British Army has been littered with thieves, murderers and ne'er-do-wells.' He glared pointedly at Blackstone. 'And, as I've said, I don't believe this baloney for one minute. Let me have him back today, and if we all come through unscathed, I'll prove his innocence afterwards.'

'He's a rapist, sir,' said Blackstone. 'You have a moral obligation to hand him over to the authorities and deal with this in the proper manner.'

'I want Tanner with me today,' said Peploe. 'And, what's more, if you insist on continuing with this farce, sir,' he said directly to his commanding officer, 'I will be left with no choice but to resign my commission immediately.'

Barclay was appalled. 'You can't do that!'

'I can, sir, and I will. I don't want to be part of a regiment that treats its men so monstrously, or to serve under a man who is prepared to believe the word of a young girl about whom we know nothing over a soldier who has repeatedly proven himself courageous, dependable and utterly loyal, a man who has already been decorated for valour in the face of the enemy and whose experience will be an invaluable asset today. I was a farmer before the war, sir. I had no need to join up, but I did so because I believe we have a moral duty to fight and defeat Nazism. I certainly did not join to find myself fighting my biggest battles with those on my own side. Now, I don't wish to add another false allegation, but let me say this: I believe there are certain elements within this company who are far bigger trouble-makers than Tanner will ever be. This nonsense has the ring of a personal vendetta about it, one that needs to be stamped on hard.' He looked straight at Blackstone.

Barclay followed his gaze. 'What the devil are you saying, man?'

'Quite enough. As I say, I prefer hard facts before I make any accusation.'

Barclay bit his lip and knotted his hands. 'Rape's a serious allegation, though. I've got to be seen to do the right thing.'

'In that case, sir, I resign.' He began to unbutton his webbing.

'Sir, you can't just ignore a charge like this,' insisted Blackstone.

Barclay groaned and stood up. 'All right, Peploe!' he exclaimed. 'I'll release him. For now.'

'And I want him to have his stripes back, sir. In Britain, a man is innocent until proven guilty. So far, Tanner's guilt has not been established.'

'This is blackmail, sir,' said Blackstone.

'Be quiet, CSM!' shouted Barclay. He went over to a dresser that stood along one side of the kitchen, picked up Tanner's stripes and handed them to Peploe. 'I was doing what I thought was right,' he said, utterly dejected. 'Let's hope Tanner proves worthy of the faith you have in him, Lieutenant.'

'I have absolutely no doubt that he will,' said Peploe.

'It's a quarter to ten, Peploe. Get Tanner and make sure your platoon are ready in a quarter of an hour.' He sighed heavily. 'But don't think this matter is closed. We've a battle to fight, but afterwards . . .' He trailed off.

Peploe and Sykes saluted, then fetched Tanner.

'Thank you, sir,' said Tanner, as he took his stripes back.

'Here,' said Peploe, delving into his pack for his housewife. 'You'd better get them sewn back on quick. Reckon you can have it done in five minutes?'

'I'll do it, Sarge,' said Sykes.

'Good. I'll go and sort out the men. Meet us by the trucks as soon as you can.'

'Thank you, sir,' said Tanner again. He then stood still while Sykes's nimble fingers quickly stitched one set of stripes, then the other into the thick serge.

'There,' said Sykes, eventually. 'Those should hold for the moment, at any rate.'

D Company set off a few minutes after ten, driving out of the square and up the hill, past the giant Canadian war memorial, erected only a few years before in honour of those killed during the last war against Germany. It gleamed proudly in the morning sunshine. Behind, pockets of mist still hung in the valley. Ahead, young pines sprouted up through the still pockmarked landscape of Vimy Ridge.

'Thank God for mobile warfare,' said Peploe as he gazed out from the cab of the Opel.

Tanner said nothing. The humiliation of the past twelve hours still occupied his mind. None of the lads had said anything to him but there had been glances and knowing looks. Blackstone had made sure they'd heard about the rape charge. Peploe had come to his rescue, but Tanner was conscious that Blackstone had still partly achieved his goal. The men in the platoon would view him differently – warily, even. The trust he had won had been undermined, just as Blackstone had wanted.

They were halted in Neuville by 151st Brigade men and directed to an open area opposite the same massive French cemetery they had passed the day before. A battery of gunners was already there, vehicles and guns lined up ready to move. A brigade staff officer ordered them out of the trucks, while Captain Barclay and his two lieutenants were instructed to take the Krupp, wheel round and head back up the ridge to Petit Vimy where they were to liaise with Lieutenant-Colonel Beart, officer commanding, 8th Battalion, Durham Light Infantry.

Tanner watched them head off. Then, as the rest of the men were getting out of the back of the Opels, he heard the tell-tale thrum of aircraft and looked behind to see a dozen Stukas peeling off and diving down on the ridge. No bombs fell, but machine-guns chattered, the sound clear and sharp. Tanner saw Ellis and Denning flinch. He hoped Mr Peploe was all right.

'Christ, will you look at that?' muttered Sykes.

'They're bloody slow, though, aren't they?' said Tanner.

'Not the Stukas, Sarge – all those bloody graves.' He pointed to the French cemetery. Row after row of white crosses stretched from the road to the ridge beyond. 'There must be thousands and thousands of 'em.'

Tanner wandered over to the small British cemetery that lay beside the French one and lit a cigarette. From the village, now that the Stukas had gone, he could hear tanks, their tracks squeaking. Soon six French light tanks were turning off the main village road towards them.

As the last one passed, Tanner stepped across the road behind it and walked to the other side of the trucks. From the far side of the Opel he could hear a group of men from the platoon talking.

'Well, I still reckon old Blackie's a good sort,' said McAllister. 'He said that bird swore the sarge had had his way with her.'

'What I don't see is why she'd lie about it,' said Bell.

'You reckon he did it, then?' said Ellis.

'I dunno,' said Hepworth. 'Maybe it was someone else. Maybe she got it wrong. It was dark, weren't it?'

Tanner clenched his fists, banged his right hand hard against the side of the truck, then walked round to confront them. A hush fell over the men as he stood before them. For a moment he glared at them, his pale blue eyes staring at each man in turn.

'Sarge, I'm sorry, I didn't mean—' began Hepworth.

'Shut up, Hepworth,' Tanner snarled. 'Listen to me, all of you. I know what you've heard, so I'm going to say this to you once. It's true that I was attacked last night and it's true that some French woman has accused me of raping her.' He eyed them all in turn. 'I did no such thing. You've had your gossip but I don't want to hear another word about it. Today we're going into battle and, believe me, when the shells start falling and the machine-guns are firing, this bollocks will seem very unimportant. What will matter is making sure we beat those bastards and that you come through it in one piece.' He stared hard at McAllister. 'Don't believe everything the CSM says, Mac. Remember this: I've known him a lot longer than you have.'

McAllister's eyes darted about nervously. His cheeks flushed. 'Sarge—' he said.

'Forget it, Mac,' said Tanner. 'Just don't let me down today, all right?'

Lieutenant Peploe could hardly bring himself to speak to Captain Barclay as they drove towards Petit Vimy. He knew the captain was not a bad man, but he also recognized some fundamental failings in the fellow. He was impressionable, not a natural leader of men, probably not terribly bright either. Or, at least, not someone who could think quickly on their feet. No wonder Blackstone had such a hold over him. That confidence, that breezy charm and quick mind – those were useful tools for someone like the CSM.

He looked out of the cab at the hordes of refugees taking cover by the side of the road and in the young woods covering the slopes of the ridge, then realized that the arrival of the Stukas had, in fact, been something of a godsend, enabling Lieutenant Bourne-Arton, who was driving, to reach the little hamlet quickly and just as the enemy attack finished.

The place heaved with troops, most of whom, Peploe thought, were exhausted. Directed to Battalion Headquarters – the village bar – they found Lieutenant-Colonel Beart and his battalion officers already in conference.

'Ah, come on in,' said Beart, ushering them to join the half-circle gathered around him. 'You're the company from the Yorkshire Rangers, aren't you?'

'Yes, sir,' said Barclay. 'We've been attached to you because we've got four Jerry trucks.'

Peploe cringed at the obvious pride with which Barclay announced this.

Beart smiled. 'Good. Then you can come under command of Captain Dixon in A Company.' He pointed to an officer several years younger than Barclay.

'How d'you do?' Dixon shook hands with each man in turn. 'Good of you to join us.'

'Right,' continued Beart. 'So, Dix, you've got a scout troop of motorcycles from the Northumberland Fusiliers, a platoon from 260th Ack-Ack Battery, a carrier platoon less one section and our new friends from across the border in Yorkshire. Captain Dixon will lead the advance guard. Dix – over to you.'

Dixon cleared his throat. 'We're going to get going at eleven hundred, then RV with Seven RTR's tanks at the village of Maroeuil.' He turned to Barclay. 'Have you fellows been issued with maps?'

'Yes,' said Barclay, pulling his from his map case. 'Yesterday, from GHQ.'

'Good show,' said Dixon. 'If you have a look you can see we're here.' He pointed to his own map. 'Here's Maroeuil, about four miles away to the south-west, and our start line for the attack is this road, eight miles further south here, running south-west from Arras to Doullens. Beaumetz is the place to keep in mind. There's been plenty of Jerry activity spotted south of there, so they're definitely lurking about. A question of flushing the buggers out.'

'Our chaps are all in Neuville at the moment,' said Barclay.

'Well, that's all right. We'll pick you up on the way. You've got a radio, have you?'

'No, I'm afraid not.'

'It'll be all right, Dix,' said Lieutenant-Colonel Beart. 'We'll just have to make do. Where exactly are you in Neuville, Captain?'

'By a large French Great War cemetery, sir,' said Barclay.

'And unless I'm much mistaken, that's *en route* to Maroeuil, isn't it?' He clapped his hands. 'Good. Well, that all seems clear enough. The rest of the battalion will follow the advance guard. One bit of bad news, though, is that we don't have any rations. Have your chaps eaten anything today, Captain?' he asked Barclay.

'They've breakfasted, sir.'

'That's something. Anyway, I'm sorry but it's those buggering refugees again. The food wagons have been held up. I hate to send fellows into battle on empty stomachs but it can't be helped.'

Beart dismissed them soon after, wishing them a cheery good luck. As Peploe followed Barclay and Bourne-Arton back to the Krupp, he couldn't help feeling that the attack plan seemed rather hastily cobbled together. It was as though a lot was being left to chance. He still had a headache, but now nausea assailed him. As a pair of collared doves cavorted above them, he wondered whether he would still be alive at the day's end. Funnily enough, the débâcle with Tanner had taken his mind off things. Ever since he'd been driven past the shell-holes of Vimy Ridge, however, the prospect of battle had been brought back into sharp focus. Fighting – killing or being killed – had seemed so remote on the day he'd joined up, full of youthful determination to play his part in ridding the world of Hitler. It had been easy to be brave then and to enjoy the sense that he was undertaking something rather noble and heroic. He'd imagined himself to be rather like a Crusader in the stories he had enjoyed as a boy, leaving his weeping mother for the Holy Land. But those shell-holes and the endless cemeteries had been an all-too-real reminder of what war could be like. And now this rather haphazard battle-plan. If he was honest, he still had no idea what they were supposed to be doing or what to expect. All he knew was that he was scared stiff.

The Durhams' advance guard rendezvoused successfully with D Company and the Rangers' trucks fell into line behind the motorcycle scout troop, two command cars, a radio car and two trucks towing two-pounder anti-tank guns, trundling at a snail's pace along a narrow road to Maroeuil. Away to their left they could see the tip of the belfry at the heart of Arras. In between and at either side of them lay open, undulating farmland.

Tanner's mood was slowly improving. He hoped that in confronting the men he had convinced them; it had made him feel better, at any rate. The awfulness of those moments when he had been under arrest in a damp scullery was past. Ahead, he could see Maroeuil being bombarded lightly from the south-east. The whistle of the shells could be heard faintly above the rumble of the vehicles, followed by a dull thud and a thin cloud of dust erupting clear of the buildings. His heart beat faster and he had a familiar sensation in his stomach and throat. Nerves, certainly, but excitement too. Fighting was exciting and, in the thick of it, his senses keen, he found it exhilarating.

Away to his right he could see the lonely ruins of a church, high on the skyline. He knew his father had fought around here – it had been 1917, he remembered – and had often talked to him about it. Now he recalled that there had been a spring offensive at Arras that year. Now, just twenty-three years later, he was marching on the same ground, ready to fight the same enemy. His father had died eight years before and not a day went past when Tanner didn't think of him. His dad had been his best friend as well as his father. Tanner smiled, remembering.

By the time they reached Maroeuil the shelling had stopped. Tanner was surprised to see some dead Germans in the village – where had they come from? – but despite vehicle congestion, the advance guard pressed on so that by twenty past two they had reached the edge of Duisans, the next village on their route to the start line of their attack.

The sounds of battle were growing more intense. Away to the west, tank and artillery fire could be heard. As they descended from a shallow ridge into the village, a bullet, then several more, fizzed above them from the wood to their right.

'Look,' said Sykes, pointing to his left. Crawling over a field up the small hill on the far side of the village were three 'I' tanks, Matilda Mark IIs with their more-than-three inches of armour. Between the sounds of gunfire, they could hear them, metal squeaking and clanking. It was such a high-pitched sound, yet with it came a deep, low rumble, promising bulk and heaviness.

More sniping whipped around them from the wood, but as they reached the centre of the village, the buildings shielded them from fire. A shell whistled overhead, and passed harmlessly above the village to explode in open country.

Ahead, a DLI officer was talking to Barclay; a minute later, the company runner came up to their cab. 'We're going to push on. We're to follow those tanks towards Warlus.'

'What about the enemy in those woods?' asked Tanner.

'B Company's being hurried forward to deal with them.'

'And why are the enemy here anyway? We haven't reached the start line yet.'

'Don't ask me. I'm just the messenger.'

They pushed on, following the three 'I' Matildas as they rumbled slowly out of Duisans and onto higher, more open country. Ahead to the south lay the village of Warlus, the slate spire of its church poking out above the trees and houses nestled around it. The anti-tank guns were unhitched and set up, then the leading cars of the advance guard turned back to Duisans.

The company runner appeared again. 'We're to stay here. They're trying to bring up more guns.'

'Make your mind up,' muttered Sykes.

To their right they could see vehicles and figures on the ridge a mile or so away. Then field guns opened fire suddenly from away to their left.

'What the hell's going on?' asked Peploe. They could hear shells hurtling over, their whistle and moan as they cut through the sky, then a series of dull crashes.

'Whose guns are those?' asked Peploe.

'Ours, I think,' said Tanner. 'They're stonking it before we go in.'

'And what about them to the right?' asked Sykes. 'Are they Jerries?'

Tanner took out his binoculars. 'I reckon they are, yes.'

'Well, I don't know about you two,' said Peploe, 'but I haven't the faintest idea what's going on. All I know is I feel bloody exposed up here.'

'I agree, sir,' said Tanner. 'Let's get everyone out until that stonk's over.'

No sooner were the men on the track, shaking their legs and stretching, than a faint rumble that soon became a roar filled the sky. Looking up, they saw waves of bombers flying over, like a giant swarm of locusts. Moments later, bombs were falling on the eastern edges of Arras, clearly visible to their left.

'Christ – look at them all!' exclaimed Peploe.

'I've counted eighty already,' said Sykes. Soon Arras disappeared under a pall of smoke. The ground shook and the sound was deafening – but all the while the British gunners continued to rain shells on Warlus and the ridge beyond. Now the church spire had disappeared under a haze of dust.

Another company of Durhams, loaded into Bren carriers, arrived on the track from Duisans, and as the artillery barrage stopped, they were ordered forward.

A few rifle shots cracked out as the advance guard entered the village, but as the smoke and dust drifted away, it became apparent that the village was empty of enemy troops. There was heavy artillery and machine-gun fire from the south and south-east, however, beyond the ridge. They paused again by a track that led towards the church. Ahead, the road climbed sharply to the next ridge and now a Mark VI light tank sped down it, a cloud of dust following in its wake. Tanner watched with interest as it stopped near them and the man in the turret hopped out. Lieutenant-Colonel Beart now arrived in his car, climbed out and the tankman hurried over to him. He was pointing behind him, showing Beart the map, then nodding furiously. A moment later, Beart called Barclay over.

'Something's up,' said Tanner, lighting a cigarette and coughing. He got out his water-bottle and drank.

Beart was now back in his car as Barclay walked purposefully towards Peploe.

'What is it, sir?' Peploe asked.

'A devil of a job, I'm afraid. Our tanks are attacking Wailly, a couple of miles to the south-east of here.'

'I can hear them,' said Peploe.

'Yes, and you can hear enemy guns too.' He took out his map. 'It seems Jerry's got a lot of guns here, Point Three, and is stopping our advance. The tanks can't get near them. Colonel Beart wants us to send one platoon over to take out as many of those guns as possible. They reckon there are four of them, and I want you and your platoon to do it, Peploe.'

Tanner noticed Barclay couldn't look him in the eye.

Peploe swallowed. 'Very well, sir.'

'Beyond this ridge is the village of Berneville, and Point Three is across the Arras–Doullens road ahead of you. I can't tell you much more than that. It's a lot to ask, I know, but . . .'

Peploe nodded. 'We'll go straight away, sir.'

'Sooner the better.' Barclay held out a hand, which Peploe took. 'Well, you'd better be off, then. Good luck, Lieutenant.'

Two trucks and thirty-six men set off immediately, the Opels labouring as they climbed the hill. As soon as they crested the ridge, past a large water-tower, they saw drifts of smoke, and the sound of battle was suddenly closer and clearer in front of them to their left.

'There!' said Tanner, pointing to a cluster of trees on the next ridge. 'They're firing from that copse. You can see the muzzle flashes.'

A moment later a shell came down in the field just fifty yards to their right, sending up a huge fountain of earth. From behind, the men shouted as bits of stone and mud landed on and among them.

'Damn it!' shouted Tanner. 'I didn't even hear that coming. What the hell was it?'

'Everyone all right?' yelled Peploe.

'Keep bloody driving, Stan,' said Tanner. 'We need to get into this village quickly.'

The road led them down to where tightly packed buildings on each side of the street shielded them from enemy gunners. It wound left, then right out of the village, still hidden from the crest of the brow ahead by trees and banks.

'We're going to have to stop, sir,' said Tanner. 'We won't get much further in these.'

Peploe nodded. 'Pull in before the end of that line of trees, Corporal,' he said to Sykes.

The road was sunken, running between ten-foot-high verges at either side. The men got out of the trucks, then, in sections, spread out either side, and walked briskly up the gently rising ridge. As they reached the Arras–Doullens road, they stopped. Inching forward with Peploe, Tanner took out his binoculars. A track, lined by hedges, led up to a farm, about two-thirds of a mile ahead. To the left of that there was a clump of trees. The enemy guns they had to capture were somewhere within it. Tanner breathed in deeply. It was possible, he reckoned. Just about. But it wouldn't be easy.

16

It had been around three o'clock when Sturmbannführer Otto Timpke had first heard the sounds of battle to the north – dull thumps, the faint rip of machine-gun fire – and immediately his heartbeat had picked up. An impatient sense of anticipation gripped him. Where were the enemy? What was happening? He experienced a stab of irritation that, yet again, 7th Panzer might be getting all the action. They had been instructed to follow Totenkopf Infantry Regiment 3 with the battalion's Panzer 38s, but infantry and artillery units of 7th Panzer were also using the same narrow roads and, with the additional weight of refugees, progress had been agonizingly slow. For several hours they had been forced to wait in the village of Mercatel, a few miles south of Arras, until Regiment 3 appeared.

The reconnaissance battalion had made the most of the wait to refuel and collect more ammunition for their tanks from a pre-prepared supply dump. Once Timpke had overseen this, however, there had been nothing to do but wait in the village square. The smell of petrol, diesel and hastily heated rations filled the still air.

He stood by his command car, an olive-grey French Army Citroën, taken the previous day in Solesmes, watching with mounting frustration as the gunfire came closer. The tepid coffee in his tin cup rippled with every boom, and he could feel the explosions pulsing beneath his feet.

He was drumming his fingers on the roof of the car and smoking French cigarettes – he had run out of Turkish – when another staff car pulled in alongside him, the rubber tyres rolling noisily across the cobbles. An army major stepped out of the passenger seat and asked for a light. 'We're not used to moving in such a big force,' he explained, gesturing towards the vehicles crawling through the village as Timpke pulled out his lighter. 'Two divisions are on the move today – so far it's been one regiment spearheading at any one time – so there's a lot more traffic than usual.' Some infantrymen were shouting at a family in a cart, trying to cross the road at the far end of the square. 'And too many damned refugees,' he added.

'Shoot at them,' Timpke suggested. 'I find that gets them moving.'

The major looked aghast. Then, clearly having decided that Timpke was joking, broke into a smile. 'Perhaps we should.'

'You should,' said Timpke, flatly. 'It would save a lot of time.'

The major smiled again, thanked him for the light, then got back into his car and drove on.

Regiment 3 arrived soon after and, having cut in front of a company of 7th Panzer infantry, Timpke's reconnaissance force followed on behind. As they progressed into open farmland beyond the village, he could see clear to Arras, some six kilometres to the north-east. A large formation of bombers thundered over and attacked the city. Black puffs of anti-aircraft barrage dotted the sky, then mushrooms of smoke rolled into the air as the bombs detonated. Nearer, though, he could hear tank and artillery exchanges. Suddenly, from over a shallow ridge behind them, a number of tanks appeared and opened fire at the column of vehicles behind them. Timpke found himself flinching as an ammunition truck blew up less than a kilometre back, the jagged sound catching him by surprise. So, too, he saw, did Kemmetmüler, sitting beside him.

'A flank attack,' said Kemmetmüler. 'What's going on? I thought we were the ones attacking.'

There was pandemonium as vehicle after vehicle was hit. Artillery and anti-tank crews tried frantically to unhitch their guns and retaliate. Above, a Feisler Storch lolled over and dropped a small canister.

'A message!' said Timpke. 'Stop!' From the scout car behind them, one of his men hurried over to where it lay in a field of young wheat. He found it soon enough and ran back and handed it to Timpke. He unscrewed the tin, pulled out the note and read, *Strong enemy armoured forces advancing.* 'I think we'd already gathered that.' He screwed up the piece of paper. 'The idiots. Wait here, Kemmetmüler.' He jumped out of the Citroën, slamming the door behind him, and hurried over to the scout car. 'What's the news, Schultz?'

'The enemy is also attacking strongly across the Arras–Doullens road towards Wailly. We're to move on towards Beaumetz and, with Regiment 2, push the enemy back towards Berneville and Warlus,' Schultz told him, handing him a hastily scribbled wireless message.

Timpke looked again at the enemy tanks. They were out of range, and seemed interested only in the 7th Panzer column directly in front of them. He unfolded his map, his eyes running over the mass of roads, villages, rivers and contours. They were five kilometres from Beaumetz and there were thick woods to the west of Berneville that would offer good cover for an attack. He could see now that the enemy armour must have swept in an arc southwards from the west of Arras; if General Rommel's artillery could stem this advance then the Totenkopf, swinging their forces wide, could outflank the enemy tanks and come round the back, ensnaring them in a deadly trap.

He took out his binoculars and looked again at the tanks crawling across the fields to the north-east. British, he reckoned. Some appeared only to have machine-guns, but others were jabbing away with their heavier guns, small flashes of fire appearing from their muzzles. Thick black smoke and flames were billowing from the 7th Panzer column behind; he could hear screams and shouting too. But already German anti-tank guns were responding and he saw now that one of the smaller British tanks had been hit.

'Schultz,' he said, climbing into the turret of the scout car, 'get a signal out. I want the battalion to rendezvous on the Arras–Doullens road to the east of Beaumetz and then we'll attack towards Berneville.'

It was already past four o'clock. With luck they'd be in position some time after five.

'Kemmetmüler!' he shouted to his adjutant. 'I'm going to stay in the scout car.' He wanted to be able to see clearly, which was impossible from the low, recessed seats of the Citroën. He ordered the column forward once more, drumming his fingers on the metal top. A memory had entered his thoughts: he had been sixteen, at a deer-shoot on his uncle's estate in Bavaria. He remembered the excitement of spotting his first stag, of watching it come closer to him. He could almost smell again the thick resin of the firs around him. And he remembered the intense thrill of capturing it in his sights, of squeezing the trigger and watching it drop to the ground, dead. He had dreamed of that moment from the instant his uncle had invited him to shoot, and when it had come, he had not been disappointed. His triumph had been every bit as thrilling as he had hoped. The Tommies might have caught the *Wehrmacht* boys off-guard, but soon they would find themselves hunted. Timpke grinned. A stag or dead Tommies, what was the difference? He was looking forward to experiencing again the sensation of triumph that had been so indelibly imprinted on his memory.

Twelve Platoon crossed the main Arras–Doullens road in sections, one man at a time. It was not a true crossroads: the men had to dash, crouching, diagonally some forty yards to their right to reach the track. Artillery fire was booming regularly, as well as from the wooded copse ahead. British tanks still lumbered down the crest to the east of Berneville, and they could hear others firing even closer.

Tanner had led the men across the road, then ducked down against the track's bank. A hawthorn hedge grew from the top on the left-hand side, but it was sparse and intermittent on the right. The road was sunk below the hedge line, but only by a few feet. As he was taking this in, Lieutenant Peploe dropped down beside him, breathing heavily.

'This side'll be all right, sir,' said Tanner. 'We'll have to crouch, but we should be able to reach the edge of the farm undetected. We don't know what's behind that ridge, though. There's a village, but we've no idea whether Jerry forces are down there, and whether it's simply a battery up in that copse or a mass of infantry taking cover and waiting to counter-attack.'

'I see,' said Peploe. He bit at a fingernail.

'And I can't quite see where that other gun's firing from.' He pointed towards the right.

'I suppose there's only one way we're going to find out.'

Tanner smiled. 'Yes, sir. I think you might be right.' The track ahead rose gently towards the farm, just under a mile away. Peering through the hedge, he could see the farm buildings – the track turned left sharply towards them near the top of the ridge and he wondered what cover the buildings might offer at that point; it depended on whether the track ran behind or in front of them. *Bloody hell.* If only they had a proper map rather than the hasty sketch Peploe had made from Captain Barclay's. It was a tall order.

Once the men were safely on the track, they moved off once more, Tanner and Peploe leading with sections following, spread out but now hugging the left. It was back-breaking work, bent double all the way, rifles and Bren in hands, ammunition pouches and packs bumping against bodies. Then, just a couple of hundred yards from the top of the ridge, they reached a railway line, a single track of old, rusting rails running across their path and parallel with the Arras–Doullens road below. Tanner had not spotted it before and, again, cursed the lack of a map. Would the enemy see them as they crossed it? He peered through his binoculars. The guns were firing ever more regularly now, the blasts sending tremors through the ground. Lying flat, he wriggled forward to the edge of the track. A British tank, some three hundred yards away to their left, had almost reached the railway, but had been hit. It was one of the more heavily armoured Matilda IIs, but it was burning, smoke and flames gushing from the turret. He wondered whether the crew had got out. Probably not. *Poor bastards.* He looked again at the copse but while he could see muzzle flashes and hear the guns ever louder, he couldn't distinguish a single enemy soldier.

'If we can't see the enemy, sir,' said Tanner, 'then hopefully he can't see us.'

'Then we must make a dash for it, Tanner,' said Peploe. He sighed. 'Come on, then.'

Platoon Headquarters went first, then Sykes's section, followed by Cooper's and Ross's, the men nipping one by one across the narrow stretch of the railway.

'Well,' said Peploe, once they were all over, 'if they did spot us, they're not letting on.'

They pushed on, keeping low or crawling, along the dusty, stony track until they reached a bend where the hedge thinned. They were now almost at the summit of the ridge. Forty yards ahead, the track forked. To the left, it ran straight to the farm, but in front of the buildings. To the right, it ran down the other side of the ridge – presumably, Tanner guessed, to the village of Wailly. He glanced around. Where was that other gun? About a mile away there was a wood – in there. Yes, he was sure of it. Those Jerry gunners would have hidden themselves well: near the edge of the trees with plenty of aerial and ground cover, but with a clear line of fire in front of them. On the far side of the wood there was another village – Beaumetz? – while directly behind them Berneville was as clear as day. Warlus must be behind the next ridge, where he hoped the rest of the company were still waiting. He could now see several burning tanks, stopped between the two ridges, their tracks having carved dark lines across the fields of young crops. Others were still wheeling about, creeping in beetling lines across the open countryside, easy targets for the German gunners now only a hundred yards or so away. The battery in the copse was doing its job effectively, round after round being fired. Past the copse, away to their left, machine-gun fire and the dull thump of the Matilda IIs' guns could still be heard amid the din of German artillery. Suddenly a shell hit the edge of a barn, knocking out a chunk of stone. Probably, Tanner guessed, a two-pound shell from one of the Matildas. *Good. They're still coming.*

'What do you think, Tanner?' said Peploe, sidling up to him.

'We need to find out what's on the other side of the ridge. Then we'll know if we can use the barns to cover our approach or even sweep round the back of the position undetected. But the less movement the better, so let me have a dekko on my own.'

'All right.'

Still crouching, Tanner hurried to the summit, past the track that veered left to the farm. Reaching the crest at last, he lay flat and squirmed forward on his stomach. He realized the track he was now on was the long side of a triangle. The fork to the farm was one of the short sides, while another led at right angles to join the main track by a walled cemetery. A number of vehicles – two Krupps, an eight-wheeled armoured car and three half-tracks – were clustered there. But no massed infantry. He looked down towards the village. Several houses were on fire, the flames dulled by the smoke. Through the haze he saw vehicles moving. The battery, still booming a short way to his left, was hidden by the farm and he breathed out heavily, the tension momentarily eased, then wriggled back a few yards and signalled urgently to Peploe to bring the rest of the men up.

'Don't let anyone go beyond this point, sir,' he said, as Peploe joined him. He glanced at the men approaching, then back to the farm. 'We've done the tricky bit – got here without being spotted – so we can cut across this pasture and take cover behind that brick barn. I reckon there's at least four guns there. Ideally, we want to attack from two different angles, but the most important thing is surprise. That means working out a good plan first, then hitting them hard and quick. I'll scout ahead now, if it's all right with you, sir, and take Corporal Sykes with me.'

'Of course. I'll wait for your signal to bring the men over.'

Tanner ran back, beckoned Sykes to follow him, then the pair climbed over the fence and ran fifty yards through a flock of anxious sheep to the edge of the barn. Pausing briefly to catch his breath, Tanner delved in his pack and pulled out his Aldis scope, unwrapping the cloth round it, then screwed it onto the pads on his rifle. Pushing his helmet to the back of his head, he said to Sykes, 'Stan, go down the other end of the barn and have a quick dekko,' then went to the nearside edge of the old brick and stone building. When he reached the rubble that had been blasted from the wall a few minutes before, he crouched as several guns boomed in succession. Another incoming cannon shell hit a building out of his line of vision. There was machine-gun fire too – a rapid chatter. *A Jerry MG.* The slower, more laboured rattle of a British machine-gun responded, but much further away, and no sooner had he caught its sound than it was smothered by battery guns unleashing yet another salvo. The noise was deafening; Tanner's ears began to ring and deaden.

Taking off his helmet, fearing the silhouette of its distinctive rim would be a give-away, he peered cautiously through a gap in the rubble. No more than seventy yards away, half hidden under a large ash tree, a small anti-tank gun, the like of which he had seen several times in Norway, was pounding out its shells. His heart began to thump, though, when he realized what stood just beyond it, partially hidden from view by the trees and foliage. It was an enormous artillery piece, resembling the 3.7-inch anti-aircraft guns they had had at Manston. The difference was that, instead of pointing into the sky, the barrel was tilted straight down the ridge to the valley below, where a number of British tanks were still groping their way towards them.

A big barrel thundered and recoiled – a double crash – then another gun boomed, and Tanner saw the tip of a second identical barrel recoil from the bushes and trees some forty yards on. Just five seconds later they fired again in staccato, their reports reverberating around the farm, shaking the ground and pulsing through Tanner's body, while the smaller gun continued hurling out cannon shells as well. Several fallen bricks near him tumbled further onto the ground. *What a gun*, he thought. They were indeed anti-aircraft guns, but were being used in an anti-tank role. A simple idea, but brilliant. He'd seen those 3.7-inch ack-ack guns fire before – they could send a shell more than twenty-five thousand feet into the sky. The velocity was incredible. And now these beasts were firing over open sights at the advancing British armour. *Christ. No wonder the tanks' advance is stalling.*

Two further guns, he now realized, were also firing – howitzers of some kind, by the sound of them – from somewhere within the trees. Several men were coming out into the open between the small and large anti-tank guns – *so there's a hollow* – and, to his astonishment, he saw that the one nearest to him wore the collar tabs and red striped breeches of a general. *Bloody hell*, he thought. *What's he doing there?*

Leaning on the fallen bricks and masonry, he brought his rifle into his shoulder. His ribs still hurt like hell; more so now that he was lying on knobbly rubble. He grimaced, which split his lip again. The general was peering through a pair of field-glasses. The two big guns crashed again and Tanner counted. *One, two, three, four, five, six. Boom-boom.* He counted again, his scope aimed at the general's head. *Two, three, four.* Breath out. *Five.* Hold breath. *Six.* Tanner pressed his finger against the trigger. The guns thundered again and his rifle cracked, the butt recoiling into his shoulder. In that instant the general turned, as though in answer to someone speaking behind him, and the officer standing next to him, slightly taller, was hit in the neck. Immediately he sank to his knees beside the smaller gun. The general swung back, crouching over the prostrate figure. Tanner pulled back the bolt, but two more men had emerged from the clearing so the general was almost hidden from view. Men were looking around, as though they were shocked and perplexed. They seemed unable to understand how, or from where, the officer had been hit.

'Damn it all,' Tanner muttered. He scrambled back from where he was crouching behind the rubble, hurried behind the barn and along to the other end. There was no sign of Sykes. Gingerly, he peered round the corner. He was looking out on to a small yard and a track that ran between the barn and an old brick farmhouse, which also gave them cover from the battery on the other side of the house but not from the vehicles some two hundred yards away down by the cemetery. Sykes was at the far side of the house, peering towards the back of the battery, when suddenly he turned and scuttled back to the cover of the barn.

'Blimey, that was close!' he gasped. 'They've got two prisoners. And there's some big cheese with 'em, too.' Sykes turned towards the rear of the battery, Tanner following his gaze. Four men were striding towards a gate below the farmhouse that joined the track leading to the cemetery: the general, then an NCO with silver chevrons on his sleeve holding a sub-machine-gun, and two British prisoners – tankmen wearing black berets.

Tanner glanced back towards Peploe and the others, motioned to them to keep low and out of sight, then brought his rifle to his shoulder once more.

'He was out front a minute ago,' he whispered to Sykes. 'The silly sod moved just as I was taking a shot at him. Got the man next to him instead.' He pulled back the bolt, and peered through the scope. A British prisoner was blocking his view. 'Get out the bloody way,' he muttered.

'Bit risky, wasn't it, Sarge?'

'Not really. I fired in time with the guns. No one had a clue where it had come from.'

'Sarge,' said Sykes, urgency in his voice. The general was now slightly behind, and Tanner could see half his head.

'Sarge,' said Sykes again, 'if you fire now you'll blow our chance of surprise. And those prisoners will probably end up getting killed an' all.'

'He's a sodding general, though, Stan. Might be a really big cheese.' The German commander's head now filled his sight. He curled his finger around the trigger.

'Sarge, our orders was to destroy the guns.'

'I've got a clear shot.'

'Don't do it, Sarge. Please. You'll scupper the mission.'

A split second. That was all it would take. His finger was on the trigger, the general's head still in his sights. The four men had now reached the gate.

'Let him go, Sarge,' whispered Sykes. 'If he comes back, shoot him then.'

Tanner closed his eyes a moment, then lowered his rifle. 'All right, Stan.' The four men were through the gate now and striding down the track towards the vehicles. The general signalled and the engine of the eight-wheeled armoured car roared into life. Tanner watched the four men slipping below the ridge and the armoured car drove slowly up towards them, its high profile dominating the track. It stopped and they clambered on. Tanner watched the general step onto the turret, the guns still booming on the far side of the farmhouse, although at a less frenetic rate of fire. *I could get you now.* He raised his rifle once more, but a moment later, the big beast was reversing down the track. At the cemetery it turned, then headed off in clouds of dust towards the smoking village.

Tanner cursed, then signalled to Peploe to bring the men over.

'You did the right thing, Sarge,' said Sykes.

'Maybe. Anyway, what do you think? What did you see from over by the house?' He looked at his watch. *Ten to six.* They needed to get a move on.

'The house is in an L-shape,' Sykes told him. 'There's some outbuildings the far side, a few bushes and small trees beyond it.'

'Before the copse?'

'Yes. They'll give cover, I think. But 'ere's another thing. That copse is just a circle of trees that overlook a kind of dip, but the land falls away to the right where there's a track leading into it. There's a bank again the far side, though. I reckon it was a quarry once. Grassed over now, but there're two 'owitzers in it. It's a brilliant position unless your attackers are right on top of you.' He grinned. 'Then it's a bloody death trap.'

'What kind of field guns?'

'Quite big. Like the ones they had in Norway when we were outside Lillehammer.'

'105s,' said Tanner. 'There are two big anti-tank guns at the edge of the copse and a smaller one.' The rest of the platoon were now hurrying, a line of ants, towards the cover of the barn.

'No one saw me, Sarge,' said Sykes. 'They're just gunners, I reckon, and bloody busy they seem too. They're firing at an 'ell of a rate.'

'There's an MG team somewhere. The far side of the copse, maybe.'

Peploe joined them. 'What was going on?'

'Just waiting for the coast to clear, sir,' said Tanner.

'Have you got a plan, Sergeant?'

'Yes, sir.' Tanner felt hot, suddenly, and wiped his brow, then tried unsuccessfully to suppress a cough – the cordite was irritating his throat. Peploe beckoned the section commanders to gather round.

'Sergeant Tanner's got a plan of attack,' he said to them. 'Sergeant?'

Briefly, Tanner explained the layout of the farm and copse. 'Rosso,' he said to Corporal Ross, 'you head out first and put your section in the bushes in front of the farm. Make sure your Bren has a really clear line of fire. Stan, I'll come with your lads round the back. Hopefully we can cross the gap without being spotted, but if we are, Rosso's section can keep them busy. At the same time, sir, you lead Cooper's section around the other side.'

'Like Hannibal at Cannae,' said Peploe. Seeing Tanner's puzzled expression, he said, 'A pincer movement. Hit hard at the front and envelop either side.'

'Exactly, sir. But, Rosso, it's important your boys don't open fire until Stan and I have got past. Sir, your lot must move under the cover of Rosso's fire – but you can use the bushes and there are some outbuildings that'll give cover. Speed and weight of fire is the key to this.'

'Good,' said Peploe. He was pale, his eyes darting from one to another. 'Brief your men and then let's go. Corporal Ross, as soon as you're ready.'

'One minute, sir,' said Tanner. His heart was hammering again. Shaky hands undid the clips on his ammunition pouches. From his respirator bag he produced half a dozen hand grenades, which he stuffed into his deep trouser pockets for ease of access. Then he walked down the line of men. Knuckles showed white around rifles, eyes stared at him. Men bit their lips. 'You'll be fine, lads,' said Tanner. 'Now iggery, all right? Once the shooting starts, keep moving. They're only bloody gunners so they'll all be deaf as posts and won't hear you coming.'

It was nearly six o'clock. He looked at the lieutenant, who nodded to him, then patted Ross's shoulder. He watched the corporal breathe in deeply, then turn the corner of the barn and sprint across the yard to the edge of the house, the rest of his section following. Tanner winked at Corporal Cooper, then said to Sykes, 'Right, Stan, let's go.'

Clutching his rifle in his right hand, he ran across the open yard, the dust kicked up from Ross's section catching in his mouth. As he rounded the end of the house he was relieved to see Ross's men already diving for cover among the bushes that perched on the lip of the hollow. He could now see the route into the quarry. Sykes had been right – it was quite a drop, some ten or twelve feet deep, and they'd have to scramble down and up the other bank. He breathed out, then waved at the rest of the section to hurry.

A glance at Ross, who raised his thumb. *Good*, thought Tanner. *Bren in position*. He motioned to McAllister to move beside him – he needed that Bren at the van of their movement. 'Mac, I'm going to count to three,' he said. 'Then we're going to make a dash for it.'

McAllister nodded, and gripped his Bren with both hands.

'One, two – three!' They were up and running down the shallow grass bank. Tanner scanned the hollow – glimpses of men gathered round the guns in a web of shadows. The big howitzers fired in turn, the recoil sending them lurching back on their wheels. Tanner gasped as he scrambled up the other slope. A shout – German – *Damn, we've been spotted* – and Ross's Bren opened fire. Tanner was conscious, from the corner of his eye, of men falling.

Rifles cracked – a yell – then Tanner urged his men on. Past several trees and then another gap, giving a view down into the pit of the hollow. *Keep going, keep going.* He was now on the other side of the hollow. The chatter of Bren fire behind, snapping rifle fire, bullets zipping, leaves and branches sliced by their passage. McAllister was still with him – *good* – and then, up ahead, across a narrow pasture, he saw men crouch-running among a further clump of bushes. A second later he heard the burp of a machine-gun and bullets penetrating the branches behind.

He raised his rifle, saw one two-man team through his scope, pulled back the bolt and fired. A head jerked backwards. More bullets spat and this time their height was better. Where were they coming from? Someone cried out, and Tanner flung himself to the ground, conscious of McAllister dropping onto the grass too, the bipod on his Bren already pulled out into place beforehand. *Good lad.* Bullets tore over his head – long bursts that were supposed to rake the ground but were firing high. *Barrel's overheating.* Gingerly he lifted his head.

Another burst of fire and this time he saw them, the dark shapes of the men manning them, a faint muzzle, from the direction of some bushes dead ahead, by the track that ran in front of the whole position. He brought his cheek to the butt of his rifle and peered through the scope, drew back the bolt and fired. Another man jerked backwards, and for a moment the splutter of bullets stopped.

Tanner leaped to his feet again, and hurtled across the grass towards the bushes. Grabbing a grenade, he pulled the pin and hurled it at the enemy machine-gun, then drew his rifle to his shoulder once more. Movement – a man crouch-hurrying ahead – another trying desperately to get behind the momentarily abandoned MG. Bolt back, fire – the grenade exploded – a man screamed and Tanner fired again. He sprinted to the MG, saw another man stretching for the weapon, kicked him out of the way, then dived into the shallow pit, lifted the machine-gun and, unable to hold the barrel because of the heat, let it plunge to the ground, drew back the bolt and fired towards the big anti-tank guns.

Bullets pinged off the metal but he was aware that none of the guns was firing now. Had they done it? He could still hear Bren and rifle fire but he couldn't see any enemy troops.

Sykes was beside him now. 'I think we've got 'em all, Sarge,' he said, between gasps for breath.

'Maybe,' muttered Tanner. Pushing himself to his feet, he said, 'Cover me,' then dashed forward to the first of the big anti-tank guns. Ten yards from it he hurled another grenade. As it landed, a terrified gunner stood up and ran for cover in the trees. Tanner raised his rifle and fired, the man falling forwards and tumbling down the sides of the hollow with a scream. He ran to the next gun and there saw Lieutenant Peploe, a stunned expression on his face. They had encircled the position.

'Hold your fire!' Tanner shouted, then turned to the lieutenant. 'Are you all right, sir?'

'I think so, Sergeant.' He laughed. 'Christ, I don't believe it – we've bloody done it! We've bloody well gone and done it!'

Tanner grinned, then wished he hadn't as his lip cracked again. 'They'll be coming up from the vehicles, sir, and maybe even the village. We need to be quick.'

'Why don't we use those vehicles?' suggested Peploe.

'Good idea, sir. Perhaps you should do that while Sykes and I make sure no one uses these guns again.'

'Yes. I'll come back straight up this track here. Meet you by the farmhouse.' He loped off, shouting to Cooper and Ross. When

Tanner turned, he saw that, without prompting, the corporal was taking out a cartridge of Nobel's, sticking in a small stretch of fuse, then lighting it and placing it in the muzzle of the first big gun. Thirty seconds later, it exploded amid a cloud of smoke and a hollow, tinny clang.

More Bren and rifle fire a short distance behind. The lieutenant's attempt to capture some transport. But Tanner now had his rifle slung on his shoulder and his binoculars to his eyes. Heart plummeting, he saw that the British tanks were no longer advancing. A number had ground to a halt, some burning, others less obviously disabled. Two stood smoking on the ridge a short way to his right. Heavy firing was still coming from the village behind and to the right, but he could see now that other tanks were pulling back, weaving slowly across the open farmland between the two ridges.

'Damn it all,' muttered Tanner. They had silenced the guns but too late. No wonder that general had buggered off. *He must have known he'd halted the attack. Damn, damn, damn.* Then movement to his left caught his eye. He swung round with his binoculars and saw, heading north to the west of Berneville, a long column of enemy troops. He looked at the second of the big guns. How hard could it be to fire one of those things? He hurried over to it. Three men lay sprawled around it, one staring up at him with wide, lifeless eyes. Large wooden shell boxes stood a short distance away. Could they really fire at that column?

'Boys!' he called. 'Here – quick!' He peered through his binoculars again. Some panzers and several half-tracks were advancing over the rolling fields towards Berneville. He looked for their own transport, but they had done a good job: they were hidden from view. Christ, not only had they silenced the guns too late, they were in danger of being cut off, stuck behind enemy lines.

'Sarge?' said McAllister.

Tanner looked at them. McAllister, Verity, Bell, Chambers and Kershaw. 'Where's Hepworth?'

'Helping the corp,' said Kershaw. A moment later there came another explosion as one of the howitzers was blown.

'Denning and Rhodes?'

'Both dead, Sarge,' said McAllister. 'Stupid idiots didn't get down quick enough when that second Spandau opened up.'

Two young men gone. Tanner sighed. And for what? He picked up a stone and hurled it angrily. 'We're going to try and fire this bastard.'

'How do we do that, Sarge?'

'Dunno,' said Tanner. He went over to the box, took out a long, heavy, twenty-pound shell and pushed it into the open breech.

'Shouldn't there be a door or something to hold it in place, Sarge?' said McAllister.

'Can you bloody well see one?'

McAllister shrugged.

'It must be a sliding breech. We need to turn it somehow. Those wheels at the side must do something.' He turned one to the right and discovered the barrel moved downwards. He reversed the action and the barrel rose. Another wheel turned the entire gun on its central column. 'See?' he said. 'Told you it couldn't be that hard.'

'That must be the firing mechanism, Sarge,' said McAllister, pointing to a lever to the right of the breech.

Tanner swivelled the gun so that it was pointing towards the enemy column, raised the barrel a few inches, said, 'There's only one way to find out,' and pressed down on the lever. In a deafening blast and a puff of choking smoke, the breech hurtled backwards in recoil, spitting out the smoking brass casing as it did so. Tanner stumbled backwards and fell over as the shell hurtled through the air and detonated a moment later in a field some distance short of the target.

'You need to elevate it a bit, Sarge,' said McAllister, lugging another shell to the breech. Tanner's ears rang shrilly as he got to his feet, raised the barrel and fired again. Another ear-splitting blast. The men spluttered and coughed, but this time the shell landed close to the target.

'Blimey, Sarge,' said Sykes, now emerging from the hollow with Hepworth, his hands over his ears.

'Grab some shells, lads, iggery,' said Tanner. 'Watch this, Stan.'

McAllister flung the next shell into the breech as Tanner raised the barrel an inch more. 'Keep out the way, Stan.' Tanner grinned. 'This thing's got a hell of a kick.' He pressed down on the lever, the great gun thundered, and this time they saw the shell explode almost on top of the enemy column some two miles to the north-west. A cheer went up, but Tanner barked at them to put another shell into the breech. He fired again, and once more found their target, then again. 'Right, Stan, time to silence her. We need to go.'

As Sykes prepared his demolition, Tanner peered through his binoculars again. He could see vehicles on fire, and others wheeling crazily around the mayhem he and his men had unleashed. Two of the panzers heading for Berneville had stopped, he now saw, uncertain, he guessed, as to what was happening and what they should be doing. He smiled grimly.

The sound of vehicles. Tanner turned towards the farmhouse and saw Peploe wave from one of the Krupps he had seen earlier outside the cemetery.

'Come on, lads,' he said. 'Time to get going.'

He ran along the track, leaving behind a mist of pungent, acrid smoke, more than twenty dead and, as the gelignite in the big gun exploded, the useless wrecks of five enemy guns. But as he clambered into the Krupp beside the lieutenant he brought his binoculars to his eyes and saw Stukas diving on Berneville and the ridge beyond. One after another, relentlessly, they screamed down, their bombs exploding amid clouds of dust, smoke and grit so that soon the entire view was shrouded in a thick pall.

Then he saw more enemy troops hurrying down the main Doullens–Arras road. Two armoured cars, motorcycles and, following behind, a half-track.

This is going to be a close-run thing. A very close thing indeed.

The last of the men was now aboard. 'Let's get out of here,' said Peploe.

'Hold on, sir,' said Tanner. He was looking again at the enemy vehicles speeding along the Doullens–Arras road. 'I've just had a bit of an idea.'

17

Sturmbannführer Timpke had managed to assemble most of his battalion to the east of Beaumetz as planned, if somewhat later than he had hoped. Once again, the narrowness and lack of roads had been the problem: his motorcycles and armoured cars – even his half-tracks – couldn't cross the soft, rich clay of the open fields. Metalled roads and firm tracks were the limit of their capabilities – and this was the case for most of the division. He had been thankful that neither the French nor the Tommy bombers had spotted their long columns on the march.

He had, however, identified three passable approaches to Berneville from the south. One track ran diagonally from Beaumetz, while a few kilometres along the Doullens–Arras road, a further track and a metalled road led off at ninety degrees directly into the south of the village. He sent Company 1 from Beaumetz and his P38 tanks off across the fields beside them, then led his remaining two companies along the main road to Arras. And thank goodness he had, because no sooner had they got going than shells were hurtling over from the ridge to the south-east. From his position in the turret of his scout car, Timpke had been startled by the unexpected explosion a few hundred yards to the north. If that had been a ranging shot, the shells that followed had soon found their mark, hitting part of Regiment 3's column pushing north from Beaumetz.

Timpke had soon spotted the source of the shellfire: a big 88mm flak gun stuck in a copse a couple of miles away. Typical wooden-headed *Wehrmacht* gunners getting carried away. The shelling didn't last long: someone had obviously pointed out the error of their ways, but to the north of Beaumetz a number of vehicles were burning, thick black smoke pitching into the air.

Wearing a wireless headset, he heard Schultz's voice crackle in his headphones from below. 'Boss, Company One are nearing the western end of Berneville. They're not drawing enemy fire.'

'Good. Order them to keep going. Where are Totenkopf Regiment Two?'

There was a pause. 'They're advancing from Simencourt, boss, along the ridge to the north of Berneville. At least six vehicles were hit by that gun.'

'Those gunners should be shot.'

As they had reached the first track into the village from the main road, he had ordered Company 2 to break from their column and advance along it. No sooner had he done so than he had heard the sound of aero-engines and, scanning the sky, spotted two dozen Stukas approaching from the east. They were flying low, one swarm of twelve aircraft stacked above another, only a few thousand feet high. For a brief moment Timpke had felt a stab of panic that they might attack their columns, but then, one by one, sirens screaming, the planes peeled off, dropping their bombs on Berneville and the ridge behind it.

'Schultz,' said Timpke, 'we'll halt until the dive-bombers have done their work. Relay the order.'

'Yes, boss,' Schultz replied. 'Company One and the panzers want to wait where they are too.'

'Agreed. But as soon as the Stukas go, get them into the village.'

When the dive-bombers finally left, smoke hid the village and the ridge. To the west, however, Timpke could see infantry pressing towards the village – men from Totenkopf Regiment 2. Mortar shells were exploding, machine-gun and small arms cracked, their tinny reports echoing across the open fields. Timpke sniffed – burned wood and rubber – as though to confirm the acrid stench of battle. He ordered his men forward once more, and a few hundred metres further on his small lead column of Company 3 turned off the Doullens–Arras road and sped towards the village.

Ahead, his motorcycles had stopped. A man had raised his hand, beckoning them on. Two others were getting out of their sidecars. Then Timpke saw them: two Opel trucks with white paint daubed across the bonnets. He knew instantly what they were – there could be no doubt.

His scout car halted in front of them and he got down, his anger rising once more. The numberplates had been painted over, but the SS runes were only partially hidden. Jaw clenched, he strode around both vehicles, looking with disgust at the British names written crudely upon them. *Yorks Rangers, BEF*. Stolen at dead of night and abandoned at the first sign of a fight. He glanced up the road to the village. Where were those men now, he wondered. In Berneville still, or dead, pulverized by the weight of the Stuka attack? Or had they fallen back further already? Dead or alive, he vowed, he wanted those men, those Yorks Rangers who had dared to take these vehicles from him.

'Herr Sturmbannführer, look,' said one of his men now.

Timpke turned back to the direction from which they had come and saw two Krupp infantry carriers rumbling down the road towards them.

'Our friends in the *Wehrmacht*,' said Timpke, walking back to his vehicle. 'If they think they're going to drive on ahead of us, they're very much mistaken.'

Timpke was getting into the scout car as the first of the Krupps pulled up alongside. To his surprise, one of the *Wehrmacht* men leaped from the vehicle onto his armoured car. He glimpsed the pale eyes of his assailant, then the man swung his forearm round his neck, choking him, kneed him in the side so hard that Timpke gasped with searing pain, and jabbed a pistol into the small of his back.

It had been so quick and unexpected that none of Timpke's men had had time to react.

'*Hände hoch!*' a man was shouting from the Krupp. '*Hände hoch!*' One of Timpke's men tried to swing round the machine-gun on his sidecar, but at a quick tap from the MG in the Krupp he jerked backwards with a cry. The rest now put their hands slowly in the air, stunned. Timpke felt the arm against his throat slacken, so that although the muzzle of his own Luger was still pressed hard against his kidney, he was able to turn enough to look at his attacker. His eyes widened. The man had a battered face, a cut on his cheek and lip and severe bruising. He wore a German helmet but, he now saw, a khaki uniform, not field grey. And on his shoulders the curved black patches bore two words in green stitching: Yorkshire Rangers. Timpke curled his lips into a snarl, then shook his head. *No!* It wasn't possible! How could they have been caught out like this? If only his men following had looked at these Tommies more carefully. German helmets – helmets! Timpke groaned. Surprise – it was one of the golden lessons of warfare, and he had let himself and his men be caught out not once but twice.

'Evening, chum,' said Tanner.

'Who are you?' said Timpke, slowly, in English, his face red with fury.

'Tell your men not to make any attempt to shoot,' said Tanner. He saw Timpke glance up the road towards the rest of his column. Tanner dared not take his eye off him, so he called to Lieutenant Peploe, 'Sir, are we all secure?'

'Yes, Sergeant,' Peploe replied. 'Can he speak English?'

Tanner nodded. 'I told you, sir. The clever ones like this fellow always can.'

Tanner pushed Timpke down against the side of the car and

said, 'Now order the men inside this car to leave their weapons and come out.' Timpke looked at him with hatred in his eyes. 'Now!' snapped Tanner.

Timpke barked an order and the two men appeared.

'Tell them to get down on the road and put their hands in the air.'

Again, Timpke did so and the men did as ordered.

'Right, Stan,' said Tanner. 'You can go down and do interesting things with their radio equipment.' He grinned, then cursed as his lip split yet again.

'Has someone got this joker covered?' he called.

'Yes, Sarge,' said Hepworth, from behind him in the Krupp.

Tanner now allowed himself to glance back to the second Krupp. As he had planned with Lieutenant Peploe, it had waited behind the small SS column. The Bren, resting on the wooden side of the Krupp, had the men in the three half-tracks and armoured car covered, while others were now hurrying over to disarm them. *Not a bad haul*. Tanner scanned briefly for another of their sub-machine-guns.

'Give me your name and unit,' he said, to the German in front of him.

'Sturmbannführer Otto Timpke, commanding officer of the reconnaissance battalion, *Waffen-SS* Totenkopf Division,' replied Timpke, through clenched teeth.

'Storm-ban-what?' said Tanner. 'What kind of rank is that?'

'Sturmbannführer,' said Timpke. 'In the *Wehrmacht* it would be the same as a major.'

'I see.'

'I do not know what you think you can achieve by this,' hissed Timpke. 'Your attack has failed. The Tommies have fallen back. Most of our division is advancing from the south and west and a panzer division is pressing forward to the east of here. You are surrounded. You might have a pistol pointing at me now but, believe me, very soon it will be you who have to put your hands in the air.'

'I don't think so,' said Tanner, taking the cigarettes from Timpke's breast pocket. 'You see, you lot are going to help us get back to our lines.' He took a cigarette, felt for his matches and, with his spare hand, struck one. *Aaah*, he thought, the swirling cloud of tobacco briefly overpowering the smell of burning that hung in the air, *I needed that*.

'Help you?' said Timpke. 'You must be mad.'

'A bit, perhaps,' said Tanner, 'but not as mad as you lot with your bloody goose-stepping and heil-Hitlers.' He grasped Timpke's neck tightly. 'Now, listen to me, Otto. We're all going to drive on through Berneville, dodging those potholes made by your mates in the *Luftwaffe*, and we'll keep going over the ridge and back down to Warlus until we find our own side again. And if we get so much as a single shot fired at us, I'll kill you all. Understand?'

Timpke glared at him, the veins at the side of his head pulsing, the muscles on his jaw flexing. Tanner tightened his grip, then said, louder, 'Understand?'

'Yes!' gasped Timpke.

Tanner relaxed his grip. 'Good. Then let's go and tell your men.' He pushed Timpke roughly so that he fell onto the road. Jumping down beside him, the Luger still in his hand, he pulled the German roughly to his feet. 'Come on, then, Otto. Be quick!'

Sykes emerged from the armoured radio car and hoisted himself into the first of the Opels, while Corporal Cooper climbed into the second. Quickly, they manoeuvred them into position between the three half-tracks. Peploe then ordered half a dozen men into the trailer of each, with a Bren and a captured Spandau pointed at the prisoners in the half-tracks.

'The motorcycles and scout cars should lead, don't you think?' Peploe said to Tanner, as he and Timpke returned to the lead vehicle.

'Yes, sir. You'll follow, will you?'

Peploe nodded.

'And shall I go in the scout car with Otto here? If we spot any of our lot we'll simply put our own helmets back on and push one of the Opels in front.'

Peploe breathed out and smiled nervously. 'Christ, Tanner,' he said, 'if I'm still in one piece by midnight, I'll be a happy man.'

Tanner grinned. 'We'll be fine, sir.' He turned to Timpke. 'I'll get in first.'

The inside of the armoured car was hot. Tanner had shoved the radio operator into one of the Opels but even with just Timpke and the driver the smell of oil and petrol was almost overpowering. Sweat ran down his neck and back; the thick serge of his trousers rubbed scratchily against his legs. When they rolled forwards, though, a breeze through the vents brought relief. To one side, the radio, with the connection leads to the transmitter, receiver and power units, had been disconnected. *Good for Stan.* He hadn't destroyed but deactivated it.

'You are finished,' said Timpke. 'Even if we reach your Tommy lines tonight, it is only a question of time. And I promise you this: I will find you, Herr Tanner, and kill you.'

'Put a sock in it, will you?' said Tanner. He noticed the sub-machine-gun hanging on cream hooks on the metal wall. He wiped his brow. His hand was clammy, the wooden grip of the Luger slippery with sweat. He stared at Timpke. Good-looking, he thought, but arrogant too – a sneering superiority was etched across the man's face. They were an efficient military machine, all right, but too many of them seemed to have been seduced by a madman with a strange haircut and an even odder moustache. He couldn't imagine feeling superior about that.

'France is falling, then so too will Great Britain,' said Timpke. 'We wondered whether you Tommies would put up more of a fight than your French allies, but after today's little exchange, it would seem not.'

Tanner ignored him. Peering through the vent, he saw they were now turning into the main street of the village. He could hear distant gunfire, but the village itself seemed quiet. He stood upright, took the sub-machine-gun from its hooks, then slung it round his neck. 'This looks like a good bit of kit, Otto,' he said. 'I took one from some of your lads the other night. At least, I think they were the same ones. They had that fancy-dress skull and crossbones on their collars.' He eyed Timpke and was pleased to see the German stiffen with anger again. 'Actually, it's funny what you were saying about the French and us because your boys rolled over easy as pie. We silenced a few sentries, nicked four vehicles and blew up half a building without so much as a cross word. Couldn't have been easier, frankly. So I'm not sure you lot are *that* good.' He examined the sub-machine-gun. 'What do you call this?'

For a moment Timpke said nothing. Then: 'It is a Bergmann MP35. Made exclusively for the *Waffen-SS*.'

'Well, your kit's definitely better, I'll give you that. We've got nothing like this. And that big anti-tank gun.' He nodded in the direction of the ridge behind them, then whistled. 'Quite something.'

Timpke couldn't hide his surprise. 'That was *you?*'

Tanner nodded. 'Actually, come to think of it,' he added, 'that lot were a bit of a roll-over too.'

He saw Timpke flush with rage but he was curious about that gun and decided it was time for some flattery. 'I really am impressed with your kit. That gun looked like our large anti-aircraft gun. What would it have been?'

Timpke shrugged. 'Probably a Flak 36. It *is* an anti-aircraft gun – 8.8-cm calibre but used in an anti-tank role.'

The driver now spoke and Tanner heard 'panzer'. Timpke spoke back to him – his words short and sharp. Tanner glanced briefly out of the forward vent again and this time saw two German tanks squeaking and trundling slowly towards the crossroads ahead of them.

'Get up into the turret, Otto,' said Tanner, 'and tell them you're advancing to Warlus.' Timpke got to his feet. 'And, Otto, don't try anything.' He pointed the Luger at the German's crotch. 'I bet a good-looking bloke like you has a lot to live for, eh?'

They drove on, Tanner's heart thudding. Beyond the tanks there were more vehicles – several half-tracks and motorcycles. *Come on,* he thought, *keep going.* As if to stress the point, he jabbed the barrel of the Luger into Timpke's crotch.

*

Standing in the turret, Timpke saw they were approaching the heart of the village, the hub into which all other roads and tracks fed. A slate-roofed house, built in the centre of the road, stood at this confluence. To the side of it, three of his panzers had ground to a halt while beyond, and from a track to his left, the vehicles of Companies 1 and 2 had now converged. The smoke was clearing although it hung heavy in the air, like a thin filter that made everything seem hazy. Several houses had been destroyed, rubble spreading onto the street. Up the hill another burned fiercely.

Seeing his forces take control of the village made him realize his envelopment had happened as he had planned – except, of course, for the unexpected ambush by these cursed Tommies. *Scheisse!* he thought. How could it be? He cursed again – but he couldn't undo what had happened. The important thing now was to resolve his predicament. A quandary: he could tell Beeck and Saalbach as he passed them what had happened and order them to rescue him, or he could do as this man Tanner had told him and continue straight to Warlus. A rescue attempt, he was sure, would be successful, but at what cost? These Yorkshire Rangers were, he guessed, some kind of British élite unit – and they were good, he had to admit. In Tanner, he knew he was up against a hard man, who would not flinch from carrying out his threat. But he was also certain that the British were beaten. The Reich's forces would soon overwhelm them so he and his men would not be held captive for long. In any case, there might be some better opportunity to escape: they couldn't keep him in this vehicle for ever.

When they reached the house in the centre of the road, he saw Beeck wave at him from his half-track, then jump down and run towards the scout car as it slowed to pass the panzers.

'We have the village, boss!' Beeck called.

'Yes – and I'm going to push on,' Timpke shouted back. 'Stay here and make sure it's secure.' An idea struck him. 'Then push on with Company Three in all strength towards Warlus.'

'Is your radio working, Herr Sturmbannführer?' Beeck asked. 'We've been trying to call you.'

'No – something's up. Follow soon, understand?'

Beeck saluted, then ran back to his vehicle.

'Otto,' Tanner shouted, tugging at Timpke's breeches, 'what was that about? You didn't tell him to mount a rescue?'

'No,' said Timpke, 'but the whole weight of two divisions will be on your heels soon. You don't have a chance.'

Tanner bent down to the vent again, and saw they were passing tanks and vehicles. Troops were searching the houses as they pressed on up the hill. Would they notice that British soldiers were driving past? The disguises hardly bore close examination. *Hold your nerve*, he told himself. *They're not expecting it. Fortune favours the bold.* They were climbing now, the road snaking out of the village towards the ridge between the two villages. Still no exclamations of surprise, no sudden gunfire. He glanced at his watch. *Nearly ten to seven.* Perhaps Otto was playing ball; perhaps they would get away with it after all.

The armoured car slowed almost to a standstill.

Tanner tugged at Timpke again. 'What's going on?'

'A bomb crater. We will drive round it.'

Once they had successfully negotiated it, they continued their climb until they reached the summit of the ridge beside the water-tower Tanner had noticed on their way to attack the copse. Through the vents Tanner saw bodies and detached limbs strewn at either side of the road – British victims of the Stuka attack they had witnessed half an hour before.

Timpke lowered himself into the car. 'Our Stukas had their fill here,' he said, and smirked. 'There are many dead Tommies.'

Suddenly a surge of anger rose in Tanner's belly. Too many times in the past fortnight he had been forced to keep it in check, to take humiliation on the chin and brush it aside. *No more.* He had had enough of this madman. Calmly he clenched his left hand into a fist then, quick as a dart, swung it into the side of Timpke's head.

The German looked at him curiously, then fell onto his side. Tanner's anger left him. His ability to hit almost equally well with both hands had always been one of his strengths as a boxer. The driver swung round, aghast, but Tanner waved the pistol at him – *just keep going.*

Now Tanner climbed into the turret himself. Behind, he saw Lieutenant Peploe. He heard small-arms fire to the left and mortars were exploding around Warlus, now just a few hundred yards on the far side of the ridge. Away to his right, but hidden from view by a dense wood, he thought he heard the clatter of tank tracks. Directly ahead there were two more bomb craters. The motorcyclists were slowing to get through them, and as one looked round, Tanner signalled to them to halt.

'Our boys must still be in the village, sir,' he called to Peploe.

'I agree,' Peploe replied. 'I'll tell Sykes to drive on in and warn them. Where's your German?'

'Out cold.' Tanner grinned. 'I'm sorry, sir, but he was getting on my nerves.'

Sykes was waved through. He raised his thumb at Tanner as he passed, mounted the verge, inched past the craters and headed on down the hill towards Warlus. Tanner waited a moment, listening, but to his relief heard no gunfire directed at Sykes's truck. He climbed back into the car and said to the driver, '*Sie gehen.*' A jolt, a jerk, and they followed Sykes's lead, clambering onto the verge and past the bomb craters.

They halted in the village. Tanner grabbed Timpke, still unconscious, hoisted him up into the turret and pushed him out, then ordered the driver to follow. As he pulled himself out, he saw that they had stopped in the wide turning towards the church, the small stretch of road they had left barely two hours earlier. It seemed a lifetime ago. A couple of trucks, several carriers and a few cars were already there. He spotted Captain Barclay and Blackstone, standing with several other men on the corner, gazing incredulously at the booty of German vehicles and the prisoners being ordered to the ground. Tanner watched for a moment, the evening breeze cool and welcome after the heat of the scout car. The air was heavy with cordite and smoke but birds were still singing in the trees around the church – last-minute wooing before they roosted for the night.

Blackstone, with Slater in tow, now walked over to Corporal Cooper, who was gathering the prisoners together.

Sykes was wandering towards Tanner, drawing on a cigarette. 'Where's 'e taking them, Sarge?' he asked, nodding towards Blackstone.

'God knows,' said Tanner, as several mortars exploded to the west, making him start. Thumps and machine-gun fire followed. A platoon of Durham Light Infantry hurried across the road by the church and disappeared behind it. More dull cracks and thuds resounded.

'Come on, Stan,' said Tanner. 'Best help me with Otto here. Then I reckon we ought to find out what the hell's going on.'

'We're under attack from the west, I'd say.'

'And soon we'll be under attack from the south as well,' added Tanner. 'Those SS-wallahs aren't going to hang around in Berneville for ever.' He sighed. 'What a bloody mess.' He tucked the Luger into his belt, rifled through Timpke's holster and pockets for any spare rounds – he found three clips – then called to Captain Barclay, who was talking feverishly with Peploe under a large copper beech that was just bursting into full leaf. 'Sir, do you want to question him?'

Barclay looked at him with a flush of irritation. 'Not at the minute, Tanner. Take him with the others. We can interrogate him later.'

'Suit your bloody self,' muttered Tanner.

Blackstone and Slater had taken the prisoners across the road to a large old-brick barn. By the time Tanner and Sykes caught up, the SS men had been corralled inside it. It was dry and dusty in there. A rick of straw was stacked at one end, but otherwise it was empty, save for a dilapidated cart, an ageing plough, a harrow and a few broken-spoked wheels.

There were, Tanner reckoned, more than forty prisoners – all SS but some had been captured earlier. One of the lance-corporals from Company Headquarters was there, keeping guard with a Bren. Tanner and Sykes laid Timpke beside the straw then turned to go.

'How's my favourite rapist, then?' said Blackstone, winking.

Tanner ignored him.

'The women of France should be quaking now his blood's up,' he continued, grinning. 'A bit of fighting today and he'll be terrorizing the ladies tonight.'

Tanner grabbed him by the throat and rammed him hard against the wooden side of the barn. Behind him, he heard the prisoners shuffling apprehensively, as though weighing up whether the time to make a bid for freedom had come. At the same moment, he heard the cock of the Bren pulled back and clicked into place. The lance-corporal was pointing the Bren straight at him.

'Shut your sodding mouth, Blackstone,' Tanner hissed.

'Let go of the CSM,' said a low, gruff voice. Tanner turned and saw Slater beside him, a Webley in his hand.

Tanner glared at him, then loosened his grip.

'Jesus, Jack,' spluttered Blackstone, 'you never could take a joke.'

'Not from you, you bastard.' He noticed the MP35 slung over Blackstone's shoulder. 'What gives you the right to carry that like some bloody trophy?'

'I see you've got another,' he answered, straightening his battle-blouse.

'Yes, unlike you, I got it the hard way.'

'It's a perk of my position, Jack, you know that. And let me tell you something else. It's not clever to go around threatening warrant officers.' He eyed Tanner carefully. 'You were lucky this morning – very lucky. But that matter hasn't gone away, you know. Rape is rape, whoever you are. And now you're showing violent tendencies towards a superior. It won't look good – it won't look good at all. And I've witnesses.' He nodded to Slater and Sykes.

'Don't think I'm one of your lackeys,' said Sykes. 'Come on, Sarge,' he said to Tanner, pushing past the two men. 'Let's leave them to guard this lot. We've got proper soldiering to do.'

Slater grabbed Sykes's shoulder and swung him round. 'Watch your lip, son,' he said. 'You and the good sergeant 'ere might 'ave been leading charmed lives but it don't pay to push your luck.'

'Let go of me,' said Sykes, wriggling free.

'Leave it, Stan,' said Tanner, ushering Sykes away. He turned back to Blackstone and Slater. 'Trust me,' he said, 'it's you two who're pushing your luck. Eventually you'll slip up and I'll be waiting when you do.'

As they walked back towards the square, they were hailed by Lieutenant Peploe. 'There you are,' he said, as they hurried over. The air was now heavy with gunfire and the sound of battle – not only from the south and west of the village but to the north as well. Dull crumps and faint machine-gun sallies were coming from a few miles away.

'Bloody hell,' said Tanner, looking northwards, 'that's Duisans, isn't it?'

'And east of there too.' Peploe rubbed his eyes and cheeks. 'Look, we've got to move into position, back up the road towards the water-tower. Then we'll dig in around the hedgerows along the edge of the village.'

'All right, sir, let's go. Shall we leave the trucks?'

'Yes, they'll be safer here, I hope.'

Tanner called to the rest of the platoon, who had been waiting by the vehicles, and they hurried back up the road that led to Berneville. Past the last of the houses, up ahead, they saw an anti-tank crew bringing their gun into position against the bank at the side of the road, men unloading shells from the carrier beside them. Away to their left, from the direction of the wood, shots rang out, while behind and to the east, guns continued to boom intermittently.

A short way forward from the anti-tank crew, a hedge extended either side of the road.

'Is anyone dug in along here?' Peploe asked one of the DLI gunners.

'No, sir. We've got forward posts in the wood but that's it.'

'All right,' said Peploe. 'Cooper, take your section and position them to the left of the road, behind the hedge. Ross and Sykes, your boys take the right. We're missing a few men now so we'll have to spread out a bit – five or six yards apart. I want one Bren by the road here opposite the gun and the other two at the end of our defensive lines giving covering fire across the whole of our front. Sykes, your section can be at the end. Ross, I want you a dozen yards in from the road. We need to watch out for any enemy infiltrating from the west but our primary task is to defend the village from the south.' He cleared his throat, then turned to Tanner. 'Happy with those dispositions, Sergeant?'

'Yes, sir.' *The lieutenant's learning fast.*

'Good – all clear? Then let's go.'

As the men shuffled along the hedgerows, the drone of aircraft thrummed away to the east. Tanner counted a dozen black crosses against the pale evening sky. In no time they were directly over-head, and then they were gone, this time to bomb some other target. To the north, fighting continued, but at Warlus, although desultory mortars continued to hit the village, it was suddenly quieter to the south and east. Tanner moved along the line, check-ing the men were in position correctly and that those manning the Brens had enough ammunition. They had lost four men during the attack on the battery, all killed, leaving Sykes's section only eight men strong and the other two with nine each. The shortfall had been made up by men from Company Headquarters, which left himself, Peploe and Smailes.

'All right, Mac?' he said, as he reached McAllister, manning the Bren at the end of their small line.

'No, Sarge. I'm bloody hungry.'

'Me an' all,' agreed Bell.

'And me,' said Tanner. He'd barely thought about food all day but now he remembered they hadn't eaten since morning. His stomach immediately began to grumble. 'Try not to think about it,' he said, to himself as much as to them.

And he was tired. For the past few hours he had barely had time to think of anything but the task in hand. Now, as the battle appeared to have died down and they lay waiting patiently, his remaining energy was ebbing. He found Peploe by the road, took out one of Timpke's cigarettes and lit it, inhaling the smoke deeply. Dew was falling. The day's warmth was seeping away as rapidly as his energy.

'Where's the rest of the platoon, sir?' he asked.

'I'm not quite sure,' Peploe admitted. 'Somewhere to the east of the village. I'm afraid we're a bit of a scratch force here. Two companies of the Eighth DLI never left Duisans – there were some enemy forces to the north-west of there – so it's only A and D Companies here, plus a carrier platoon and a few mortars, and they've lost a fair few during the day. Lieutenant Bourne-Arton is missing and we're down a dozen men so far today – and that's not including the four from this platoon. The Durhams have had it worse – half their number are gone.'

Tanner shook his head. 'Mostly to dive-bombers?'

'You would have thought so, but no. Only about ten went in that. The worst casualties happened when they tried to push forward earlier, and since then there have been others – mortars, small arms and so on.'

'Not good. How long are we expected to stay here, sir?'

Peploe shrugged. 'Colonel Beart's missing too, and so is Captain Dixon. One of the advance-guard motorcycles went back to Duisans to try and get information but hasn't been seen since.'

'It's ridiculous, sir, trying to fight mobile battles with no radio. These SS-wallahs we picked up today, you should've seen their kit. Sykes disabled a beauty in the scout car.'

'I know. I'm beginning to think we're not really prepared for this war. That gun was something, wasn't it?'

'Actually, sir, I found out what it was. An ack-ack gun, all right, but it seems they use them in an anti-tank role. It's something called a Flak 36, 88mm calibre. I think we should take a leaf out of their book and start using our ack-ack guns in that way.'

'Beasts to move around but they certainly make our little twenty-pounders look a bit feeble.'

'The twenty-pounder's all right, sir, just so long as you use it over short distances. If anything comes over that ridge tonight, I'd back those boys to see it off, but over longer distances – well, that 88 caused mayhem, and we were firing more than two miles.'

'And the pair of them saw off our tank attack,' added Peploe.

They were silent for a moment, and then Peploe said, 'I know we did what we were asked to do today, but that it was all for nothing sticks in my gut. Four good men lost. To think they were eating and breathing and living their lives this morning and now they're lying beside some copse on a French hill.' He sighed. 'I can't help feeling responsible for them – guilty, even. It wasn't something I ever considered when I was at OCTU.'

'You might have lost more men if we'd stayed here, sir. And we learned a lot from that attack. Do you remember our conversation when we first got to Manston, about experience being the best training? Don't you feel a better soldier now than you did this morning?'

'You're right.' Peploe smiled. 'But another thing they don't teach you at OCTU is how confusing battle is. Most of today I haven't had the faintest idea what's going on. I still don't.'

Tanner grinned. 'I don't think anyone does. You just do what you can in your own part of the battlefield. Try to deal with whatever's flung your way.'

It was quiet now on their front, although to their rear gunfire still thumped intermittently.

'Did you see the CSM?' asked Peploe.

'He's looking after the prisoners. He had Slater with him and another lad from Company Headquarters.'

'Dangerous job.'

Tanner smiled wryly. 'Like I said, he's a coward. All bullies are,' he said. 'He won't get in the firing line unless he absolutely has to.'

'Did he say anything to you?'

'Not really.'

'Tanner, I'll make sure this rape charge is forgotten, you know.'

'Thank you, sir,' said Tanner, 'but we've got to get out of this mess first. If Jerry doesn't attack in the next hour, I reckon he'll wait until morning. He doesn't like attacking at night. But the fact is, sir, I think we're more or less surrounded. If we don't pull out tonight, we'll be in the bag tomorrow.'

'We've been ordered to hold the village, though. What else can we do?'

Tanner sighed. 'That's what's worrying me, sir, because it's a lost cause.'

18

When Sturmbannführer Timpke came round he couldn't understand where he was or how he'd got there. He was lying on straw and it was dark – not completely but enough for him to realize he must have been out for several hours. His head was pounding with a sharp, throbbing pain.

He saw that he was in a large old barn. Aged, dusty beams, hewn and fitted together centuries before, hung above him. He could smell dust and straw, but something else too – something sweet and cloying. For a moment he couldn't think where he had come across it before. Then, pushing himself up on his elbows, he gasped. Bodies – lots of them. Totenkopf men. His mind raced. Not ten yards from him Schultz lay on his back in a large dark pool of blood. And there were others he recognized too. *No*, he thought. *They've shot my men.*

Suddenly he heard voices – English ones – and saw two men standing in shadows by the open door. Soundlessly, he lay down again and closed his eyes.

'It's Tanner, all right,' said one of the men.

'Sergeant Tanner,' said the other. 'And Corporal Sykes. They've murdered the lot of them. And look.' The man kicked something – a weapon. 'Tanner was carrying one of these earlier.'

'Tanner,' said the first man. 'How could he do this?'

Timpke heard them leave, but waited where he was for a few minutes. His brain reeled. He had overseen a number of executions in Poland but the victims had been partisans, resisters and Jews. That was one thing, but to kill fellow soldiers in cold blood – it was incredible, horrifying, beyond comprehension. And it had been Tanner, the piece of scum who had sat with him so coolly in his scout car. He had recognized then that Tanner was a hard man, but now he had done this. Him and that small, wiry man who had disabled the radio. Sykes. When he dared to get up, he staggered as he saw the dead. Some stared up at him, their eyes still open; others lay on top of their comrades. Flies buzzed around, gorging on the blood. Timpke clutched his head, staggered again, then turned towards the entrance. A sub-machine-gun lay on the dirt floor. He bent down and picked it up to examine the markings. Yes, there could be no doubt. Two circles and a square inside, with the letters W-SS, engraved on the breech. A Bergmann MP35 Mark I. Exactly like the one Tanner had taken from him.

Leaving it where it was, he reached the door, looked around, saw no one, and ran across the yard to the farm's main entrance. Carefully peering around the gateway, he saw the end of his scout car parked across the road. To his surprise, no one was around. For a moment, he crouched in the shadows, thinking. It was almost dark; above him, the first stars were twinkling. He could hear occasional gunfire from the north, but he was certain the Tommies still held the village. He wondered why the rest of the battalion hadn't followed and attacked as he had ordered Beeck. But then, of course, they would have realized that he and the bulk of Company 3 had been taken prisoner. Units of Regiments 2 and 3 would have caught up; any orders Beeck tried to implement would have been overruled. They would have probed forward this evening, would send out patrols tonight and then, having made sure a sufficient weight of fire was in place, would attack the following morning. *Yes. That's what's happened*. If the Tommies remained where they were, they would have no chance.

And then a plan took shape. All he had to do was disable the vehicles. If he did that, they would struggle to get away. And he wanted them to stay. He wanted them to stay so that he could exact his revenge on this *Unteroffizier*, Tanner.

So long as Tanner and Sykes were not killed, they would almost certainly end up as prisoners of war. Then he would take personal charge of them. There would be no simple bullet to the head – no, Timpke was already planning something far more drawn out than that. He allowed himself a thin smile. The mere thought of it helped lift his spirits.

It was around ten o'clock when Sykes heard movement. He lay stock still until he heard a chink about fifteen yards in front. He hissed at McAllister to hold his fire, then carefully pulled a grenade from his haversack, drew out the pin and lobbed it over the hedge. The night air was so still that he heard it land with a dull thud among the young shoots of corn and a few seconds later it exploded with a blinding crack of light. A man cried out and fell backwards. Then McAllister opened up with the Bren.

A moment later a German machine-gun fired from just below the ridge. Bullets whizzed above them, splintering the tops of the hedge, then mortars were falling, but exploding some distance behind them.

More small-arms fire came from the direction of the wood to the south-east, then mortars.

'Give them another burst,' Sykes told McAllister, 'just in case.'

Tanner joined them, crouching beside Sykes.

'I think it's only patrols, Sarge,' said Sykes.

'Maybe. Sounds to me like they're trying to clear that wood of our posts, though.' More mortar shells fell and a tree now caught fire. They could hear the spit and crackle of burning timber. A flickering orange glow shone from the southern end of the wood and shouts rang out, followed by yet more mortars and small arms. Then, from the village, they heard an engine and the sound of a vehicle driving away.

'Someone scarpering?' asked McAllister.

'Hopefully to fetch some bloody relief,' muttered Tanner.

'It's not looking good, is it, Sarge?' said Sykes. 'We should all bloody well scarper if you ask me.'

Tanner sighed. 'I know, but we've been given specific orders to stay.'

Fighting continued in the wood, while mortars fell regularly on the village. Several houses were burning, so the crisp night air grew heavy with smoke. Apart from occasional bursts of machine-gun fire, the enemy were quiet to the south. Tanner checked on the rest of the men and, as he was doing so, heard engines turning over. None would catch. Again, they whined, like bleating sheep, but none would start. *Bloody hell.*

'Sounds like our vehicles are on the blink, sir,' he said, as he reached the lieutenant once more.

'I might go and find out what's happening,' said Peploe. 'It seems pointless to stay here.'

'Who exactly is in charge, sir? Who gave the orders to stay put?'

'I'm not sure. I was given my orders by Captain Barclay.' As though this had confirmed his thoughts, he said, 'Yes, I'm going to head back quickly into the village. See what's what. All right with you?'

'Yes, sir. Good idea.'

Peploe slipped away, but was back within twenty minutes.

'I saw Captain Barclay,' said Peploe breathlessly. 'He's in a bit of a dither, I'm afraid. Colonel Beart's been found – he's wounded in the leg and should be all right – but Captain Barclay's now the most senior fit and able officer. They think Captain Dixon's dead and the OC of D Company's missing. Anyway, the posts have been forced out of the wood, so to the east and south-east there's just a skeleton force holding the perimeter of the village.'

'And us.'

'Yes.'

'What about the vehicles?'

'That's what's really got the OC. They won't start. It seems someone's taken the rotor arms out of the distributors.'

'Sabotage. Must be one of the prisoners. What's happened to them?'

'I don't know. I must admit, I'd forgotten about them.'

'And where the bloody hell are Blackstone and Slater?'

'Presumably still guarding the prisoners. They weren't with Captain Barclay.'

'Damn it all,' muttered Tanner. 'Does the OC have a plan?'

'He does now.' Peploe chuckled. 'Did you hear that vehicle go off about half an hour ago?'

'Yes.'

'It was an armoured car – one of the DLI's – attempting to get help, or so the OC told me. I suggested to him that we wait here until midnight and if there's still no sign of help we evacuate on foot.'

'And he agreed?'

'Er, not entirely.'

Tanner sighed. 'Bloody hell. And I'm absolutely starving.'

'Here,' said Peploe, passing him his hip-flask. 'I managed to get a refill in Givenchy. Nothing like as good as the single malt I brought out with me, but when in Rome, eh?'

Tanner took a swig. 'What is it, sir?' he asked.

'Calvados. It's French – made from apples.' He took a swig himself. 'Cheers, Sergeant. Here's to getting out alive.'

Tanner's exhaustion was growing but he knew he had to keep awake and alert, and make sure the men did too. Twice he shook Hepworth, while he had to cajole, back-slap and urge the others to think not of food and sleep but of Jerries pouncing on them if they weren't watchful. Time seemed to have slowed, and he found himself repeatedly looking at his watch. Desultory mortar fire fell on the village, but otherwise the front remained quiet. Yet with every passing minute, Tanner felt sure their chances of escape were melting away. His cheek still hurt, his lip kept splitting and his ribs – no, his entire body – ached. Fighting was tiring. What wouldn't he do for a bed?

Eleven o'clock passed, then eleven thirty. *So no one's coming.* But then, just before midnight, they heard the tell-tale squeak and rumble of tanks approaching the village from the north.

'Hear that, sir?' said Tanner.

'Yes,' said Peploe. 'What do you think? Friend or foe?'

'I'm hoping it's the bloody cavalry – if it's Jerry, he's acting out of character.'

'Well, you go this time, Tanner.'

'All right, sir.'

'Fingers crossed.'

Tanner hurried down the road, exhaustion forgotten. The centre of the village glowed from another burning house so that the vehicles, dark and looming, were silhouetted against the flickering light. Several Durham men stood around, smoking and flinching every time another mortar hurtled over.

'Seen any officers?' Tanner asked them.

'Your skipper's in the church, mate,' said one.

The sound of tanks grew louder, then Tanner heard other vehicles rumbling with them. He ran down the road, and there, two hundred yards ahead, a column of tanks was approaching, their bulky shapes silhouetted against the now dull glow of the sky. Not British but French. He recognized them as the same models he had seen earlier that day in Neuville-St-Vaast. *Thank God.* He turned and ran to the church.

He found Captain Barclay sitting on a pew at the front. A number of candles had been lit.

'Sir?' said Tanner.

'Sergeant Tanner,' said Barclay. 'I was just trying to think and, er, offering a few prayers. Silly, probably, but I thought it might help.' He scratched the back of his neck.

'It might have done, sir. Some French tanks are here.'

'Really?' said Barclay, surprised. 'I must say, I'd always hoped there was a God.' He tapped his foot on the stone floor. 'There's a bunch of civvies down below, you know. They've been praying all night.'

When Tanner and Captain Barclay hurried outside, the tanks were in the centre of the village, and rolled to a halt by the other vehicles.

'*Bonsoir.*' A French officer saluted. 'We heard you were in difficulty,' he said in English, 'so we have come to take you out.'

'But my orders are to stay here and defend this village,' Barclay replied.

Tanner clutched his head in exasperation. 'But, sir, we haven't got a hope of holding out.' He counted six tanks and two tracked troop carriers. 'There are two entire enemy divisions out there.'

Barclay ignored him. Instead he turned to the Frenchman and asked, 'Where have you come from?'

'From Duisans. A German tank formation attacked from the north-east but they have moved further east now. Your battalion is still holding the village but they will be falling back soon, I think.'

'And what are your orders?'

The French officer shrugged. 'To help you.'

'Very well. We stay.'

'Sir – please,' said Tanner.

'No, Tanner. I'm the senior officer and those are my orders. Our armoured attack will no doubt take place in the morning. If we lose this ground they'll have to start all over again.'

'But, sir, how do you know there's going to be any more armour?'

'These boys are here, aren't they?' Barclay snapped. 'Now get back to your platoon, Sergeant.'

A renewed barrage of mortar fire fell on the village as Tanner loped back up the road. At one point, he flung himself to the ground as a mortar crashed forty yards from him. Then another building was burning, angry flames crackling into the sky.

'It's madness, sir,' he told Peploe, on his return. 'We're getting stonked to hell, all part of Jerry's softening-up process. Keeps us awake, hopefully causes a few casualties and frays nerves. At first light they'll send over some Stukas, and when they've gone they'll storm the place with all guns blazing. To stay here now is suicide.'

'All right, Tanner,' said Peploe, 'but this is a hell of a stonk. I reckon we're safer here than in the village. Let's wait for it to die down and then I'll talk to Captain Barclay.'

Mortars continued to rain on the village and more houses blazed. Tanner's agitation and anger grew. He knew the men felt much the same.

'This is madness, Sarge,' said Bell. 'Let's pack up and get the hell out of here.'

'Calm down, Tinker,' he said, moving on down the line.

'I'm cold and damp, tired and hungry, Sarge,' said Sykes. 'I wouldn't mind so much if I could see the point of it. Has the OC gone mad, then?'

'God knows.'

But at one a.m. news came that they were to move back into the village. One of the French carriers rumbled forward to hitch up the twenty-pounder while, muttering and cursing, the Rangers walked back down the road, rifles at the ready, circling regularly to check that no one was following them. At least a dozen houses were now ablaze and the centre of the village was lit up as though by gas-lamp. One of the captured SS trucks was also burning, destroyed by a direct hit. The air was thick with the stench of burning wood and rubber.

Men were taking cover by the vehicles, some DLI, others from 11 Platoon. Peploe told the men to wait and set off in search of Captain Barclay.

'Bloody hell, Sarge,' said Sykes, beside him. 'We need to get everyone together and bugger off sharpish. Where's old Barclay?'

'God knows,' said Tanner. He lit one of Timpke's cigarettes. 'And where's Blackstone? I can't believe he's been patiently guarding those SS-wallahs all this time.'

'There's one way to find out,' said Sykes.

Another mortar crashed near the church as they hurried across the road and into the yard. The place was dark, the glow of the flames shielded there by the walls and height of the barn. Slowly, Tanner pushed open the wooden door, which creaked on its hinges. 'Hello?' he called. Silence answered him.

'They've been moved, I reckon,' said Sykes.

'Hang on, Stan. What's that smell?' He felt into his pack, took out his torch and switched it on.

'Oh, my God,' said Sykes. 'Christ alive, what's happened here?'

'They've been shot, Stan. They've been bloody shot.'

'You mean murdered, Sarge.'

Tanner shone his torch across the prostrate bodies. Buttons undone, pockets rifled. *Jesus.*

'Blackstone?' said Sykes.

'Who the bloody hell else would have done it?' Tanner snapped. 'That bastard – that absolute bastard! And where the hell is he?' He strode out of the barn and back across the yard.

Two more mortars fell, one a short way behind them, another further on. Tanner ducked, but continued towards the vehicles. Barclay was there now, cowering beside one of the French tanks, Peploe too. The French officer was gesticulating – *Let's go, Monsieur Capitaine.*

'Sir,' Tanner said directly to Barclay, 'where are Blackstone and Slater?'

'Good God, man, can't you see I'm busy? How the devil should I know?'

'Sir,' insisted Tanner, 'they had taken charge of the prisoners. But they're not in the barn. The prisoners are and they've been shot, sir.'

'What the devil are you talking about?' said Barclay.

'Oh, Christ, no,' said Peploe. 'All of them?'

'Yes,' said Tanner. 'Every single one.'

'Show me.' Peploe turned to Barclay. 'Sir, you should come too.'

Tanner saw the panic in Barclay's face. The OC was struggling – it was clear as day. *He doesn't know what to do. And now this.*

'Yes – yes, all right,' he snapped. His right eyelid was twitching.

They ran back across the road and over to the barn. Once more, Tanner shone his torch upon the dead SS men.

'No,' murmured Peploe. Barclay retched and vomited, then left them. Tanner and Peploe followed, but he waved them away, hurrying back across the road. Tanner watched him lean against one of the German half-tracks, wiping his mouth with his handkerchief. Then he took a swig from his water-bottle, straightened and went to the tanks.

'Sir?' said Peploe, walking towards him.

'What, Lieutenant?' Barclay's hand gripped the edge of the French tank.

'The best part of forty Germans have been shot. What are we going to do about it?'

'We're going to leave.'

'But I thought you wanted to stay here.'

'I've changed my mind. We'll withdraw. Back to Château Duisans. Help round up the men.'

'But, sir, we can't just leave those bodies there.'

'And what else do you propose we do, Lieutenant? Bury them? How long will that take?'

'But you must find out who did this. Those men were murdered, sir.'

'Yes, but what can I do about it?' He was shaking now, his voice rising. 'We're being mortared like mad and we've lost God knows how many men. I simply can't think about that now.'

'Sir, when Tanner left those men, the CSM and Sergeant Slater were guarding them.'

Barclay looked at him with a mixture of anger and incredulity. 'Blackstone? You're saying he did this? He wasn't responsible.' He turned to Tanner. 'I do hope, Sergeant, that this is not some warped retaliation for what happened earlier.'

'Sir, really,' said Peploe. 'Sergeant Tanner hasn't accused anyone. But where are they? You have to admit it's odd they're not here.'

'Not at all,' said Barclay. 'I sent them back with Lieutenant Worthington from A Company and four of his men an hour or more ago. They took the DLI's armoured car. Worthington thought he and his little group were the only survivors of A Company. I told him he should try to get help, but he seemed a bit washed out so I told Blackstone and Slater to go with them. I wanted someone I know and trust for such a task. And, frankly, it seems to have paid off because our French friends have now arrived.'

'That doesn't mean anything, sir,' said Peploe.

'Look here,' said Barclay, prodding Peploe in the chest, 'you listen to me. Those men are dead and I cannot undo that, but I have to make sure as many of our troops get out of here as possible. That's my main concern, not the fate of forty enemy dead. You may not approve, but I can't help that. Now, get your men ready, Lieutenant. Check the far side of the church and château grounds for stragglers. We leave in five minutes.'

Peploe glared at Barclay. 'Yes, sir,' he said, and shouted to the men to load themselves onto the tanks and into the carriers. Tanner began to follow, then ran to the church and into the manor-house gardens. One of the outbuildings was on fire. Moving between the trees to the edge of the house, he saw figures and shouted, only to realize they were not British but German. Running for the cover of a tree, he crouched and peered around. The light of the flames was in front of him, not behind. Inexperienced enemy troops had not grasped that they were silhouetted in perfect clarity. He could see them, moving forward, half crouching between the trees. How far away were they? Forty yards? He unslung the sub-machine-gun and glanced at the length of the muzzle. It wouldn't be much use at distances of more than that but at thirty yards, he reckoned, it should do the job perfectly. 'Come on,' he whispered to himself. There were only a few – ten, perhaps, a patrol, nothing more. Cautiously, they continued forward, and then, when the lead man was just ten yards away, Tanner stepped around the tree and opened fire. He saw four men drop immediately while others dived for cover. He took a grenade from his haversack, pulled the pin and hurled it. Seconds later it exploded and a man cried out. Tanner fired another burst then ran back, through the trees and bushes, past the church until he saw the six tanks and carriers. Another mortar shell crashed behind him, near the church, but he barely flinched. He saw Sykes and Hepworth clinging to one of the tanks and Sykes held out an arm. The engines were running, clouds of exhaust fumes mixing with smoke and cordite.

'Come on, Sarge!' Sykes shouted. Tanner gripped his hand and hauled himself aboard the iron body of the tank. A moment later, it jolted and moved off.

'Not before time,' said Tanner, breathing heavily. 'Not before bloody time.'

Sturmbannführer Timpke had watched their departure. He had hidden in an abandoned house opposite the vehicles. It had a strong, deep cellar in which he had sheltered during quiet periods, while on the ground floor there was an open window from which he could see and hear what was going on without being spotted.

A short while before he had been congratulating himself for successfully disabling the vehicles – it had been almost ridiculously easy. No one had been around – no guards – and it had been dark, too, unlike now with so many houses blazing. Then, to his annoyance, he had heard first one, then two vehicles start up and head northwards. He had not spotted them earlier – they must have been parked in a different part of the village. Nonetheless, he had remained optimistic that the bulk of the small British garrison would be trapped.

Such hopes had fallen away when the French tanks had turned up. However, watching from an open ground-floor window, Timpke had followed events with mounting incomprehension. Why had those Tommies not left immediately? Then he had seen the officer in charge and had recognized a man promoted beyond his capabilities. The fool had been paralysed by the weight of responsibility on his shoulders and unable to make a decision.

Then the dead prisoners had been discovered, and from that

moment on, the Tommy officer had not been able to leave soon enough. *He's walking away from it.* Timpke's anger had risen once more. He had seen Tanner standing beside two officers and then, as men had loaded themselves onto the tanks, run off towards the church and disappear from view. As the engines started and still he saw no sign of Tanner, his hopes rose. He was sure he had heard gunfire from beyond the church, but then that tall figure had emerged from the gloom, running towards the tanks. An arm was outstretched and Tanner had scrambled on.

'No!' hissed Timpke to himself. 'No!' In a kind of stupor, he had walked out of the house and stood in the middle of the road, watching the last of the vehicles disappear from view, until all he could hear of them was the faint squeak and rattle of tracks. Then a mortar shell whistled over and landed on the roof of the big barn where so many of his dead comrades still lay. A moment later, a second and then a third followed. In what seemed like no time at all, the building was aglow, angry flames rising from the broken roof, wooden timbers cracking and spitting.

Timpke felt the rotor arms in his tunic pocket under his camouflage smock. At least he had his vehicles back, but that was small consolation. Only one thing would give him peace, and that was revenge. Revenge for his humiliation. Revenge for his dead comrades. *Revenge. Revenge. Revenge.*

It was a slow journey. Near the edge of the village, the survivors from Warlus had had to stop to clear burning debris from the road but, thankfully, they had met no resistance. It was still dark by the time they reached Duisans, but the stench of battle was heavy on the air. The château and village were now deserted; whatever had remained of B and C Companies had clearly fallen back.

On they trundled, back up the ridge that ran between Duisans and Maroeuil where earlier they had seen British tanks advancing. By the time they rumbled into Neuville-St-Vaast, the first streaks of dawn were creeping over the horizon. Smoke still drifted over Arras, but the distant tower of the belfry still stood. Despite the discomfort of sitting on the back of a moving French tank in the crisp cold of early dawn, Tanner dozed, imagining a big plate of bacon, egg and bread fried in beef dripping, as he and his father had eaten when he was a boy. When he woke again, it was nearly six and they had driven back over Vimy Ridge and come to a halt in Vimy village.

Seventy-four men and officers were all that remained of nearly three infantry companies, an anti-tank battery and a carrier platoon. Exhausted, they slid off the tanks, scrambled out of the carriers and collapsed at the side of the road. Men milled about. Vehicles – trucks, carriers and several cars – lined the road beneath a row of young horse-chestnuts. Tanner smoked the last of Timpke's cigarettes as Captain Barclay and the lieutenant headed off towards Brigade Headquarters.

'What happens now?' Sykes asked Tanner. It would be another sunny day, and the air was filled with birdsong.

'God knows. Hopefully get some grub.' Several of the men were already asleep, stretched out on the dewy grass beneath the horse-chestnuts. Tanner wondered when the fighting would start again. Enemy bombers would be over soon, and those two German divisions would be gearing themselves up for the next surge forward. It was supposed to have been a counter-attack – an attempt to push the enemy back, but here they were, one day on, in exactly the same place as they had started, but with good men dead, wounded and taken prisoner. In their own company, they were now down to just two officers; 11 Platoon were short of eighteen men – half their number. He wondered whether Timpke had been among the dead in the barn; he'd not seen him, but then again he'd not looked that hard either. But, Christ, all those bodies. Prisoners were a pain in the backside when you were busy fighting, but killing them in cold blood – he could barely believe it, even now. He closed his eyes. No doubt Blackstone would turn up, winking and slapping the lads on the back, everyone's mate. The murdered Germans would be swept under the carpet while the accusations of rape would be brought to the fore. And, overhead, the *Luftwaffe* would be swirling, diving and dropping their bombs. *Damn them.* Barclay was a bloody fool. How could he not see through Blackstone? Good leadership required many things but the ability to judge character was one; another was the guts to take clear-headed decisions. Squadron Leader Lyell had been right: the captain was a hopeless soldier.

Sykes nudged him now. 'The lieutenant's coming.'

Tanner glanced up and saw Peploe approaching.

'Tanner,' he said, 'come with me a moment, will you?'

Tanner stood up and went to him. Dark circles surrounded Peploe's eyes and a growth of gingery beard covered his chin. It was amazing, Tanner thought, how much fighting a war aged people.

'Captain Barclay wants to talk to us,' said Peploe, 'with Blackstone.'

'Bloody hell.'

'He wants to clear the air.'

Tanner eyed him, expecting to see an ironic smile, but the lieutenant's face was set hard.

They found Captain Barclay and CSM Blackstone standing outside a bar that had evidently been requisitioned as part of 151st Brigade's headquarters.

'Ah, there you are,' said Barclay, taking his pipe from his mouth. His eyelid flickered and he rubbed it self-consciously.

'Morning, Jack,' said Blackstone. 'How's the head?' He circled a finger around his own face.

Tanner didn't answer. 'You wanted to see me, sir.'

'Yes, all three of you, actually,' said Barclay. 'We've had a difficult twenty-four hours and we've probably got some difficult days ahead. Jerry's snapping at our heels and we've lost some damn good men.'

Tanner wished he'd get to the point.

'Now, I know that you, Tanner, and the CSM are not exactly friends, but I want you to bury the hatchet. I don't want to hear any more about this girl or the dead prisoners.'

'But, sir,' interrupted Peploe, 'you can't just sweep it under the table. Forty men were murdered.'

Barclay smoothed his moustache. 'Blackstone has given me his solemn word that neither he nor Slater had anything to do with it, and his word is good enough for me.'

'But Tanner's word wasn't good enough for you yesterday morning.'

'I've told you, Lieutenant, that I consider both matters closed.'

'We handed over guarding the prisoners to some of the DLI lads,' said Blackstone.

'Who?' Peploe asked. 'Don't you think we should be speaking to their commanding officer?'

'Colonel Beart's been sent to hospital,' said Blackstone.

'For God's sake, someone must have taken over – Major McLaren. He was second in command yesterday. Sir, war or not, it was an appalling crime that cannot go unpunished. I mean, damn it, I thought we were fighting to stop the tyranny of the Nazis. Condone this and we prove ourselves no better than they are.'

'Peploe, my dear fellow,' said Barclay, attempting a more placatory approach, 'the Durhams have lost nearly half their men. Their OC is in hospital and two company commanders are in the bag. I hear Sixth Battalion has suffered similar losses. How well do you think it will go down if we march in there accusing their men of slaughtering forty Nazis – and, let's face it, they were all SS men, the very worst of the worst. I know this probably sounds a bit cold-hearted but, personally, I can't help feeling the world is better off without them.'

Tanner saw the flush in Peploe's cheeks. The lieutenant's jaw tightened and for a moment Tanner wondered whether he should simply steer him away before he did something he might later regret.

'Shame on you, sir,' said Peploe at last. He swallowed hard. 'Because we are at war and because of the situation we find ourselves in, I will continue to serve under you to the best of my ability. But I want you to know, here and now, that when we get home I shall be reporting this disgraceful episode and I will make sure the perpetrators are caught and that justice is done.'

'That, of course, is your prerogative,' said Barclay, stiffly. 'But now I want you, Tanner, and you, Blackstone, to shake hands.'

Blackstone thrust out his hand, smiling amiably at Tanner.

'Christ alive,' muttered Peploe.

'Tanner?' said Barclay.

'Is it an order, sir?'

'Yes, damn it, it is.'

Tanner held out his hand and felt Blackstone's grip it.

'Good,' said Barclay, smiling at last. 'That wasn't so hard, was it?' He stuffed his pipe back into his mouth, relit it, and then, as sweet-smelling tobacco wafted around him, he said, 'Now we've got that straight, I can give you our orders. We're to join the line between here and the Canadian war memorial on the left of Eighth DLI, or what remains of them. They're covering the line all the way up to Givenchy.' He cleared his throat. 'We lost a lot of tanks yesterday and there's going to be no more offensive action for the time being. Our job is to stop the enemy getting any further.'

'I thought we were going to rejoin the rest of the battalion, sir,' said Tanner.

'Nothing doing, I'm afraid. They're still down on the Scarpe to the east of Arras, but with the DLI's losses, we're to stay and help them. In any case, we no longer have any M/T.'

'And what about food?' asked Tanner. 'The lads haven't had anything since yesterday morning.'

'Eighth DLI's B Echelon have set up a kitchen a short way back up the road in the wood. We've been ordered to pass through it, rather than using roads – Brigade's expecting heavy air attacks. We're to pick up rations on the way to our positions. All clear?'

Tanner and Peploe nodded.

'Oh, and one last thing,' added Barclay, 'I've made CSM Blackstone Eleven Platoon commander. He's taking over from Lieutenant Bourne-Arton with immediate effect.'

Tanner willed himself not to look at the triumph on Blackstone's face, but something within compelled him to do so. Standing a little way behind Barclay, Blackstone lit a cigarette and, as Tanner glanced at him, he smiled and winked – just as Tanner had known he would.

19

Four thirty p.m., Thursday, 23 May: orders had arrived that D Company, 1st Battalion, the Yorkshire Rangers, along with A and D Companies of 8th Battalion, the Durham Light Infantry, were to move out of the young woods at Petit Vimy along the ridge to Givenchy, and from there to join the line on the right of the rest of 8th Battalion to the north-west of the village.

It was raining, and had been since mid-morning, alternating between drizzle and a heavier, more persistent downpour. Some of the men wore their green oilskin anti-gas capes as mackintoshes, but Tanner felt too restricted in his so he had put on his leather jerkin. It meant his body was dry still but the damp serge of his trousers and battle-blouse sleeves scratched his skin.

The weather did nothing to improve his mood. Being forced to shake Blackstone's hand had been a humiliation too far. Back at Manston he had promised himself he would make no concessions until he felt the man had earned his respect and trust. Now he had been ordered to renege on that vow and forced to shake hands with a man who, two days before, had had him beaten up, who had accused him of rape, and who had possibly shot more than forty prisoners in cold blood. A man, he had once felt certain, who had already tried to kill him at least twice before. To make matters worse, Barclay had made it quite clear that he felt Tanner and Lieutenant Peploe were being difficult and churlish, rather than Blackstone. Tanner had not expected effusive praise, but he felt he had acquitted himself well enough on the twenty-first; he and the platoon had done everything asked of them, and more. In contrast, Blackstone had kept his head down and scuttled off at the first available opportunity. That alone had hardly merited promotion.

Blackstone had clearly been preying on Peploe's mind too. The lieutenant had made no secret of his disgust. 'I shouldn't be saying this to you, Tanner,' he had fumed, as they had walked back to rejoin the platoon, 'but the OC is treating this like some bloody playground spat. I swear on all I hold dear that I will not let this matter drop. When we get home, I'm going to make sure it's properly investigated.' Since then, Peploe had been subdued, not at all the cheerful, easy-going man Tanner had come to like and respect.

In truth, however, it was not only Blackstone and the weather: for nearly two days now they had heard increasingly heavy gunfire to the south, from the eastern side of Arras, where they supposed the rest of the battalion were still dug in, and from far to the west. Moreover, it seemed that the *Luftwaffe* had singled them out for particular punishment. Enemy aircraft had buzzed over almost continually. Already that day they had been dive-bombed twice. The trees of the young wood, just twenty years old, had offered some protection, as had their hastily dug slit trenches, but the attacks grated on the nerves. Every time a Stuka dived, screaming, or a Junkers 88 flew over, roaring, the men crouched into the earth – which was wet and muddy with all the rain – and prayed no bomb would land on them. Lethal shards of splintered wood and shrapnel hissed over their heads, while clods of soil and fragments of stone clattered on top of them, rattling their steel helmets and working their way down the back of their necks.

They had seen no British or French aircraft.

'Where's bloody Lyell and his lot?' Sykes had muttered at one point. 'Surely he's back by now?'

'Just like sodding Norway,' McAllister had complained. 'Why does Jerry always seem to have more of everything than us?'

'Search me,' said Sykes.

'I'll tell you what's really getting on my nerves,' McAllister had said. 'It's this place. Graves everywhere and sodding shell-holes. The sooner we're out of here the better. Gives me the creeps.'

Tanner agreed. His father had fought near by and wouldn't have thought much about his son being bombed on the same stretch of troubled land that had been battled over some twenty years earlier. Through the trees near Petit Vimy, they had seen the tall, white Canadian war memorial. It was a stark reminder that Tanner could have done without.

And they were losing – the German gains could no longer be seen as mere temporary setbacks; rather, Tanner recognized, the British had most probably been plunged into an irreversible defeat. He had sensed it in Norway, and he sensed it again now. Of course, he had little idea of what was really going on, but he'd put money on it that few of the top brass did either. There never seemed to be enough forces in the right place to stem the flow. Lieutenant Peploe had told him they would be attacking south of Arras with a composite force of more than two divisions, but there had been nothing of the sort. As far as he had been able to tell, there had been two infantry battalions, a handful of tanks and some field and anti-tank guns. Where had the rest been? And what could they possibly achieve now? They were sitting on this ridge, supported by a few anti-tank guns, being bombed and blasted and waiting for Jerry to bring himself up to strength. It was hopeless.

It was still raining as they set off, in companies, platoons and sections, heads bowed and gas capes glistening, through the woods towards Givenchy. They passed across the Canadian national park, with its warnings of unexploded shells, then wove past the memorial and towards Givenchy. As they trudged down the ridge,

Tanner noticed an anti-tank gun battery to the south-east of the village, below the memorial, and was struck by how poorly camouflaged it was. An easy spot for any reconnaissance plane, even on a rainy day.

It was as though the *Luftwaffe* had read his thoughts. They were nearing the edge of the village when he heard the familiar rumble of aero-engines, faint at first, then growing rapidly in volume, until two dozen Junkers 88s swooped low out of the cloud. 'Take cover!' he shouted. Men flung themselves into the sodden grassy bank at the side of the road. A moment later, bombs were falling, a brief whistle then an ear-splitting crash as they exploded. Tanner lay on the trembling ground, his hands over his ears. A bigger detonation now ripped the air. More bombs whistled. One man was screaming. Some in the village were firing, shooting rifles and Brens. The ground shuddered again and Tanner pressed his head to it, breathing in the scent of wet grass and earth.

The bombers were soon gone, disappearing into the cloud. Tanner, with the rest of the men, got to his feet, brushing off damp blades of grass, and gazed at the village, now shrouded in a veil of dust and smoke. Several houses were burning, flames flickering through the haze. In the centre of the village a column of angry black smoke swirled. Cries and shouts could be heard.

Up ahead, from A and D Companies, orders were barked. Blackstone gave the command for the Rangers to fall in, and they stood there for a few minutes, watching the flames, hearing timber burn and masonry collapse while Captain Barclay went forward for further instructions. He reappeared a short while later, his face set, and spoke with Blackstone and Peploe.

'What's happening, sir?' Tanner asked, as Peploe rejoined the platoon.

'A and D Companies are moving into position cross-country avoiding the village. We're to go in and help clear up.'

'Better than sitting still in the rain, I suppose.'

In places it was hard to get through. A number of houses had disintegrated, rubble spewing across the road. The men worked their way around it and eventually reached the centre of the village. The church was still intact, but half a dozen homes around it had been destroyed. Choking dust and smoke filled the air. Tanner wetted his handkerchief, then tied it round his mouth, encouraging the others to do the same. Near the square, where he had been attacked three days before, the blackened skeletal frame of a truck smouldered while at either end of it two more vehicles were ablaze. A sudden gust swept down the street and the flames leaped, black smoke billowing into the sky. Soldiers and civilians were coughing and stumbling about, disoriented. An officer – a signals captain from 5th Division – was scrabbling at bits of fallen brickwork. 'Come on, give me a bloody hand!' he yelled. 'My men are under this lot.'

Tanner hurried over to him. 'Sir,' he said, looking at the wreckage, 'there's nothing we can do.'

'Can't just leave 'em here,' he said, and Tanner noticed the tears that streaked the grime on his face.

'Sir,' he said again.

The officer stood up and stared at the sky. 'The murdering bastards,' he said, his voice cracking. 'I had six good men in that house.' He picked up a broken brick and hurled it.

In the main square there were several large bomb craters. A few women were screaming while an old lady knelt outside the church, praying. Tanner saw Peploe and went to him. 'Sir, what are we supposed to be doing? We can't clear all this rubble.'

'God knows.' He looked up as Captain Barclay and a major approached.

'Peploe, this is Major McLaren,' said Barclay. 'He's taken over as battalion commander of Eighth DLI.'

Peploe and Tanner saluted.

'You can help the wounded,' said McLaren, 'but I don't want you wasting too much time here.' He nodded towards the burning vehicles. 'Bastards hit an ammunition truck. Fifth Div artillery were passing through – damned unlucky timing.' His eyes rested on the debris. 'In any case, there are still enough of them to sort this place out. I'd rather you were in position on D Company's flank.' He looked at his watch. 'Half an hour, no more. Jerry's only a few miles away so we might see some action later.'

It was a grim task collecting the dead and wounded. Tanner found an old man weeping over his wife, who had lost a leg, shorn clean off. He and Smailes had lifted her but she had died as they tried to hoist her into their arms. Then Smailes had been called to the anti-tank battery on the south-east of the village and Tanner followed with Corporal Cooper's section. Several large craters now pockmarked the field where they were positioned. Two of the guns had been put out of action, and one of the gun crews had been blown to smithereens, body parts flung in a wide arc to hang in trees and hedgerows. One young gunner was wandering about, his face and body covered with another man's blood. Two of Cooper's men vomited and Tanner couldn't blame them: it was one thing seeing an animal torn to pieces, quite another a human and a comrade. *They'll get used to it.* He certainly had, and while Smailes administered what help he could, Tanner removed bits of flesh from the hedges and branches near the guns, placed them in a pile a short distance away, then covered them with soil and stones from the craters.

'Thanks,' said an ashen-faced lieutenant. 'Very good of you.'

'It's easier for me, sir,' said Tanner. 'I didn't know them.'

The lieutenant swallowed. His uniform and face were filthy. 'It was all s-so sudden. One minute they were there, the next they'd g-gone.'

'They wouldn't have known a thing about it, sir.'

The lieutenant nodded. 'No. I suppose not.'

Tanner offered him a cigarette from a packet he had been given at Petit Vimy. He took it gratefully, but his hands were shaking so much he could hardly put it into his mouth.

'We'll help get the wounded back, sir.'

They took six men to the church, which had become a temporary field dressing station. Tanner had just helped set down a gunner with a bad groin wound when he saw Sykes and

Hepworth carrying the body of a young woman. Her face, clothes and dark hair were covered with dust but even so he recognized her immediately. 'That's the girl,' he said, as they laid her down on the ground.

'Which girl?' asked Hepworth.

'Mademoiselle Lafoy,' said Tanner. Dark blood had matted her hair and run down her face. 'The girl who accused me.'

'It's a shame, Sarge,' said Hepworth, 'but at least she can't testify against you no more.'

'For God's sake, Hep,' snapped Tanner. 'I'd far rather have seen her alive and found out who persuaded her to set me up.'

'And for how much,' added Sykes.

'Yes. I wonder what it would take to persuade a hungry, home-less girl to do that.' The rain, which had stopped for a short while, now began again. Fat drops landed on her face and arms, cleaning away the powdery layer of dust. Tanner looked away, and heard Blackstone order everyone to fall in.

'Come on, boys,' he said. 'Let's get going, iggery, eh?'

Later that evening there was another air raid, but by that time D Company was dug into the north-west of Givenchy, and the bombs were directed further along the ridge. At ten, orders arrived that they were to hold Vimy Ridge to the end. Twenty minutes later, enemy tanks were reported to be no more than six hundred yards away. They heard the squeak and rattle of tracks but it was too dark to see. The men were restless and jittery but Tanner reckoned they were safe until the morning. Then just after midnight new orders arrived. They were not going to hold the ridge after all: instead they were to head back to a new line of defence behind the La Bassée canal, some ten miles to the north-east.

Wearily they got to their feet, gathered their kit and tramped back through the woods, Bren carriers clattering through the trees on their flank covering their withdrawal. At Petit Vimy, trucks and transport were waiting for them. Desultory gunfire boomed across the night, but otherwise the violence of the previous day had been left behind. Tanner sat at the back of a large fifteen-hundredweight Bedford, Sykes beside him. The rain had stopped and a dense canopy of stars twinkled above them. Tanner's clothes were still damp and he shivered. Behind them, he could hear carriers wheeling about, but of the enemy panzers there was no sign. By one a.m. on Friday, 24 May, the column was trundling down through Vimy, vehicles nose to tail. A snail's pace, but better than walking through the night on exhausted legs.

Withdrawing again, thought Tanner. Even so, he was glad to be getting away from that place, a part of France that seemed haunted by death. He lit a cigarette and smoked it in silence, watching the pale smoke disperse into the cool night air. When it was finished, he flicked away the stub, closed his eyes and fell into a deep sleep.

By mid-morning on the twenty-fourth, the men of D Company were digging in yet again, this time in a large, thick wood a mile or so behind the La Bassée canal near the main road between Carvin and Libercourt, some fifteen miles north-east of Arras. Still attached to 151st Brigade and the 8th Durham Light Infantry, they were told to rest there for as long as possible. However, no sooner had they begun to dig their new slit trenches than they were joined on the opposite side of the road by large numbers of French troops, who had moved in with the *Luftwaffe* seemingly on their tail like a swarm of angry bees. The planes began dive-bombing and strafing almost immediately.

'Some bloody rest this,' muttered Sykes, as Tanner squatted with him in their slit trench.

'Could be worse, Stan,' said Tanner. 'Could still be raining. And at least we're getting our rations.'

The delivery of food had done wonders for the men's mood. Earlier, near Carvin, they had been given breakfast in a disused factory. This had been followed by the establishment of B Echelon's kitchens and the smell of tinned stew floating to them through the wood. Much to Tanner's relief, supplies of cigarettes had also arrived.

By evening that day, enemy air activity had melted away and the sound of the guns to the south lessened until a strange quiet descended over the wood – so much so that as dusk was falling, Tanner heard faint birdsong a short distance away. 'Hear that, sir?' he said to Peploe, as they walked along the platoon lines. 'It's a nightingale. I haven't heard one since I was a boy.'

Peploe smiled. 'They didn't have them in India, then?'

'No, but they always used to sing back home. At least, there was one part of a wood where you could always hear them. Especially at this time of year – May and early June.'

'It's always been my favourite season on the farm – the leaves on the trees out at last, everything so damned green and lush, the whole summer stretching ahead. And cricket. Lots and lots of cricket. You play, Sergeant?'

'I do, sir. Love the game. That was one thing that linked India with home – and, of course, in India, you could play pretty much all year round.'

'And here we are getting bombed and strafed and shot up. I must have been mad to join up.' He grinned. Tanner was glad that his mood had improved. 'Still,' Peploe added, 'at least it's quiet tonight.'

'And we should make the most of it, sir. God knows what'll happen tomorrow.'

The following day began with orders that rations were to be cut by fifty per cent. Then, early in the afternoon, came the news that another counter-attack was to take place: 5th and 50th Divisions, with four French divisions, would thrust southwards towards Cambrai, which meant 151st Brigade would be very much involved. The first obstacle – a preliminary to the main attack that would go in the following day – was to get back across the La Bassée canal in the face of what was expected to be heavy enemy opposition. By four in the afternoon, a troop-carrying company had arrived, dispersing its trucks and vehicles through the wood ready to move the men forward to the start line of their night-time assault.

Tanner never enjoyed the hours before an attack. Apprehension gnawed at him, replacing hunger with an uncomfortable sensation in his stomach. He cleaned his weapons – his rifle and the MP35 – then cleaned them again, and took on more ammunition, although less was available than he would have liked. He checked his kit, smoked and brewed mugs of sweet tea. He knew the others were in the same boat – if anything, they were probably more nervous than he was; scared, even. Certainly their drawn, pale faces suggested so.

A little under twenty miles away, as the crow flew, General Lord Gort was reaching a decision that would reprieve the Yorkshire Rangers and all those troops involved in the proposed attack. Three days earlier he had moved his command post to the small village of Premesques, north-west of Lille. The British commander-in-chief and his advance staff had occupied a rambling old house in the heart of the village. Now, in a wood-panelled ground-floor room, with thick beams and a low ceiling, Gort was staring at the maps of northern France and Belgium that had been hung on the walls when he had moved in.

The day had brought little cheer. Following on from the news that the Channel port of Boulogne had fallen the day before, it now seemed that Calais was all but in German hands too. His promised 1st Armoured Division, attempting to move north from Cherbourg, had made no headway. Supplies of everything, but especially food and ammunition, were running low. General Dill, deputy CIGS, had arrived, and let him know that the BEF was being criticized at home for its performance. Throughout the day, disquieting news had reached them from the northern front, where it seemed the Belgian line was deteriorating; apparently, Belgian forces were drifting northwards towards the river Scheldt – reports suggested that a gap was developing between them and the British. Then, half an hour ago, details of some German documents captured by a British patrol on the river Lys, on the northern flank, revealed that the enemy intended to bolster its front there and attack between

Ypres and Commines – precisely at the link between BEF and Belgian forces. If reports of the gap were true, the Hun would be able to outflank the BEF in the north with potentially catastrophic consequences.

Gort studied the mass of roads, towns, villages, rivers and canals – images and names that were now so familiar to him. His forces were dangerously overstretched, of that there could be no doubt, and even though they had intercepted the extraordinary message that German troops had halted their attack towards Merville and Dunkirk, it was clear this respite could not last.

Lord Gort fingered his trim moustache and cast his eyes towards his southern flank. General Weygand had demanded there be a properly co-ordinated counter-attack southwards – with which the War Office had concurred – but only a few days earlier he had attempted precisely the same thing at Arras, and, as he had feared, their allies had barely contributed. Admittedly Weygand seemed to have a bit more verve than poor old Gamelin, but Gort was loath to push two divisions into the attack unless he knew for certain that the French would honour their commitments to the battle, especially now that his northern front was so shaky. And therein lay the quandary that had troubled him this past half-hour: should he let down his French allies and move 5th and 50th Divisions north to bolster his front there, or should he go ahead with the Weygand plan in the hope that, this time, the French would pull their weight? *Damn it.* He sat down at his desk, put his hands together and stared ahead.

A knock on his door startled him. 'Come,' he said.

'Excuse me, my lord,' said Major Archdale.

Gort motioned him to a seat. 'What news from Army Group One? How are their battle plans?'

'Down to three divisions, not four, my lord.'

'So already they're reneging. Give me strength.' Gort sighed. 'You know, Archdale, I've had a damned rum deal from our allies. The Dutch copped it from the start, but the French and the Belgians – you can't get a straight answer from 'em. The French are always complaining that they're too tired to fight, their staff work's a bloody disgrace, and there's been no firm direction or proper co-ordination whatsoever from the high command. Now I hear that the Belgians are drifting away and that a dangerous gap is emerging between our chaps and them. Tell me this, why are the Belgians retreating north? If they fell back southwards, they'd be able to preserve a decent front and lines of communication.' He felt himself flush, but was too angry to care – too frustrated by the impossible position in which he was placed, everyone pulling him in different directions, the Belgians tugging him north, Weygand urging him south, Churchill and the war cabinet sticking their oar in. 'Well, Archdale?' he said.

'I wouldn't like to say, sir, it's not my place, but I wouldn't be surprised if the Belgians feel rather as we all do about the French. Perhaps they think it's better to fight with their backs to their coast than retreat towards France.'

'You think they'll throw in the towel?'

Archdale shrugged. 'It may come to that. More than half their country's already in enemy hands. General Blanchard has gone to Belgian GHQ, though. Perhaps he can put some steel into them.' He didn't seem convinced.

'And what's the mood at Blanchard's HQ? Tell me frankly. Is it any better now that Billotte's gone?'

'There's faith in Weygand, my lord, but General Blanchard is the same man he was before.'

'In other words, no commander at all.'

Archdale looked apologetic.

The telephone on Gort's desk rang and he dismissed Archdale, then picked up the receiver. It was General Adam, commander of III Corps, whose troops were earmarked for the southern counter-attack. 'Tell me some good news,' said Gort, trying to sound cheerful.

'I wish I could, my lord,' said the general. 'I've just been to see Altmayer. He told me he can only provide one division for the attack.'

'One?' Gort began to laugh.

'Sir?' said Adam.

'But, my dear Adam,' said Gort, 'that *is* good news. Don't you see? We'll have to call off the attack. It can't possibly succeed – one division! My God, it's unbelievable. Yesterday it was four plus two hundred tanks. Now the best the French can offer is one lone division!'

He rang off and strode next door to see Pownall. 'Henry!' he said. 'Do you know how long I've been agonizing over what to do about our northern flank? I've had a call from Adam saying the French are only planning to put in one division!'

'Surely not?'

'It's true. So that's made my decision for me. Brookey can have his two divisions. Get Franklyn up here smartish. We need to stop Fifth Div from moving south and get them and Fiftieth up to plug the line between Ypres and Commines right away.'

'Of course, my lord,' said Pownall, 'but what about Blanchard?'

'We'll tell him that, because of this, the attack would be doomed to fail and we'll no longer play a part in it. It's no more than giving them a dose of their own medicine.'

'What about the PM and the war cabinet?'

'Don't get 'em involved. They'll only throw a spanner into the works. They've asked me to command the BEF and that's what I'm doing – commanding, damn it. We'll simply present it as a *fait accompli.*'

'Very wise, my lord. In any case, we don't have enough ammunition to carry out such an attack. I was never very keen on the idea.' He shook his head wearily. 'The whole thing really is a first-class mess, and what's frustrating is that I don't think it's much of our making.'

'I agree, Henry. But it's important that, from now on, we think for ourselves. We can't rely on our allies, and I think we may have just saved the BEF from annihilation. What we must do now is ensure that as many of our boys as possible are saved – saved to fight another day.'

'You mean the evacuation, my lord?'

'Yes, Henry, I do. We've talked about it as a possibility, but now it's a necessity. I've no doubt we'll still lose a great many men, but we have to think about getting our forces to the coast, making sure that as many as possible are lifted off the beaches and taken safely back to Britain. A staged withdrawal to the coast – here.' He stood up and pointed to the stretch between Dunkirk and Nieuport on the wall map. 'We might have stemmed the flow for a while, but we must be realistic. We cannot stay here in northern France without being surrounded – Hitler's tanks aren't going to lie idle. His armies are closing in on the Belgians and they've got Calais in the bag. There's no other direction for us to go.' He stroked his chin. 'You know, Henry, it's funny but for days past – and particularly the last few hours – I've been agonizing over the right thing for us to do. I've felt quite paralysed, if I'm honest. But now everything seems perfectly clear. It's time to look after ourselves. It's our only course.'

20

Three a.m., Monday, 27 May. In driving rain, D Company clambered aboard three trucks of 8th Battalion's Troop Carrying Company, parked, with engines running, in the main square at the north end of Carvin. They were thirty-hundredweight Bedford OYs, large enough to take the forty-eight remaining Rangers plus a section from 8th DLI.

'Come up front with me, Tanner,' said Peploe, holding the dark green door open for him.

Silently, Tanner hauled himself aboard, rain dripping from his tin hat, his MP35 clanging against the door frame as he settled on the canvas seat. There was a musty smell – of damp canvas, oil, rubber and stale tobacco – but at least it was dry in the cab. He thought of the men at the back of the truck, the open canvas covering. Hepworth would be cursing.

'Leave the window open, will you, mate?' said the driver, an RASC corporal. 'Otherwise we'll get steamed up in here.'

Rain continued to spatter Tanner's face. From the south a gun boomed, but it was quieter again now: the Germans had never liked fighting at night.

'Where are we going, Corporal?' asked Peploe.

'Steenvoorde, sir. It's not too far – forty miles at most. As long as the roads aren't too clogged we should be there for breakfast.'

A few shouts and barked orders came from the squares, then the corporal ground the truck into gear and they lurched forward. Tanner smoked a cigarette, then took off his helmet, rested his head against the door and closed his eyes. His body was jolted by the movement of the lorry, his ears alive to the thrum of the engine and the rhythmic squeak of the wipers.

It had been a day and a half of orders and counter-orders. Late on the twenty-fifth, they had been stood down, the attack across the canal cancelled, with no explanation as to why. Of course, they had been relieved, but Tanner had felt irritated too – all that tension and apprehension for nothing. But something had been afoot, for all night heavy shelling had continued from both sides of the La Bassée canal, and had continued as dawn had broken. No shells had fallen near their own positions but there had been an enormous explosion to their right. Later they discovered the gas-works at Libercourt had received a direct hit. As the morning had worn on, machine-gun and mortar fire had been heard to the south; rumours had spread that the enemy had crossed the canal and were advancing.

The Rangers had watched 8th DLI's carrier platoon rumble off, rattling down the main road, heading to the south edge of Carvin. The men were restless and fidgety, especially when the French battalion in the woods opposite had begun to move out. No one had seemed to know what was going on, but all the time the sound of guns and small arms was drawing closer although, in those woods, still frustratingly out of sight. Above, enemy reconnaissance aircraft had circled ominously. Soon the bombers would arrive.

Orders to move came a little before nine o'clock. They were to head to Camphin a few miles to the north. No sooner had the lead companies moved off along the main road than the dive-bombers had swooped, engines and sirens screaming, dropping their bombs on the column. The Rangers, the last to leave, were unharmed to a man, but several vehicles had been put out of action and the road was badly cratered. Some of the men had been quite shaken. Tanner noticed that a couple – Verity from Sykes's section and Dempster in Cooper's – were a bit bomb happy, cowering more than the others and taking longer to recover their composure. They'd all have to keep an eye on them. Yet it was interesting that a dozen Stukas had attacked their column and only four from A Company had been wounded. Two trucks had been destroyed and another's radiator and front tyres had blown, but the damage had been comparatively light, all things considered. As Tanner was increasingly aware, Stukas were not especially accurate despite their alarming sirens. The biggest inconvenience had been the craters in the road – it had meant they had been ordered to debus and then tramp cross-country on foot while the M/T had been forced to risk going through the centre of Carvin, which had been coming under regular and heavy shellfire.

They had reached Camphin in one piece, and, at last, out of range of enemy guns. Immediately the men had been ordered to dig in yet again, at the edge of the village, but after they'd made slit trenches, new orders arrived. The Rangers were to join B Company of 8th DLI and occupy Provin, a village a few miles to the west where 9th DLI were now based. With the men grumbling about pointless digging, they set off again. When they finally reached Provin, there had been no sign of 9th so they had been sent back to Carvin, where the rest of 8th was now attacking beside the French and a couple of platoons from 5th Leicesters who had somehow become detached from the rest of their unit.

Footsore, hungry and in no state to fight, the Rangers had reached the edge of Carvin as a storm broke overhead. Guns boomed, their reports mixing with the cracks of thunder. In the pouring rain, the Durham and Yorkshire men had headed south towards the fighting, scrambling over the rubble and fallen masonry of destroyed houses. The shriek of shells could now be heard, whooshing like speeding trains through the rain-drenched air. And then, ahead, they had seen trucks and cars, tanks and carriers, all crammed with men.

'My God, is that the enemy?' Barclay had asked, wiping rain from his face.

'No, sir,' Tanner had replied. 'They're French.'

Silently, they had watched them trundle past. Most were Moroccans, who glared at the Tommies. Their officers seemed dejected. Tanner could hardly blame them – their country was falling. Defeat hung in the air. Thunder continued to crack. For the first time since he'd arrived in France, he'd begun to think they might never get out.

Not long after, the rest of the battalion had fallen back too. Shelling had continued with nightfall but the enemy had not stormed the town, and shortly after midnight, word reached them that they would be pulling out – and this time not falling back a few miles. Rather, they were being transferred to the northern flank. Out of one cauldron and into another.

Now Tanner sighed and sat up. Through the faint beam of the blinkered headlights, he could see the rain and, just ahead, the tail of the lead truck, with Captain Barclay, Blackstone, the rest of Company Headquarters and 11 Platoon. He had avoided Blackstone as much as possible, which in itself had been frustrating. It wasn't in his nature to shirk confrontation, but dealing with Blackstone was like facing a boxer who forever moved about the ring – always there, in your face, but upon whom it was impossible to land a punch. In truth, they had been on the move so often in the past couple of days that there had been little need for their paths to cross, but Tanner was ever mindful that unfinished business lay between them. He had, however, detected a subtle change in the men's attitude towards the CSM – at least in 12 Platoon. If any of the lads had resented the CSM's early departure from the battlefield at Arras, they had not said so; Blackstone had made it clear to them that it was thanks to him and Slater, bravely dodging roving enemy panzers, that the French tanks and carriers had made it to Warlus to rescue them. Yet Tanner had noticed that the men had been less effusive about him, not so quick to laugh if he stopped to speak to them. *Blackstone.* Always at the back of his mind, a menace he was unable to shake off. Tanner thumped a clenched fist into the other palm. Well, they might be losing the battle, but somehow, some way, he would nail him. *If it's the last thing I do.*

They reached Steenvoorde at around eight a.m., halting in the cobbled town square. Peploe and Tanner got out of the cab, and while the lieutenant went to speak with Barclay, Tanner ambled to the back of the truck, lighting a cigarette on the way. McAllister was playing cards with Hepworth and Chambers, but most of the others were just sitting on the wooden benches that ran down each side of the carriage. Their faces were dirty and smudged with rain. Those old enough to shave had two days' growth of beard. Clearly they were tired and fed-up.

'What's going on here, Sarge?' said Sykes, getting down beside him.

'This is Steenvoorde. It's where we're supposed to be.'

'Apart from us an' the Durham lads it seems deserted.'

'Probably some cock-up,' said Tanner. 'Maybe the front's moved.'

Ten minutes later, Peploe reappeared. 'We're off again,' he said.

'Where to now, sir?' asked Sykes.

'Not far. A couple of miles the other side of town.'

Once they were back in the cab Peploe confided, 'Colonel McLaren's furious. He'd been expecting someone at least to meet us. Apparently some of our boys are at Cassel, a few miles further on, so he's ordered us to dig in and hide up halfway between the two while he tries to find out what on earth's going on.'

The road between Steenvoorde and Cassel was heavy with refugees, the same sad mass of people trudging to nowhere in particular so long as it was away from the fighting. Slowly the trucks jerked forward.

'Get out of the bloody way!' yelled the driver, as a cart blocked the road, his cheery bonhomie of the early hours long since gone.

'Shouting at them's hardly going to help,' said Peploe. 'They're homeless, the poor sods. Here,' he added, taking out his silver cigarette box, 'have a smoke and calm down.'

'Sorry, sir,' said the corporal, accepting. 'It's so bloody frustrating. I've had it up to here with refugees. If these people had all stayed at home, maybe we'd have been able to get around a bit better, like, and we wouldn't be losing this sodding war.'

He took them to the edge of a dense wood west of Cassel and there they got out. They were at the end of the line, several hundred yards to the left of A Company. The trucks reversed into an equally clogged track a short distance further on, then turned back in the direction of Steenvoorde. As the Rangers tramped across an open field towards a hedge a hundred yards or so from the road, Tanner watched the vehicles chug slowly through the mass of people.

They began to dig in yet again, this time in an L shape, facing south and west, behind a hedge on one side and a brook on the other. Soon they heard gunfire to the south-west and west. Once, a cloud of smoke drifted over the wood, but their view of Cassel, and whatever fighting was occurring there, was blocked. In a short time, Tanner and Smailes had dug a two-man slit trench big enough to lie down in. In Norway Tanner had cursed the uselessness of the latest standard-issue entrenching tool for its lack of pick on the reverse end of the spade, but here, in the rich, soft Flanders clay, it did the job well enough, especially since Tanner had sharpened the edge so that it would cut better through turf. He was also pleased to see Lieutenant Peploe digging his own slit trench again. He was never too proud to get his hands dirty and Tanner liked that in him. 'Do you need a hand, sir?' Tanner asked, his own dug deep enough.

'It's all right, thanks, Sergeant,' Peploe replied. It was no longer raining and between breaks in the cloud the sun shone warmly. He paused to wipe his brow. 'Go along the line and check the chaps are all right, will you?'

'Yes, sir.' Tanner wandered down the line of freshly dug trenches, pausing first by McAllister and Chambers.

'Any idea how long we're here, Sarge?' said McAllister, his Bren already set up.

'No, Mac. Not the faintest.'

'It must be time to move on again now, isn't it, Sarge?' said Chambers, manning the Bren with McAllister. 'I mean, now that we've dug in an' all.'

'Just you keep watching ahead of you, Punter.'

He walked on, pleased to see how quickly the men had completed the task. They had staggered themselves well, making good use of natural cover; the Brens of each section were positioned in such a way that each gave the other covering fire. And he'd not said a thing. They had done it almost without thinking. Tanner smiled to himself. Three weeks ago, half of these boys had been little more than raw recruits. They were fast becoming soldiers.

He paused by Verity, who had dug a deeper hole than any of the others and was squatting inside it, his hands clasped around his rifle.

'Are you all right, Hedley?' Tanner asked him.

'Fine, Sarge.'

Tanner offered him a cigarette.

'Thanks, Sarge,' said Verity, taking it.

Tanner lit both. 'Do you bowl anything like him, then?'

'Hedley Verity?' He grinned sheepishly. 'I wish, Sarge. I try, though. I can certainly turn it a bit. Mind you, I've seen him play.'

'I'd pay good money to do that.'

'Last summer at Headingley when Yorkshire won the championship for the third time on t' trot,' said Verity, brightening. 'Sarge, it was brilliant. He got a five-for that day. I live in Leeds, see, and it's only a short way to the ground.' His expression dropped. 'Seems like an age ago now.'

'Well, I've always been a Hampshire supporter, it being the nearest county to Wiltshire.'

'Wiltshire?' said Verity. 'Is that where you're from?'

'Born and bred.'

'So why are you in the Rangers, Sarge?'

'It's a long story.'

Verity thought for a moment. Then, smiling once more, he said,

'Well, Sarge, since you're a Ranger, you really should switch allegiance. Yorkshire are the best side in the country by a mile.'

Tanner patted his shoulder. 'All right, Hedley, maybe I will.'

As the morning wore on, the enemy shelling grew louder, but by early afternoon it had quietened again as the fighting appeared to move south. The Rangers ate what was left of their half-rations and remained in their positions, waiting.

'Sir,' Tanner asked Peploe, 'don't you think we should try to find out what's going on? It's too quiet for my liking.'

Peploe thought about it. 'It's after three,' he said eventually. 'Maybe – yes. Let me go and see the OC.' He returned a short while later with orders for them to sit tight. 'He said someone would have told us if they wanted us to move.'

But when another hour had passed and there was still no communication from the rest of the 8th DLI, Barclay agreed to send a runner over to A Company to find out what was going on. A quarter of an hour later the OC came to Peploe. He was fuming. 'I don't bloody well believe it,' he said. 'A Company's damn well gone and buggered off without us.'

'Really, sir?' said Peploe. 'Are you sure they haven't just moved back or forward a little?'

'No – they've gone!' He took off his cap and mopped his brow. 'It's unbelievable. The buggers have gone and forgotten us – and they've taken all the damned M/T.'

'Must have been when that shelling was going on,' said Tanner. 'We'd have heard them otherwise.'

'Well?' said Barclay, looking at Peploe.

'What, sir?'

'What do we do, damn it? I mean, I can only think of two things. Either we stay here or we head back towards Steenvoorde.'

'As I understood it, sir,' said Peploe, 'we were never supposed to be here in the first place. Major McLaren moved us here while he tried to find out where the rest of the brigade was supposed to be.'

'They certainly can't have gone west, sir, because we'd have seen them,' added Tanner, 'and we were heading for the northern front, weren't we? But we're at the southern front here. At least, it sounded like it.'

Barclay nodded. 'All right, then,' he said. 'We'll pack up and head back to Steenvoorde. See what we can find out there. Get your men ready, lieutenant.' He shook his head. 'Honestly, it's unbelievable. The whole thing's a complete cock-up.'

A quarter of an hour later, they were marching, not along the road but through a field beside it. Refugees stared at them with a mixture of resignation and resentment. To the south, guns were firing again. Tanner noticed a young woman with two children flinch in alarm, then her daughter began to cry. He wished she would stop.

''Ere, Sarge,' said Sykes, alongside him. 'Just thought you should know – the lads in Eleven Platoon are getting really fed up.'

'Aren't we all?'

'Yes, but they're blaming Captain Barclay.'

'How do you know?'

'I've been walking just behind some of them, listening. It's Blackstone, Sarge – he's been telling them that the OC's nerves are frayed.'

'You heard them say that, Stan?'

'Clear as day. They believe it too. And, what's more, they're not all that happy about it neither.'

'Bloody hell,' muttered Tanner. 'That's all we need, mutiny in the ranks.' Something made him pause to listen. Then Sykes heard it too.

'Aircraft.'

Both men stopped to scan the sky. 'There!' said Tanner, pointing to the east beyond Steenvoorde. A formation of aircraft was already beginning its initial dive, the roar of engines louder with every second. In moments the now familiar gull-wing and locked undercarriage of the Stuka was clear. Tanner counted twelve. 'Where are the bastards heading?' he said.

'Looks like directly at us,' said Sykes.

'I doubt it. I bet they're on the way to Cassel. They know we've got troops around there.'

'Come on, boys!' Barclay shouted from the front of their small column. 'Let's show the bastards!'

All too quickly, men were unslinging their rifles. Tanner saw a Bren gunner from 11 Platoon bring his machine-gun into his hip and aim it skywards.

'No,' said Tanner. 'No!' He ran to Peploe. 'Sir, you've got to get the men to put their weapons down.'

Already a Bren was chattering. Rifle shots were cracking out.

'Sir, please!' said Tanner again. 'We're sitting ducks out here. These things are like wasps – there's no point in making them angry. In any case, it's a waste of ammo. We'll never hit them at that height.'

Peploe looked at him – *yes, you're right* – then yelled, 'Lower your weapons – *lower your weapons*!'

But it was too late. Some men from 11 Platoon heard him but others continued to fire, their bullets hurtling harmlessly into the sky. The Stukas were almost past when two peeled off and, rolling over, dived towards them, their death wail growing louder and louder until the planes were almost upon them, their sirens and engines seeming to envelop those on the ground below. On the road, women and children screamed and men shouted in panic, while the Rangers ran for what little cover they could find.

'Just get down and keep still!' shouted Tanner, and dropped to the ground.

As the Stukas pulled out of their dives, two lone bombs whistled towards them. The first fell on the far side of the road, the second fifty yards into the field in which the Rangers had been marching. Tanner saw two men thrown into the air by the blast. But the dive-bombers had not finished. Both were now banking sharply and turning back. Tanner watched as Captain Barclay got to his feet then, too late, realized the Stukas were swooping towards them again. Tanner could see the bombs still hanging under each wing, but they were not going to drop those. Instead, the first opened fire with a two-second burst of his machine-gun. The pilot's angle of attack was not quite right, but as he swung across the road, bullets scythed through the hedge, kicked up spits of earth, and the captain spun around, his arms flung into the air, and collapsed. As the first aircraft hurtled past, the second opened fire with another brief burst, this time hitting two more Rangers. And then they were gone, climbing away to the west. In the distance, towards Cassel, the rest of the Stukas were now diving, their sirens screaming.

Frightened civilians were dusting themselves down and getting to their feet, but as far as Tanner could tell, not a single one had been hit. He saw Peploe and Blackstone get to their feet and run towards Barclay. Tanner ran to two others who had been hit. The first was dead, the second nearly so. His face was white as chalk, and dark blood frothed at his mouth. He had been hit by at least three bullets – one in his leg, one in his stomach, the last in his chest.

Ross was running towards the crater of the second bomb and, leaving Smailes with the dying man, Tanner followed. There were two casualties. The first, Walker, a young fair-haired lad, was lying on the ground, saying, 'Am I alive? Am I alive?'

'Yes, you are, mate,' said Ross, 'but let me look at you.'

Tanner, meanwhile, had hurried to the second. He found him on his belly, and felt for a pulse. There was none. Tanner rolled him over. There was no obvious mark on him. He took off the man's helmet, and pulled open his battle-blouse and shirt, but still nothing. 'The bloody fools,' he muttered. Others had reached them now.

'What's the damage, Sarge?' said Sykes.

'Three dead. Walker seems to be fine. A lucky escape. Get the bodies back to the edge of the field,' he said. 'Iggery, all right?'

Now he ran to the prostrate Captain Barclay. Peploe was kneeling beside him, Blackstone and Slater standing over him. As Tanner reached them, Peploe looked up. 'He's gone.'

Tanner saw the stain of blood spreading across Barclay's chest.

The flush in his cheeks had gone, leaving his skin pale and waxen. He crouched beside Peploe. 'There's three others dead, sir. I've told the men to bring them to the edge of the field. I suggest we carry them into the town.'

In a state of numb silence, the men tramped back into Steenvoorde and laid the four dead men by the church. The town was eerily quiet. There were no troops, although civilian refugees were now passing through. The priest emerged from the church and told them that a number of British soldiers had been there earlier and had headed out on the Poperinghe–Ypres road.

'But if I remember rightly,' said Blackstone, as they stood outside the church, 'that means they went east. The coast is that way.' He pointed. 'We should head north.'

'Hold on a minute,' said Peploe. 'I'm the only officer now and I'll decide what we do.'

'Yes, sir,' said Blackstone. 'But in case you hadn't noticed, we're getting a beating. What can forty-four men do to help? Do you really think we can stop the rot? I say we head to the coast. For all we know, the rest of the battalion's already there.'

Peploe stared at him. 'Don't speak to me like that. Show some bloody respect.'

'We've got to go north, sir. It's obvious.'

'I'll decide that, Sergeant-Major, not you. Now go and organize a burial party, will you? We can't do anything until we've got these poor men buried. Right away.'

Blackstone gave him a half-hearted salute, then issued orders to the men. 'More digging, I'm afraid, lads,' he said. 'Not too deep, because they won't be here for ever. Get to it now, and I'll make it up to you later.'

'Jesus,' Tanner muttered to Peploe. 'What a bloody mess.'

'I'm going to have my hands full with Blackstone, I can see,' said Peploe. He took off his tin hat and ran his hands through his hair. 'It seems so incredible that the captain should be dead. A bloody silly thing to do, I know, and he had his faults, but he was a decent sort, really.'

Tanner didn't want to think about Barclay or any of the other three dead men. Now was not the time to be worrying about them; it had happened and couldn't be undone. Rather, quick, firm decisions had to be made. 'We need a map, sir. We don't have one of this part of Flanders.'

'I know. It's ridiculous.' He sighed. 'Bloody hell. We're in a bit of a fix, aren't we?'

'We'll be fine, sir. We just need to think calmly and clearly.'

Peploe glanced at the priest, who was hovering around the men as they dug the graves. 'Hold on a moment, Sergeant,' he said, then strode over to the man. Tanner watched them talk, then cross the cobbled road to a small house. A few minutes later Peploe came out again and hurried back to where Tanner was waiting with Sykes and the rest of Sykes's section.

'I've got a map,' said Peploe, as he reached them. 'It's only a road map and about ten years old at that, but it's better than nothing. Sykes, will you and your chaps give me and the sergeant a moment?'

'Course, sir,' said Sykes, moving his men a short distance away.

Peploe opened out the map and held it up.

'Ypres is almost due east from here, sir,' said Tanner, 'about fifteen miles away, and Poperinghe's about half that.'

'No huge distance, then.'

'No. The DLI must have gone in that direction.'

'And while Blackstone's quite right in as much as we're hardly going forward, no one's mentioned anything to us about falling back to the coast yet.' He rubbed an eye. 'We've been attached to 151st Brigade and my instinct is that we should at least try to find them. We're bound to run across some British troops eventually, if not Eighth DLI. And if we don't, or if we find ourselves approaching the enemy, we can take another view then, surely?'

'All the guns we've heard today have been from the south and west, not the east, sir. I agree with you. I think we should make for Poperinghe and Ypres.'

'But we'll take the back roads. We don't want to get ensnared in more refugee traffic.'

'Good idea, sir.'

Blackstone now came over to them. 'Sir,' he said to Peploe, 'if you're going to consult Sergeant Tanner, you should discuss things with me first.'

'Yes, all right. We're going to head for Poperinghe and Ypres and try to find the rest of the brigade,' said Peploe, stiffly.

'What a surprise,' said Blackstone. 'I might have known that whatever I said Jack would say the opposite.'

'It wasn't Tanner's decision. It was mine. Sergeant-Major, I really don't want to have to remind you again about insolence. I'm the officer in charge, and I've made up my mind. We're not running back to the coast – those are not our orders. Our orders are to stand and fight with Eighth DLI and the 151st Infantry Brigade.'

Blackstone reddened. It was the first time Tanner had seen him look really angry since he'd arrived at Manston. 'Very well, sir,' he said slowly, as though he was trying to control his fury. 'But everyone's hungry. I would strongly suggest we don't march for too long.'

'It's half past four now. We'll march for a couple of hours and see how far we get.'

Guns boomed out again to the west. Faintly, in the distance, small arms could be heard. More aircraft buzzed overhead, but this time they were high, mere specks in the sky. Tanner flicked away his cigarette, took out his water-bottle and had a swig. The enemy were closing in and the net was tightening. The lieutenant had made the right decision, he was certain, but not all the men would agree. He had a feeling Blackstone might find willing listeners should he make clear his own views on the matter. *Bollocks*.

'Cheer up, Sarge,' said Sykes, walking over to him. 'It might not happen, you know.'

Tanner smiled. 'Maybe not, Stan.'

'We've got ourselves out of tight spots before.'

'Always look on the bright side, don't you?'

'I try to, Sarge. I reckon we've still got some fight in us yet.'

'I'm sure we have.' He patted Sykes's shoulder. 'But it's not Jerry I'm so worried about.' He nodded towards Blackstone. 'It's him.'

*

From the edge of Creton Farm, Sturmbannführer Timpke peered through his binoculars down the track to the neighbouring house, some two hundred metres away. Beside him, at the back of the brick farmhouse, stood his half-track, a single motorcycle and side-car, and a large French Somua tank, now daubed with the German cross and, on its front, the Totenkopf death's head. Kemmetmüler and others from his battalion headquarters were waiting behind the cover of the farmhouse while his old friend Hauptsturmführer Knöchlein stood beside him. It was about five o'clock in the after-noon and the day had turned grey, with a light drizzle.

'I'm certain I saw a white flag, Fritz,' Timpke told Knöchlein.

'It's about time those Tommies gave up.'

'Order another burst and see what happens,' suggested Timpke.

Knöchlein stepped back and signalled to the men spread out on either side of Creton Farm, and Timpke watched them signal in turn to the men beyond, then heard several bursts of machine-gun fire. They had the place surrounded, so it was just a matter of time before the British troops still in the Duries farmhouse were forced to give up – after all, their ammunition couldn't last for ever. Nonetheless, they had caused far too many casualties. That was the problem of fighting in this flat, open countryside – there was never enough cover. Every time Knöchlein's men scrambled to their feet, more rifle and machine-gun fire rang out and another good soldier collapsed to the ground.

Timpke had been asked to help here at Paradis only half an hour earlier by Regiment 2's commander, Sturmbannführer Fortenbacher. On hearing that Knöchlein's company were bearing the brunt of the Tommies' resistance, he had decided to come forward in person with his battalion headquarters from nearby Le Cornet Malo, which had just fallen. He had reached Creton Farm only a few minutes before but now it seemed his men were hardly needed.

As the firing died down, he stared again through his binoculars, and this time there was no doubt: what looked like a white towel was tied to a pole.

'They're definitely surrendering, Fritz.' He shook his friend's hand. 'Well done.'

Knöchlein grinned, then signalled to his men with a wave, urging them forward. A spontaneous cheer rang out as his troops now picked themselves up from where they had been lying in the fields and ditches round about and ran towards the battered remains of Duries farmhouse. Timpke put away his binoculars then strode quickly back to his half-track. There he took off his helmet, replacing it with his cap. Keeping on his camouflage smock with his replacement Luger – taken from a dead comrade – at his waist, he began to walk down the track towards the scene of the Tommies' resistance. He wondered how many prisoners there might be – forty-two at least, he hoped.

It had, he reflected, been a hard few days – even frustrating at times – but he couldn't deny that he'd enjoyed it. From the moment his comrades had found him in Warlus early on 22 May, his fortunes had improved. Pressing north-west, they had swept all before them until they had reached the La Bassée canal. And during that thrust towards Béthune, he had been able to recoup some of his earlier losses, including the Somua, captured intact and undamaged.

Then had come the order – from the Führer himself, so rumour had it – for the advance to halt. At the time, it had seemed inexplicable – and certainly no reason had been given. Eicke had been furious: he had personally led Regiment 3 across the canal and had won a hard-fought and costly bridgehead, only to be ordered back. Timpke had never seen Papa Eicke so mad, and had his own reconnaissance troops been involved in the assault he would have shared their commander's dismay and fury.

Since the halt order had been rescinded the previous day, however, the entire division had been in action. Timpke's task had been to assist whichever of the attacking units needed his help. A company had been assigned to each of the three infantry regiments. Timpke and his battalion headquarters had roved between them, hacking cross-country in his half-tracks from Hinges to Locon to Le Cornet Malo and now Paradis.

As he approached the Duries farmhouse, he saw the Tommies being directed onto the track. They were bloodied, unshaven and exhausted, hands clasped on their heads. With rifles and sub-machine-guns pointed at them, they were pushed and prodded into a line. In contrast, Knöchlein's men were bright and fresh, laughing, sharing cigarettes, enjoying their moment of victory. Timpke smiled. He shared their exhilaration. Victory was sweet, as he had known it would be, but so was revenge, and as he walked along the column of prisoners he counted them. *Forty-one, forty-two* – he had barely reached halfway. *So much the better.*

He counted ninety-nine men of the Royal Norfolk Regiment – it was a shame they were not Yorks Rangers but that would have been too much to hope for. He stopped a young *Untersturmführer* who was directing his men.

'Are you in charge of these prisoners?' Timpke asked.

'Yes, Herr Sturmbannführer. I'm taking them to the field beside Creton Farm to search them.'

'Good,' said Timpke. He watched the column trudge past, then followed until they had been led down a right-hand fork in the track into the field next to the farm. Seeing Knöchlein, he now called to him.

Knöchlein waited, watching as his men began to search the prisoners. 'Yes, Herr Sturmbannführer – you wanted me?'

'I do, Fritz,' said Timpke, putting an arm round his shoulder. 'You may have heard what happened to some of my men the other day.'

'The Tommies put them in a barn and shot them.'

'They were prisoners of war, Fritz – they were my men. Shot in cold blood.'

'I'm sorry. The bastards who did that should pay for it.'

'You know, Fritz, I survived that massacre of my comrades. I was lucky. But I swore then that I would avenge it. They were my men, sure, but they were also Totenkopf men. Your comrades too.'

Knöchlein faced him. 'You want me to shoot these Tommies now?'

'Yes, Fritz. The British must pay for what they did. This will show them that in future they must not mess with the Totenkopf. That if they play dirty we will play dirty too, but twice as harshly.'

Knöchlein nodded. 'You're right, Herr Sturmbannführer. The Tommies dishonoured us and they must pay the price.'

Timpke smiled. Knöchlein had always been impressionable. He had known the simple fellow would agree. 'Good,' he said. 'I knew you'd understand, Fritz. I'll have the vehicles moved, then we can line them up against the farmhouse. Get a couple of machine-guns prepared.'

'Right away, Herr Sturmbannführer.' His eyes glinted. 'Yes. It's the justice our comrades deserve.'

Five minutes later, they were ready. The big Somua had rattled out of the way, and the half-tracks, while two machine-gun crews had set up their MG34s, with full belts of ammunition feeding into the breeches. Timpke stood with Knöchlein behind the machine-guns, watching the British prisoners being marched towards the farmhouse. The Untersturmführer leading them now came towards them. He looked nervous, his eyes shifting between the prisoners and the officers before him. Timpke stared at him. *It is an order. Do it.* The Tommies at first seemed not to know what was going on, but then some spotted the machine-guns facing them and panic spread among them.

When the first of the British soldiers had reached the end of the brick building, Knöchlein glanced at Timpke, who nodded. A moment later, an order was barked and the machine-guns opened fire.

21

Somehow they had managed to get lost. Thick cloud had rolled in, the sun had disappeared and, with it, the opportunity to navigate their way easily due east. Before long, it had begun to drizzle, and the flat, featureless Flanders landscape had been consumed by a dull mist. The inaccuracy of their road map had compounded their difficulties. The Rangers had certainly avoided refugees but instead had found themselves tramping a web of tracks and narrow roads, none of which seemed to correspond with what was shown on the map.

After a couple of hours, and still no sign of Poperinghe, Tanner was frustrated. He prided himself on his sense of direction yet, to his extreme annoyance, he had lost his bearings – not that he wanted to admit this to the lieutenant who, he knew, was feeling much the same. The men's spirits had been low when they had left Steenvoorde, but now they were plummeting rapidly. Heads were dropping, feet were dragging; there was grumbling among the ranks. *Just one more crossroads, another couple of hundred yards*, Tanner kept telling himself.

'Sarge,' said Sykes, after they had been tramping for nearly three hours, 'we've got to stop. Old Blackie'll be feeding off this one. Admit defeat, and let's stop for the night.'

Tanner nodded. 'All right, Stan.'

The lieutenant agreed, but added, 'Let's keep going for another half-hour. Poperinghe can't be far now.'

But no cluster of buildings or high-spired church appeared through the mist. Poperinghe remained as elusive as ever, so when, at just after eight o'clock, a large white farmstead loomed ahead, Peploe called a halt.

'Chaps, I'm sorry this has been a difficult afternoon,' he said to them, from the road leading to the farm. 'The lack of a good map and particularly the weather haven't helped. I'd hoped to get us to Poperinghe, but it's not to be, so we'll stay here for the night.'

It was a large, rambling place of whitewashed brick and grey slate, built around three sides of a square, with a narrow moat-like pond running along one edge. The farmhouse itself had a high-pitched roof, with a collection of different-sized barns and outbuildings, presumably added on at differing times but which, over the years, had moulded together, and now spread round the inner yard.

As the Rangers walked across the flat wooden bridge over the pond and into the yard by the front of the house, a few chickens scurried about – an encouraging sign. As Peploe approached the main door, a man appeared. Wearing a dark jacket and well-cut trousers, with thick greying hair and a moustache, he gazed defiantly at the exhausted, footsore and hungry men before him.

Immediately Peploe stepped up, offered his hand, and began to speak to him in French. Tanner watched carefully, trying to gauge the farmer's response. A shrug, a finger pointing towards one of the barns.

'Do you think he's playing ball, Sarge?' said Sykes, beside him.

'I don't think he's got much choice. But Mr Peploe's a well-brought-up fellow. I'm sure he's asking very nicely.'

Now they saw Peploe smile, shake the farmer's hand, then trot back down the steps. 'Monsieur Michaud is kindly allowing us to stay here tonight,' he told the men. 'He suggests we stay in the long barn, which is mostly empty except for straw and hay. He's going to see what food he can find, and we'll cook in sections. The well water in the yard comes from a natural spring so it's perfectly safe to drink and, indeed, wash and shave with. We'll sort out food now, but try to clean up a bit and then we can get some rest.' He glanced around at them. 'All right, dismissed.'

The farmer offered them cheese, milk, half a dozen old chickens and a bag of the previous season's apples and potatoes. Men from each section were issued the rations, then left to cook a meal, either on Primus stoves or on small fires made with logs from the woodshed. The drizzle had stopped, but it was cool, the air damp, as the men huddled round their fires and stoves. Savoury aromas soon wafted across the yard, mixing with the smell of straw and animal dung, reminding Tanner of how hungry he was. Seeing the lieutenant standing by the entrance to the farm, he wandered over to him.

'We should post some sentries, sir,' he said.

'Oh, yes – I suppose we should. I hadn't thought of that.'

'Shall I sort it out?'

'Thank you, Tanner – yes, please.'

As Tanner turned, Peploe added, 'I think morale's picked up a bit now, don't you?'

Tanner smiled. 'I'd say so, sir, although it'll be even better when they've eaten.'

He had just organized the sentries when he heard a vehicle approaching. Stepping out into the road he saw a British ambulance driving towards him. As the truck drew level, the driver, a sergeant with a Red Cross armband, leaned out of the window.

'Boy, am I glad to see you,' he said. 'We're horribly lost. Any idea where we are?'

Tanner looked at him, then at the passenger sitting next to him, a woman wearing the grey uniform of a Queen Alexandra's nurse and a tin hat. She stared at him as though she recognized him, then caught his eye, smiled and looked away.

'Er, not entirely sure, I'm afraid,' he said. 'We're lost too. We were trying to get to Poperinghe.'

'You stopping here for the night, then?'

'Yes. Where are you headed?'

'Ypres. We've been on the go non-stop since yesterday evening, taking wounded blokes up to Dunkirk and back. This is our third run but we were trying to be clever and avoid the civvies on the roads. The plan backfired rather.'

'Same happened to us,' said Tanner. 'Have you any idea what's going on at the moment?'

'Has anyone?' He grinned ruefully. 'The evacuation's begun.'

'Evacuation?' said Tanner. 'Really?'

'Yes. From Dunkirk. Bloody mayhem there – you've never seen anything like it. Men are falling back and making straight for the coast while other divisions hold the Jerries back. Yorkshire Rangers, eh?' he said, looking at the black and green shoulder flash on Tanner's battle-blouse. 'We had one of your lot in the ambulance this morning.'

'Where from?' said Tanner eagerly.

'Just south of Ypres somewhere. Wijtschate, I think it was.'

Tanner pushed his helmet to the back of his head. 'How many are they hoping to lift?'

'Search me. Not too many, looking at the place. Dunkirk's been badly knocked about. The port's absolutely had it.' He turned to the nurse beside him. 'What do you think, Lucie? Shall we stop here tonight? No point getting even more lost and we need a rest.'

She yawned. 'Yes, let's. I'm done in. I won't be any use to anyone until I've slept.'

The medic turned back to Tanner. 'Something smells good.'

'We're just cooking some food up now. Ma'am, I'm sure there's room in the farmhouse for you – and your name was?' he asked the sergeant.

'Greenstreet, Jim Greenstreet. And this is Lucie Richoux of the QAs.' He held out a hand.

Tanner shook it. 'You all right dossing down with us in the barn, Jim?'

'Perfect, mate.'

Despite the now fading light, Nurse Richoux received a fair number of stares and glances as she stepped out of the ambulance. Tanner introduced her and Sergeant Greenstreet to the lieutenant. 'The evacuation's begun, sir,' Tanner told him. 'It sounds like First Battalion is one of the units helping to keep a corridor open until the rest have passed through. I bet that's where 151st Brigade were heading – to help keep the Jerries at bay in the Ypres area.'

'Christ,' said Peploe. 'I can hardly believe it. It's not even been three weeks.' He sighed heavily. 'So we were right, then, to head in the direction of Ypres.'

'Sounds like it, sir.'

'Then we'd better try and join them tomorrow. Or at least look for them.' He knocked on the farmhouse door and ushered the nurse forward. 'We'd better make the most of this rest.'

By half past ten the men, Tanner included, were asleep in the barn, their appetites sated. One man, though, was still very much awake. Sergeant-Major Blackstone couldn't sleep. Instead, he lay on the straw drinking a bottle of wine he'd taken earlier in Steenvoorde. The news of the evacuation was the final straw – and still that bloody upstart of a lieutenant wanted them to head to Ypres in the morning. Peploe, Tanner and Sykes – the trio seemed bent on ruining everything. He'd had the whole company eating out of his hand – especially that idiot Barclay. The captain had been just the sort of man Blackstone had wanted as OC. A weak character, suggestible and easily persuaded.

It had been almost ridiculously easy, Blackstone reflected. He'd laid it on pretty thick that he was a highly experienced soldier while subtly yet repeatedly reminding Barclay of his own shortcomings. He'd won over the men in no time, through a combination of charm, easy-going affability and sudden savage threats. A tried and tested formula. In no time at all he'd been running the show, enjoying an easy life and a satisfying amount of power. And when they were thrust into action, as he had known at some point would surely happen, it had been his intention to steer them – and, of course, himself – away from the fray. He saw no reason to get himself killed for King and country when plenty of others were willing to do so.

And there had been rich pickings, too. He'd been building quite a nice little nest egg. When the war was over, he planned to retire in style. It was by chance that he had discovered Slater's criminal past but the two men had quickly come to a working agreement. Blackstone's influence created opportunities that Slater's criminal mind could exploit. Together they were quite a team. The fuel racket at Manston had proved particularly lucrative.

Then Tanner had turned up. *Damn him to hell.* He'd been just the same in India – full of misplaced honour and tediously in-corruptible. Of all the sergeants in the world, why had Tanner had to join his nice little set-up? He'd groaned the moment he'd seen him again and his forebodings had been justified. Everything had started to go wrong the moment the bastard had arrived and started sniffing around their fuel scam. He'd tried charm, he'd tried threats – Christ, Slater had tried to kill him and that interfering sidekick of his in the stores at Manston – but the idiot wouldn't take the hint. He'd taken a shot at Tanner on the canal but he'd never been much good with a gun and had missed. Then he'd suggested they split up the company. For once, he'd thought he'd got through to him, but Tanner had gone and spoiled everything with his damned heroics. Next, Blackstone had bribed that silly French bitch to accuse Tanner of rape and that hadn't worked either. Then Slater had killed all those SS monkeys in an attempt to implicate him. Blackstone had balked at the idea, but it had been a good plan – and, anyway, they had been SS Nazis. Who was going to mourn them? The first part had been to make sure Barclay and the rest of the company remained in the village. With a bit of talk to the captain about duty and honour and obeying his orders to the letter, that had been easy enough. The second part of the plan was to wake the unconscious SS officer and talk about Tanner loudly; and the third was to make sure he and Slater got the hell out of there – which they had by telling the OC they were going to get reinforcements. It had all been working perfectly until they'd discovered another vehicle had got away – and that the stupid bastards in it *had* got reinforcements. Rather than Tanner being left to a slow, painful death at the hands of the SS, his nemesis had turned up again with the rest of them the following morning. Blackstone had felt like shooting him down there and then.

Now he got up and walked out of the barn into the yard, still clutching the bottle. It was a still, cool night, with just the hint of a breeze. For a moment, he wondered whether he and Slater should take the ambulance and scarper with the loot they'd acquired since they'd been in France, but he knew that wasn't the answer. After Warlus, he wouldn't make the same mistake of assuming the lads would all end up dead or captured. In any case, the survivors would be bound to report them. No, he needed to get the boys on his side, which he'd been working hard at the past few days. He reckoned he'd done quite well, too, but with the lieutenant now in charge, his authority had been weakened. And he was all too aware that most of them, especially those in Peploe's platoon, still respected Tanner. Somehow he needed to get Peploe out of the way. *Yes.* Peploe first, and then he'd sort out Tanner once and for all.

A light at the top of the house caught his attention and he looked up to see the nurse standing at the window in her underclothes, drawing the thick curtains. He felt his loins stir and took another glug of wine. An idea occurred to him – a plan that would not only get rid of Peploe, but would allow himself a bit of fun with the girl. There were, as far as he knew, only four people in the farmhouse: the farmer and his wife, the lieutenant and the nurse. He took another glug of wine. *Courage, lad. This little plan might just work.* A bit reckless, perhaps, but the wine was making him feel so, and the sight of the girl had awakened in him the urge to find female company. *Let's see what Ted makes of it.* Returning to the barn, he trod softly among the snoring men and woke Slater, who followed him silently outside.

'All right,' said Slater, once Blackstone had explained his plan. 'But we should leave it another hour. Make sure everyone's properly asleep.'

'All right. You can have the girl after I'm done.'

'Not my type,' muttered Slater. 'And there's a shotgun in the kitchen. I saw it earlier. I'll get that and I've got the captain's Webley too.' He grinned. 'Hang on a minute. I bet there are supplies in that blood-wagon. Some chloroform could come in handy.'

Blackstone chuckled. 'I like it. I'll go and talk to the sentries outside the front while you have a little rummage.'

It was a quarter to midnight when they crept into the dairy next to the house and, from there, found some steps and an open door that led into the kitchen. Using their torches they soon spotted the shotgun resting in a corner by an old oak dresser. Both barrels were loaded. Slater smiled. 'They were always going to be,' he whispered. 'After all, this is a time of war.'

They trod softly up the stone stairs. From the landing there were a number of rooms but they had already guessed from the open windows they had seen in the yard where the farmer and his wife, and the lieutenant, were sleeping. Stealing down the corridor, Blackstone saw, to his relief, that the lieutenant's door was ajar. He listened and heard his slow, rhythmic breathing, then nodded to Slater. Putting on his respirator, Slater took out a two-ounce tube of chloroform and entered the room. Blackstone waited breathlessly, but half a minute later Slater reappeared, taking off his gas mask. 'He's out for the count. You go and get him, then have your oats,' he whispered. 'I'll sort out Mr and Mrs Farmer.'

Lieutenant Peploe was laid out on his bed, still wearing his trousers and shirt. Blackstone listened to the faint breathing, then hoisted him onto his shoulders with a gasp, staggered out of the room and up the second flight of stairs to the top of the house. He was hot and breathing heavily by the time he got there, and, he realized, his senses weren't quite as keen as he would have liked. He'd had too much of that damned wine. He shook his head, then moved towards the door at the end of the short passage.

It opened before he had reached it, and there, before him, was the nurse, hastily buttoning the neck of her dress. 'What's the matter?' she asked. Her dark hair, he noticed, was cut short and hung to her shoulders. She had a trim, shapely figure.

'It's the lieutenant,' he said. 'He's unwell.'

She switched on the corridor light, then glanced up at him guardedly. 'All right,' she said. 'Put him on the bed.'

He did so, then stood back. At that moment, there was a commotion from below. The farmer's wife screamed, then there was a crash and the farmer himself began to shout.

'My God, what on earth's going on?' said the nurse, alarm in her voice.

'Never you mind,' said Blackstone, grabbing her wrist.

'Let go of me!' she shouted, but Blackstone had both her wrists now and pushed her to the floor. She was wriggling and kicking as he heard Slater and the farmer thumping up the stairs.

'You nearly done, Will?' Slater called.

'No, I'm bloody not,' he gasped. 'Keep still, will you, lass?'

'Too bad,' said Slater. 'I'm coming up.'

Blackstone saw the girl's eyes widen as Slater entered the room. Turning, he saw his friend's hand was over the farmer's mouth and the shotgun was pressed to his side. Now he flung the man against the wall, then calmly pulled the trigger. Plasterwork fell as Monsieur Michaud slumped to the floor. Blackstone was momentarily stupefied, then felt a violent pain in his groin. Rolling over in agony, he was conscious of the nurse jumping to her feet and running out of the room.

'For God's sake, Will!' snarled Slater. He took off after her, and as Blackstone, still wincing, got to his knees, he heard a second blast and then, faintly, a splash.

*

Tanner had been awake the moment he heard the shotgun. Others were stirring too, but he grabbed his MP35 and ran out of the barn, across the yard and into the house. Flailing in the dark, he was halfway up the stairs when the second shot rang out. Flinching, he hurried on.

'Sir!' he shouted. 'Sir!'

It was not Lieutenant Peploe coming down from the top landing, but Slater.

'Sergeant Tanner,' he said, his voice more animated than Tanner had ever known it. 'I never thought I'd say this, but thank God you're here.'

'What the bloody hell's going on?' He noticed the sergeant was holding a Webley revolver.

'It's the farmer,' he almost gabbled. 'He tried to have his way with the nurse. Too much grog. He's whacked his wife, struck the lieutenant with his shotgun, then Blackie and me got there and we had a bit of a tussle. I'm looking for the girl.'

'What? Where did she go?'

'I don't know – I think she may have jumped out of a window. I heard a splash.'

Tanner glanced up to the landing, then into the room nearest him. He went in and ran to the window, forced it wide and leaned out. Then there was a crack on his head and his mind went blank.

In the top room, Blackstone could hear men shouting and talking outside as they hurried across the yard. The pain had eased, and so he moved Peploe from the bed and swung the door into the lieutenant's head. Looking up, he saw Slater at the top of the stairs.

'We've got be quick, Will,' said Slater, urgently, as he ushered him back into the room. 'You need to go out into the yard and tell the men what's happened. The sky's cleared and the stars are out. Explain to them that the best course for them is to start heading for the coast. We can use the Pole Star, but my guess is we've been heading north anyway. Make it convincing, all right?'

Blackstone nodded. 'What about Tanner?'

'I don't think we need to worry too much about him. I coshed him over the head and pushed him out of a window into the pond. He's probably drowned. You can tell them he jumped after the nurse. I'll go and search for them now. If either of them's found, they won't be making any trouble, that's for sure.'

'And the farmer's missus?'

'I've dealt with her.'

Blackstone swallowed. 'All right, Ted.'

'Good – you do the talking, and I'll hunt for Tanner and the nurse.'

He hurried off, leaving Blackstone in the top bedroom. The CSM glanced back at Monsieur Michaud's lifeless body and tried to think clearly. He could hear the men in the yard and in the house downstairs. Slater spoke to some of them as he passed. Hurrying to the window, he leaned out and said, 'All right, boys, everything's under control.' Then, as he dashed for the stairs, he saw Sykes, McAllister and Greenstreet, the medical orderly.

'What's going on?' said Sykes.

'A bit of a to-do with the farmer, lads,' said Blackstone. 'Can you come up here and give me a hand with the lieutenant? I'm afraid he must have been coshed.'

Sykes pushed past and hurried to Peploe. 'Sir?' he said, and then, as he checked the lieutenant's breathing, he noticed Monsieur Michaud's bloodied body. 'Christ alive!' he said, jolting backwards.

'Slater got him,' said Blackstone, then turned to Greenstreet. 'I'm sorry, mate, but the bastard was trying to have his way with your nurse friend.'

Panic spread over Greenstreet's face. 'Where is she?'

'She got away from him – kneed him where it hurt most, I think. We got here just after he'd fired a shot at her on the landing. Then Ted pounced on him and eventually managed to shoot him. We never saw her, but I think she jumped out of the window in the adjoining bedroom.'

'Oh, my God,' said Greenstreet, leaving Peploe to run down the corridor and into the next room. 'Lucie!' he shouted, from the window. 'Lucie!'

Following him, and deliberately blocking the top of the stairs, Blackstone said, 'Slater's taken some men to look for her.'

'Then I must go and help,' said Greenstreet.

'No. You stay here and make sure the lieutenant's all right. There's enough people already searching for her.' Blackstone ran down the stairs.

'Sergeant,' Sykes called to Greenstreet.

'Sorry – yes, I'm coming,' Greenstreet replied. 'This is bloody unbelievable.'

Sykes saw him glance at Monsieur Michaud as he came back in. Then Greenstreet cleared his throat and said, 'We should take the lieutenant back to his room. Can't leave him to come round in here with – with all that blood.'

Sykes and McAllister lifted Peploe, carried him down the stairs and laid him on his bed. Greenstreet felt his pulse, then put his ear to Peploe's mouth.

'He's still breathing, all right.'

'What about his head?' asked McAllister.

'A bad bump, that's all. He's out cold, though.' He stood up. 'Look, I'm sorry, but I've got to find Lucie.' Muttering under his breath, he hurried from the room.

When he had gone, Sykes said, 'There's something going on here, Mac.' Now he remembered Tanner. 'And where's the sarge – where the bloody hell is he?'

'I don't know,' said McAllister. 'I haven't seen him.'

'Jesus Christ,' muttered Sykes. 'Right. You stay here, Mac, and keep an eye on the lieutenant. I'm going to look for the sarge.'

He ran from the room, down the stairs, across the hallway and out into the yard. 'Has anyone seen Sergeant Tanner?' he said, grabbing at the others. 'Where's the sarge?'

'It's all right, boys,' said Blackstone. 'Sergeant Tanner jumped out after the nurse, but there are men looking for them.'

'Sod that,' said Sykes. 'Three Section! To me!'

He ran from the yard, around the front of the house and down to the moat, his men following. As he ran he took his torch from his pocket, although up ahead, lights were already flickering along the pond's bank. He slowed now, sweeping his torch across the narrow strip of water. It was still and dark, thick with weed and bulrushes.

'Keep your eyes peeled,' said Sykes.

Slater came over to them. 'I'm sorry,' he said. 'We've searched the whole length but there's nothing.'

'There must be,' said Sykes. 'Didn't the sentries see anything?'

Slater shook his head. 'They came into the yard when they heard the shots. We've looked – we've had half a dozen torches on it, but there's a lot of weed and God knows what else in there.' He called over the rest of his men. 'Come on,' he said. 'I know the CSM wants to talk to everyone.'

'We'll just have another quick look,' said Sykes. 'He is our sergeant.'

'I'll stay too,' said Greenstreet.

Slater nodded. 'Be quick about it.'

Once Slater and his men were out of sight, Hepworth said, 'Bollocks, Corp, there's only one way to find him,' and began to take off his boots and trousers.

'He's right, Corp,' agreed Bell, following suit. When they had undressed to their underwear, both men lowered themselves into the water.

'Jesus, it's cold!' said Hepworth. 'Wherever he is now, I hope the sarge appreciates what we're doing for him.'

'How deep is it?' asked Sykes.

'Not very,' said Hepworth. 'Five foot maybe.' They waded up to the bridge, then back again and down the length of the farm buildings. But there was nothing.

'Where can they have gone?' said Greenstreet. Sykes thought he seemed close to tears. 'She was a great girl, Lucie, plucky as they come.'

Slater called to them from the bridge. 'Come on, you lot! The CSM wants to speak to you.'

While Hepworth and McAllister dried themselves with their battle-blouses, Sykes looked into the dark still water. As he did so, a thought occurred to him. 'Hang on a minute,' he mumbled to himself. Then he turned to the others. 'Hey, boys, I don't reckon we need to feel too gloomy just yet. Hep and Tinker haven't had a dip for nothing.'

'What do you mean?' said Bell.

'Well,' said Sykes, in a low voice, 'think about it. If he's not there and neither is Nurse Richoux, they must be somewhere else, which means one or other must be alive. They're not both going to vanish into five foot of a ten-foot-wide pond, are they?'

Hepworth's face brightened. 'Bugger me, Corp, you're right!'

'Ssh!' said Sykes. 'Keep your flaming voice down! Now, listen, don't let on that the pond's only five foot deep, all right? Not yet, at any rate. Me and the sarge have had our suspicions about the CSM and Slater for some time and if we're right then something fishy's going on and I don't think it'd be a good idea for Slater to think they're still alive.'

'You think Slater and the CSM tried to do 'em in?' said Bell.

'I'm not sure, Tinker, but maybe, yes.'

Bell whistled.

'Jesus,' said Greenstreet.

'But listen to me. If you want to help the sarge and Nurse Richoux, you follow my lead, all right?' He shone his torch at them. 'Yes?' They nodded. 'Good. Then let's go.'

Blackstone had assembled the men in the drawing room of the house, a large space with electric lighting where antique tapestries and old portraits hung on the walls. He explained what had happened – how he and Sergeant Slater had been in the yard and had heard a commotion inside the house; how they had found the lieutenant unconscious and the farmer assaulting the nurse. The lieutenant had been hit on the head. It was all very unfortunate.

'So, boys,' said Blackstone, solemnly, 'it means that, for the time being, I'm in charge. And things have changed a lot for us since yesterday. We've lost our skipper and the lieutenant's out of action. More than that, we know what's going on. We've all sensed the battle hasn't been going our way, but it's now a fact that the BEF is being evacuated. It seems likely that Fifth and Fiftieth Divs are doing a hell of a job holding back the enemy in the Ypres area while the rest of the boys in between make a dash for the coast. But what the hell can we do? Forty-odd men aren't going to make any difference. Our battalion walked out and left us behind in Belgium and now Eighth DLI have deserted us too. We've done all that's been asked of us, and more, but right now, it's time we thought of ourselves.' There was a shuffling of feet and a murmur of agreement. 'Look,' he continued, 'we're all awake now, we've got some grub inside us – and it's not as if we haven't had a rest, is it? The rain's gone and we've a clear sky above us. I know it wasn't what we intended, but last evening we were heading north – you know, maybe someone's trying to tell us something. If we get going now, we can follow the Pole Star and make good progress before all those refugees are on the move. We'll be there by lunchtime and we can rest all we like. With a bit of luck, we'll be back in Blighty by the following morning.' There were further murmurs of agreement. 'The alternative is that we wait here until morning, battle against the flow of refugees, eventually get to Ypres, find our boys have already gone and end up in the bag. Or, worse, dead.' He paused again. 'So, who's with me?'

Hands were raised, and Blackstone smiled. 'Good,' he said. 'We leave in five minutes.'

'Hold on a mo', Sergeant-Major,' said Sykes, as he and McAllister entered the room. 'I know my section would rather wait here until Lieutenant Peploe comes round.'

'But there's an ambulance,' said Blackstone. 'Sergeant Greenstreet can take care of him.'

'We'd still rather stay here. It sounded to me like you were givin' us a choice a moment ago. What's more, there's also Sergeant Tanner,' Sykes continued. Another ripple of murmuring from the men. 'You see, that pond's not very deep and we've trawled it pretty carefully and found nothing. That makes me think that the sarge and the nurse got out.' The room had gone quiet now as the men listened to him. 'There's no way I could let my men leave this place until we've found both of 'em, and I'd like to think Rosso and Coop would feel much the same way.'

Cooper and Ross nodded.

'If they're still alive why aren't they here?' said Blackstone.

'Perhaps they're fearful for their safety, Sergeant-Major,' Sykes replied.

'That's ridiculous. Why on earth should Tanner feel that?'

'Maybe because he's been nearly burned to death, shot in the side, and falsely accused of rape. I'd have thought that's reason enough.' There was an audibly sharp intake of breath from the others.

Blackstone cursed to himself. He was losing them. *Damn Sykes to hell.* They'd taken care of Peploe and Tanner but overlooked the third man in the trio. *Careless, very careless.* And now the Cockney runt was on the point of ruining everything. 'And you think I was responsible for all that?' Blackstone said, hoping his feigned incredulity was convincing. 'Don't make me laugh.' He jabbed a finger at Sykes. 'Corporal, you're talking out of turn.'

'What I'd like to know,' said McAllister, suddenly speaking up, 'is where Madame Michaud is?'

'The farmer's wife?' said Blackstone. Panic now coursed through him. He glanced at Slater – *help me out here.*

'The farmer killed her, then attacked the nurse,' said Slater.

'You know what?' said McAllister. 'I reckon that's a load of old bollocks. I reckon the whole story's bollocks.'

'You – be quiet!' said Blackstone.

'No, I won't,' said McAllister. 'Why would a gentle old farmer suddenly do his wife in and cosh an officer when he's surrounded by that officer's troops? It don't bloody well make sense.' The men were all talking now. Blackstone had his hands in the air trying to silence them when a shot rang out. The effect was immediate. All the men stopped talking and stared at Slater, who held a revolver pointed at the wooden floor.

'Listen, all of you,' said Slater, and Sykes noticed that several men from Company Headquarters had positioned themselves by the door, fully armed. One held a Bren at his waist. 'We're leaving now. All those coming with us, move to the door. The rest stay where you are. I'm going to count to three. One.'

Half a dozen men from 11 Platoon stepped forward, but the rest, including all of Peploe's platoon, remained where they were.

'What are you going to do now?' said Sykes. 'Shoot us like you did those Jerries?'

'Shut up!' said Blackstone, then said to Slater, 'Don't even think of it, Ted. We'll put them in the cellar.' He wondered for a moment whether Slater might ignore him and shoot them all anyway. *Christ alive*, he thought, and his stomach lurched. It was one thing killing Nazis, but to slaughter men on your own side – men you'd lived alongside for the past couple of months? That was a step too far.

'If you insist,' said Slater, pushing past him. 'Right,' he said, waving his Webley, 'those of you with weapons, drop them on the floor and get into single file.' He shoved several men forward.

The entrance to the cellar was in the kitchen across the hall from the drawing room and the men, most of whom were stupefied by the turn of events, were led there at gunpoint, then shoved through the door. Ten feet below, at the bottom of a flight of stone steps, there was a large, cold, musty cave, its vaulted bays partially stacked with wine. 'There,' said Slater, as he followed them. 'Have a drink on us.' He grabbed a couple of bottles. Then, satisfied that the men were all there, he walked backwards up the stone steps and shut the door.

'How can you do this?' protested a corporal from 11 Platoon.

'More easily than you'd think,' said Slater, and closed the door.

From the cellar, the only light the men could see came from the outline of the door. In silence, they heard a padlock click shut across it. Then there was a heavy scraping sound as furniture was moved in front of it. Finally, the lights went out, and a minute later, they dimly heard the ambulance being driven away.

*

Tanner heard the ambulance leaving, too, opened his eyes and wondered where the hell he was. Lying on straw with a pounding head and, he realized, someone close to him with their arms round him. He jolted into full consciousness.

'You're awake,' said a voice.

The nurse. 'Where am I?'

'In one of the stables.' She unfolded herself from him and Tanner felt a wave of cold as her warm body moved away from his. 'I'm sorry for the intimacy, but you were wet and cold. I didn't want you to get hypothermia. How's your head?'

'Sore.' He propped himself up on his elbows. 'What happened?'

'One of your men tried to rape me,' she said, her voice catching. 'I got away and jumped from a window into the pond. I saw you looking for me but you were hit from behind and pushed out.'

'Slater hit me with his pistol. Knocked me out.'

'I saw you fall and pulled you out – only just in time. One of them – the man who killed Monsieur Michaud – he came looking for us with some other men. They had torches, so I dragged you behind this barn. There was a strut sticking out that hid us. Then I saw this door and inside found all this straw.'

'You saved my life – thank you.'

'I've never been more terrified.'

'You're very brave.'

'We need fresh clothes,' she said, 'but I daren't go out. I've used up my courage quota for one night.'

Tanner stood up, stumbled, then steadied himself. 'Wait here,' he said. 'Don't move a muscle. I'll be as quick as I can but I must find out what's going on.' He crept out of the door at the back of the farmstead, then saw he was beside the long barn in which they had been resting. He paused to allow his eyes to adjust to the dark. In moments, shapes emerged – the looming bulk of the house, trees and bushes, stars reflected in the pond. He made his way back down the track, round the house and into the yard. The ambulance had gone and there were no longer any lights on in the house – had Blackstone and Slater left? It seemed likely but he couldn't be certain. He ran to the yard, entered the barn and found no one there. Yet his kit and rifle were. He put on his webbing over his wet shirt, felt in his pack for his torch and switched it on, then hurried back across the yard and into the house. Immediately he heard banging and muffled shouts from the kitchen.

'Help! Get us out! Help!'

Tanner went into the kitchen, shone his torch and saw that the dresser had been moved in front of the cellar door. He moved it clear, then smashed the door with the butt of his rifle until at last it swung free. He shone his torch on the stairs. 'Stan?' he said, seeing his friend. 'What the bloody hell's been going on here?'

Despite the pain in his head, Tanner's spirits were higher than they had ever been since he'd arrived at Manston. Blackstone and Slater had gone. An enormous weight had been lifted from his shoulders.

He ordered the fire in the kitchen to be relit, brought Lucie in from the barn and led her to a chair in front of the fire. Then he detailed Corporal Cooper to organize a burial party for the bodies of Monsieur and Madame Michaud. Everyone else was sent back to the barn. They would rest until morning, he told them, by which time he hoped Peploe might have recovered. Sergeant Greenstreet had agreed to remain with the lieutenant, who was already showing groggy signs of coming back round to consciousness.

Having overseen the burial of the farmer and his wife, Tanner staggered back into the kitchen, where he found Lucie wrapped in a rug and warming herself by the fire; her uniform hung over a chair.

'There's some brandy on the table,' she said. 'You should have a glass. It'll do you good.'

Tanner poured himself a tumbler, then sat in an armchair next to her. 'I'm sorry about what happened,' he said. 'Those two have been making life very difficult for some time. I just couldn't nail anything on them. But I'm truly sorry you should have been caught up in it.'

'It was frightening but, actually, he'd barely laid a finger on me before I hit him hard between the legs.'

'A good place to go for – it's always painful,' said Tanner.

'Yes, well, it did the trick. Far more upsetting was seeing Monsieur Michaud killed like that. I've seen some terrible things since coming to France and I've got a strong stomach, these days, but that was just so – so brutal, so cold-blooded.' She shivered.

Tanner sipped his brandy, the liquid searing the back of his throat. Christ, his head throbbed. He gazed at the flames and noticed steam coming from the thick serge of his still-wet trousers and shirt, then saw that Lucie was staring at him. He met her gaze and smiled. She was undeniably pretty – slight, with large deep-brown eyes. There was vulnerability in them, he thought. 'Richoux,' he said. 'Jim said your name was Richoux. Doesn't sound very English.'

'It's not. My father's French. My mother's English, though, and I was sent to school in England. But I think of myself as French, really. It's home. And now it's overrun with Germans.'

'What will you do if France falls?'

'Go back to England, I suppose. I joined the QA in London.'

'And what about your parents?'

'They're still here. At least, I hope they are. We live near Cherbourg – I don't think the hysteria's reached there yet.' She sighed. 'You should take off those wet clothes and let them dry. I must look at your head – you might need a couple of stitches.'

'Maybe,' he mumbled. He took off his webbing, then undid his boots and put them before the fire.

'And the rest,' said Lucie. 'Don't be shy on my account.'

He knew she was right; wet clothes were to be avoided if at all possible. He needed to be fit in the days to come. Even so, he felt self-conscious as he took off his trousers, then his shirt.

'What happened to you?' she asked, seeing the mottled yellow and purple bruising across his right side.

'Nothing much – a bullet graze and a bit of a kicking. All thanks to those two.' He yawned. 'Maybe we should get some rest now. There are plenty of bedrooms upstairs.'

'Yes, you're right. But I'd rather not go back to that room at the top.'

'Of course not,' said Tanner, standing up. 'Come on. We'll find you a room on the first floor.'

They crept upstairs. The house was still once more, the only sound the gentle snores coming from Peploe's room.

'That's Jim,' whispered Lucie. 'I've heard him snore even louder than that.'

The bedroom door opposite was open. It was the same room from which Slater had thrown Tanner. The window was still open, and there was a large, unused bed. 'Why don't you sleep here?' he suggested. 'I'll get your kit from upstairs.'

'Thank you.'

He returned a minute later. 'Goodnight,' he said, having placed her kit on the bed.

'Sergeant,' she said, 'just let me look at your head first. Really – I should.'

Tanner sat on the edge of the bed, conscious of his near-naked-ness. Lucie knelt behind him, her delicate fingers parting his hair. He winced as she touched the wound.

'Sorry,' she said. 'It does need a couple of stitches. There's no point leaving it open and letting it get infected. And you've some old stitches too that should be taken out. What have you been doing?'

'Soldiers tend to get bashed about a bit,' he said.

'But not usually by your own side.'

'You'd hope not.'

She delved into her surgical haversack, took out a syringe and a phial, then a rolled cloth pouch that reminded him of his house-wife. 'I'm just going to give you a small injection of procaine,' she said. 'It'll numb your head a bit.'

'Good,' said Tanner. 'You can give me a big one if you like.'

She laughed, a soft, infectious sound. 'Just keep your head still. This won't take long.'

When she had finished, she ruffled his hair, then put away her surgical scissors and thread. Something made him linger, then turn to her. She gazed at him a moment, then ran her hand across his cheek. 'You remind me very much of someone,' she said. 'Someone I used to know.' She leaned towards him, lips parted, and kissed him. 'Stay with me,' she breathed. 'Stay with me tonight.'

22

Six p.m., Tuesday, 28 May, Wijtschate, Belgium. What was left of
D Company, the Yorkshire Rangers, stood sheltering at the edge of
a wood a short distance from the village. The passage of shells
could be heard easily amid the crumps and sharper detonations,
whistling as they hurtled through the air. Short but plentiful bursts
of machine-gun fire and the lighter explosions of mortars indicated
that this was not merely an exchange of artillery fire but that front-
line infantrymen were actively engaged against one another. Every
so often a larger shell – a 105 or 155 – exploded and the men felt
the ground below them shake. Despite the damp and the rain that
still threatened, the air was heavy with cordite, burning and dust.
Wijtschate, once a pretty Belgian village, had had the misfortune to
find itself on the front line twice in the space of twenty-five years.
In the Great War it had been destroyed and now it was on its way
to being destroyed again. Several houses were burning; many more
had crumbled. Shell craters pocked the road that led into the village square. Ahead, a column of men were picking their
way through the rubble of a collapsed building. Another shell

hurtled over, this time from the western side – British gunners.

Tanner looked up as a despatch rider sped down the road a hundred yards in front of them and turned into the farmhouse that was now home to 13th Brigade Headquarters. A few minutes later another motorcycle raced off. Messengers had been coming and going – by motorcycle, bike and on foot – at regular intervals. Taking out a cigarette, he glanced at the men. They looked fed up. It had rained on and off for most of the day, and although gas capes were more or less waterproof, they couldn't stand up to prolonged rain. Moreover, they were hot, especially when marching. Tanner had discarded his hours earlier, but now his uniform was damp again. Khaki serge was certainly warm and strong, but when wet it was heavy, scratchy and a bugger to dry. Tanner wondered why he'd bothered to put his trousers in front of the fire the night before, and pleasanter thoughts of Lucie sprang into his mind. She'd been a sweet girl – passionate, too – but there had been a wistfulness about her he'd not been able to put his finger on. Perhaps it was just the war – and the inevitable loss of France. They had left her and Sergeant Greenstreet in Poperinghe, and he wondered whether he would ever see her again; he hoped so. She had got under his skin more than he had expected. The girl who had saved his life.

The roads had been heaving all day, with French and British troops going in the opposite direction from their own small band. Their progress had prompted numerous jibes: 'You're heading the wrong way!' 'Dunkirk's the other direction!' It had got on their nerves and more than once Tanner had questioned whether he and Peploe had made the right decision. The men had carried on marching, standing aside to let vehicles through, weaving past troops and civilians, but by the middle of the afternoon, heads were sagging. At least the lieutenant was fit, apparently none the worse for the crack on his head. 'I must have a very thick skull,' he had joked.

He and Peploe had inevitably talked about Blackstone and Slater. Peploe was of much the same opinion as Tanner – that their flight was a weight off his mind. Tanner wondered where they were now. Back in England already? It wouldn't have surprised him.

'Don't worry, Sergeant,' Peploe had told him that morning, 'they're facing a life on the run now. I swore I'd make sure they paid for what they did in Warlus and I mean it even more now. And if for any reason I don't make it back and you do, you must promise me you won't let them get away with what they did.'

Tanner had promised. He wondered what had become of the Pole, Torwinski. Christ, but that seemed a long time ago now. And Lyell? Had he made it back?

A hundred yards away the column of men had now halted by Brigade Headquarters. Tanner guessed there were two hundred or more. He watched them fall out, collapsing wearily on the side of the road, and wondered what Peploe was up to. He glanced at his watch as two shells landed only a few hundred yards away. 'Come on, Mr Peploe. Either let us dig in or get us out of here.'

The brigade staff had been pleasantly surprised when Lieutenant Peploe had walked in and announced his arrival with thirty-three other ranks.

'You're just in time,' said Captain Ross, one of the Brigade staff officers. 'The Yorkshire Rangers have just been pulled back.' He explained that every battalion in the brigade was horribly depleted, including the 1st Yorkshire Rangers. Since D Company had been left by 1st Battalion on the Brussels–Charleroi canal, the brigade had not been idle, having seen fierce fighting east of Arras and almost continually since then. For two days, the entire 5th Division had been fighting desperately to hold the canal line between Ypres and Commines; 13th and 17th Brigades had managed to stave off every German attack, but not without crippling casualties. 'It's been one bloody crisis after another,' he said. 'You've heard about the Belgians, I suppose?'

'No, sir.'

'They've thrown in the towel. Yesterday evening, just like that. The whole of Third Div had to move last night from south of here to north of Ypres to fill the gap in the line. They did it, though. Bloody miracle.'

There was a feverish atmosphere inside the farmhouse. Brigade staff had been whittled down to a bare minimum, which meant every man had more work than he could reasonably manage. A map was spread on a table in the kitchen and Peploe saw the brigadier and his GSO 1 standing over it. Despatch riders hurried in and out, delivering and taking messages. Every so often a shell landed uncomfortably close and the house shook. Peploe noticed a pile of plaster on the floor in the kitchen. And there was an almost choking quantity of cigarette and pipe smoke.

Another despatch rider came in and passed a message to the brigadier, who read it with a faint smile. He was a lean-faced man, with slightly hooded, intelligent eyes and a fair moustache. Looking up, he noticed Peploe and extended his hand. 'Hello,' he said. 'Brigadier Dempsey. And who are you?'

'Second Lieutenant John Peploe, D Company, First Battalion, Yorkshire Rangers. How do you do, sir?'

'D Company were cut off from the rest of the battalion eleven days ago, sir,' said Ross. 'They fought alongside Eighth DLI at Arras and on La Bassée canal, got cut off again, but have eventually found us here.'

'That's rather impressive, Peploe,' said Dempsey. 'I think most people in your boat would have hot-footed it straight to Dunkirk.' He scratched the back of his neck. 'I'm afraid poor comms have been one of the biggest failings in this campaign. Anyway,' he smiled, 'while I hate to make you go back the way you came, that's exactly what I'm going to do. We're about to withdraw – it seems we've done what was needed here, thank goodness, and we're now the last in the line. Most of the brigade are to head to the river Yser and from there fall back within the Dunkirk perimeter, but the Yorkshire Rangers are being transferred.'

'To where, sir?'

'First Guards Brigade. You see, Lieutenant, although your lot are down to just over two hundred and fifty men, that's a bit more than the Wiltshires and quite a bit more than the Inniskillings and Cameronians. Just luck, really – the Yorkshire Rangers have had a less busy time than the other battalions in the brigade. Your task will be to help hold the Dunkirk perimeter until all the other troops have safely passed through.'

'And been evacuated.'

'Well, that's the general idea at any rate,' continued Dempsey. 'I'm sorry, it's rather a devil of a job.'

'There's M/T waiting a couple of miles from here on the far side of Mount Kemmel,' added Ross. 'It'll be a bit of a squeeze, but better than walking, I'd say.'

'And when will we be leaving?' asked Peploe.

'We're expecting Colonel Corner and the battalion at any moment.'

Brigadier Dempsey shook Peploe's hand. 'Good luck, Lieutenant,' he said, 'and pass on my best wishes to your men. I hope our paths cross again.'

The journey north was desperately slow. The thirty-four men of D Company as well as a much depleted seven-man platoon from A Company were crammed into one Bedford OY truck, and since the A Company platoon commander, Lieutenant Lightfoot, was one of the seven, Tanner was forced to squeeze into the back with the rest of the other ranks. Every road they took was clogged with troops, and while the British tried to head north, the French, many of whom travelled by horse-drawn cart, seemed to be cutting across them to the west. And still there were refugees with their barrows and carts, bicycles and pitiful piles of belongings. It was as though the whole of northern France was on the move.

Poperinghe had looked badly knocked about when D Company had passed through earlier, but by dusk it was worse. Rubble had spilled into the streets and had been only partially cleared, while the main bridge across the canal was cratered in two places. British sappers were trying to repair it while around them the traffic ground to a confused halt. From the back of the truck, Tanner peered out at the darkening skies and prayed the *Luftwaffe* had called a halt for the day; they would find rich pickings in Poperinghe.

By the time they had eventually got through the town, it was dark. Progress was hardly much faster, however, the truck jerking forward, then frequently coming to a halt, sometimes for a few minutes, often for much longer. As the first streaks of dawn appeared, it was clear that the battalion's column had become separated, so that when they eventually halted for good at Rexpoede, a village half a dozen miles south of the perimeter, C Company and half of B Company had been caught up in the traffic stream heading for Dunkirk and were nowhere to be seen. Instead of supporting the 1st Guards Brigade with two hundred and fifty men, they were now only around a hundred and forty strong.

Tanner had barely slept – the crammed, jolting truck had been too much even for him. All the men were exhausted but especially those from the rest of the battalion. He watched the men of A Company lead off. Most would have been just boys a few weeks before but nearly three weeks of war had aged them – three weeks of marching hundreds of miles, of being shelled, bombed and shot at, of retreating, of getting too little sleep and not enough food. Dark rings framed hollow eyes; smudges of oil and grime covered their faces. Uniforms were filthy, and often torn. They stank, too.

Ahead lay countryside that was as flat as a board. Rows of poplars and willows lined the hundreds of dykes and waterways. Here and there red-brick farmhouses rose against the skyline. Above, thunderous skies rolled – rain again in the air – while on the horizon, for all to see, there were thick clouds of oily smoke, drifting high above the coastline.

'So that's Dunkirk,' Sykes said to Tanner. 'Charmin' lookin' place.' He began to sing, ' "Oh, I do like to be beside the seaside . . ." '

Tanner laughed, then Hepworth and McAllister joined in, and in a few moments the whole company was bellowing it out, singing the same verse over and over again.

'Sarge?' said Hepworth, when they had eventually stopped, 'do you think there'll be donkey rides and a band and everything?'

'Probably, Hep. Deck-chairs for hire and fish and chips.'

They reached the Bergues–Furnes canal just before eleven o'clock. 'Jesus, Stan,' said Tanner, gazing at the mass of abandoned vehicles that ran the length of the road. 'Will you look at that?'

'We need to get scavenging, Sarge.'

'There better be something worth nicking, because I tell you, Stan, that lot are going to be more useful to the enemy than to us.'

'But surely they've been immobilized, Sarge,' said Hepworth. 'No one's going to be stupid enough to leave them for Jerry to use.'

'Not to drive, Hep,' said Tanner, 'but as cover. Look at this place. It's flat as a pancake, and here's a long line of British Army trucks to help Jerry as he crawls up to the canal. Bloody hell, it's enough to make you weep. I tell you, there's not enough thinking ahead around here.'

Colonel Corner was waiting for them on the bridge, so the men were given the order to fall out along the road while the battalion OC had a conference with the company commanders. 'I don't suppose I'll be long, Sergeant,' said Peploe.

'All right, sir. We'll see if we can scrounge some ammo and supplies.'

Peploe nodded, then hurried off towards the bridge.

'All right, boys,' said Tanner, calling the company around him, 'have a quick dekko at these vehicles. Any weapons, ammo, grub – take 'em, all right?'

Most of the vehicles had been run off the road. Their engines had been wrecked, windscreens broken and tyres slashed, but while their former owners had been careful to make them unusable to the enemy, most seemed to have left on board whatever was there. By the time Peploe returned twenty minutes later, Tanner and Sykes had found two Brens and some crates of unopened ammunition. Several others had been equally successful.

'There's a stack of stuff here, sir.' Tanner grinned. 'Look at all this – and we've barely started.'

'We're going to need it, I think.' Peploe was grim-faced. 'We've just met up with Brigadier Beckwith-Smith – the chap commanding First Guards Brigade – and he announced to us that we were among the luckiest men in the British Army because we had been given the honour of being the rearguard here at Dunkirk.'

'And what did you say, sir? That it wasn't *that* great an honour?'

'No. I just swallowed hard and tried not to look as terrified as I felt.'

'What does it mean exactly?'

'That we've got to hold this line until we're told to do otherwise.'

'Christ. Sounds like a suicide job to me.'

'I don't know. I hope not. The Second Coldstream Guards will be on our right up to this bridge, the battalion's got fifteen hundred yards to the left of the bridge and then it's the First Duke of Wellington's – they're part of Third Brigade.'

'And what about the company?'

'I thought we might be amalgamated, but the colonel wants us to stay as we are. A Company's going to be next to the bridge, then us, then B Company. The bridge will be blown once the last stragglers are across but it's fairly obvious the enemy will concentrate on it, so we'll be supporting A Company's defence. We need to dig in and see what cover and observation points we can use. Battalion HQ will be with the Coldstreams at that windmill back there at Krommenhouck.' He pointed to it, standing out from the flat ground a mile or so to the north.

'And what about C Company and the rest of the missing men, sir?'

'The colonel was furious about that – and rather blaming the French for cutting across our withdrawal lines and mucking everything up in Poperinghe. Poor old French – everyone's got it in for them at the moment. Anyway, he wants to send someone into town to look for them. The obvious person is Captain Hillary, the OC of B Company, but the colonel wants a couple of men to go with him.

Hillary said he'd rather not send his own chaps as he was under-manned. I said I'd send along a couple from D Company.'

'But how long will it take? Sir, we've got a job to do here. The Germans might arrive at any moment.'

Peploe shook his head. 'No one's expecting them until to-morrow, and even if things go disastrously wrong not until tonight. Don't forget the rest of Fifth Div are defending the Yser to the south of here and even then the Germans have got to pack up and follow us. I think we do have a bit of time to prepare, actually. And we're taking the OC's car, so it shouldn't take long to get there.'

Tanner thought for a moment, then said, 'Sir, let me go. I'll take Sykes.'

'I'd rather have you here, overseeing things.'

'Sir, please. I'd like to get a look at the lie of the land. If we do eventually fall back, it'll probably be during the night so a bit of orientation will come in handy.'

Peploe screwed up his face. 'Oh, all right,' he said eventually. 'But try not to be too long.' He pointed out Captain Hillary, who was talking with one of his lieutenants beside the bridge. 'You'd better go and speak to him now.'

Tanner nodded and looked about for Sykes.

'And, Sergeant,' said Peploe, 'what are your thoughts about our position?'

'Some kind of building would be useful. We can use it as an OP.' He glanced along the canal bank. 'There's a few cottages along there. Then it's a question of digging in. We've been lucky with the soil so far and I reckon it'll be good along here too – nice and easy to dig out. But, sir,' he added, 'we need to stockpile stores. We need some men digging in and others scrounging for supplies.'

Peploe clasped his shoulder. 'Thanks, Tanner. That sounds like good advice. Good luck – and if you see Blackstone or Slater, make sure you take them straight to redcaps.'

Tanner grinned. *So the lieutenant guessed.* He grabbed Sykes and they hurried over to Captain Hillary, a tall man, with a square, clean-shaven face – one of the few in the battalion to have shaved over the past couple of days. 'This is awfully good of you both,' he said amiably. 'I'm afraid it'll be rather a bore.'

Taking the car, they drove through the fields and network of dykes and canals towards Dunkirk, passing reams of soldiers heading for the coast. Some still looked fit and spry but many more trudged northwards, heads down, with various pieces of equipment and uniform missing. Aircraft droned overhead, and even from the confines of the car they could hear bombs falling and exploding beyond the town. The pall of smoke still hung heavily over the darkened buildings.

The town was a wreck. Broken and abandoned vehicles were everywhere. Tram wires lay twisted and curling on the roads. Craters pocked the streets. A number of houses were burning, and all of them had suffered some kind of damage. Walls had tumbled into the streets; half-destroyed roofs shorn of their tiles hung above exposed bedrooms or attics. Debris lay everywhere – masonry, rubbish, weapons, even dead bodies, of troops and civilians alike. The stench was appalling – of decaying flesh, dust and smouldering rubber. Troops scurried past. Many, Tanner noticed, were drunk, swaying awkwardly as they tried to dodge the detritus of war.

'Damn me!' exclaimed Captain Hillary. 'Where the hell do we begin?'

'We need to get to the port, sir,' said Tanner. 'We'll get a better picture there.'

They were stopped several times, and forced to reverse down blocked streets, but eventually they reached the seafront at Malo-les-Bains and saw, for the first time, the true scale of the evacuation. Thousands of men were crammed onto the beaches like ants. Others drifted in lines from the beaches out to sea where a number of small boats and whalers were coming as close to the shore as they dared. Yet more vehicles had been driven onto the sand. Trucks, guns, carriers stood abandoned, with endless piles of boxes and discarded kit. Out at sea, ships of all sizes filled the horizon. The sound of battle, now that they were free of the noise-deadening effect of the buildings, was deafening. Guns from warships were firing, the pom-pom-pom of Bofors mixing with the heavier, thunderous sound of bigger artillery. Further out to sea, a ship was burning; they could just see its hull tilting, angry flames and thick black smoke pumping skywards. Aircraft swooped and dived overhead, engines racing. A number of Stukas were attacking the port behind them to their left, while machine-gun fire could be heard above. On their left, a sea wall ran behind the beach to a long pier. More than half a dozen ships were moored alongside this delicate mole, while a dense column of men spread out along the wall onto the pier. For more than a minute, the three sat in the car, speechless, staring at the scene before them.

'It's pandemonium,' said Captain Hillary at length. 'Utter, bloody pandemonium. I'll take out the rotor arm and then I suggest we leave the car here for the moment. I'll have a look on the beach. You, Corporal, try and get along the sea wall, and Sergeant, go into the town. They'll only have been here a short time, so hopefully they won't be too far along in these queues. But let's face it, the chances of us finding them can't be high. We'll give it a go, then head back.' He looked at his watch. 'It's a quarter to one. Let's meet back here at two.'

Tanner slung his rifle across his shoulder and brought the MP35 to his waist. Since his ducking in the moat, he had stripped and cleaned the sub-machine-gun twice, then dried and oiled the bullets in the magazine he'd had loaded at the time. Now it worked perfectly. Like the Spandaus they had captured in Norway and in France, he reckoned the weapon was a masterpiece of engineering – nicely balanced, beautifully put together and with some fine touches of workmanship, like the safety catch above the trigger that was so easy to click on and off. He still had another half-dozen magazines in his respirator bag, but after that the sub-machine-gun would be useless, unless he could find some more of the same calibre bullets. Perhaps, he thought, he would hand it over to someone at Enfield or in the War Office if he ever made it back – he reckoned the British Army could do with a weapon like it.

He wandered along the seafront a short distance, then cut along a back-street towards the centre of Dunkirk. Electricity cables lay on the ground, while halfway down another house had been blown out. He trudged on towards the port and saw some British troops coming towards him. Glancing at their sleeves he saw they were gunners, not Yorkshire Rangers.

'Who are you looking for, mate?' one of them asked.

'Yorks Rangers. Seen any?'

'Try the cellars. Most people have been hiding in them. It's the only safe place around here.'

'Cheers.'

He entered the nearest building, and immediately heard men coughing. A cellar door ran off the main hallway and it was open. He nearly gagged at the stench of alcohol, sweat, damp and stale urine. He shone a torch inside but blank faces stared back at him, not just soldiers but women and children too.

'Any Yorks Rangers here?' he asked. No one answered.

He tried several more buildings near the port, but got the same empty reply from each, then headed back towards the seafront at Malo-les-Bains to check the cellars there. *This place*, he thought, as half a dozen Junkers 88s swept over. He crouched in the middle of the road, and a moment later the bombers dropped their loads, which whistled, then exploded. The ground quivered and, not a hundred yards away, he heard a great crash of tumbling masonry, wood and glass.

At the sound of footsteps he swung round. A group of soldiers was running towards him and at the end of the street three men were hurrying in the direction of the mole. His heart raced. In a moment the three men had passed out of his view but he was sure that two of them had been Blackstone and Slater. *They couldn't have been*, he told himself, but already he was running back down the street. At the end he looked back towards the seafront and the mass of soldiers. 'Where the hell did they go?' he muttered, and set off again. Other troops were walking along the street, blocking his view, but suddenly he saw them again, eighty yards ahead. He ran on, faster, then lost them once more as another group of soldiers cut in. 'Damn it!' Tanner cursed. He ran on, pushing past some, swerving between others, then paused briefly to look into one of the streets that ran parallel with the seafront. Nothing.

'Sarge!' came a shout. He turned to see Sykes thirty yards away, coming towards him.

Waving for him to follow, Tanner ran on until he reached the seafront and saw their car still waiting at the side of the road. He stopped again to scan the troops wandering mindlessly along the corniche.

'Who have you found?' panted Sykes, as he reached him.

'Blackstone and Slater,' said Tanner, still craning his neck. 'I'm not a hundred per cent sure but it looked like them.'

Sykes joined him in gazing along the seafront. 'There! Sarge, up ahead! It *was* them! It *was*!'

Tanner set off again, Sykes following. Now he could see them too. They were walking quickly, not running, and Tanner and Sykes were gaining on them. Suddenly, the three men stepped off the road and into a building under a shredded café awning, but as Tanner and Sykes drew level they saw that the awnings covered not one but two cafés, and that there were two more doors as well.

'Damn!' said Tanner. 'Where have they gone?'

'Let's try the cafés first. I'll go into this one and you check next door,' said Sykes.

Tanner nodded. Inside, at least thirty men sat either drinking or sleeping. Bottles lay smashed on the floor, while the mirror behind the bar was also broken. 'Anyone see three men come in?' Tanner demanded.

'Cellar's next door,' a soldier replied. 'You're not redcaps, are you?'

Tanner hurried out and through the door to the side. A corridor ran along the café wall, and at the end a staircase led up and down. He went up first, searching each room of the house above the café. On the second floor, he opened a bedroom door to find a soldier with a French girl. She screamed, as though she was more terrified of him than of the bombs. Apologizing, he backed out and, having finished his search, went down to the ground floor and descended the stairs to the cellar.

There was light down there from several hurricane lamps, the same stench of sweat and urine. 'Did three men just come in?' he asked again.

'They've gone on down,' said a bloody-faced man. 'These cellars are deep.'

Tanner thanked him and picked his way through the bodies coughing and wheezing on the damp floor. Seeing more steps down, he took them. There were men below, but the light was dim. Taking out his torch, he now saw there were several chambers. 'I'm looking for three men that have just come in,' he said. Shining his torch on the man at his feet he was startled to see the black and green shoulder tab of the Yorkshire Rangers. He grabbed the man's collar and recognized him immediately as one of Blackstone's group.

'Where the hell are Blackstone and Slater?' he demanded.

'What?' mumbled the man and Tanner smelled the alcohol on his breath.

'Come on, wake up!' he said. 'Where are Blackstone and Slater?'

A footstep behind, and suddenly something was prodding into his back. *I've found them.*

'Well, well,' said Slater. 'Jack Tanner. You just keep turning up, like a bad penny. I can't tell you how fed up I am of seeing you. Why won't you ever die?'

Tanner half turned. Slater wore an ugly snarl. 'Because, Slater,' he said, in a low, measured voice, 'if you want to kill someone, you have to do it properly and you have to do it face to face. But you and Blackstone never do that – you always leave too much to chance.' He stood up slowly, his back to the other man. The revolver muzzle pressed harder into his side.

Slater chuckled mirthlessly, then breathed into Tanner's ear, 'Do you know what? I think you're right.'

Tanner heard the click of the cock and at that moment jerked his head backwards, hard. The rim of his helmet hit flesh and Slater screamed, instinctively bringing his hands to his face. At that moment, Tanner jabbed his left elbow into Slater's head. He cried out again and fell to his knees. Still clutching his pistol he now tried to straighten his right arm, but before he could fire, Tanner punched him in the temple – a hard, sharp, crushing blow. In the flickering light, he watched him topple over, blood pouring from the long gash across his nose and cheeks. Lifeless eyes stared ahead as he hit the ground, dead.

'Jesus – what's going on here?' said one man.

'What are you doing killing your own bleeding side?' said another.

'He was a murderer many times over,' said Tanner, 'and he was about to kill me. If anyone deserved to die it was him. Now, where did the other two go?' He bent to pick up the revolver, then shone his torch at the men huddled on the floor. Most, he realized, were drunk too. He stepped forward down a passageway from which wine bays extended on either side. After about five yards, it turned ninety degrees and continued in a square. As he cautiously turned the first corner, he heard a slight commotion behind him and ran back, only to see a pair of legs disappear up the steps.

Blackstone? He darted after him, stumbling over Slater's prostrate body. He gasped, recovered, and sped up the steps. In the brighter first chamber he saw Blackstone hurtle up the staircase to the ground floor. Tanner followed, kicking another man as he tried too quickly to dodge between the mass of soldiers. 'Sorry,' he called back, 'but I've got to catch that man!' Up the staircase, into the corridor, and there was Blackstone by the door. Tanner saw Sykes step into the doorway, but Blackstone was running hard at him and knocked him out of the way. Tanner ran on, then tripped again, sprawling on the pavement next to Sykes. 'Get up! Get up!' shouted Tanner and, scrambling to his feet, saw Blackstone race across the road and down onto the beach, running like a madman towards the sea.

Tanner followed, unslinging his rifle as he tore after him. At the edge of the beach, he stopped and raised his weapon. Blackstone was sixty yards away now, nearing the water. Tanner aimed, then a group of soldiers walked in front of his view. He cursed, but realized what Blackstone was thinking. A short way out to sea a small whaler was turning away from a line of men on the beach and being rowed to a waiting tramp steamer further out. But as it broke away from the line of men, it moved initially almost parallel to the shore. Blackstone was now in the water, wading out towards the wooden vessel. Tanner followed, Sykes beside him, a clean, clear shot now out of the question. Men were shouting at Blackstone from the beach, but he waded on undeterred.

'He'll get pushed back, Sarge,' said Sykes, now standing breathlessly beside Tanner, the sea lapping at their feet. 'There's a system here, of sorts. Queue-barging ain't allowed.'

'Don't you believe it, Stan.'

Blackstone was now at the whaler, a lone arm raised and gripping the gunwale. Tanner and Sykes saw the Royal Navy officer at the tiller shouting at him to let go, but then he seemed to change his mind because two Tommies began to heave Blackstone aboard – *Oh, let him on, then.*

'Bloody hell,' said Sykes.

'The bastard,' muttered Tanner.

They watched as Blackstone sat up in the boat and looked towards them.

'Cheers, boys!' he shouted. 'It's been good knowing you, Jack!'

Tanner watched a moment, then turned away. 'Come on, Stan,' he said. 'Let's get back to Captain Hillary.' Slowly, they trudged off the beach, neither man speaking as they wove through exhausted waiting soldiers and past the debris of a broken army. But then, as they climbed off the beach and walked back along the seafront, they heard two aircraft roar overhead. Looking up, Tanner glimpsed two Junkers 88s as they flashed through the smoke and low cloud. Then bombs were whistling through the air, evidently aimed at the tramp steamer, for the first exploded in a mountain of spray just to her stern. The second and third fell near her port side, but the fourth fell further away, some forty yards from the vessel.

'My God, Stan,' said Tanner, 'the whaler.'

More bombs fell beyond the steamer, detonating harmlessly in the water, but as the spray subsided there was no longer any sign of the small boat, or of the twenty-odd men crammed into it. For a minute, Tanner and Sykes stared at the disturbed sea. Of the men and the whaler there was almost no sign, just a few bits of wood. Tanner took out his German binoculars. A few bodies bobbed on the surface but he knew that most of the men, if not blown to bits, would have sunk; their lack of life-jackets, heavy uniforms and webbing would have seen to that. Seagulls were circling like vultures, then swooping towards the water.

'Damn,' muttered Tanner.

'But he's dead, Sarge. I'm sorry for those other poor buggers, but to Blackstone, good bloody riddance.'

Tanner grunted and continued to peer through his binoculars.

'Sarge?' said Sykes.

'I'd like to see a body.'

'There's no way he could have survived that. Look – the bloody thing was obliterated.'

It was true. Tanner could see no sign of life – except the seagulls. 'I suppose you're right, Stan,' he said, lowering the binoculars.

'He's not going to trouble us any more,' said Sykes. 'On that you can rest easy.'

Tanner nodded.

'And Slater?' said Sykes.

Tanner told him. 'Useful thing, a Tommy helmet,' he said.

'So that's it, then, Sarge? Blackstone and Slater?'

'Yes, Stan.'

Captain Hillary was waiting for them by the car. 'Find anyone?' he asked.

'Not really, sir,' muttered Tanner.

'Nor me. Still, no use crying over spilt milk. We tried, eh? Now we need to go back and get on with it. Make the best of what we've got.'

Tanner pulled out a cigarette, exhaustion seeping over him. *Just a few minutes' kip.* Blackstone and Slater might be dead, but there was still an enemy to fight, and he knew that if he was ever to see England again he'd need all his wits about him for the battle to come.

23

Wednesday passed into Thursday, 30 May, and still the enemy did not come, but all along the canal that marked the Dunkirk perimeter, the men made the most of the respite, strengthening defences and preparing for the battle. D Company had occupied an abandoned farm four hundred yards from the bridge. The main house, a solid old brick building with a typically Flemish high-gabled tile roof, overlooked the canal. It had not only a first floor with good views to the south but also an empty attic with a gabled window to the rear. Behind it was a large barn, also with a second storey, offering views both east and west along the canal, and some outbuildings. A track led out of the farm then dog-legged back to the road between the bridge and Krommenhouck.

The men had been digging hard. As Tanner had guessed, the soil was rich and soft, and between them they had soon created a trench system that ran back from the farm and extended along the canal front as far as A and B Companies to either side of them. As the hours passed, it was widened, deepened and strengthened. The sluices all along this drained section of Flanders had been opened in an effort to slow the German advance, and by the morning of the thirtieth, the fields on either side of the road to Krommenhouck lay beneath shallow water. Even so, by using the excavated soil as a makeshift dyke, the Rangers managed to hold at bay most of the rising water along their front; although the trenches were soggy underfoot, they were by no means flooded.

More importantly, the wait had allowed them to stockpile ammunition and supplies. From the abandoned vehicles along the road in front of their position, D Company had requisitioned another fifteen Bren guns, one Lewis gun, two Boys anti-tank rifles, eight wooden boxes of twelve No. 36 grenades, numerous spare rifles and some twenty-five thousand rounds of .303 ammunition. In addition, Sykes had scouted out some more explosives.

'If I'm honest, Sarge,' he confessed to Tanner, 'I didn't look all that hard for those C Company lads in Dunkirk. I got a bit distracted, you see, by some sapper boys who showed me an abandoned truck of theirs a bit further down on the beach. Anyway, they had a wooden box of Nobels and all the gear, so I 'elped meself. I managed to stuff in five cartons of 808, plus detonators and safety fuse.' He grinned. 'You never know when it might come in handy.'

However, it was not only weapons and ammunition they had found but food and other supplies too. The larder in the farmhouse was soon stacked high with tins of bully beef, condensed milk, fruit, vegetables, biscuits, beer, wine and cigarettes. The men would no longer be expected to fight on empty stomachs. Tanner found a new battle-blouse, and also a compass – something he had rarely used before because he had generally relied on the sun and the stars and his own sense of direction, yet he now vowed never to be without one again. Lieutenant Peploe and Kershaw, meanwhile, recovered a No. 9 wireless set from an abandoned carrier. Setting it up in Company Headquarters in one of the outbuildings at the back of the farmhouse, they soon managed to pick up the BBC and, for the first time since they'd arrived in France, were able to hear the news from home. They also discovered some of what was happening in France. The evacuation, it seemed, was going better than had been expected.

That Thursday was a glorious day – warm, sunny, with a deep blue sky and just a few summery white clouds. Late in the morning, stripped to his shirtsleeves, Tanner led a six-man patrol across the canal, partly to see if there was any sign of the approaching enemy but also to scrounge yet more supplies. At L'Avenir, a hamlet a mile or so to the south, they struck gold when they found two abandoned Royal Engineers eight-hundredweight Humber trucks. In the back of the first, sitting there waiting for the enemy to help themselves, were two wooden crates of Nobels as well as an intact fifty-cap blasting machine.

'Blimey, Sarge!' exclaimed Sykes. 'Just look at all those lovely explosives!'

'But we've already got more than enough, haven't we?' said Tanner.

'Sarge, you can never have enough gelignite.'

'Actually, Stan, you're right. I've just had an idea – with all this we can blow the approach roads, can't we? A few big craters'll annoy Jerry something rotten because he won't get too many vehicles over the fields, will he?' The water had not risen as high to the south as to the north of the canal, but the ground either side of the raised roads and tracks was wet and waterlogged. 'He'll have to send his infantry forward on foot,' Tanner added. 'That means no tanks and no artillery pieces until he's mended the roads. And that'll take time.'

'True enough.'

'So let's fetch some of the others and get to it.'

Four roads fed into L'Avenir, two from the south and two from the north. Heading south first, they stopped two hundred yards beyond the hamlet and Sykes got to work. He laid a packet of five cartridges of gelignite on the road, placed a detonator at one end, then crimped a four-foot length of safety fuse and lit it. That done, he ran back to the others waiting some hundred yards away. Two minutes later, the gelignite blasted rock, tarmacadam and dust high into the air. They watched the debris clatter to the ground and waited for the dust to settle. A hole had opened across the width of the road. Sykes grinned. 'One down,' he said. 'Dr Nobel does the trick again.'

'Nice job, Stan,' said Tanner. A lone shell screamed over and they ducked. It exploded harmlessly in the fields several hundred yards to their right. 'Someone's getting twitchy. Tinker,' he said to Bell, 'you'd better go back to Battalion HQ and tell them what we're doing. And iggery, all right?'

They paused while Bell trotted off, scrounging some more tins of food and cigarettes from another abandoned truck, and waited some more while a newly arrived column of fifty or so troops trudged past on their way to the perimeter. An almost constant stream of men, both British and French, had poured through the day before. The previous evening, one column of French infantry had thrown all their weapons in the canal as they had crossed over into the perimeter. The Rangers had watched them, appalled, from their part of the line. 'Sergeant,' Peploe had said, 'I take back what I said earlier about the French. That was a bloody disgrace.'

Since then, however, the stream had petered out so now there was just a trickle of stragglers.

Tanner watched the men stagger down the road, their uniforms torn and filthy, their faces haggard and drawn. 'Which lot are you?' he asked.

'DLI,' came the reply.

'Which battalion?' Tanner asked them.

'Eighth.'

'We were with you lot at Arras,' said Tanner.

'Arras?' muttered one bloodied sergeant. 'That was a lifetime ago.'

'Here, have some beadies,' said Tanner, handing him a packet of French cigarettes.

'Cheers, pal,' said the sergeant, pausing to open the packet and light one.

'How far back's Jerry?' Tanner asked him.

'Not far. Must have crossed the Yser, I reckon, and that's eight or ten miles away. He'll be here by nightfall, that's for sure.'

'Cheers,' said Tanner. 'Good luck.'

'Good luck yerself.'

'Right,' said Tanner, turning back to the others. 'We'd better get a move on.'

By midday, they had blown the three approach roads and those leading into L'Avenir in at least two places and were crossing back over the bridge when they saw, parked just on the north side, a large staff car. A British general was standing beside it, talking with the colonel of the Coldstreams, their own OC and a captain. He wore a distinctive high-peaked cap, breeches and immaculately clean cavalry boots, while above his top lip was a neat moustache.

Tanner recognized him at once – Brigadier Alexander, as he had been last time they had met. 'Better look sharp, boys,' he said, and as he neared the general he saluted as crisply as he could.

The general acknowledged him, then said, 'Excuse me, Sergeant, we've met before, haven't we?'

Tanner brought his men to a halt and stood to attention before him. 'Yes, sir, in Waziristan.'

Alexander smiled. 'Of course – Tanner. And a sergeant now.' He stepped forward and tapped on the ribbon of Tanner's military medal. 'He's a brave man, this one,' he said, to the officers beside him. 'Should have got a DCM for what he did at Muzi Kor.'

Tanner reddened. 'There were others a lot braver than me, sir.'

'Well, it's jolly good to see you fit and well, Sergeant. Do you think we can hold the Hun for a bit?'

'Yes, sir.'

'Are you the chaps who've been blowing the approaches?' said Colonel Corner.

'Yes, sir,' said Tanner.

'Well done – that was smart thinking.'

'Thank you, sir. Hopefully it'll take Jerry time to bring the bulk of his heavy fire-power to bear. I can't speak about his indirect fire but our boys are well dug in, we've got a good OP, and we can certainly deal with the infantry for a while.'

'Good gracious, Sergeant Tanner,' laughed Alexander. 'I rather think I ought to have you on my staff, although I can see you're needed here. Anyway, well done, and good luck, all of you.' He saluted, and Tanner responded, then marched his men back towards their positions.

'Blimey, Sarge,' said Sykes, once they were out of earshot. 'I've never seen a general before. He certainly looked the part, didn't he?'

'He was a damned good brigadier, I'll say that for him.'

'What did you do then, Sarge,' asked Ellis, 'to get your MM?'

'Nothing much, Billy.'

'I'd love to have a ribbon on my chest,' Ellis went on. 'Sets you apart, doesn't it?'

'Trust me, Billy, you don't want to worry too much about gongs. Lots of people get ribbons they don't deserve and many more don't get the ones they should've got. It's a bloody lottery. Just concentrate on doing your job and keeping alive. Much more important than glory-hunting.'

Bren teams had been placed all along D Company's front and there were two in the attic of the house. Tiles had been knocked out of the roof in several places and two tables, one from downstairs and one hastily knocked together in a shed at the back, brought up for the Brens to rest on. An old wooden bucket had been filled with water for cooling the Bren barrels. Meanwhile, the Lewis gun had been set up on the first floor of the barn behind the farmhouse. Stockpiles of ammunition were left beside the weapons or in freshly dug cavities beside the trenches. Along the canal, the abandoned vehicles were set on fire. Each charred chassis still offered decent cover for the enemy, Tanner thought, but less so than before. At around six o'clock that evening, once the last of the stragglers appeared to have passed through, the bridge was blown.

A couple of hours later Tanner stood with Lieutenant Peploe in the attic of the farmhouse. Gunfire sounded to the east, dull and persistent. Behind, black smoke still rolled high above Dunkirk.

Tanner had been watching a dogfight from the dormer window to the rear, high above the town where the sky was clear, blue and free of smoke; he had seen a German fighter plunge into the sea. It had been the first enemy plane he had seen come down in France. Perhaps the RAF boys were learning.

Now he and Peploe were at the front of the farmhouse, peering through binoculars at a calm summer's evening. Long lines of poplars were bursting into leaf and the evening sun shone on the watery fields, casting dramatic reflections.

'We're ready, aren't we?' said Peploe.

'I think so, sir,' said Tanner.

'I just wish they'd get on with it. All this waiting – it's getting on my nerves, rather.'

'I can live with it. I want those bastards to leave it as long as they can. With every hour that passes, we can get more men away. The more that get away, the better the chance we have of making it home.'

'You're right, but you have to admit the waiting's the worst part.' He bent and pulled a bottle of French white wine from the Bren cooling bucket and offered it to Tanner. 'It's *très rustique*, I'm afraid, but serves its purpose.'

Tanner smiled. 'Thanks.' He took a glug, and then, as he passed it back, he saw something glint in the distance. Immediately he brought his binoculars to his eyes again. Ahead, several miles away, he spotted movement – vehicles – and wished now that he and Sykes had blown the roads even further back.

'Can you see them, sir?' he said. 'Dead ahead.'

'Christ,' said Peploe. 'Ignore what I said a few moments ago.'

'Don't worry, sir. I'll doubt they'll attack tonight. They'll be setting up their artillery, that's all. I reckon we can expect some shells but the infantry won't attack, I'm sure. Patrols, perhaps, but that'll be it.'

A short while after, a few shells did follow, but fell beyond their position. Later, once darkness had fallen, they heard small-arms fire from the area around the bridge.

'Damn me,' said Peploe, 'the idiots are using tracer. Look at it, Tanner – you can see lines of the stuff sparking across the canal. Why would they do that? All they're doing is giving their positions away.'

But Tanner saw it differently. *Cunning bastards.* 'They want us to fire at them, sir. They're just testing the strength of our defences and working out where our blokes are.' He turned to the lieutenant. 'Sir, if they open fire on us, I think we should tell the men not to respond. Not unless we see or hear them trying to cross the canal. I'm certain this isn't a major attack.'

'All right, Tanner. Quickly, then.'

Tanner was crouching along the trench to the right of the farmhouse when the enemy opened fire on their positions. Small bursts of machine-gun fire zipped above their heads, but in their trenches the men were quite safe.

'Don't fire back!' hissed Tanner to Corporal Ross. 'Don't let any of the lads fire back.'

He was impressed by how well the men maintained their fire discipline – not a single shot was returned and, within twenty minutes, the enemy had slithered away from the canal. In the east, towards Furnes, the artillery continued to sling shells through the night, but for the Yorkshire Rangers, the hours of darkness slipped past quietly. Hours that brought them closer to a possible withdrawal.

By morning, the vehicles and guns Tanner had seen moved into place had gone. He couldn't understand it. All night he had been bracing himself for a heavy assault, but while the battle seemed to have intensified to the east, the fields to their front seemed as empty and calm as they had the previous morning. It was another bright early-summer's day, warm again, too. The water levels had risen higher and now, behind them as far as the coast, the countryside had become a large, shallow lake, through which roads and houses, lines of trees, farms and churches could be seen. It was difficult country through which to attack. Their defences were good and the twenty-yards-wide canal provided a superb anti-tank ditch. Yet they were only thirty-four strong in their part of the line; the entire battalion had fewer than two hundred men, and he had heard the Coldstreams had barely more. It was probable that equally hard-pressed infantry companies and battalions were holding the line all the way from Bergues to the coast, yet soon the might of the German forces, flush with their sweeping victories, would be upon them. Through the gap in the roof, Tanner peered through his binoculars, but saw nothing. He went down to one of the bedrooms, lay on an empty bed and closed his eyes. If Jerry was going to make them wait, he'd get some sleep.

Six miles away, General Lord Gort was eating his last meal on Belgian soil. It might have been a sunny summer's day, and it was true that he was having a half-decent lunch in the not unattractive surroundings of the Belgian king's summer palace at De Panne, but his heart was heavy as he toyed with his food. He had been ordered home to Britain, lest the Germans use his possible capture for propaganda, but to leave before his men ran against all the principles of soldiering he held dear. Outside, across the dunes, the beaches led down to the sea; beaches on which tens of thousands of his soldiers still huddled. Some ingenious engineers had built a makeshift jetty out into the water from otherwise unwanted trucks and vehicles, but it made a pitiful sight, as did the mass of small boats bobbing on the water crammed with too many troops.

Major-General Alexander sat opposite him, eating with measured precision and making polite small-talk with Brigadier Leese as though nothing out of the ordinary was going on. He looked utterly imperturbable, and Gort thanked God he had accepted Montgomery's advice and relieved General Barker of command of the rearguard. Monty had been right: Barker was a hopeless case. At conference the night before the general had seemed nervy and Gort had noticed his hands shaking. When he had spoken, he had gabbled and told a poor joke about dining soon in a *Schloss* overlooking the Rhine. Gort had originally chosen Barker for the job because he had been the most expendable of his generals; he had accepted that most of the rearguard might eventually be forced to surrender and taken into captivity, but there had been something rather galling about hearing Barker's passive acceptance of their fate. The rearguard was made up of fine fighting men, and while their surrender had to be considered, it most certainly did not have to be accepted as inevitable. Monty had pointed out that in Alexander he had a first-class divisional general, with a calm and clear brain; he wouldn't flap or be rushed into making hasty decisions. With him in charge, Monty had urged, there was no need for anyone to surrender.

Gort took a sip of his wine. He didn't much like Monty – he was an irritating, conceited little man – but he knew his stuff, and when it came to organization there was no one to beat him. The way he had moved 3rd Division overnight to cover the gap left by the Belgians had been stunning. And Monty wasn't a bad judge of character either – as he watched the man in front of him, he felt certain his remaining troops within the bridgehead were in the safest possible hands.

Even so, he hardly envied Alexander the task. After lunch he handed him handwritten notes of the orders he had given him earlier. Alexander was to remain under the command of the French Admiral Abrial, whom Gort believed to be out of his depth physically and metaphorically; he knew the admiral hadn't emerged from his bunkers in Bastion 32 since the crisis had begun. Furthermore, it had been agreed by the French and British governments that French troops should share the chance for evacuation, an order with which Gort instinctively disagreed. Not for the first time, he had cursed the French as he had written those instructions. Only one French general had agreed to fight on at Dunkirk – de la Laurencie with his III Corps; that damned fool Blanchard had sacrificed his entire army at Lille. He couldn't help feeling that the war would be a lot more straightforward once the French were out of the fight.

Gort led Alexander into the palace drawing room; for the past couple of days it had been his office. He offered him a cigar and brandy. Then, as they puffed out clouds of smoke, he said, 'There's far too much politicking going on, Alex, with London trying to placate Paris and so on. HMG thinks it's essential that we're seen to be helping the French to the last. You'll find Abrial's a decent enough fellow but, like so many French commanders, not really in touch with the reality of what's going on here. You must be respectful but firm with him. Yes, we'll help the French escape, but your prime task is to defend the bridgehead for as long as possible in order to allow the most men to get away. We've done well so far – more than I'd ever hoped – but we mustn't throw in the towel now.'

'I understand,' said Alexander. 'How long should I hold the perimeter? I've toured First Division's sector and the men are keen and reasonably well stocked, but they won't be able to hold out for long. Thankfully, the Hun seems only to be attacking in any kind of strength from the east, but that won't last.'

'That's for you to judge, Alex. Only you can make that call now.'

Near by, several bombs exploded, shaking the palace. From the drawing room, Gort saw high plumes of sand thrust into the air. Alexander barely flinched.

'Good luck,' said Gort, holding out his hand. 'May God be with you and I pray you may return safely to Britain.'

'Thank you, sir,' said Alexander. 'I'll do my best.'

Dawn, Saturday, 1 June. Tanner had done no more than catnap and at three a.m. had woken for good. He helped himself to some breakfast in the farmhouse kitchen, then roused the rest of the slumbering men and told them to get some food inside them. Half an hour later, with the first hint of dawn streaking the horizon to their left, he walked up and down their line, making sure the men were awake, alert and at their posts. Enemy troops had been spotted moving into position the previous evening and long-range artillery had opened fire soon after. Desultory shellfire had continued ever since, screaming over their heads towards the coast.

Now he accompanied Lieutenant Peploe to the attic where

McAllister and Chambers were waiting beside their Brens. Ahead, the fields beyond the canal were shrouded in mist. A row of poplars half a mile to the south rose spectrally above it against the pink and pale orange early-morning sky.

'Another beautiful day,' said Peploe.

'Those bastards are out there, though,' said Tanner. 'If they've got any bloody sense they'll attack now, while they've got some cover. This'll burn off soon enough.'

But, apart from continued artillery fire, the enemy did not attack and when, at around eight o'clock, the mist lifted, they saw, to their amazement, large numbers of German infantry standing several hundred yards away in the waterlogged fields of young corn.

'Bloody hell,' said Tanner, bringing his binoculars to his eyes. 'They're digging in. They've got spades, not rifles. Mac, Punter, five hundred yards – get firing!'

Both Brens opened, spewing bursts of bullets. To begin with, they fell short, cutting into the corn in front of the startled enemy, but both men adjusted them and Tanner watched as German troops were mown down. Men fell to the ground, some hit, others desperate to find cover in the corn, but Tanner kept the two machine-guns firing until he could see no further movement.

Cordite from the Brens filled the attic, and several empty magazines now lay on the bare wooden floor. Tanner delved into his haversack, took out his Aldis scope and fixed it to his rifle.

'I can see Germans moving into those cottages six hundred yards in front of us,' said Peploe, his binoculars held to his eyes. He turned to Tanner. 'Time for some sniping?'

'Absolutely, sir.' Tanner was already poking the barrel of his rifle through a hole in the roof. He could see two small guns being brought up, infantry scampering behind them, most with rifles but others with machine-guns. He aimed at one of the gunners, pulled back the bolt, made adjustment for the range and squeezed the trigger. The man fell back, and the others threw themselves onto the ground. Tanner pulled back the bolt again, saw a machine-gunner run forward, and pulled the trigger again. He, too, stumbled to the ground. 'Mac,' he said, 'wait for my word but get a bead on the approach to that cottage ahead, all right? I reckon it's six hundred yards, but the moment I give the word, open fire.'

'Yes, Sarge.'

Tanner peered through his sight, waiting for the enemy soldiers to get up and move again. Sure enough, before long anxious helmeted heads lifted and then, when no sniper's bullet arrived, the men got to their feet.

'Fire!' said Tanner, and McAllister sent out another withering burst. More enemy troops tumbled.

For the next two hours, Tanner sniped while the Brens and the Lewis gun in the barn kept up their harassing fire. Despite their best efforts, however, it was clear that enemy troops had reached and occupied the half-dozen cottages and buildings that dotted the open fields in front of them. The attackers were using the elevated camber of the roads as cover, and although from the attic the Rangers could see glimpses of half-hidden moving enemy troops, their fire could only slow their progress, not prevent it entirely. By mid-morning enemy guns were in place all along the Hondschoote–Bergues road, which ran parallel to the canal some two miles in front of them. Shells began to hurtle over and gradually found their range. Mortars were also in action, and shortly after eleven, several hit the road on the other side of the canal. Then a flurry landed in and around their positions.

'We're not going to able to stay up here much longer, sir,' said Tanner. 'One shell in the right place and we'll be lying under a pile of rubble.'

'What do you suggest?'

'I'm not sure. This and the barn are the only place where we can really see the enemy, but the buildings stand out like a sore thumb. If only those damned vehicles weren't in front of us we might have a better line of fire.'

No sooner had he said this than two large shells screamed over in quick succession and hit the barn. Someone yelled, and then there was a grinding crack of breaking timbers, tiles and brick.

'Oh, Christ,' said Peploe, his face ashen. He stared at Tanner, then sped down the stairs. Tanner ran to the rear window and saw that half of the barn had collapsed. *Jesus*, he thought, *how many were in there? Half a dozen?* McAllister and Chambers were firing again, the burst of bullets deafening in the narrow confines of the attic. Suddenly McAllister's Bren stopped and he cursed. 'Sarge, I think the firing pin's melted. Bastard won't fire any more.'

'Go and get another. How are we doing for ammo?'

'Running quite low, Sarge,' said Chambers.

'Mac, get another MG and send someone up here with more mags.'

'Sarge,' said McAllister, hurrying downstairs.

Tanner now stood at the embrasure in the roof once more and, raising his rifle, saw several German artillerymen running down the road from the cottage towards the canal, towing a small anti-tank gun. Quickly, he drew back the bolt, adjusted his aim and fired, hitting the first man clean in the chest. The other three ducked, but he hit them, too, with his next four shots, then saw one man, evidently wounded in the leg, hobbling off the road. He aimed again, fired, and saw him trip over the edge of the road and into the ditch. Already, though, another anti-tank gun was being run off the road and into the cover of some poplars.

'Did you see that, Punter?' called Tanner. 'Get some fire over there – quickly!'

Chambers gave out a burst but not before the anti-tank gun, some three hundred yards away, had opened. Tanner saw the flash of the muzzle and a split-second later a shell shot past one end of the house.

'Quick, Punter, time to go!' said Tanner, and then a second shell burst through the roof to hit the central beam. It bounced off and landed on the floor. 'It's an anti-tank incendiary!' yelled Tanner, almost pushing Chambers down the stairs. 'Out! Out!' he shouted, to Hepworth and Ellis, who were still manning a Bren on the first floor. Together they raced down the stairs as two more shells hit the roof. Hurrying to the back of the building they saw Peploe running from the barn with Sykes. Half of the building still stood, including part of the first floor. A ladder had already been leaned up against it and Tanner saw Corporal Cooper climbing it with another Bren.

'Four dead from Cooper's section and another two badly wounded,' said Peploe.

'I'm sorry,' said Tanner, 'and now the attic's been hit.' He looked up and saw smoke wisping from the damaged roof, but there had been no blast.

'Hold on,' he said, ran back inside the house, up the stairs and cautiously to the attic. Three shells were smouldering on the floor, apparently spent, so he ran across to the bucket, poured water over them liberally, then dashed back downstairs again. 'I think we might be all right up there,' he said, as he rejoined Peploe at the back of the house, 'but the bastards have got guns on it now, so the moment we start using it again we'll be in trouble.'

Another mortar crashed behind them, hitting one of the sheds, and causing them to dive to the ground.

'The problem is that we can't see them clearly enough,' said Tanner, as they got to their feet again. 'If only we could get across to the other side of the canal we could use that cottage fifty yards up the road and get stuck into them from there.'

'There's that dinghy, Sarge,' said Sykes, 'by the woodpile the other side of the farmhouse.'

'Don't be mad,' said Peploe. 'You can't use that.'

'Why not, sir?' said Tanner. 'We can take a couple of Brens and the Boys. If we get a move on we can occupy that cottage before Jerry does, let rip, then come back again. It might just delay him a bit more.'

'I'm not sure – it seems horribly risky to me.'

'No more so than staying here,' he said, gesturing to the remains of the barn.

'I'll rig up something for Jerry to remember us by in the house as well, sir.' Sykes grinned. 'Maybe put something interesting in those vehicles too. Don't know why I didn't think of it before.'

'I suppose there's something to be said for that,' agreed Peploe.

'Good,' said Tanner, taking that as his cue. He turned to Hepworth. 'You can come too, Hep.'

'Why do you always pick on me, Sarge?' said Hepworth.

'I'm doing you a favour, Hep. It's better to be doing something than sitting here getting stonked.'

Having picked up the Boys anti-tank rifle, a Bren and some spare magazines, they found the dinghy, ran to the front of the farmhouse and lowered it into the water. They rowed the short distance across, scrambled onto the far bank, secured the boat and hurried, crouching, along the road to the cottage. It was only a one-storey building, but had a small, neat garden and a hedge that ran round the back, protecting it from the fields beyond, and a willow tree in the far corner.

Intermittent shells and mortars continued to rain on their positions along the canal, but now, from the direction of the destroyed bridge, there came a sudden escalation of small-arms fire from both sides.

'Sounds like Jerry's making a play for the bridge,' said Tanner, as they crept to the back of the cottage. 'Stan, get to work on the cottage, will you? We don't want any Germans using it. Hep, come with me.'

They ran, in a crouch, across the lawn to the far corner beside the willow and, lying on the ground, Tanner peered between the hedge and the tree. He could see the road from L'Avenir leading to the bridge but a track went to a farmhouse by the bridge. German troops were scurrying forward, either side of the road and track, using it as cover. At the end of the track, perhaps two hundred yards away, there was a small cottage and a barn. From where he was, Tanner could just see a mortar team and another anti-tank gun behind it.

Pulling the big Boys rifle into position so that it poked through the hedge, he brought the padded shoulderpiece tight against him and lowered the front support. He had already fitted a five-round magazine and, having adjusted the backsight to two hundred yards, pulled back the bolt, lifted the safety catch and aimed straight at the enemy anti-tank gun.

'Hep, you ready with that Bren?'

'Yes, Sarge.'

'Good. The moment I fire, open up on those Jerries advancing towards the bridge, all right?'

'Sarge.'

Tanner squeezed the trigger and felt the big gun kick hard into his shoulder, then immediately fired again. To his relief, he saw both .55 bullets smack into the gunshield and topple it. He fired another and one of the gunners was almost sheared in half. The mortar team now looked around nervously – *where the hell had that come from?* – but before they could react, a third bullet had ripped into the weapon. 'That's got you,' muttered Tanner. He jumped up and ran to the other side of the garden while Hepworth continued to fire short, sharp bursts from the Bren.

Peering through the other side of the hedge, Tanner saw the gun that had been firing at the attic. Quickly bringing the Boys into position again, he was conscious of bullets ripping through the hedge, and twigs being spat onto the lawn beside him. He fired several rounds, saw the bullets strike home, then called to Sykes. 'Stan – you nearly done?'

'Yes, Sarge.'

'Good, let's go. Hep, time to call it a day.' More bullets flew through the hedge, so he crawled to the side of the cottage, then turned to see Hepworth make a dash for it. He had not gone two paces before he fell forward with a cry.

'Hep!' called Tanner.

'Bastard's got me in the back of the leg!'

'All right, I'm coming to get you.' Tanner crawled back to him, grabbed his shoulders, then pulled him towards the cover of the cottage. Keeping Hepworth flat on his belly, he pulled out several field dressings, tore open the thin linen casing and wrapped them tightly round Hepworth's bleeding leg. 'We need to get him back quickly,' he said.

'Let me plant some jelly mounds in some of the vehicles, though, Sarge. You think you can carry Hep?'

'I'll have to.'

From the safety of the front of the cottage, Tanner heaved Hepworth over his shoulder and grabbed the Boys in his spare hand while Sykes took the Bren. Hurrying onto the road, praying that no German would see them, he hastened past the line of burned-out trucks to the boat, groaning at the combined weight of Hepworth, the Boys and his webbing.

'Come on, Stan!' he called, as he squatted with Hepworth on the bank.

A moment later, Sykes slid down beside him and got into the boat, which rocked. Passing him the Boys, Tanner said, 'Have you got her steady?'

'I think so.'

Tanner cursed, then almost lost his balance, with one foot in the boat and the other still on the bank. A shell hit the canal thirty yards further towards the bridge and he almost fell over again, but then, with Sykes's help, he lowered himself, Hepworth still over his shoulder, into the dinghy.

On the other side of the canal, Peploe and Ellis were there to help pull Hepworth, crying out with pain and fear, from the boat. Having passed up the weapons, Tanner and Sykes followed, then scuttled the dinghy and ran along the trench to the rear of the farmhouse.

'We knocked out a couple of anti-tank guns and a mortar,' said Tanner breathlessly, 'and Hep got some Jerry infantry but there's so many of them.'

'Like the hydra's head,' said Peploe. 'You chop off one, and more grow in its place.'

'A bit like that, yes, sir.'

Peploe took a swig from his hip-flask and offered it to Tanner. 'Calvados. I just filled up.'

'Thanks,' said Tanner, taking it.

'We've got two more wounded – two men from Ross's section.

That's five now. We need to get them out of here and back to the beaches, but I can't think how.'

'Can the others walk?'

'One can.'

'Get a runner to go down to Battalion HQ. Maybe they can send a car up for them.'

'But we're already down to twenty-five men.'

'I know, but all we can do now, sir, is sit in our trenches and wait for enemy troops to appear. We can't do any more about the artillery and mortars apart from pray they don't land directly in any of our trenches.'

'All right. I'll send Ellis.'

Tanner went to see Hepworth. He was laid out with the other wounded men behind the last of the outbuildings, his face drained of colour. Smailes was with them, binding wounds and injecting morphine.

'I'm sorry, Hep,' he said.

'My fault, Sarge,' he croaked. 'Should have crawled like you.'

'At least you'll get away from here. Billy's gone to get some transport to take you to the beaches.'

Hepworth smiled weakly. 'I'd rather have stayed,' he said. 'We've been through a lot together the past few weeks.'

Tanner clasped his shoulder, then went back to the canal.

The enemy's assault on the junction with the bridge was successfully repulsed by the Coldstreams and the Rangers, and for the next few hours the German infantry made no further attempt to attack. There was, however, no let-up from their artillery and mortar teams, and shells rained down on their positions throughout the afternoon. Nonetheless, Ellis successfully reached Battalion Headquarters, and just before three o'clock two carriers made it to the back of the farm and took not only D Company's wounded but A and B Companies' too.

Unpleasant though it was to be crouching in damp, muddy trenches as mortar and artillery shells exploded around him,

Tanner knew that in soft ground the enemy ordnance was, for the most part, ineffective. Plumes of water and earth ballooned into the air, but apart from a regular shower of mud, the men were safe, so long as no shell landed directly on top of them. As the afternoon wore on, he and Peploe hurried up and down the trench, making sure the men were all right and that they had enough cigarettes and food.

Most were holding up well, but Tanner was increasingly concerned for Verity, who seemed paralysed with fear in the trench to the right of the farmhouse. His face was ashen and he would accept no food, drink or cigarettes; instead, he clutched his knees, trying to make himself as small as possible.

'I don't know what to do about him, sir,' Tanner said to Peploe. 'He's better off out of here, to be honest.'

'It's too late for that. We should have sent him out with the carriers.' He ducked as another shell tore into the upper part of the farmhouse amid a cloud of dust, grit and tumbling masonry. 'Hell. The poor fellow.'

'I didn't think of it then, sir,' said Tanner, 'but I'm worried he's going to be hard to shift. He can't do anything.'

'Well, I don't know what to suggest.' Peploe sighed wearily and took another swig from his flask. 'I never knew it was so exhausting being shelled like this. What do you think will happen? I can't bear the thought of us all ending up in the bag. Such a bloody waste.'

'I don't know, sir. But I'm sure Jerry's preparing for another attack. Maybe we'll hold him again, but we can't keep on doing so for ever. There's simply too many of them and not enough of us.'

The attack, when it came, was every bit as hard as Tanner had known it would be. Just after six o'clock, enemy troops were spotted moving to their front, and soon after, bursts of machine-gun fire were spitting towards them. The battle for the canal had begun once more and time was running out for the defenders. Fast.

24

'This is no good, sir,' said Tanner to Lieutenant Peploe as bullets hammered into the mound of earth immediately in front of them. 'I need some height.'

They were in the trench beside the farmhouse and although the barn to the rear was now completely destroyed, Tanner reckoned the main house still offered some decent firing positions. 'Sir,' he continued, 'if it's all right with you, I think it's time to risk going back into the farmhouse. I'll do some sniping from the first-floor windows.'

'What about getting some Brens up there too?' said Peploe.

'Good idea, sir. We've still got some ammo left.'

'Right – use Sykes's section. Get a couple of men up there with the boxes of ammunition and two more on the Brens. I'll stay here with Cooper and Ross's sections.'

As the enemy infantry advanced closer to the canal, the artillery lifted their fire deeper into the perimeter, so that now it was just small-arms and mortars that were directed at the defenders. Even so, as Tanner ran along the trench to the back of the farmhouse, he could hear bullets snapping into the brickwork. Bursting through the back door, he ran to the staircase as another bullet pinged through a broken ground-floor window and ricocheted off the hall wall next to him. Upstairs, the roof and most of the first-floor ceiling had collapsed, but the walls were thick and looked firm. Entering a now open-roofed bedroom, he ran to the window, cleared the worst of the broken glass out of his way with his boot, crouched and drew his rifle to his shoulder, resting the barrel on the window ledge.

Platoons of men were advancing across the ground in front of him, using as cover the young corn in the fields, the lines of poplars and willows and the raised banks at either side of the approach roads. He saw a machine-gun team hurry forward alongside the road on the left that led towards the canal, then drop to the ground beside a poplar and set themselves up to cover their comrades' advance. Immediately, he drew a bead, aiming at the head of the man now feeding a belt into the breech. Even without his scope he could see the figures distinctly, although their features were not clear. The light was still bright, he was looking slightly down at the two men, and the ground between them was level – all factors that could lead to underestimating distance. Taking that into account, he guessed they were around three hundred and twenty yards away. Quickly adjusting the range drum on the scope to three hundred yards, he peered through the lens, fractionally raised the point of aim, let his finger squeeze until it reached the first point of pressure on the trigger. Holding his breath, he gripped the rifle tightly and pressed hard against the second pressure point. A crack, a jolt, and the first man rolled over. Pulling back the bolt, he aimed at the second. The enemy soldier was now twisting his head round in panic – *a sniper or a lucky shot?* – so Tanner aimed at his body, rather than his head. *Aim, breathe out, steady, squeeze the trigger.* As the Enfield cracked out shrilly in the narrow room, the second man slumped forward, as dead as his comrade.

He drew back the bolt again, aimed and fired, and again and again, using his scope to spot officers and NCOs. Although he was not entirely certain what the German uniforms and insignia denoted, officers were easy enough to spot, with their leather holsters and baggy twill breeches – he wondered why armies insisted on making their officers so damned obvious. German NCOs wore chevrons on the upper sleeves similar to their own, although on a triangular black patch. He reckoned he'd felled at least seven men with his first magazine, including an officer, one NCO and the machine-gun team.

As he had been firing, the others had joined him, McAllister and Sykes setting down Brens at the windows along the front of the house. Kershaw and Bell were bringing in boxes of ammunition and unloading Bren magazines. Already, the open rooms were heavy with cordite, which irritated the back of their throats.

'Thank God the roof's blown off, Sarge,' said Kershaw. 'Gives us a bit of fresh air.'

'Call that fresh?' said Tanner, pressing two more five-round clips into his magazine. The two Brens were chattering now.

'Watch it, Stan,' warned Tanner. 'Short, sharp bursts, all right? We need to keep those weapons working – can't afford to overheat them.'

'We could do with another bucket of water, Sarge,' said Sykes.

'Do you want me to find one?' asked Bell.

'Yes – but keep your bloody head down back there.'

Now the enemy had located them, so machine-gun and rifle bullets were whacking into the walls. Tanner peered around the edge of his window, then jerked back as a bullet hissed past his shoulder and struck the wall behind him. Then, inching around the window-frame again, he saw more men crouch-running down the track on their left that led to the canal.

'Stan, get a burst over here,' he shouted. 'Those bastards nearing the road, ten o'clock.' He fired, then noticed another stream of Germans scurrying towards the cottage on the far side of the canal, no more than a hundred and thirty yards away. He adjusted his scope. All along the canal to the ruined bridge the Rangers were firing, Brens and rifles cracking out, bullets from both sides whining across the narrow stretch of water. Most, he guessed, were passing high – he could even see a line of German tracer arcing well over the trenches. He had been right to try to gain height; the only danger now, he reckoned, came from a stray bullet or mortars, which had yet to be directed towards them.

He fired again towards the men approaching the cottage, then saw several make a gap in the hedge into the garden, then more hurrying through. 'Go on,' he muttered, then called, 'Stan, they're in the cottage garden.'

Sykes stopped firing and pulled the magazine from the top of the weapon. He crawled across the floor to Tanner. 'I've got to see this.'

A moment later a huge explosion ripped apart the sky and the cottage disappeared behind a livid ball of flame. For a brief moment, the firing along their section of the line stopped as soldiers on both sides, caught off-guard by the detonation, paused to take cover from the debris. Quickly, Tanner brought his rifle to his shoulder and picked off another handful of startled enemy soldiers.

'I reckon that was one of my better ones.' Sykes grinned. 'Nice little bang, that.'

The Germans' assault faltered, as men took cover in the fields and behind buildings further back from the road, towards L'Avenir. It gave the defenders a brief chance of a breather. The Brens cooled, more magazines were loaded, and Tanner sent Ellis and Kershaw downstairs to find some food and drink. They returned a short while later with several tins of bully beef, condensed milk, a tin of jam and some biscuits. Tanner opened one of the cans of milk, drank some, then crushed a handful of biscuits into the remainder and added a large dollop of jam. Stirring it all together, he began to spoon it hungrily into his mouth. 'I needed this,' he said.

Peploe appeared, clutching several bottles of wine. 'You should all have a swig,' he said, then went over to Tanner. 'You all right?'

'Yes, thank you, sir,' said Tanner. He sat down against the wall, his helmet on his knee.

'I've some good news. Captain Moresby's been up to see us from Battalion. We're withdrawing tonight.'

Tanner sat up. 'Tonight? When?'

'At ten o'clock.'

'Twenty-two hundred,' repeated Tanner. 'A little under three hours.'

'Yes, and then straight to Dunkirk. Apparently in the east we've already pulled back to the border.'

'Bloody hell – I'd not thought about the rest of the line.'

'It's hard to when there's so much going on in front of us,' said Peploe. Three mortar shells in quick succession burst on the far side of the farm. No one flinched.

'Jerry'll have at least another attack in him, don't you think?' said Tanner, after a gulp of wine. 'How is it down on the canal?'

'We're holding up. Ross has lost three men, though. Direct hit from a mortar. Dempster's been hit in the shoulder.'

'And Verity?'

Peploe shook his head. 'Poor fellow. We've moved him to the back of the house – he's properly bomb-happy.'

'It can happen to anyone, I suppose,' said Tanner. 'So, we're down to the last twenty men.'

'And ammunition's a bit low.' He turned to Sykes. 'That was good work in the cottage, Corporal.'

'Thank you, sir. And we've got a few jelly bombs prepared in the vehicles too.'

'Jelly bombs?'

'Gelignite, sir,' said Sykes. 'The sergeant here takes a pot-shot with a tracer round and boom – up they go.'

Peploe smiled.

Tanner looked at his watch. 'Nineteen twenty,' he said. 'Well, every minute that passes . . .'

'It's going to be tight, though, isn't it?' said Peploe.

'Yes, sir. It is.'

*

The enemy renewed their attack shortly after eight o'clock. More mortars had been brought up and the enemy's approach was in part masked by a barrage of shells aimed towards the canal. Miraculously, they all missed the crumbling remains of the farm-house, and because many landed in the canal or the waterlogged fields behind, their effect was significantly reduced. Nonetheless, more enemy troops than ever were now working their way forward, some attempting to bring anti-tank guns with them, but the Boys, on the first floor now, and some sniping from Tanner knocked them out. Suddenly, a platoon-scale attack burst out on the canal road to their left – the men had clearly managed to creep along the adjoin-ing track – but Sykes had spotted them and got most of them with his Bren. It was the weapon's last gasp: the firing pin had com-pletely worn away.

'We need another,' said Tanner. 'Billy,' he turned to Ellis, 'find the lieutenant and get another Bren up here.'

Ellis turned to go, but as he did so a bullet caught him in the shoulder. 'I'm hit!' he cried, and fell to the floor.

'Christ, Billy,' said Tanner, beside him. 'Stan – and you, Kay,' he said to Kershaw, 'get him out of here and fetch a Bren.' He ripped out two packets of field dressings. The bullet had gone clean through Ellis's shoulder, but although he was bleeding profusely and his face was ghostly white, he was breathing regularly. 'You'll be all right, Billy,' said Tanner, pulling open the young man's battle-blouse and pressing the dressings to his wound. 'It's missed your lung. Brave lad. Someone give me another field dressing.' Sykes handed him a pack and he wrapped it round Ellis's shoulder and under his armpit, then tied it in a tight knot.

'Sorry, Sarge,' mumbled Ellis, and passed out.

Tanner left him and returned to the window. More men were crawling through the corn, so all he could see were the tops of their helmets and the green stalks moving. Another Spandau was firing at the house now, lines of tracer arcing slowly, then seemingly accelerating as they smacked into the walls. The burst stopped, and Tanner poked his head around the edge of the window. More lines of tracer pumped towards the house, but this time he had the machine-gun marked. It was by a willow next to the track to the left. A hundred and eighty yards, he reckoned.

'Mac!' he called.

'Sarge?'

'I need you to fire a burst at eleven o'clock, a hundred and eighty yards away. There's a Spandau by a willow tree,' he said, as he adjusted his scope and pulled back the bolt.

'Got it, Sarge.'

'On three – one, two, now!'

Swinging around to the window, his rifle butt already into his shoulder, he found his target, aimed, fired, and saw the man behind the weapon slump forward. A second shot, and another machine-gun crew had been silenced.

Sykes and Kershaw returned – with another Bren – but by now ammunition was running critically low. Tanner glanced at his watch and was astonished to see that it was nearly nine. Where had the time gone? Mortars continued to crash towards their positions. He wondered what was going on elsewhere – whether the Coldstreams were holding their part of the line – or those either side of them, for that matter. The light was fading, although the sky above was still clear, and away to their right, the last tip of the sun, deep orange, cast its rays across the flooded fields and canal. Tanner cursed the lack of cloud: it would have been almost dark now, had there been the low grey skies of a few days before.

He fired another magazine from his rifle, then turned to see a lone box of twelve Bren magazines. He delved into his pouches and discovered he had just twenty rounds, plus ten tracer rounds. 'Is that all we've got left?' he called.

'Yes, Sarge,' said Kershaw.

'Well, get downstairs iggery and find some bloody more.'

He continued firing but when Kershaw got back, ten minutes later, he was empty-handed. 'That's it, Sarge,' he said. 'Mr Peploe says there's no more spare boxes left.'

'Bollocks,' muttered Tanner. Outside, the light was fading fast, but the enemy continued to press forward.

'Sarge!' called Sykes. 'Look. Two o'clock. They're reaching the vehicles.'

Tanner strained his eyes into the gloom. German troops were hurrying to the edge of the road now. Some were hit by fire from the canal, but many more were reaching the cover of the abandoned British vehicles.

Sykes left his Bren and rolled over towards Tanner. 'Go on, then, Sarge, now's the time.'

'Hold on a moment longer,' said Tanner. At the side of the window he brought his rifle to his shoulder and peered through the scope until he spotted the first pack of gelignite resting on the near-side wheel arch of an abandoned Morris Commercial truck. He swept along the row of vehicles, making sure he could see each of the prepared jelly bombs. Emptying his magazine, he replaced it with two clips of tracer he'd prepared earlier and pressed them down into the breech.

'There's more reaching them, Sarge,' hissed Sykes.

'All right.' He turned to Bell. 'Tinker, go down and find Mr Peploe. Tell him to make sure everyone gives whatever they've got the moment the jelly bombs blow. You've got less than a minute, so iggery.'

'Yes, Sarge,' said Bell, disappearing down the stairs.

'Stan,' continued Tanner, 'get back to the Bren and be ready to fire. Mac!' he called. 'Be ready to open up when I say. Boys,' he added, turning to Chambers and Kershaw, 'get whatever grenades you can and go downstairs. When I tell you to throw, hurl 'em across the canal.'

Tanner aimed his rifle at the furthest of the jelly bombs, then fired. As the first exploded, he swept his rifle past several others, and fired again. Another blast erupted, detonating the charges in the vehicles at either side. Tanner moved along the line to the first jelly bomb and fired again, hitting the gelignite, which exploded immediately. In the space of five seconds, the vehicles along an eighty-yard front were a cascading tumble of flame and oily black smoke.

'Fire those Brens now!' shouted Tanner, to McAllister and Sykes. He picked up his German MP35, squatted by the window and fired off four of his remaining magazines. 'Now grenades!'

A devastating wave of explosives and bullets poured across the canal. Tanner fired at any figure he could see through the rapidly descending dusk. The Brens continued, with short, sharp bursts of fire. By the road, vehicles burned and men screamed. A blazing man staggered towards the canal but was shot before he reached the water. Tanner continued to fire. His shoulder ached, and a blister was swelling on his trigger finger. His throat was as dry as sand, his nostrils burning from the acid stench of cordite.

Sykes's Bren stopped, then McAllister's. Tanner delved into his pouch – just two clips left.

'I'm done, Sarge,' said Sykes. 'That's it. No more.'

All along the line, the firing lessened as though every soldier had released their last rounds at precisely the same time. Overhead, a flurry of artillery shells screamed, but apart from the still burning vehicles and the occasional mortar shell, the front was strangely quiet. Tanner strained his eyes, staring across the canal to the fields and tracks beyond. The poplars and willows stood dark now against the last glimmer of light. 'Where are they?' he said. 'Where are the bastards?' And then against the glow of the burning trucks, he saw several figures moving – in the direction they had come. The enemy was falling back.

Tanner let himself slide to the floor. It was 2145. Fifteen more minutes and they could leave this bloody place. He closed his eyes, then felt for his water-bottle. There were only a few drops in it, which he swallowed, savouring the soothing fluid as it trickled down his throat.

'Sarge!' said a voice, and there was Chambers. 'We're going! We're falling back to the beaches!'

*

At a little after five thirty a.m. on Sunday, 2 June, Squadron Leader Charlie Lyell was leading B Flight on their first patrol of the day over Dunkirk. Since the weather had improved, the bulk of the evacuation had taken place during the night and for the past two days fighter patrols had been concentrated at dawn and dusk when Allied shipping was either approaching or leaving Dunkirk. Even at first light, it was easy enough to see the port almost from the moment their Hurricanes rose into the sky – or, rather, the huge plume of smoke that stood permanently above it. This morning, however, a haze hung over the Channel, shielding the vast expanse of northern France and Belgium that could normally be seen stretching away from them as they approached the French coast.

Still, the smoke was a useful visual marker. Over the Channel, Lyell had led his six aircraft up to eighteen thousand feet, heading north-east to avoid the worst of the glare from the rising sun, then turned inland before heading back west with the sun behind them.

'This is Mongoose Leader,' he said, speaking over the R/T, 'make sure you all keep your eyes peeled.'

He had been back for more than a week. From Arras, he had been given a ride to Lille-Seclin and from there passage in a Blenheim to England. Then he'd got a lift to London and caught a train to Manston. His return had been marked by a sensational night in the pub, in which his pilots had made it touchingly clear that they were very pleased to see him come back from the dead. After two more days – spent hanging around the airfield with a bandage round his head – the MO had given him the all-clear to fly. A brand-new Hurricane had arrived, which he had immediately claimed as his own, and with 'LO-Z' painted on the fuselage, he had been back in the air leading the squadron once more.

He had returned a better pilot and squadron leader. Being shot down had taught him valuable lessons, and during that long journey to Arras he had had time to think. It had dawned on him that while there were some very talented pilots among the *Luftwaffe*, those in the RAF could be every bit as good. It was just that some of the tactics and formations that had been drummed into them were not necessarily the best way to fight a war in the air. Prescribed formation attacks didn't work because the targets always moved; nor did flying wingtip to wingtip make sense because the pilots were spending so much time concentrating on keeping formation that they couldn't see when the enemy was bearing down on them. And to hit an enemy aircraft, you had to get in close – as close as you dared. Last, and this he had learned from Sergeant Tanner, surprise was the best form of attack. With the sun behind them and plenty of height, it was possible to knock anything out of the sky.

On his first sortie back in charge, Lyell had ordered his vics to spread out more, and above cloud level he had made a point of leading his squadron high enough to position themselves with the sun behind them. When they had spotted a formation of enemy bombers approaching Dunkirk from the east, they had swooped down on them, in no particular attack formation but with Lyell leading, and had opened fire. Within seconds they had shot down two Heinkels and one probable.

Since then, the squadron had claimed a further seventeen enemy aircraft and Lyell had four confirmed kills to his name. Just one more and he'd be an ace. An ace! It was ludicrous, really. What did it matter who shot down what, so long as they were knocked out of the sky? But he did care: personal pride made him want it but, more than that, he felt it was important that, as commanding officer, he should be seen to show the way.

He wondered how many men were left in France. It had been a miracle that such an extraordinary number appeared to have been lifted and he liked to think that the RAF had played no small part in that success. There had been reports of fights in Ramsgate between returning soldiers and Manston airmen on account of the RAF's poor showing, but that was nonsense. Anyone doubting it had only to climb above the smoke and cloud where they would have seen a very different story. When Lyell had been shot down, he had been keenly aware of how outnumbered they had been. The men on the ground had grumbled that the *Luftwaffe* had ruled the skies, and during those few days with the Yorkshire Rangers, Lyell had understood why they had felt that way; if he was honest, he had barely seen an Allied plane himself. Over Dunkirk, however, it had been different. Not only 632 Squadron, but many other RAF fighter squadrons had fought well. It was as though they had all been forced to learn quickly and were now reaping the benefits.

Now they flew back towards the coast, the rising sun bursting high above the haze below. Above, the deep blue canopy was clear and promising. Lyell turned his head: behind, ahead, below, behind, ahead, below.

A glint caught his eye, below, off his port wing, and then he saw them clearly: three formations of four twin-engine bombers, a squadron of a dozen Junkers 88s, probably flying around ten thousand feet, heading unmistakably towards the column of smoke rising high above Dunkirk.

'This is Mongoose Leader,' he said. 'A dozen bandits, ten o'clock, angels ten.'

He gunned his throttle and turned so that he could follow them dead ahead.

'Spread out, boys,' he added. 'Don't want to make too big a target. Keep your eyes peeled behind you, but I'm going to take us down to make the most of the sun.'

He watched the altimeter fall as the enemy bombers grew larger. On the Junkers flew, apparently oblivious of the six fighters stalking them. They were now half a mile away and just two thousand feet below. Lyell pressed on, glancing at the rest of the flight, their two vics now nicely spread.

Seven hundred yards, six hundred, five hundred, and then just five hundred feet below them. Behind, the sun glinted off the Perspex of his Hurricane's canopy. Lyell flicked off the safety catch on the stick, then said, 'Tally ho, tally ho,' and pushing the control column forward, dived below the lead formation and, at less than two hundred yards, opened fire. The Hurricane's frame juddered as the eight Brownings spat bullets, and long lines of tracer hurtled towards the leading Junkers, streaking across the fuselage, over one wing and hitting the portside engine, which burst into flame. Immediately, the rest of the formation broke up but not before the other five Hurricanes had torn into them. Lyell flew underneath his Junkers and banked to the left, aping the stricken bomber, which had tried to climb but was now diving towards the haze.

Glancing around to check that the skies were clear, he flipped over the aircraft and followed his Junkers. It was not good practice, he knew, but he wanted to make sure: if it disappeared from view still flying, however badly, the best he could hope for was a probable – and that wouldn't make him an ace. Only a confirmed kill would do. A wave of exhilaration swept over him. And then he was through the haze, flying over the beaches of Dunkirk. Directly in front of him was the crippled Junkers. 'Got you!' he muttered, with satisfaction.

At twenty-five minutes to six in the morning, the Isle of Man ferry *Manxman* was slipping away from the east pier at Dunkirk, crammed with a hundred and seventy-seven, including most of the surviving members of the 1st Battalion, the King's Own Yorkshire Rangers. Footsore and exhausted, they had reached the port just before midnight and had discovered the pier heaving with men. Four destroyers and a steamer had arrived and lifted a large number of the remaining men but at three a.m., as the Rangers had neared the front of the queue, they had been told by a naval officer there would be no more ships until the following evening.

As dawn broke, Tanner had seen the scale of the devastation once more. Abandoned vehicles littered the port area beside the mole and all along the beaches as far as the eye could see. Half-sunk ships stood out of the sea. An oily stench filled the air as the dark-green water lapped lazily at the pier's struts. But compared with two days before, the small number of men still wandering the beaches was nothing short of a miracle. The crowds had almost all gone, most presumably taken back to England. Tanner saw two short lines of men waiting at Malo-les-Bains but otherwise the port and the beaches seemed eerily empty. Had all those men really gone home? It seemed too incredible to be true.

They had returned to the end of the pier, and the men had collapsed onto the ground, smoking or sleeping almost instantly, while those still left to lead them decided what they should do until nightfall. Then salvation had arrived. A small ferry had come into view, and as it eventually drew alongside the pier, the Rangers realized they had been rewarded for waiting at the foot of the mole. Trudging forward along the wooden walkway, they had numbly boarded the little ship.

Tanner and the rest of D Company had made their way to the back. Two more men had been killed in the last attack by the enemy and a further three wounded. No one knew what had happened to Hepworth and the others who had gone with the carriers, but Peploe insisted that the remaining wounded would be taken to England; with makeshift stretchers, the men had enabled him to keep his word. Nineteen men, Verity included, were all that remained of D Company. Only sixteen still stood.

'Well,' said Sykes, as the ship slipped its moorings, 'we made it.'

'We've still got to get across the Channel, Stan,' said Tanner, exhaling a cloud of tobacco smoke. At that moment they heard the clatter of machine-guns above the haze. 'Bloody hell,' said Tanner. 'That's what comes of counting your sodding chickens.'

Suddenly a Junkers broke through the cloud. It was only a few hundred feet above them and astonishingly large, the black crosses and streaks of oil on the underside of the wings vivid. The port engine was on fire and the second was spluttering as though on its last gasp. A moment later a Hurricane burst into view and opened fire at less than a hundred yards' range. Immediately there was a loud crack, a burst of smoke and the second engine caught fire. The bomber whined and, amid gasps from the watching men, plunged into the sea. From beneath the waves they heard the mournful creak of tearing metal. The men cheered.

'Look!' shouted Sykes. 'Look – LO-Z!'

'Damn me!' muttered Tanner. 'Lyell.'

The Hurricane roared past them, banked, then turned back, just a hundred feet above the surface of the sea. As it flew over the ship, it rolled, not once but twice, then climbed and disappeared back into the haze.

It was six days later, on the evening of Saturday, 8 June, that Lieutenant Peploe, Sergeant Tanner and Corporal Sykes climbed into Squadron Leader Lyell's newly repaired car.

'All set?' said Lyell.

'Yes, thank you, sir,' said Tanner.

They drove out through the main gates and, on the cliffs above Ramsgate, were waved through a roadblock.

'Not quite so keen as you were, Sergeant,' said Lyell, as they motored on towards Kingsgate Castle. 'And, what's more, no one gives us a hard time about coming here either.' He grinned into the mirror.

Lyell parked outside the hotel entrance and led them into the bar. The rest of the squadron were already waiting, clapping and whistling as they entered. Tanner noticed four shots and four pints already lined up on the bar.

'Drambuie and beer,' said Lyell. 'Drambuie first, then the beer. Come on, let's be having you.'

'Bloody flying wallahs,' muttered Tanner, bringing the shot to his lips.

'Humour them, Tanner,' said Peploe. 'Just go with the flow.'

Tanner had downed both his drinks when suddenly he noticed a familiar face smiling in front of him.

'Torwinski?' he said.

'I've been accepted into the RAF Volunteer Reserve,' he said. 'Do you like the uniform?'

Tanner laughed. 'Very smart. You're not with this lot already, are you?'

'Not yet. Squadron Leader Lyell has tried to pull strings but I have to do flying training first. I don't mind so much – I'll soon show them what I can do in an aeroplane.'

'It's bloody ridiculous,' said Lyell. 'This fellow flew against the Germans last September and they still don't think he's qualified to fly. It's a joke. We took him up in the Maggie and he showed us up horribly. I'd have him like a shot, but there's no reasoning with the top brass. More fool them.'

'I hadn't realized you were a pilot,' said Peploe. 'You never said.'

'Myself and the other two in our hut.' He looked down. 'We all wanted to fly again against the Nazis. Thanks to you, at least I will have that chance. I appreciate what you did before you left for France and on your return.'

'It's a promise I made to myself,' said Peploe. 'I'm only glad I was able to honour it. And at least we know the truth now. I'm sorry.'

'And the bastards got what they deserved,' said Tanner. 'I always knew Blackstone was a nasty piece of work, but Slater was leading him on. He was behind the fuel scam and I wouldn't mind betting it was his idea to frame you three.'

'I just hope I can honour my friends' memory by shooting down many German aircraft.' Torwinski raised his glass.

'It's certainly going to be up to you pilots now,' said Peploe.

'And I don't envy you,' added Tanner.

'Really? You don't fancy flying, Sergeant?' asked Lyell.

'No, sir, I don't. I like having my feet firmly on the ground.'

Lyell laughed. 'I think we can safely say that about you, Tanner.'

Tanner smiled ruefully. He wondered what would happen in the weeks and months to come. The BEF had been beaten, and although he'd heard that more than a quarter of a million British troops had been lifted from Dunkirk, most of their kit had been left behind. That stuff didn't grow on trees – it couldn't be replaced overnight. And a lot of good men had been left behind too. Just twenty-two from D Company had made it back – including Hepworth. Tanner had been glad to know Hep was all right. Would the Germans really try to invade Britain? Christ only knew. No doubt there would be other battles to fight, but for the time being, he decided, he would make the most of the pause and the leave he had been given. Bloody hell, he deserved it.

Historical Note

On the whole, the British Expeditionary Force performed rather well in France in 1940, even though it was forced to evacuate at Dunkirk. Most of the troops were bewildered by the rapid series of withdrawals that took place in order to keep in line with the French and Belgians as they fell back, but as the German net closed around them, the British fought with considerable gallantry and determination despite the enemy's superior numbers and fire-power. As the Germans would discover later in the war, fighting on the ground when the enemy commands the skies is not much fun.

Most of the characters depicted at BEF Headquarters were real and, thanks to diaries, testimonies and copies of messages and con-ferences, it has been possible not only to gather a fairly clear picture of what was going on at Gort's command post but also to use words spoken verbatim. I have, however, probably been a bit generous to General Lord Gort. He had many fine qualities, and it must have been an exasperating and extremely depressing time, but he also had his faults, not least his insistence on having far more staff officers than were necessary. Both GHQ and his advance headquarters were heaving with them, which made for a slow dissemination of orders and did nothing to improve the already parlous state of Allied communications. Nonetheless, his decision to act swiftly and unilaterally to evacuate as much of the BEF as possible, and his system of maintaining strongpoints as the bulk of his force fell back towards Dunkirk, was courageous and deftly handled.

I'm conscious I have been quite hard on the French, although I should make clear that any criticism applies more to the commanders than to the fighting men. Unfortunately, however, the French commanders have a lot to answer for. In May 1940, France had a bigger army, navy and air force than Germany, and when one considers that accepted military doctrine suggests you should not attack unless you have at least a three-to-one advantage in manpower and matériel, it seems incredible that the Germans should have rolled over the French so easily. Furthermore, it was an extraordinary gamble on the part of Germany to launch such an attack against not only France, but Belgium, Holland and Britain as well. There is not the space here to explain why the German panzer thrust was so successful, but it is certainly true that France – and, indeed, many German commanders – thought the war would soon become largely attritional just like that of 1914–18. Only a few on the German side ever envisaged the kind of fast-paced highly mobile campaign that became the reality: as has been proved convincingly by the German historian Heinz Frieser, there was no 'blitzkrieg' concept as an agreed and fully formed strategy at this time.

It was because the war was expected to be attritional that most of France's aircraft were spread out across the country and held in reserve rather than being near the front. It is also why the French went to such lengths to build the infamous Maginot Line. No one (apart from one French government minister) suspected that Sedan, the hinge between the end of the Maginot Line and the manoeuvrable front that was to enter Belgium the moment the Germans attacked, would be the point of the German spearhead.

As a result, it was horribly under-defended, with no active mine-fields whatsoever, poorly trained troops and incomplete, scarcely manned bunkers.

Despite this, all the French really needed to do was stand firm at the key nodal points – bridges, key road junctions and so on – and the German lines of supply would have been cut off, isolating the thrusting panzer divisions. As it happened, just six German panzer divisions and four motorized divisions were largely responsible for defeating a French Army of some two million men; panicking commanders, unable to move their cumbersome, defensive-minded troops quickly enough, and lacking sufficient radio sets, became like rabbits caught in headlights. General Gamelin, the French commander-in-chief until he was sacked, General Billotte, commander of First Army Group, General Blanchard, Commander of First Army, and General Altmayer, Commander of French V Corps, were all reported to have broken down in tears at various points. General Ironside, the British chief of the Imperial General Staff, even grabbed Billotte's jacket and shook him to try to knock some steel into him. What *was* needed was resolve, determination and clear thinking; blubbing was certainly not the answer. I have made the point in the novel about the comparative ages of the British and French commanders and I think it's valid. Most of the French commanders were a bit long in the tooth, and not only far too ingrained with the military thinking of the First World War, but physically and mentally too old to deal with the enormous stresses of commanding a modern army. Few generals have won decisive battles aged sixty-five plus.

I have tried to depict the main events described in the book as accurately as possible and all the locations, dates and timings of events are written as they were. The *Waffen-SS* Totenkopf Division was one of only two SS divisions to see action in France, and both Eicke and his frustrations in trying to convince the *Wehrmacht* of his division's worth were much as depicted. The reconnaissance bat-talion's bulldozing through a retreating French column was also based on a similar episode, although it was a reconnaissance unit from 7th Panzer Division, rather than the Totenkopf, who were responsible. Timpke, however, is fictional, although the reconnaissance battalion is not. The real-life commander was Sturmbannführer Heimo Hierthes, but I did not think it fair to give him Timpke's many disagreeable qualities when I could find out nothing whatsoever about him.

Actually, there were French troops in the area near Hainin where Tanner and his men stole the Totenkopf's trucks; that is, a part of the French 43rd Division had been trapped to the north of Mauberge after heavy fighting against the 5th Panzer Division on 17 May. Most of the division had fallen back to Bavay and then across the Escaut, but those trapped continued to fight on stubbornly while German troops advanced around them. This was not an uncommon scenario in the battle for France and it is quite possible that on 19 May, Timpke's reconnaissance battalion would have missed them entirely.

I have tried to recount the British counter-attack at Arras as accurately as possible, but it was complicated and the precise details are often contradictory. Although the British knew that the Germans were concentrating forces south of Arras and vice versa, neither Major-General Franklyn nor Major-General Rommel knew that the other was going to attack in precisely the same place. Thus, the 25th Panzer Regiment, Rommel's main tank unit in his 7th Panzer Division, had already thrust successfully north-west of Arras towards Acq by the time the two British columns were moving south. This was why German forces were spotted west and north-west of Maroeuil as they moved south; 25th Panzer hung around near Acq during most of the afternoon of 21 May, until Rommel ordered them south-east again at around seven p.m. so as to cut off the retreating British. This is why the 8th Durham Light Infantry, still in Duisans, and the accompanying artillery found themselves under renewed attack from the north-west that evening.

It is true that Rommel personally directed the German battery at Point 111. The guns were situated in an old quarry next to Belloy

Farm, just north-west of the village of Wailly, and it is not only still there, but clear to see why they had positioned themselves in such an ideal spot. It is also true that Rommel's aide-de-camp, Oberleutnant Most, was killed while standing right next to him; also, Rommel, in his diary, expressed surprise as to how it had happened because he was not aware that the position was under direct attack – rather, the British tanks in front of them and on their right were aiming at the troops moving either side: the SS Totenkopf on their left and his artillery and 6th Rifle Regiment on his right.

Tragically, the massacre of the Royal Norfolks at Le Paradis also occurred much as described, although there was no Timpke egging Knöchlein on to carry out such an appalling deed. There have been all sorts of suggestions as to why he ordered the executions. One – entirely unconfirmed, I hasten to add, and without any evidence at all – asserts that it was a revenge attack for the death of a number of Totenkopf prisoners at Arras. Two men survived and escaped, although wounded, and were later recaptured and spent the rest of the war in PoW camps. Afterwards, however, they revealed the truth of what had happened. Knöchlein, who had survived the war, was tracked down, put on trial, found guilty and hanged.

One brief note about the weapons. Interestingly, an MP28 sub-machine-gun – almost identical to the *Waffen-SS* MP35 – was brought back from Dunkirk and handed over to the Admiralty. With the RAF, they decided to commission a new sub-machine-gun. The Lanchester, as it became known, was an almost like-for-like copy of the German model.

Had the French not lost their heads and panicked and instead dealt with the German attack logically and calmly, the Second World War would, no doubt, never have become a world war in the way that we think of it today and would very likely have been over that summer. Sadly, that did not happen. France was vanquished, and by the signing of the armistice on 22 June 1940, all of continental Europe, from the top of Norway in the Arctic Circle, all the way down to the southern tip of Spain, lay in Nazi or Fascist hands. Britain faced five more years of war and the men of the Yorkshire Rangers had many more battles to come. Jack Tanner and Stan Sykes were needed again all too soon.

Glossary

choky	prison
CIGS	chief of the Imperial General Staff (head of the armed services)
croaker	badly wounded or dying
CQS	Company Quartermaster Sergeant
dekko	look around, observe
DLM	Division Légère Méchanique, i.e. a Light Armoured Division
GSO3	General Staff Officer 3 – a British staff officer
HMG	His Majesty's Government
housewife	small standard-issue linen wallet containing needles, thread, spare buttons, darning wool and thimble
iggery	get on with it, move it
Irvin	thick sheepskin flying jacket made by the Irvin company for the RAF
IO	intelligence officer
Maggie	RAF slang for a Miles Magister aircraft
MO	medical officer

M/T	motor transport
O4	German divisional general staff officer
OC	Officer Commanding
OCTU	Officer Cadet Training Unit
on the peg	under arrest
OP	observation post
ORs	other ranks (i.e. not commissioned officers)
poilus	old First World War name for French infantry
puggled	drunk
QA	Queen Alexandra Imperial Military Nursing Service
RASC	Royal Army Service Corps
RTR	Royal Tank Regiment
R/T	radio transmitter
RV	rendezvous
sitrep	situation report
Spandau	German light machine-gun; in May 1940, most were MG34s, but British troops tended to call all such weapons 'Spandaus' after the location stamp marked on the German Maxim guns of the First World War
Snowdrops	RAF Military Police
stonk	a sustained artillery barrage
vic	V-shaped formation of three aircraft, with the lead plane at the point of the 'V'

My thanks to the following: Roger Baker, Oliver Barnham, Dr Peter Caddick-Adams, Clive Denney, Rob Dinsdale, Richard Dixon, Phil Harding, Professor Rick Hillum, Lalla Hitchings, Staff Sergeant Steve Hurst, Steve Lamonby, Peta Nightingale, Hazel Orme, Bill Scott-Kerr and all at Bantam, Lieutenant-Colonel John Starling, Jake Smith-Bosanquet, Patrick Walsh, Guy Walters, Major Steve White, Rachel, Ned and Daisy.